Over and Under

ALSO BY TODD TUCKER

The Great Starvation Experiment: The Heroic Men Who Starved So That Others Could Live

Notre Dame Vs. the Klan: How the Fighting Irish Defeated the Ku Klux Klan

Over and Under

Todd Tucker

Thomas Dunne Books *New York*

St. Martin's Press

This is a work of fiction. All of the characters, organizations, and events portrayed in this novel are either products of the author's imagination or are used fictitiously.

THOMAS DUNNE BOOKS.
An imprint of St. Martin's Press.

www.thomasdunnebooks.com
www.stmartins.com

Library of Congress Cataloging-in-Publication Data

Tucker, Todd, 1968–
Over and under / Todd Tucker.—1st ed.
p. cm
ISBN-13: 978-0-312-37990-2 (alk. paper)
ISBN-10: 0-312-37990-0 (alk. paper)
1. Boys—Fiction. 2. Male friendship—Fiction. 3. City and town life—Fiction 4. Labor disputes—Fiction. 5. Indiana—Fiction.

PS3620.U33 O94 2008
813'.6—dc22 *2008012472*

First Edition: July 2008

10 9 8 7 6 5 4 3 2 1

Pandora
An Imprint of HarperCollins*Publishers*
77–85 Fulham Palace Road,
Hammersmith, London W6 8JB
1160 Battery Street,
San Francisco, California 94111-1213

Published by Pandora 1994
10 9 8 7 6 5 4 3 2 1

A catalogue record for this book
is available from the British Library

ISBN 0 04 440901 X

Printed in Great Britain by
HarperCollinsManufacturing Glasgow

THE WOMEN'S QUIZ BOOK

Jennifer Gourley

Pandora
An Imprint of HarperCollins*Publishers*

Jennifer Gourley was born in Newcastle-upon-Tyne. She taught in Manchester primary schools for eight years and hopes to begin a masters degree in the near future.

THE WO[illegible]
QUIZ BOOK

For my son

Andrew Jackson Tucker

The trigger pull of the M6 Scout is a bit stiff for the smallest youngsters, but using four fingers at first, and later two on the unique squeeze bar trigger works well. The gun's accuracy is quite good, too—a helpful trait in preventing discouragement in a young shooter.

—*Hunting Digest*, "The Best Guns for Kids," Fall 1977

Over and Under

Prologue

I was eight years old when Mack Sanders lost a nut in the mill room of the Borden Casket Company. Dad told me a vague version of the story the night it happened, but along with the rest of the town, I soon knew every gory detail. It was 1973, the day before the Kentucky Derby, and Sanders had tickets to the big race.

Sanders was right out of high school, so new at the plant that maybe he hadn't yet developed a proper respect for the horrible things that can happen to a man in a building full of industrial woodworking machinery. Maybe if he'd made it even one more week, he would have started to notice the large number of men around him with fewer than ten fingers, or ragged purple scars across their cheeks. Vern Schumacher in payroll, for example, cheerfully delivered Mack his paycheck every two weeks with an empty sleeve safety-pinned to his shoulder; he was waiting out retirement in a desk job he'd gratefully accepted after a run-in with a band saw. Who knows what Sanders might have learned given a little more time. I just know that what did happen to Sanders made even Vern Schumacher count his blessings.

Sanders had been assigned to a noisy green Torwegge ripsaw, a machine powered by a five-horsepower motor

bolted to the concrete floor. The motor was old, but like every piece of rotating machinery in the plant, it was lovingly maintained by a cadre of meticulous German mechanics who believed with moral certainty that all machines could last a century or more with proper care. Just days before the accident, responding to a barely audible rattle, maintenance man Oscar Schmidt had checked the speed of that very motor using a strobe light designed for the purpose. Waiting until after sundown so that the ambient light would be low, he pointed the light at the chain and adjusted its speed until the rapidly moving links appeared frozen in space, their speed synchronized perfectly with the blinking of the strobe. Oscar thus verified the speed of the motor: 1,600 revolutions per minute, exactly as designed. He concluded that the noise he'd heard was caused by the metal chain that connected motor to saw in a rapidly moving, well-oiled loop. Some of the links had become worn and barbed with age, causing noise as the malformed links meshed and unmeshed with the sprockets of the saw and motor. Oscar made a note to order a replacement chain from Louisville Mill Supply as he returned to the shop.

Sanders worked the day shift in the mill room, where he was pulling down the highest wages a new guy could anywhere in the plant. As shitty as the work could be—hot, dusty, and loud—Sanders knew he was lucky to have it. Especially as his unemployed, pot-smoking buddies from the class of '72 proved irresistible to the local draft board. With his pride, six dollars an hour, and a free yearlong vacation in Southeast Asia at stake, Sanders threw himself into the job every day, attacking his pile of wood in a sweaty frenzy. The day before the Derby was no exception

as he fed the ravenous saw, sweated through his Neil Young T-shirt, and tried to avoid looking at the clock.

Late that afternoon, a small forklift delivered to Sanders the day's last load of wood. Eager to begin his big weekend, Sanders grabbed the biggest board off the top of the stack, and, in an attempt to keep up with the men on either side of him who had been doing the work for decades, Sanders fed too much lumber into the saw at once. The large maple board got cockeyed and jammed itself with a squeal between the saw blade and the housing. The powerful motor groaned with displeasure but kept running. Sanders tried to muscle the board out, but couldn't. From where he stood, he had a hard time getting a good angle; the big motor on the floor was right where he needed to stand.

Sanders should have just turned the saw off and asked for help at that point, but he didn't. He'd gotten wood stuck before, and had always managed to get it out by himself. Turning the saw off would cause a bell over his machine to ring, an alert designed to get maintenance men or the foreman over to see what was wrong: everybody called it the "idiot alarm." A new guy took enough crap in the plant already without inviting it on himself like that. He also didn't want to give anyone an excuse to move him to a lower paying, less demanding job in the finish room or the trim line. As the outside of the saw blade spun against it, the board started to heat up, and Sanders knew that soon the smell of wood smoke would draw more unwanted attention than a clanging bell.

Knowing he had just a few minutes left before the foreman made his way over to see what was impeding the flow of lumber through the plant, Sanders decided to try

something different. To reach a better position, he stepped atop the motor housing, about two feet off the ground, with one foot on each side of the rapidly moving drive chain. Now the offending board was sticking out right at his navel, and he was able at last to get a good, solid grip on the thing, and pull.

He had positioned himself so well that the wood popped right out, surprising him. Holding on to the big heavy plank, Sanders tried to keep his balance, but he overcompensated when shifting his weight forward. His feet slipped on the motor housing, which was made slick by a coating of sawdust as fine as talcum powder. He fell hard, landing with his full weight on the rapidly moving metal chain, a leg on each side.

It all happened in an instant. With a buzzing sound, the jagged metal links ripped through the denim crotch of his jeans like a chain saw. Sanders instinctively put his hands down, gashing them badly on the chain. Events were now unfolding at 1,600 revolutions per minute, and even in his panic, he had no hope of reacting in time. The chain chewed through his jockey shorts as easily as the denim, and then moved on to the tender flesh of his scrotum. With those three scant layers of protection removed, one of the lightning-fast metal links, its outer edge worn into a hook-shaped barb, snagged his left nut, ripped it off his body, and flung it twenty yards through the air.

They say there wasn't a place in the plant where you couldn't hear the screaming. Guthrie Kruer, another new employee who was working nearby, was one of the few men present to act fast. He sprinted over and hit the big red emergency stop button, but by then the nut was flying

across the mill room, never again to be a part of Mack Sanders. It hit the far wall with a splat, left a bright red starburst of blood, and fell straight down into a pile of wood shavings.

From his hospital bed the next morning, Sanders told his brother to go on to the Derby without him. He also gave him a week's wages and strict instructions: bet it all on Secretariat to win. Danny Sanders, however, convinced that he had received a heavenly sign, bet every dime on Forego, the only gelding in the field. Forego finished just out of the money. We all know what Secretariat did. Six years later, when Tom Kruer and I went into the woods searching for Mack Sanders, he was still pissed off.

One

The strikers cheered as the tractor dragged the ancient Chrysler Newport in front of the main gate. Virgil Stemler, his long skinny arms straining with the effort, sloshed gasoline all over the car from a dented metal can. Mack Sanders followed closely behind him, jittery and playing to the crowd as he tossed a lit match onto the hood, then another, then another, jumping backward with each attempt, until *whoosh*, the rusty car burst reluctantly into flames. Sanders threw the matchbook to the ground and whipped around to accept our applause as the fire swelled behind him. There was something scary about his enthusiasm, and I wondered how many were like me, clapping only because I didn't want Sanders to pick me out of the crowd. Tom and I watched, along with half the population of Borden, Indiana, as a streak of greasy black smoke climbed straight into the sky, almost high enough to be seen beyond the heavily wooded walls of the valley that surrounded us.

Tom and I, both fourteen years old, pedaled around the edges of the crowd on our dirt bikes. It was August 1979, the second week of the strike, just before the start of ninth grade and high school. Like almost every other kid I knew,

my dad worked at the plant, but I had somehow up to that point been unaware of the tectonic forces that had pulled and pushed us into our respective roles that summer. My ignorance met its end at about the same time that doomed Chrysler did. Before the summer was over, I would learn the differences between management and labor, scabs and thugs, and see the most amazing gunshot of my life.

My best friend's full name was Thomas Jefferson Kruer. I'm Andrew Jackson Gray. That's not as strange a coincidence as it might seem outside the valley; I had many friends named for the heroes of democracy. I also knew an Elvis, an Aron, and a Presley, a smattering of John Waynes, and two grown men who went by "Peanut." I couldn't remember a time when Tom and I weren't friends, and we had been around each other so much that I often knew his thoughts, and he more often knew mine. That's not to say Tom couldn't surprise me. Frequently he would suggest an idea so crazy or so dangerous that I would stare in disbelief as he grinned and waited for me to come around to his way of thinking.

Tom and I wheeled around the outside of the crowd to get a better look, popping wheelies as we went. There were quite a few other kids from school there. I waved to Steve Koch, a classmate whose brother had died in Vietnam when we were all in kindergarten. I remembered him proudly showing us a set of dog tags in the cafeteria. Steve was laughing and wrestling Mark Deich, who was tossing Steve around like a rag doll. Mark had for some unknown reason a droopy, half-paralyzed face, but despite that affliction he was the undisputed strongest kid in our class, and one of the happiest.

With a start, I spotted Taffy Judd at the edge of the crowd, as always in her faded Pink Floyd T-shirt, the one with the rays of light coming out of the prism. I wanted to get a better look at her, but she was moving quickly along the perimeter of the crowd, almost as if she didn't want anyone to get too good a fix on her location. Taffy and I sat next to each other in second grade, and were for a time madly in love with each other. When we were given an assignment to write about what job we wanted when we grew up, I guaranteed myself weeks of unmerciful teasing by scrawling in crayon that I wanted to be a doctor, with Taffy as my nurse. Taffy agreed with that vision of the future, and drew a neat picture of herself in white holding hands with a smiling Dr. Gray. Our brief romance ended the next week when she caught me sharing my sandwich with Theresa Gettelfinger and hit me in the head with her lunch box. As brief as it was, my friends still occasionally gave me shit over Taffy. That was one of the reasons I tried to be subtle as I watched her.

As we got older, Taffy got harder and harder to spot in a crowd, lingering in the background as she did on the picket line, elusive and on the edges of the action. She lived in a trailer on a sliver of swampy land between Muddy Fork and Highway 60. Her dad, Orpod Judd, worked at the plant when he wasn't faking workmen's comp injuries or doing time for some variety of drunken mayhem. Poverty was easy to hide in Borden, where even the very few of us who were certifiably middle class chose to live simply. Taffy had all the telltale signs, however, even beyond the limited wardrobe and the run-down trailer home: she didn't have to drop change into the pie plate for her school lunch every

day, she seemed to fight the same cold all winter without a doctor visit, and in the school directory she shared a phone number with all the poorer kids of Borden. It was the number of the pay phone in front of Miller's General Store, the common phone for those in the nearby trailers who couldn't keep one of their own turned on.

"It's already junk," Tom said critically of the burning car, snapping me out of my thoughts about Taffy. It was true. Even as they reveled in their unfamiliar roles as labor firebrands, my flinty German neighbors would no sooner destroy a functioning automobile than they would torch a church. Besides, along with strawberries and Christmas trees, junk cars in Borden were always a surplus crop. I followed him up to a rough-looking trio of older strikers in lawn chairs, all with Local 1096 ball caps and bulges of Skoal in their lips. They used the sticks of their picket signs to push themselves noisily backward as the fire grew too hot.

"Why are we burning a car?" he asked them. His directness impressed me. I was afraid to admit that I found the whole ceremony a little mysterious. Like me, Tom was shirtless, tanned to a dark brown, and wearing shorts made from last year's jeans. His young body was on the verge of carrying knotty, showy muscle like his father, and he looked athletic and efficient, his body honed by exploring every corner of our valley with me every day, on bike and on foot. His hair was bushy and long, not because that happened to be the fashion of the moment, but because his mom couldn't get him to sit still on the front porch for the twenty minutes she needed to give him a proper trim. His eyes were bright and alert, more so than mine, a giveaway to the reasonably perceptive that he was the smarter one of our pair. Other

than that, on those rare occasions when we ran into strangers, they often thought we were brothers. So I guess we looked alike.

"Why are we burning a car?" Tom asked again. The old men looked at one another, almost as if for a moment they couldn't think of a good reason themselves.

"That Sanders kid is nuts," said one of the men in what was not quite an explanation.

"He ain't been right since . . . the accident," said another. We all took a moment to be thankful for our intact testicles.

Tom persisted. "So why are we burning a car?"

"To keep the scabs out!" said the third man, as if the official answer had suddenly dawned on him. He looked to his friends for affirmation and the bills of their caps dipped in agreement. I didn't know what a scab was, but it didn't seem to me that we were in any danger of being overrun by them. The parking lot of the Borden Casket Company was empty, except for the old Ford truck that belonged to Don Strange, the plant's general manager. I presumed he could see the car's flames from somewhere inside the empty factory, though we could not see him.

Tom was fascinated by the vocabulary of the strike. He shared with me each term he picked up—that morning he had explained "cost of living" to me. He knew by heart his father's shifts on the picket line as well, six hours every day and a half. I couldn't help but feel the sting of being left out when he talked about that. For reasons that had not yet been explained to me, my father was never on the picket line.

"Will the sheriff come?" he asked. I was curious about

the same thing. Sheriff Kohl was famously stern—he once ticketed New Albany High School's basketball coach for cursing during a sectional championship game. I, too, was surprised that he would allow car burning in broad daylight along our busiest road. At the same time, the sheriff was a mysterious source of tension inside my home. I would not have brought the matter up on my own.

The striker threw a gap-toothed leer to his friends at Tom's mention of the sheriff. He leaned forward. "Ain't you Gus Gray's kid?"

"Yes," I said.

"The sheriff won't come here. Don't you worry about that."

He was right. That old Newport burned right down to the wheels and Sheriff Kohl never came.

I was well into adulthood before I realized just how isolated we were up there in Borden, deep in the Hoosier Valley, at the edge of Clark and Washington counties. The rest of Indiana had been scraped clean by an advancing glacier during the last ice age, leaving the land geometrically flat and ready to divide into rectangular fields of beans and corn. Right at the Washington County line, the glacier stopped and retreated, so the primeval hills to the south were spared, all the way down to the Ohio River. Like parallel rows of barbed wire, the hills wrapped us up tight in protective layers of rolling, inconvenient geography that kept road-pavers and subdivision-builders at bay. When I doubt it now, and think that the isolation was some figment of my imagination, an idealization of a rural childhood when the size of my world was limited by how many miles I could

ride my dirt bike, I remind myself of some of the creatures that Tom and I used to trap, shoot, and pull from the floating snares we made out of milk jugs and treble hooks. There were critters in Borden you just wouldn't see anywhere else.

Silver Creek wound back into the hills across giant banks of freshwater mussels. I don't mean one or two lonely shells clinging to rocks; I'm talking about sheets of the things, thriving generations crusted on top of one another in porous layers that the water ran through with a distinctive, high-pitched sizzle. At Indiana University, in Bloomington, not all that far from Borden as the crow flies, I read once that freshwater mussels were endangered. I laughed out loud right there in the Main Library—Tom and I used to fill our backpacks with the empty shells and pretend they were money in our games. Downstream from the mussel banks, Silver Creek widened and slowed, and on still summer days freshwater jellyfish paraded by, almost invisible to the untrained eye—they looked like pieces of Kleenex drifting just beneath the surface. Boys at school brought giant caterpillars stuffed into Mason jars for show-and-tell, behemoths as big around as Coke cans, with orange horns and elaborate fake eyes imprinted on their backs by the Creator. Between our steep hills sat small, deep, wedge-shaped ponds, home to croaking amphibians we called "mud puppies," and slime-covered primitive fish with twitchy, stunted legs. My parents had spent good money, they periodically reminded me, on the set of red junior *Encyclopedia Britannicas* in my room. They stood in regal alphabetical order above my Springfield M6 rifle in its gun rack, my two most valuable possessions displayed on

the same windowless wall. Those encyclopedias showed in exquisite color plates the grotesque Sargassum fish from the Red Sea, and Hawaii's beautiful Moorish idol, but none of Borden's local wildlife. It was too exotic to be included.

The strange biosphere continued below our feet. The valley was riven with limestone caves. Some were roped off, domesticated, and turned into tourist attractions for the Louisville families not worn out by their daylong harvest of whatever U-Pick crop was in season. Each had its own unique attraction. The tour of Marengo Cave finished in a chamber where visitors were encouraged to throw coins straight up, where they would stick in a muddy ceiling sheathed by years of captive pennies and nickels. Wyandotte Cave featured the footprints of prehistoric Indians leading to cold fire pits. Most spectacularly, Squire Boone Caverns contained the bones of Daniel Boone's brother, Squire Boone, who had asked to be interred in the cave he had discovered. Every year of grade school we field-tripped there, where somber teachers warned us in vain to be respectful as we passed the dusty coffin. I'd made the trip so many times I knew Squire's epitaph by heart: *My God my life hath much befriended, I'll praise him till my days are ended.*

What Tom and I had discovered during the summer of the strike was that these weren't isolated, distinct caves, each with its own exit turnstile and gift shop. The whole thing was a system, a giant network of caves that ran wild throughout the region, connecting the tourist traps, the National Forest's caves, and the pristine caves opening in the middle of the woods that only Tom and I knew about. There was really just one giant cave. Inside it lived a community

of giant white crickets, albino crawdads, and even eyeless white fish, creatures mutated to complete blindness by eons of dark isolation. I couldn't help but feel sorry for them.

Exploring the caves had become a passion of Tom's that summer, and he seemed to find something almost magical in the way they could lead us from one end of the valley to the other. When the Chrysler began to smolder, and boredom returned to the picket line, he suggested we head underground. The thought of that cool, dry air was tempting, and he had a theory he wanted to pursue. I turned to get a last look at Taffy as we left, but she was gone.

Two

Many major events of that summer were determined by the migration paths of ancient buffalo. The Buffalo Trace was a trail pounded into the southern Indiana soil over thousands of years by enormous herds of American bison. These giant communities of buffalo marched every year from the salt licks of Kentucky, across the Ohio River at its shallowest point in Clarksville, and across Indiana into their pastures in Illinois. The herds were just about gone by the time the first white settlers arrived in our state, although there are a few shocked accounts from the earliest pioneers who stepped back in wonder to watch the woolly, grunting masses of buffalo splash their way across the Ohio River. While the buffalo had been gone for two centuries by the time Tom and I came along, their trail remained, a testament to the hardness and determination in those hooves. Large sections of the trail remained wild, and provided a remarkably smooth and straight corridor through the woods for two kids on bikes. Other sections of the trace were so wide and smooth that they had been adopted by the pioneers as a ready-made frontier road, which in turn became State Highway 60, the major road through Borden. Tom and I

sped down Highway 60 on our bikes after the car burning.

We rode hard, enjoying the speed that we could gather on the asphalt. Our legs were accustomed to much harder pedaling on dirt, up hills, and through mud. We zipped through Borden's tiny town proper, starting with Miller's General Store and its fading RC Cola sign. Next came the three schools—elementary, junior, and high—each in ascending order up the side of Daisy Hill. Next to them rose the Victorian eminence of the Borden Institute, still grand and hopeful even in its old age. The barber shop and the hardware store marked the end of Borden's minuscule retail district, and the post office marked the end of the town's incorporated limits. Just past the bridge, but before the cemetery, we veered sharply off the highway to the left, like jet fighters in formation, and let our momentum push us through two feet of thick brush in the state right-of-way. We dodged the thickest tree branches as we penetrated farther, but couldn't avoid the low-lying thorns grabbing at our bruised and scabbed legs. Just as the vegetation threatened to bring us to a stop, we burst into the clear again, like rockets pushing clear of gravity's pull, onto the smooth path cleared for us hundreds of years ago by the buffalo.

The trace narrowed as we rode on, forcing Tom and me into single file. We then left the easy riding of the trace and turned again into the brush, as we stood up on our pedals to gain traction. Finally, when pedaling was no longer possible, we laid our bikes down, satisfied that they were sufficiently hidden by the weeds. We continued on foot.

I felt the cave entrance before I saw it—a thin ribbon of cool dry air that felt like air-conditioning in the middle of the sweltering woods. Tom and I walked a short distance to a shelf of limestone that hung over a cave entrance we knew well. From even just a few feet away, the entrance looked like no more than a shadow under the outcropping.

I had suspected this was our destination when we left the picket line. The rest of Tom's plan, like most of the cave, was a mystery to me. We ducked to enter and let our eyes adjust. The hole was smooth and the dirt floor well-traveled—we were far from the first kids in Clark County to explore the more accessible portions of this particular cave. The chamber widened a little after the entrance. We walked hunched over across the main chamber, toward a small chute that led deeper. Directly above the chute, growing from the dirt, a knobby, thick stalagmite stood guard, the first recognizable cave feature, a smooth pillar of stone pushing through a tangle of dusty tree roots. Tom reached behind it and pulled out two red plastic flashlights that he kept hidden there, and handed one to me. We clicked them on and climbed on down the chute, past two slumbering bats who ignored us.

Fewer people had preceded us into this second chamber, judging by the dwindling number of beer cans and cigarette butts on the ground. We finally got to the far wall, the apparent end of the cave, where Tom turned and smiled, looking slightly demonic, underlit as he was by his flashlight.

"Listen," he said. His excited voice echoed slightly. I closed my eyes, but still heard nothing but the blood rushing in my ears. I shook my head.

"Down here," Tom said. I stooped over and put my head next to a hole about the size of a basketball where he was pointing. I had never noticed it before. The room we were in was not large, but I could only ever see what was inside the narrow beam of my flashlight, and it had never fallen on this particular spot before. The hole looked like someone had dug it out and enlarged it, but it was impossible to say when. Time froze in caves, with their constant temperature, low humidity, and eternal shelter from the elements. The hole could have been dug out the week before by some bored kids, or centuries ago by a wandering Shawnee mystic.

With my head next to the hole and my eyes closed, I heard what Tom was talking about: swiftly running water. Water was blood to a cave, and running water meant a living cave: spectacular formations and strange creatures, our eternal quests.

"I think we can get to Squire Boone through there," said Tom.

"No way."

"I'm not shitting," he said. "We get through that hole, and it'll connect."

I shook my head. Squire Boone was almost to the Ohio River, just a short trip from the interstate and from Kentucky. I had heard Tom say repeatedly that all the caves were connected, but this notion strained my considerable respect for his knowledge of our local geography and geology.

"Come on," he said, impatient with my doubts. Even as the rational part of my mind braced itself halfheartedly to debate Tom about his theory and the wisdom of pursuing

it, the rest was assessing the beam coming from my red plastic flashlight: steady and strong, ready to go exploring, at least until suppertime. Tom was already digging at the hole, enlarging it one handful of gravelly dirt at a time. I heard rocks falling through it, out the other side, and landing some distance below. Soon, the hole was almost big enough to fit through, and Tom started climbing into it feetfirst.

"Wait, you don't know how far down that is on the other side," I said. "You could fall two hundred feet."

He hesitated. "What should we do? Just walk away? Let's try it and see."

"Come on out, I've got an idea."

Tom reluctantly stepped back while I sifted through the gravel he'd dug out, until I found a rock about the size of a Ping-Pong ball. I shoved my arm through the hole as far as I could, up to my shoulder, until my ear was up against the wall. Then I released the rock.

I listened to it roll. When that sound stopped, when the rock was falling through open space, I counted in my head "one Mississippi" to mark the seconds. Before I could say "miss," the rock struck the bottom, a hard, high-pitched crack that echoed sharply.

"Let me try that again." I grabbed another rock from the cave floor.

"That's bigger," said Tom. "It'll fall faster."

"No it won't," I said. "But it will be louder." I rolled it down the chute again, and counted the brief fall.

"So how far is it, professor?"

"It takes two seconds to fall fifty feet," I said, standing up and brushing the dirt off my hands.

"And it doesn't matter how big the rock is?" He sounded as doubtful as I had about reaching Squire Boone.

"Nope. You'd take two seconds to fall fifty feet, too. And that rock fell in less than a half-second."

"So . . ."

"It's hard to say. I'm guessing around ten feet."

"Then it's like jumping off your porch roof," said Tom. "That's about ten feet. Let's go."

He resumed climbing into the hole, forcing himself through it backward. At one point before he completely disappeared, he looked up at me with only his head visible, like a grinning human hunting trophy that had been mounted to the wall of the cave. Then he popped through and was gone. When I didn't hear any screams or breaking bones, I knew I had to follow.

It was a tight squeeze, even for wiry kids like us. I had to put my hands over my head to fit through. I pushed backward, slid for a few feet, and then fell straight down through a brief, terrifying emptiness, before landing squarely on my ass. Stars traced tiny curls in the blackness. When they faded, I pointed my flashlight straight up, to see where I had landed, but realized with awe that the size of the chamber was too large—my beam couldn't reach the top. Tom and I had discovered something massive.

"Holy shit," I said, the leisurely response of my echo another indication of the room's giant size. I swept my flashlight around; I saw Tom's beam moving in the distance as he did the same.

Surrounding us like the trunks of redwoods were the

biggest stalagmites I had ever seen, ropy columns of pink stone that looked like molten wax, each identical, each at least twenty feet around at the base and rising straight up. They were wet—alive—still growing as water dripped onto them from the unseen ceiling, depositing tiny amounts of dissolved limestone with each drop, growing each massive column a few molecules at a time. Right through the middle of the room ran the stream we'd heard from the other side, burbling in from a hole at one end and crashing into another at the far wall. The stream had cut a trench through the stone floor as straight and true as an irrigation ditch.

"Think how old these are," shouted Tom from across the room. I knew I wasn't supposed to, I had been warned in countless school field trips that the oil from our hands could kill the cave formation's growth, but I reached out anyway and put the palm of my hand against the side of one of the columns. It felt preternaturally immovable and solid, as if the columns were holding the whole surface of Clark County above us in place.

Tom was less transfixed than I. He quickly worked his way to the other side of the chamber. "Check this out," he shouted in the distance, his voice echoing more sharply. I walked toward his flashlight beam. It felt strange to be so far away from him in a cave, where usually things were more compact. "Look," he said when I reached his side at the edge of the chamber.

He had called me over to a wavy sheet of rock growing up from the floor. It was as thin as paper, thin enough that we saw the yellow glow of a flashlight held to it on the other side. Its folds and curves looked like a curtain blowing

over an open window. Tom and I stood on each side, facing each other, examining it—we'd never seen anything like it in all of our explorations. Water dropped onto it from above, growing the wall microscopically, imperceptibly between us. I was lost for a minute, watching a perfectly spherical drop of water fall onto it and roll along its edge.

"Over here," Tom yelled from far away—he had darted away from me again, moving on with his exploration. At the end of the chamber, one of the giant treelike stalagmites had fallen. I tried to imagine what it would have been like to be in the chamber when that thing had tumbled over. It was broken into three even sections, looking like a column from a ruined ancient temple. Tom scurried up the ragged broken end of one of the pieces, using the jagged nubs for handholds. He soon stood atop the fallen column, which put him within reach of a horizontal crack in the wall.

The crack was about two feet high, and ran the length of the chamber, at least as far as we could see with our underpowered flashlights. Tom hoisted himself into the crack, and lay down inside of it, looking down at me, where I still stood on the cave floor. "Come on up," he said.

I hesitated.

"Come on up," he said again. "This crack'll take us to Squire Boone."

"Wait, don't you want to check this out? This room is better than anything at Squire Boone, even the five-dollar tour."

Before I was done even saying it, Tom was crawling forward, endlessly enthusiastic about finding the next chamber, learning how they all tied together. I climbed up the broken end of the column, peered inside the crack, and

pulled myself up and in. Tom didn't say anything; he continued scurrying forward, into the darkness. I paused just a moment to look ahead. The crack was rough and dirty, with no formations—it really was more of a fissure in the dirt than what we typically called a cave.

We crawled until I completely lost track of time and distance. Gradually, the ceiling above and floor below turned back into smooth, damp limestone. I hustled to keep Tom in my light. The crack shrunk as we progressed, a millimeter at a time, until eventually I felt my back scraping against the ceiling and my belly on the floor as I moved forward. Soon, I was pushing hard through the crevice. Then I was stuck.

I watched as Tom, slightly smaller than me, continued forward a foot more, until he, too, was stuck fast. I could see only the soles of his shoes, struggling, his toes scraping the hard stone in an attempt to push forward. His shoes scraped a line into the thin film of watery mud that coated the rock. Then, just as I had, he tried to move backward. "Shit," he said.

No one knew where we were—that was my first thought. Both Tom's parents and mine accepted that on fair summer days we would both disappear into the woods all day, returning home filthy and tired but always in time for supper. Local folklore about boys killed in the caves began racing through my mind. Being trapped in a chamber as it suddenly filled with water was one popular motif. Tom had once explained to me that a dusty cave was safe, while a wet cave like this might get flushed out once in a while by a lethal flash flood. And drowning wasn't the only way to die in a cave. Sheriff Kohl sang lead in a gospel group around

town, and I suddenly remembered a lyric he sang at the Harvest Homecoming about a Kentuckian who had died in a cave long ago: *I dreamed I was a prisoner, my life I could not save.* The man in that story, Floyd Collins, had died of "exposure," a word I found horribly vague and descriptive at the same time. Without even a T-shirt to protect me, the stone on all sides leached warmth from my body. My teeth started chattering.

"Are we screwed?" I asked, trying not to sound like too much of a puss. Tom stopped struggling just long enough to let me know that we were.

The fear seemed to make my body swell, fixing me even tighter in the crack. I knew better than to try and muscle my way out—I wasn't stronger than all that limestone. I could tell by watching Tom's feet that he had not given up. His shoes twisted and twitched. The crack, I noticed, was barely as high as one of his shoes. One of those shoes came off, then the other, and he continued the struggle in just his socks.

I fought harder to move, completely unsuccessfully, and the frustration allowed me to completely give in to the fear. I could move my arms, and kick my feet about an inch up and down, so I did both as fast as I could in a kind of swimming motion that I couldn't stop once I started. In my panic, I actually wondered how long it would take me to shrink a little, how many days might pass before I starved enough to slide freely backward the way we came in. Long before then, I knew, my flashlight would die, and I would somehow have to remember which direction to crawl in the total darkness. As I flailed, sweat combined with the dirt and stung hard as it dripped into my eyes.

I stopped long enough to rub my eyes. I noticed then that Tom wasn't thrashing. He was digging his toes into the dirt and pushing in a very deliberate, determined way. It was hard to see at first, but he was moving infinitesimally forward. The motion was almost imperceptible because his denim shorts remained in place—Tom was pushing himself right out of his Wranglers. I watched as his feet went up inside the legs and disappeared and the shorts collapsed, as if Tom had wanted out of the crack so badly that he had willed himself into vapor. His dimensions reduced by the thickness of one ply of well-worn denim, he shot forward, past the range of my flashlight's beam.

"Got it!" I heard him say at the other side. By the echo and the strength of his voice, I could tell he was in a chamber large enough to stand in upright. I didn't shout for Tom to come back and help me. There was no possibility that he wouldn't.

He crawled back to me without his flashlight so that his hands would be free. I saw his white face like a rising moon when he came within range of mine. He stuck out both hands, and I let go of my flashlight to grab them. With a hard yank, Tom pulled me forward. I tumbled out of the crack, leaving behind in the crevice my flashlight, as well as Tom's shorts and shoes.

I took in the new room where we found ourselves, my senses heightened by the receding panic. Tom had left his flashlight sitting on a ledge in the chamber, pointing more or less at the crack that almost swallowed us forever. The walls of the new chamber were high and smooth. Inviting paths led out from two sides. The packed-down dirt made them look oddly well-traveled.

"Holy shit," said Tom, as we slapped the dirt off ourselves. It was the peculiar bright orange mud that was characteristic of our local caves. We were coated in the stuff from head to toe.

"That sucked," I said, trying to sound unfazed.

Tom moved across the chamber, to where the crack entered at the other end. "I wonder if there's a better way through," he said, eyeing the length of it across the wall. I remained silent in a way that let him know I had no intention of crawling into that crack ever again. "It looks wider over here," he said.

"Not to me."

Suddenly Tom heard something I didn't. "What was that?" he whispered.

A moment later, a dozen smiling, jabbering tourists rounded the corner, led by a man in the faux park ranger's shirt and wide-brimmed hat of the Squire Boone tour guide. As they came into view, hidden electric lights clicked on, dramatically underlighting the chamber's formations in garish green and blue. The guide was walking backward, talking to the group, so the paying customers saw us before he did: two filthy, orange boys squinting at the light, one of them wearing nothing but his Fruit-of-the-Looms.

The guide turned to face us and there was a split second when we all just stared at one another. Then Tom and I sprinted directly toward them as the group eagerly parted.

We hauled ass down the well-lit tour path. Ahead of us we heard the squawk of someone shouting through a walkie-talkie and saw the herky-jerky movement of a flashlight in the hands of someone at a dead run. Tom took a quick right and I followed him, into a room that was lit

with green and red lights, a room whose theme I remembered from a past school trip as having something to do with a pile of rocks shaped like a Christmas tree. Through that room and into the next: we ran directly toward the dusty coffin of Squire Boone, propped up on what looked like sawhorses, when Tom took another sharp turn. We splashed across a shallow, slow stream—I wondered what the sad blind fish might think of the commotion—and into the safety of an unlit, untraveled passageway, where deep, loose gravel made running tough. I knew the tour guides would hesitate before following us this far off the path. I also knew from Tom's speed that he must have had some notion of where he was going. I trusted him completely; his sense of direction in the caves was uncanny.

We ran like scalded dogs up the path, until I saw narrow lines of light ahead of us, the unmistakable, welcoming brightness of natural sunlight. The two lines of light intersected at a perfect right angle, a beacon of something that had to be man-made. We got closer and I saw that the light outlined a metal door set into the rock by some enterprising cave owner, an attempt at keeping nonpaying customers like us out. It was not, however, designed to keep anyone in. Tom and I hit the door with our shoulders at the same time and it flew open, hurling us into the blinding sunlight, the heat, and the blanketing humidity.

We slammed the door behind us and quickly assessed the situation. We were alone, for the moment. Tom and I ran to the top of a low ridge to get a better look at the landscape and to figure out exactly where we were. We saw the tall knobs in the distance, heard traffic on Highway 60, and saw the slightest discoloration of sunset on the western

sky. We knew that the Ohio River, and beyond that Kentucky, must be just over the next ridgeline. A small aluminum fishing boat with a Kentucky license sticker on its bow was turned over by the cave door, another indication that the big river was nearby. As we ran by the boat, we stopped long enough to lift it up, to confirm that there were good oars stored beneath it, and that it looked generally river-worthy. Despite our mad rush, taking inventory of a discovery that valuable in the woods came automatically.

Having fixed our position in the woods, we ran all the way back to my house, staying off the roads and hidden in the trees because of Tom's pants-less condition. At my house, both cars were in the driveway, meaning both Mom and Dad were home, which I still wasn't used to at this early hour. Tom and I snuck in the back door when I heard Mom vacuuming in front. We didn't have to sneak by any siblings—to my perpetual dismay, I was an only child, a rarity in a land of sprawling German-Catholic clans. In my room, Tom put on a pair of my pants and old sneakers over his orange-stained socks. Tom's pants and shoes, I knew, would be forever preserved in the cave, or at least until disturbed by another reckless boy or some wondering archaeologist centuries in the future.

I walked with Tom to the intersection of Cabin Hill Road and our driveway, the relief from having gotten away unscathed starting to settle in. I saw a turkey hop deeper into the woods as we approached, effectively disappearing into the green. Had it been winter, after the leaves fell and the scrub died off, we could have watched that turkey run for a thousand yards, and followed its tracks in the snow for miles. We could have seen right through the trees down to

Highway 60, perhaps even to the black smudge on the road where the Chrysler had burned. It was August, though, and the woods were choked with vegetation; the turkey could feel secure. I couldn't even see the deep gorge that marked our property line, barely a half mile away.

"Want to eat supper here?" I asked.

"Nah. I'm eating with my dad on the picket line—they're cooking burgers."

"Cool." I was insanely jealous. "Hey," I asked, always eager to be part of the strike conversation. "What's a 'scab' anyway? Are they the guys that beat everybody up?"

"Nah," said Tom, "those are the thugs. The scabs are the guys that steal everybody's jobs."

With that, Tom walked off, occasionally reaching back to hike up my slightly too-large jeans.

As I walked into our house through the basement door, I heard that the vacuuming had stopped. My parents were in the kitchen arguing in tense low voices. They fought so seldom that I could tell they weren't very good at it—their rhythm was off, inexperienced as they were in disagreeing with each other on any matter of substance. It was far more common, if I came home unexpectedly early, to find them blushing on the couch and straightening their clothes.

"I don't want you turning our home into some kind of headquarters," my mother whispered. My ears perked up at this. I imagined midnight gatherings, code words, and trench coats: a speaking role finally in the strike drama. My father laughed in a way that let both my mother and me know we were being ridiculous.

"Cricket, he wants to talk to me here. What was I supposed to tell him? He's been over here a thousand times."

"Tell him he can come over for supper any time he likes, but to keep work at the plant. Where it belongs."

My father muttered something that sounded like a muted capitulation as I reached the top of the stairs. Despite the strike, Dad was in his work clothes: a short-sleeved white dress shirt; a striped, wide tie hanging loosely around his neck; and some kind of eyepiece on a lanyard, a device that measured the degree of gloss on finished caskets. Stacks of folders and envelopes embossed with the Borden Casket Company logo were on the kitchen table in front of him. Mom turned away from both of us and began noisily stacking clean glasses in the cupboard.

My mother was from Kentucky, but other than that her childhood was almost a complete mystery to me. Not only had I never met a single blood relative of my mother's, I'd never even seen a family photograph. I didn't know how many siblings she had, what her father did for a living, or what town she'd called home. Once in a great while Mom would drop some tiny clue about her past: a story about a brother in a bloody fistfight, a family legend about a relative's coffin washed away in a flood, a sad memory of charity packages at Christmastime. I grabbed each fragment as it came my way, hoping someday to assemble them into a full mosaic that would tell me her story, which was, after all, half of my story. I was entitled to it.

Not all the gaps in my mother's story took place in the murky past. She was an ardent admirer of Sheriff Kohl's, had worked on his campaign, and Sheriff Kohl had the

honor of being the only nonfemale candidate for office to ever have a sign in our front yard. The sheriff admired my mother as well, singling her out at campaign events for praise and long, laughter-filled conversations. Mom periodically took calls from him in the middle of the night, quick calls that resulted in her hurriedly leaving us, sometimes until the next morning when she would come home frazzled and exhausted. I tried and tried, but could never think of a single good explanation for Mom's behavior. And I knew from Dad's example that I was not to ask about her secrets, no matter how much they bothered me.

Because she was not from Borden, my mother was also a mystery to our neighbors. Without their ancestors knowing her ancestors, they could only make vague guesses about her true nature, about whether she might be prone to cancer, drinking, or dishonesty. Her self-taught feminism kept the neighbors off-balance as well—she went to meetings and rallies in Louisville, she liked to loan books by Kate Millett and Betty Friedan to the unsuspecting, and she confused cashiers everywhere with Susan B. Anthony dollars. Let it be said, however, that in Borden, Indiana, in 1979, her feminism was too bizarre to seem threatening. Down Old Township Road, Red Vogel liked to paint welcoming messages to UFOs on the roof of his mobile home; my mom's behavior was regarded similarly. It was strange, but more or less harmless. My mother was beautiful, well-liked, and active in church and at my school. Cricket Gray was just somewhat unknowable to my neighbors, as she was to me.

My father, on the other hand, was an open book, born and raised in Borden, but educated at Purdue where he

received a degree in aeronautical engineering—he used to say that he was too dumb at the time to realize it was a smart guy's degree. I had heard repeatedly all the mild escapades of his youth, not just from him, but from all of our neighbors who had grown up with him and witnessed it all: the time he tripped on the stage at junior high school graduation, the time he'd gotten his car stuck in the mud on prom night, the successful carpet cleaning business he'd run during summers home from Purdue. Neil Armstrong had been a classmate of his in West Lafayette. Everybody in Borden knew it.

Although my father had employed his degree for twenty years making wooden coffins instead of rocket ships, he still liked to pepper his speech with space-age terminology. When people asked him why he had gotten a good education like that only to return to Borden, he would say that he had "failed to achieve escape velocity."

He spied me on the steps. "What's going on, my man?" Mom didn't turn around from the cabinets she was furiously organizing.

"Nothin'," I said. He could tell I was happy to see him, hours before he usually got home, and this in turn made him happy. He grabbed my arms and pulled me closer in a kind of half-hug. "What's going on?" I knew my dad had a tendency to be pathologically honest under direct questioning.

"I've got a little meeting here tonight," he said. "No big deal."

"Here?" I said. I knew it had to have something to do with the strike. "Who with?"

My father suddenly noticed my orange hue, and took the opportunity to change the subject. "Good Lord, you

are filthy," he said with real admiration in his voice. "What have you been doing all day?"

I tried to think of what I had done that day that would alarm my parents the least. "Tom and I saw them burn up a car down at the picket line."

"You watched?" His grip on my arms tightened. Mom turned around, real concern in her eyes.

"Whose car did they burn? Don's?" she asked.

"It was a junk car," my father said dismissively, overcompensating in his attempt to sound casual about the whole thing. "I heard it didn't even have an engine in it."

"Did Sheriff Kohl come?" my mother asked me.

"Of course not," Dad said sourly, "they could burn that plant to the ground and Kohl wouldn't risk losing a vote by turning his siren on." His comment seemed designed to piss off Mom.

"I guess you think he should go down there and crack some heads," my mother snapped. "You want him to break out the clubs? Beat some people up to save a junk car?"

"I want him to keep the peace," my father said. "I think I heard him say he'd do that in one of the eight hundred campaign speeches I had to sit through."

The whole exchange had confused the hell out of me. "Don't we want the strikers to win?" I asked. "Tom's dad says they work their butts off and the owners make all the money."

There was an extended tense silence. I could tell I had said something wrong. In a spastic kid's errant strategy, I decided it was best just to keep talking. "Tom's dad says they deserve doctor cards, and that they have to do something now if they ever want to get ahead."

My mother put her hands on her hips and eyed my father. Dad chose his next words carefully.

"What none of us want," he said in measured tones, "is for that factory to close. The strikers don't realize that a lot of factories like ours are going south, or to Mexico, or even further."

"How could the Borden Casket Company move away from Borden?"

"It will if the owners wake up tomorrow and decide that keeping the plant here isn't worth the trouble," he answered. "Then where will Borden be? Where will Tom's dad be?"

"Oh," I said. Everything I had heard on the picket line suddenly seemed wrong. "Maybe you should go down on the picket line and tell them all that."

"Son, they won't listen to me down on that picket line. I'm management."

Now I was really confused. "I thought . . ." I strained for the right words. Unlike Tom, I had not mastered the vocabulary of collective bargaining. "I thought you *worked* there."

After a pause, Mom and Dad both burst out laughing. Although I was still confused, I was happy that my words had somehow swept the tension out of our little home just as I had brought it in. Dad began talking in a more relaxed, instructive tone, the same tone he used to explain to me why water towers were necessary, how the refrigerator worked, or why all rocks, no matter how big, take two seconds to fall fifty feet.

"I'm management, Son—they pay me a salary. I'm not in the union. Tom's dad gets paid by the hour, and he belongs

to the union. The union negotiates his wage, and that's what the company has to pay him."

"Did the union tell him to go on strike?"

"That's right," said Dad.

"Only after the company refused to negotiate the contract," said Mom pleasantly. She had made her way over to the table and was laying down our three plates. Behind her, pork chops sizzled on the skillet and biscuits cooled on a wire rack. I looked back at Dad.

"You're mother's right," he said. "The company came to the table with a fair offer, the union refused it, we refused to negotiate anymore, and they decided to go on strike. Many of those men thought it was a mistake."

"Why do they stay in the union then?" I asked.

"If they want to work in our factory, they have to," said Dad. "That's what's called a closed shop."

Mom jumped in. "People join unions because they have more power if they work together." Dad smiled right back at her.

"That's true, too," he said. "Of course."

"Have we ever had a strike here before?"

"Lord, yes. Back in the forties when they first unionized the plant, they had to bring soldiers up here to keep the peace—there are pictures of it in the library. Right after the war, they had strikes so regular people used to plan their hunting trips around them."

That made me feel better, to think that all this had happened before, and that somehow everyone had gotten through it.

"Does that clear everything up?" he asked.

"I guess. But I'm still not sure: are we for or against the strikers?"

Dad started to answer when Mom interrupted. "Go wash up. Dinner's almost ready."

As I went into the bathroom I heard Mom and Dad both laughing. I washed my hands and arms up to my elbows, watching the orange dirt spiral down the drain, to our septic tank, back to the southern Indiana underground. Mom was putting the pork chops on the table when I came back downstairs, along with baked beans, kale, and biscuits. Dad said grace and before his hands were unclasped I was digging in. My parents shook their heads as always at the amount of food I could cram into my small body.

After we ate, I helped clean up. Our normal after-dinner card game would have to wait because of Dad's meeting. Instead, we sat down together to watch the news on WHAS-11, one of three Louisville TV stations we picked up—we were blessed with good reception on top of Cabin Hill. The big story was about the court-ordered busing of schoolkids in Louisville, which had just begun. Rocks were thrown, signs carried, and overflowing Catholic schools with names like Trinity and Saint X were turning away panicked white families in droves. The broadcast ended with Chuck Tyner's forecast: hot and humid.

"How come they're not saying anything about the strike?" It was the only news in Borden; every night I was surprised it wasn't covered on TV.

"Things have to get pretty bad way out here before we make the Louisville news," my dad said.

The doorbell rang. Before my parents could react, I sprang from the couch. Anybody who really knew us came in through the back door, by the kitchen. An actual ring of the doorbell was always startling and a portent of drama. I opened the door so fast that our visitor's finger was still on the doorbell button. He looked at me through his thick safety glasses and smiled.

"Well, hello, Andy," he said. "You're growing like a weed!" It was Don Strange, the plant manager.

Three

Don Strange was my dad's boss at the coffin factory. I suppose he was everybody's boss. I had never thought of him in that way, however, until the strike began forcing me to divide everyone into the categories of labor and management. Before the strike, I thought everybody in the factory had some unique and equally important individual skill, like the Superfriends, or the members of KISS. Some men went into the woods to cut trees down. Some men, like Tom's dad, worked on the trim line, screwing in handles and hinges. My dad was an engineer on the finish line—he could look at a coffin rolling out of the oven and tell you immediately if the primer was weak, if there was dust in the clearcoat, or if the oven temperature was off by ten degrees. Mr. Strange's skill was making them all work together.

Dad had been correct in saying that Mr. Strange had been to our house many times, but those suppers always retained a certain formality, as indicated by his coming to the front door. Mr. Strange and Dad always began and ended each evening with a handshake, and Mr. Strange always brought some small wrapped gift for my mother, items that would be meticulously displayed the next time

he came to visit, small fancy soaps or a set of brass coasters. Those evenings were a lot like the suppers that Tom's mom would cook for their parish priest. They were friendly, even congenial, but not quite comfortable.

Dad and Mr. Strange did spend one day a year together outside the factory. For as long as I could remember they'd attended the Oaks together, the traditional day for locals to enjoy the festivities at Churchill Downs one day before the complete mob scene of the Derby. And every year after the race, Dad would come home and regale us with the story of how Mr. Strange would carefully study the horses in the paddock, and bet only on the horse taking the biggest prerace shit.

"Hello, Mr. Strange," I said, offering my right hand to shake, just as he had once coached me in his office. His grip was gentle, but his skin was rough from having handled a million board feet of fine lumber over a lifetime, eyeing each piece for knots and feeling the grain as it came out of the mill room. He was elfish, shorter than me, with ears that stuck out and giant glasses that accentuated the smallness of his head. Like a lot of tiny old men, he seemed to be cold all the time. On that steamy August evening, he wore a red-and-black-checked flannel hunting jacket. I knew from past visits that the inside pocket of the jacket was lined not with shotgun shells but with rolls of wild cherry Life Savers.

"My Lord, you're getting big," he said. I felt my dad walk up behind me. Mom marched up the stairs without greeting our visitor, a breach of courtesy that startled us all. Mr. Strange gave my father a look that told me he understood what was going on far better than I did.

"Well," he said.

"Come on in, Don," said my dad.

"No, wait a minute." The twinkle returned to Mr. Strange's eye. "I want to talk to this young man here for a minute. Are you still runnin' around in those woods every day?"

"Yessir, near every day."

"You huntin' squirrel?"

"In season." He had clear blue eyes for an old man, even through the thick lenses.

"Fishin'?"

"I just went fishing on Sunday."

"What'd you get?"

"Nothing but a gar." I held my hands up to indicate the size. A gar was another of our peculiar indigenous species, another I didn't know was peculiar at the time. It was a long, thin stone-age fish with an alligatorlike snout and hundreds of needle-sharp teeth. It liked to cruise right below the surface, sometimes snapping at our fishing line where it touched the water, spitefully severing it with its impressive chops.

"You know how to cook a gar?" asked Mr. Strange.

I turned to look back at my dad, who had always told me that you couldn't eat a gar. Their bones were like their teeth, sharp and plentiful. Dad was smiling in a way that told me I was about to hear a joke he had heard a thousand times before.

"Well, I'll tell you how," continued Mr. Strange. "First, you nail it to a board, you got that?"

I nodded.

"Then, you leave it out in the sun for two weeks, okay?"

"Okay . . ."

"Then, you throw away the gar and eat the board!"

I laughed hard. It might have been an old joke, but I had never heard it. I couldn't wait to tell Tom.

"You keep an eye on those trees for me while you're out in the woods, okay?" said Mr. Strange as my laughter subsided. "Especially the small ones."

"I will."

"And let me know if you spot a mahogany. I need one of those down at the plant, okay?"

"Okay," I said, laughing again. I knew mahoganies came from some jungle somewhere, one of the few hardwoods we had to import.

"Here's an advance reward for when you find one." He handed me a two-dollar bill from his shirt pocket. I'd never seen one before, and at first I thought it was some kind of joke, like those million-dollar bills with Jimmy Carter on one side and a peanut on the other.

"Don, don't," my dad said seriously. He had that small-town tendency that found all exchanges of money somehow dirty. Mr. Strange shushed him away. "They gave me that crazy thing at the bank this morning. Don't you think the boy deserves some kind of reward for finding me a mahogany?"

"Thanks, Mr. Strange," I said, folding the bill in half after briefly studying the engravings on both sides.

"Go hide that where your daddy can't find it," he said.

I stepped back to let Mr. Strange into the house. He passed in a fragrant cloud of Old Spice and pipe tobacco. Dad had arranged his files neatly on the coffee table, each stack topped with a chart drawn in mechanical pencil on graph paper, along with some neat drawings of equipment

lineups and tooling arrangements. My father, like many engineers of that precomputer generation, was a wonderful illustrator, evidence of his ease with the physical world. I walked upstairs before suffering the embarrassment of being told to leave, but I stopped to look down at a comforting scene.

Both men were hunched over Dad's drawings, both with their glasses down on the tips of their noses, both pointing to precise positions on the paper with the sharp tips of their pencils. They looked serious, but utterly natural, and not at all worried. I had seen my dad attack problems that way countless times before, an engineer's technique: charting, calculating, and dissecting the data until out of sheer exhaustion, the solution surrendered itself. Now, I assumed, the problem they were working on was how to keep the plant from moving to Mexico.

"So we could produce with as few as fifteen men?" said Mr. Strange. He seemed pleasantly surprised.

"With the right fifteen men. For a little while. Until we use up the preassembled boxes we've got in storage."

"How many of those do we have?" asked Mr. Strange.

"Two hundred and seven. I counted them myself."

"Well, that's something," said Mr. Strange with a sigh. "We could fill some orders, anyway. Keep the wolves at bay for a little while longer. What about bringing in outside men?"

My dad shook his head vigorously. "No. They wouldn't know what to do—it would take weeks to train them."

"Plus, you don't want to bring in scabs," said Mr. Strange.

"No, I do not. Do you? I don't want to be responsible for

that. I'd rather just wait a little bit and see if we can't get some of our own to cross the line. I've got some men in mind I might call, men I think might be willing to go back to work. Fellows I know need the paycheck. I'm not sure Cricket would ever talk to me again if I hired scabs, not to mention what the good men of Local 1096 would do to them."

"Trust me, Gus," said Mr. Strange, "the good men of Local 1096 won't take it any easier on their own when they start crossing that line."

After a pause, their talk began to focus again on the various ratios, coefficients, and tooling arrangements necessary to start making coffins flow again through the factory. I retreated up the stairs.

In my room, I started reading a library book about the great maritime explorers: Magellan, da Gama, Captain Cook. Like many kids in the heartland, I was fascinated by the whole idea of an ocean. Exhausted by my own explorations, and comforted by the rumble of deep voices coming from downstairs, I fell asleep before it was dark, the book still in my hands.

I had a nightmare that night about being stuck in the cave. I was in the crevice, unable to move, the light from my flashlight slowly dimming as the batteries died. Dad was somewhere in the cave, unaware of the danger I was in or unable to help. Just as my light winked out for good, Tom tapped three times on my bedroom window, waking me, rescuing me.

I shook my head as I regained my bearings. I saw only a silhouette through my window, but I knew it had to be Tom. He had climbed up our porch railing and onto the porch roof, which went right up to my bedroom. Before my

heart had even slowed down from the nightmare, it began to race again in a familiar combination of dread and excitement, the way it always did before I blindly followed Tom into the unknown.

There comes a time in every boy's life where his capacity for getting into trouble suddenly exceeds his ability to get out of it. For Tom and me, that moment had arrived that spring, when we discovered we could sneak out of our bedrooms in the middle of the night. We had performed the feat exactly three times. The first two times we didn't go anywhere. We'd skulked a few feet into the woods, listened to the owls hoot and the crickets chirp, and reveled in our daring. Then I had carefully climbed up to my window and gone back to bed. The third trip was more dramatic. That time we'd been scared so bad that we'd gone almost the whole summer without sneaking out again. That was in May, before the strike, on a night when Chuck Tyner had warned in his six o'clock forecast that the atmosphere was "unstable."

It had seemed peaceful enough when we set out. The moon was out but hidden by thin clouds, a white smudge against the sky. "Where are we going?" I asked. It was clear Tom had a destination in mind.

"The railroad tracks out by the cemetery," he said excitedly. "Dad said when he got home from work that a train full of tanks was stopped there." His dad worked swing shift before the strike, getting off at midnight.

"Tanks?" I was picturing cylindrical tank cars full of ethanol, or corn oil, or any of the other agroproducts that constantly rolled through town. "What's the big deal?"

"No: tanks. Army tanks, Sherman tanks."

We sped up to a trot, not wanting to miss the tanks if they were only stopping briefly in Borden. I was skeptical. I'd seen hundreds of trains pass through town, and I'd never seen a tank onboard. I had a hard time even picturing such a thing. Still, strange things had been known to roll through town. There was the time, for instance, when the Ringling Brothers Circus train stopped for an hour in the middle of the night on its way to their winter home in Florida—Patsy Miller still talked about the bearded lady and the tired-looking midgets who ambled down from their car and into the store to buy coffee and cigarettes. If there was a train full of tanks, we both wanted to see it.

We jumped over the low stone wall that surrounded the cemetery, and by the light of the graveyard's single security light I saw that Tom's dad had not exaggerated. It was a whole train full of them, one per flatcar, gun barrels raised jauntily and pointing in the general direction of the high school. The tanks extended as far as we could see in both directions.

"Holy shit," we both said. We dodged gravestones as we sprinted to get closer.

The tanks were painted a dark forest green—we were still painting our tanks for jungle duty rather than the sandy colors of the desert in 1979. We got close enough to one to read the indecipherable sequence of white numbers stenciled on its body. It was beautiful, unblemished. The wheels were fascinating to me. I had seen tanks on television, and drawn them on notebooks, so I knew what they looked like in a cartoonish, GI Joe kind of way. Up close, though, I saw how the wheels linked into the track, and how heavy-duty that track appeared. I had always imagined the

track of a tank to be a kind of conveyor, like one of the soft belts that carried caskets around the factory. In fact, the belt was a complicated interlocking flat metal chain, a machine unto itself. The pieces of the belt looked like steel teeth, and they fit together as precisely as a mosaic. It looked like a device designed to crush rocks into powder.

A ladder of steel rungs led up the side of the tank. The second I saw those rungs, I knew where Tom would end up.

"Let's go on up," he said, reading my thoughts.

"No. No damn way."

"Why not?" He was astonished that I would pass on such an opportunity.

"Too dangerous."

"What's dangerous about it?" he asked. "We've gone up on train cars before. Dozens of times."

That was true—once we had spent an afternoon climbing inside musty L&N boxcars looking for hoboes. All we found was a used condom, the meaning of which Tom had to explain to me.

"These are tanks!"

"What's the difference? The thing ain't gonna start shooting just 'cause we climb up on it."

"No way." I shook my head.

He reached for the bottom rung and started climbing up.

"Tom!" I said, a little loudly. He didn't look down as he continued on up.

He climbed all the way up to the turret, the highest point. He scurried all over it, examining the thing in detail, searching for weaknesses in the armor. "Look here,"

he said pointing, "there's little windows in this thing." He peered inside. "I bet I can get in there." He began tugging on the hatch. That was more than I could take. I followed him up.

It truly was irresistible for a couple of hillbilly kids like us: all the appeal of a new gun and a new car combined. There were hooks and loops all over it, everything made from thick steel, every component looking indestructible, right down to the thick glass of the armored searchlight. Tom was straining against the top hatch with all his strength, trying to muscle it open. What kind of trouble Tom could get us into from the inside of an army tank I could not imagine. Fortunately, the army's prudent tank designers had made it difficult for attackers to open from the outside. Still, given enough time, I think Tom would have gotten us in.

The car suddenly clanked forward as the train began moving, onward down the line to Fort Knox, Kentucky, I suppose, or farther. Tom and I scrambled down, and at the bottom of the tank jumped well clear, a practiced maneuver designed to avoid an awkward landing with an arm or a leg across the tracks.

The cars jerked forward again, and again, groaning and creaking until finally the whole train was rolling slowly forward, the massive power of the unseen engine overcoming the inertia of a hundred army tanks. Tom watched a little wistfully as the tanks rolled past, while I tried to hide my relief. The flatcars clickety-clacked by us with increasing frequency, then the caboose, yellow light pouring from its windows, through which we glimpsed two tired-looking men hunched over a cribbage board.

Then it was gone, leaving behind in Borden only the lonely sound of its whistle.

It wasn't until the whistle faded that we first noticed the lightning in the distance. It was always harder to detect incoming storms at night, when you couldn't see the approaching line of dark clouds, but even in darkness the quickness of this storm's approach was alarming. Tom and I weren't scared of getting struck by lightning or swept away in a tornado; we'd weathered plenty of storms outdoors and knew how to take shelter and survive. But neither of us wanted to sneak back into the house soaking wet at two o'clock in the morning. Tom and I began a slow trot across the cemetery in the direction of home. I noticed it wasn't windy, which was also odd, given the amount of lightning to the south.

By the time we reached the stone wall of the cemetery, it was raining steadily. We heard thunder, still in the distance but getting closer with each rumble. The temperature dropped so noticeably that I visualized the blue line of the cold front moving across us on a weather map. The lightning was so steady that it was like a strobe light, making Tom look robotic as he ran beside me. The trees themselves were still curiously motionless—my experience told me that the wind should be howling in ahead of the rain as the storm barreled down the Ohio Valley like a marble in a pipe. The storm was weird, and that made us run faster, sometimes slipping on the dirt path that was rapidly turning to mud.

We came to a small clearing in the woods, a recently cut patch of forest peppered with low, fresh stumps. Tom saw something and grabbed my arm. I skidded to a halt with him.

In the middle of the field in front of us, four yellow balls of light rolled erratically along the ground. Each was roughly the size of a grapefruit. They weren't rolling with the light wind—they zigzagged in random directions, sometimes jumping a few feet into the air before dropping back to the ground.

"What the hell?" whispered Tom. I won't lie—I was a little afraid. More than that, I felt a real sense of wonder, even when one of the balls began rolling directly toward us.

It rolled almost to our feet, and then floated up to eye level. It was not blindingly bright, only about as intense as a sixty-watt lightbulb. A low buzzing sound came from inside it. All around us I smelled ozone, the smell of electrical failure, a Lionel train set gone bad. As that ball hovered directly in front of our eyes, I was afraid, but I also wanted to feel it. Somehow I knew it would be cool to the touch. As I started to reach out, the ball fizzled and disappeared with a pop.

That snapped us out of our trance. It also announced the onset, finally, of a raging, severe, dangerous storm. We resumed our headlong run, now through the driving rain and constant flashes of lightning that illuminated trees bent over at impossible angles. Occasionally the rain paused to give way to hail, which made a sound like popping popcorn as thousands of icy beads pelted the muddy ground. Thunder crashed, and then echoed a dozen times as the sound bounced from one side of the valley to the other and back. Once or twice I thought I saw more of the light balls bouncing along with us through the woods, but we didn't stop to investigate. When we got to my house, Tom kept running without a word, and I felt bad that he

had to continue on by himself even though that sort of thing didn't seem to bother him. I shot up my front porch, through my window, tossed my soaking wet clothes in a pile on the floor, and jumped into bed.

Even as I got between my blankets, I heard the bleating weather radio alarm in my parents' room—a not uncommon occurrence during the spring tornado season. What happened next, however, was unusual.

Dad burst into my bedroom, wearing just his pajama bottoms, his eyes wild. "Get to the basement!" he yelled, making no attempt to hide his own fear. I ran down the steps with Dad so close behind that I worried he might trample me. Mother was waiting there with a flashlight and a portable radio tuned to 840 WHAS.

The state police had confirmed the touchdown of a powerful tornado in Henryville. It was heading our way. The frantic late-shift weatherman counted down the minutes until the twister reached Borden, his words disappearing into static with each burst of lightning. Suddenly it was there, and the screaming wind all around us really did sound like a train, just like people always say. We had an old Buck stove in the basement, and at the wind's peak, the stove's little iron doors flew open and a blast of cold, wet ash shot across the floor. Then, just as quickly, the storm was gone. The exhausted weatherman began a new countdown, the minutes until the tornado reached Pekin. I peeked inside the stove. It was pristine, sandblasted clean by the ash and the freak wind.

After things quieted down in the basement, and we all caught our breath, Dad led me back up to my bedroom with his hand on my shoulder. I think he felt bad about not

keeping his cool when he woke me up. "Good night," he said softly as we reached my room. Just as he was getting ready to step out, he saw the soaking wet pile of clothes in the middle of my room. A puddle had formed around them. He looked at me, then back at the clothes. He shook his head, shut my door, and never said a word about it.

Neither the news nor my junior *Britannica* said anything about the strange glowing spheres. I learned from old-timers and other less authoritative sources that it was a natural phenomenon called "ball lightning." Some books said that ball lightning was a myth, but I'm here to tell you that it's not. After scouring the library, I did manage to find one other reliable eyewitness account: *On the Banks of Plum Creek*, by Laura Ingalls Wilder. During a raging blizzard, three balls of light rolled down the Ingallses' stovepipe. Ma chased them around the house with a broom before they disappeared. It's one of the more dramatic episodes in the whole Ingalls saga not depicted by a Garth Williams sketch. I presume that's because he had no earthly idea how to draw such a thing.

Our close call with the Daisy Hill tornado kept Tom and me content and safe in our bedrooms at night for almost the entire summer. This August night looked clear, however, and Tom had reason to give covert operations another try.

I slipped out of bed, trying to avoid floor creaks that would give me away. I pushed open the window.

"Hey," I whispered.

"Hey," he whispered back. "Come on, there's something

going on down at the picket line tonight." I quickly slid on my shoes, which Mom had arranged by my bed.

I climbed out the window, closed it behind me, and followed Tom silently down the porch roof. The porch light put the front yard in a yellow oval. From the porch, everything beyond that arc seemed invisible in the darkness. I had learned, however, in our past expeditions, that once beyond the reach of the porch light, my eyes adjusted so that I could see pretty well. In that weird way, the electric light actually blinded us, and I was eager to get beyond it and into the dark woods where I could see again.

"What time is it?" I asked once we were safely in the trees. There was always a feeling of relief when we could talk normally and not worry about waking a parent. The moon was bright and the sky unusually clear. The humidity that could press down on Borden for weeks at a time in the summer had lifted, leaving the night crisp and beautiful, a preview of the rapidly approaching fall.

"I think it's about one in the morning," he said.

"What's going on?"

"I don't know," he said, his eyes glowing with excitement. "I went down to eat a burger during my dad's shift on the picket line, and he sent me right back home—wouldn't let me listen to anything anybody was saying. When he got home, I heard him mumbling something to my mother, and the way she acted, it must have been pretty bad, whatever it was."

I could tell there was something else. "And?"

"And . . ." he said, pausing to build the suspense. "I'm not the only one who snuck out of the house tonight."

"What?"

"I heard my dad start his truck and drive away about a half hour ago."

We cleared the deep gorge that marked our property line, taking turns to briskly walk across a large fallen ash that spanned it, our arms extended for balance. We then picked up the Buffalo Trace, walking side by side again. We remained silent for the next half mile down into the bottom of the valley.

We came off the Buffalo Trace and fought our way through a few feet of undergrowth, and then carefully stepped over an old barbed-wire fence into a well-tended field of soybeans, a carpet of the bushy low plants stretching into the darkness. Across the field loomed the back wall of the factory, well-illuminated by the moonlight, but still forbidding with all the big sodium arc lights turned off. Tom and I knew that the graveyard shift was normally the most hectic time in the big back parking lot, as the eighteen-wheelers were loaded and unloaded in a chaotic scene that resembled some kind of military evacuation. At the eastern end of the lot during happier times, empty trucks with the Borden Casket Company logo ("dedicated to the dignity of life") backed up to the loading docks to the tune of their grumbling engines and unintelligible amplified announcements. When the light above each bay turned from red to green, the trucks were loaded with expensive wooden caskets swaddled in elaborate shipping containers. At the other end of the lot the lumber trucks maneuvered, flatbeds weighed down with tree trunks, one type of wood per truck. In the middle of the lot the drivers met in small, jovial groups, drank coffee,

smoked cigarettes, and laughed their asses off, enjoying what I was sure was the coolest job in the world. I knew from Dad that the coffins they manufactured went all over the world. It amazed me to think that those drivers, neighbors of ours when they weren't on the road, might finish their coffee, rub out the butts of their Kools on the ground, and then drive to Los Angeles, New York, or any of those other large cities I knew from TV.

On that night, though, because of the strike, the place was dark. Tom started walking toward the plant, carefully stepping between the soybean plants to avoid crushing them.

"What are we doing?"

"I want to sneak up on the picket line to see what's going on." He pointed toward the back of the plant.

I processed what he was saying, and understood right away. Sneaking up on the picket line from the front of the plant would be impossible—we'd have to cross Highway 60 and another soybean field, which offered little natural cover, especially in the bright moonlight, and especially a hundred yards away from a group of bored men whose eyes had thoroughly adjusted to the dark. The logical alternative was to sneak through plant property and approach the picket line from behind, from inside the plant's gates. I knew how Tom meant to do it. He was already in motion by the time I realized it.

We crossed the soybean field quickly, very aware of how exposed we were in the bright moonlight. At the back of the plant a railroad spur entered through a massive sliding chain-link gate. It was shut and locked.

"Pull on it," said Tom. I pulled at the gate as hard as I

could, and Tom tried to slide through the tiny gap I created, but couldn't. There were two sets of chain wrapped tightly around it, and judging by the shininess of the chain, I guessed that it was a new security measure in place because of the strike.

Tom lowered himself to the ground and tried to slide under the gate between the rails of the tracks. He could almost make it, but not quite. I saw the bottom wires of the fence dig into his belly as he tried to slide by. He pulled himself back, bleeding and frustrated.

We trotted around the fence looking for other ways inside. Climbing over it was impossible—the fence was topped with a swirl of razor wire. Tom looked thoughtfully at a drainage pipe that penetrated the berm beneath the fence. I saw where it came through on the other side, a distance of about twenty feet. Without hesitating, Tom dove into the pipe. I followed.

Although it hadn't rained in weeks, there was about two inches of stagnant water in the bottom of the pipe. It smelled like an old basement, with an underlying chemical sourness that made me wonder what this pipe might be carrying away from the factory besides rainwater. Small, sharp gravel covered the bottom, like rocks in a creek bed. The pipe itself was corrugated, and the hard ridges also made it painful to crawl along. Because of the small diameter, I could only move my elbows and knees a few inches forward with each step, falling on an elbow when I raised a knee and vice versa as I made slow, uncomfortable progress. There was no way to hurry. It was completely dark. Halfway into the pipe, I couldn't see anything. I just

kept telling myself that if I crawled forward long enough, I would eventually come out the other side.

Finally, I did, rolling out of the pipe and unfurling my cramped limbs. Tom was waiting for me patiently, pulling some tiny rocks out of his elbow. With that, we were officially trespassing on Borden Casket Company property.

I had been to the plant many times, and was vaguely aware of the major functional areas: mill room, assembly, trim, and finish. Inside the fence, though, I was as confused and disoriented as I had been in the cave—and Tom was just as sure-footed. I followed him around two buildings, stopping when he stopped, listening when he listened, until we turned a final corner and saw the picket line, across the asphalt expanse of the front lot. The strikers were just outside of the fence.

There were four men standing around a dwindling fire in a fifty-five-gallon drum. We were too far away to hear the conversation, but something in their stances made it clear that two of the men were arguing. In profile, all four men had the same lean build, and a ball cap pulled down low. The two antagonists were standing rigidly, facing each other directly across the barrel. The lawn chairs were pushed back out of the way. One man pointed his finger with a jabbing motion at the other, who stood unflinching with his hands on his hips. The two noncombatants stayed silent and took turns taking off their ball caps and rubbing their heads with concern. An upside-down picket sign leaned untended against a chair and in the firelight I read 1096: LOUD AND PROUD! A knot popped in the barrel and sent a covey of orange sparks into the air.

Tom ran across the parking lot until he reached a stack of steel drums organized neatly under a sheet-metal roof. I followed him. In our new location, we were close enough to hear the men but well hidden by the barrels.

"So help me, those crazy assholes are going to get themselves killed," said the man pointing his finger. "Those boys don't have a lick of sense between 'em."

"No one thinks it's a good idea, Ray," said the other. That was him—the man with his hands on his hips was Tom's dad. He was speaking slowly to Ray Arnold, trying to calm him down. Arnold was a well-known hothead; a skinny, nervous guy who was always ready to start a fight, no matter how many times he got his ass kicked.

"That's a crock of shit, *Kruer*. Lots of people thought it was a good idea, all that tough talk. People *loved* it. *Ate . . . it . . . up!* Funny how none of those pussies managed to show up here tonight."

"Let's all settle down," said Tom's dad quietly.

"Why's that?" said Ray, leaning toward the drum. "You think it's a good idea, too? Tear up some company shit? Break the law? You want to help those dumb-asses shut this factory down forever?"

Tom's dad didn't say anything, but I felt the two of them glaring at each other. Ray's blood was up.

"So help me," pronounced Ray, "if they show up down here for any goddamn reason, I will use that thing." He pointed to an object beneath his lawn chair, something Tom and I couldn't see from our hiding place. "Union or no union, I will use that thing. Then I will get on that CB in my truck, I will call the cops, and I will tell the whole damn

world who thought this bullshit up, and who thought it was a good idea."

"We don't know if they're going to do anything," said George Kruer. "It just sounded like a lot of big talk to me . . ."

"They sounded pretty serious to me," interrupted Ray.

"Let George talk, Ray," said one of the men who had mostly been quiet.

Tom's dad continued. "It's just a lot of big talk from some pissed off kids."

"What if it wasn't just talk?" said Ray. "What if you're wrong? Maybe I should call the sheriff right now and tell him who's saying what at the union hall these days."

There was a long silence before George Kruer spoke again. "Ray, I'm going to strongly recommend you don't say a goddamn word."

Tom and I turned to face each other. Neither of us had ever heard his dad speak that way before. He had done two tours in the army, we knew, and he would have looked tough, with his muscled arms and their smeared, indecipherable tattoos. It was all mitigated normally by his perpetual smile and the somewhat girly Bruce Jenner haircut that Tom's mom gave him on the front porch. From here, though, behind the drums, we heard a different George Kruer, the Kruer we'd seen in yellowing Polaroids with bandoliers of ammo crossing his chest and jungle foliage in the background. He sounded like a pure badass. I once again felt myself getting jealous over our fathers' relative positions in the strike.

Unfortunately, as I turned back to face the picket line,

hunched over as I was, I lost my balance slightly and put my hand out to brace myself, as if I unconsciously thought the drum in my face was as solid and immovable as a tree of the same diameter. The fifty-five-gallon drum in front of me, however, was completely empty, nearly weightless, and I pushed it firmly into the empty drum in front of it. The two drums banged together with a sound as loud and resonant as a church bell.

"Shit!" said Ray. "That's them!" He ran over to his chair and grabbed what was beneath it. For a split second, as he aimed it at us, I was certain it was a gun. Then he turned it on.

It was a spotlight, the kind of million-candlepower thing that hooked to a car battery and was used by poachers to stun deer. It sure as hell stunned us. Tom and I ducked back down behind the drums, temporarily blinded. I knew we couldn't be seen, shielded by the drums, but as my night vision slowly returned, I saw we were trapped by two impossibly bright bands of white light streaming by each side of the shelter. If we moved, we'd be spotted immediately.

"It's them!" screamed Ray. "Stop! I'm calling the police!" The light jerked as he shouted, the shadows cast by it dodging and weaving crazily. I heard a rattle as he banged against the chain-link fence. The light was so bright individual pebbles cast long shadows in the parking lot. We were pinned.

And then suddenly we were free. Ray briefly turned the light on Tom's dad, either in his excitement or in an unwise act of aggression, giggling as he did it. Tom's dad promptly smashed it to the ground, where it shattered

and extinguished with a loud pop. He and Ray Arnold immediately began the fistfight they had both been preparing for all night, and the other two men began their equally anticipated pulling of the men apart. As much as we both wanted to watch George Kruer kick somebody's ass, Tom and I took the opportunity to skedaddle.

I was sure the whole time we ran that murderous guards were following us, running right behind me with guns drawn. I was paranoid, out of my element on the treeless asphalt instead of in the woods where I knew what the hell I was doing. In the woods, we had to evade pissed off people on occasion: farmers from whom we borrowed watermelons, an occasional Department of Natural Resources ranger, and, of course, angry Squire Boone Caverns tour guides. That was fun, and it even felt slightly heroic, just a more exciting form of the escape-and-evade games we had always played in the woods, whether we called it Capture the Flag, Cowboys and Indians, or Outsmart the Commie Invaders. Running with Tom across the company parking lot felt radically different. As the chain-link fence raced by in my peripheral vision, I felt like a juvenile delinquent, and that made me feel vulnerable.

Tom dove into the drainage pipe and I followed right behind. As we crawled, I saw that Tom had refined his technique. He was shooting through the pipe twice as fast as I could, stagnant water flying up in his wake. He disappeared in front of me and I was alone, about halfway through, with Tom standing outside whispering frantically at me to hurry up, his voice amplified and metallically sharp inside the pipe. Maybe it was my slightly longer limbs, but no matter how hard I exerted myself, I couldn't speed up, I

could only lift my elbows and knees a few inches, move them forward, and do it again, making exhausting, painful, slow progress.

I felt something beneath my thigh move as I trudged forward. I was so out of breath and hell-bent to escape that I ignored it at first, until I put down my leg again, and felt it farther up and probing urgently, toward my head. There was something alive with me in the pipe, something big, and I knew with a bolt of pure, nauseous dread what it had to be. It was racing forward with the exact kind of panic I felt, both of us determined to get out and get away from each other. I pushed up on my elbows as far and as fast as I could, smashing the back of my head into the top of the pipe. My face was still just inches from the snake's head when he slithered forward from under my chest.

He was a copperhead. As dark as it was inside the pipe, the snake was big enough and I was close enough to see that clearly: the penny-colored head, the hard cat's eyes. He was huge, too; even as his head came even with mine, I felt him tugging his tail beneath my knee. With that knee, I had unintentionally pinned him, enraging him, but I couldn't raise my knee without lowering my face, already just inches from the snake. He began to spasm with panic, his tail jerking under my knee with surprising force. He twisted and turned his head toward mine, and I saw in the slits of his eyes something more primitive than hate. Ready to strike, he stretched his mouth open wide, exposing his bone-white, hook-shaped fangs.

I shot my hand out and grabbed his neck, which caused the rest of my body to fall on top of him. The full length of my torso was now pressing on him, as he contorted crazily

beneath me. I was holding the head away from my face, but barely, and he was jerking toward me with his mouth open, trying with every instinct in that tiny brain to sink his fangs into one of my veins. I tried to kill him with the hand I had around his neck. I squeezed as hard as I could but it didn't have any affect other than wearing out my grip, and I knew that whatever I did, I could not let go. I tried to press my thumb through his skull, but the thing had been engineered too well to be killed that way—it was like trying to push my thumb through a walnut. I tried pulling his head away, while keeping the rest of him pinned beneath me, to see if I could pull him in half, but again, the constraints of the pipe, the sturdy design of the snake, and my inadequate strength made it impossible.

Abandoning the idea of pulling the snake apart, I pulled up my knees, and discovered that with snake in hand, I had still advanced six inches or so down the pipe. I went to my belly again, this time anticipating the feeling of the snake fighting beneath me, and moved forward farther, keeping eye contact with the snake the entire time. I worked my way down the pipe with snake in hand, and finally realized that Tom had been yelling at me the entire time—and not all that much time had passed. By moving like a snake myself, I slowly, painfully, slithered to the end of the drainage pipe.

At the end of the pipe, I put the snake out first, and then tumbled after, keeping him at arm's length. He sensed freedom, the sudden open space and cooler air, and as I tumbled out of the pipe he wrapped his tail around my arm.

"What the . . ." Tom tried to take in what was going on. Before he could help, I threw my arm down as hard as I

could and let go of the snake's head, flinging it to the ground.

It could have hung on to my arm with its tail, turned, and sunk its teeth into me at last, but my instincts were correct in sensing that the snake wanted to be separated as badly as I did. It quickly slid into the high grass, disappearing in seconds.

"Let's go," I said, as Tom stood staring. I wanted to get away as fast as I could. The factory seemed a very dangerous place for us.

We flew across the soybean field, to the edge of the woods before we stopped and turned around for a last look to make sure we hadn't been followed.

We watched the backside of the factory, breathing hard, knowing that we were relatively safe where we stood. One step into the protective canopy of the forest, at night, on a path we knew by heart, and no one alive could catch us. Another close call with Tom, another escape.

"Oh, hell, I stink," I said, catching my breath. Oily musk covered me; the snake had emitted torrents of it as we fought.

Tom was about to respond when he saw something, and my eyes followed his. Against the brown wall of the factory, barely visible, were the black silhouettes of two men running as fast as they could toward us, their arms pumping, a ball cap flying off one of their heads. They were chasing us, I was sure.

We both braced, ready to turn and run into the woods.

We saw the explosion before we heard it. I had to completely shut my eyes against the flash. In the second it took my eyes to adjust, the sound reached us, a massive *whomp*

that moved across the soybean plants like a gust of wind. Steel drums lifted by the blast crashed to the ground, some of them spilling their contents in a gush, then bursting into flames themselves. In the nucleus of the fireball, we saw the men still running toward us, their silhouettes growing as they neared.

I felt a swell of heat on my back as we turned and bolted into the woods. We took the same path we had taken on the way down, our feet barely touching the dirt on the trace as we flew up the hill. When we reached my house, Tom continued running, as we parted ways without a word. I shot up the porch railing, onto the roof, and through my window. I stripped down and attempted to control my breath as I jumped into bed.

I forced myself to calm down. My breath slowed, my heart stopped racing, and I settled down to the point that I could once again hear the ticking of the clock in the hallway. Except for that, the house was quiet, and I felt profoundly sad that because of what I'd seen, the quiet would not last. I reeked because of the snake, and something else, something bubble gum–sweet that took me a second to identify. It was the odor of burning varnish.

Finally, inevitably, I heard the muted ringing of the telephone next to my parents' bed through the wall. It rang again, and again, finally pulling my father from sleep. I heard him fumble for the handset and answer with a hoarse "hello." More mumbling was followed by a wide awake "Jesus Christ!" He hung up. Mom asked a question. Change spilled from his pockets as he pulled on yesterday's pants. I heard heavy footsteps across the bedroom, and then a pause.

Into that series of familiar noises came a sound unusual but still recognizable. I heard my father drag a heavy box out from under his bed, open it, close it, and then slide the box back. I knew the sound. My father was getting into his footlocker, the only private space he had in the house. The footlocker contained two old love letters from Mom, four Purdue yearbooks, three issues of *Playboy*, and one .38 Smith & Wesson revolver.

Don Strange was dead. He had returned to the plant after the meeting with my father. Dad said that he had no idea why, that ever since his wife had died Mr. Strange had trouble sleeping and was always going to the plant at odd hours, to catch up on paperwork or look over some piece of machinery that had popped into his head in the middle of the night. My mother needed reassurance that Mr. Strange wasn't working at the plant that night because of her, that he hadn't followed her order, as relayed by my father, to keep plant business at the plant. My father swore up and down that he had ignored my mother's request, an oversight for which she was profoundly, tearfully grateful. It was almost dawn by then, the woods outside our house turning from black to washed-out gray. Mom poured coffee as Dad told us what he had seen down the hill.

"By the time I got there, every volunteer fireman in Borden was standing along Sixty," he said. "Their trucks were blocking the road, every one of them with its light on top, swirling around, making it hard to see anything." Dad's voice was scratchy. "The hook and ladder was through the gate already, all their hoses were running through the front door by the lobby. Something was leaking—there was a

huge puddle of water that almost covered the front lot. I fought my way to the front of the crowd by the fence, and found Dave Grosheider," he said. Grosheider was our fire chief.

"Dave told me there'd been some kind of explosion, a hole blown in the back wall, and that they had extinguished a small fire out on the back loading dock. He asked me about hazardous materials in the plant, that kind of thing, told me that he had three search parties inside the factory already, looking around, making sure there weren't any more fires. I started to tell him where the gas shutoffs are, the main breaker panels, where the drums of naphtha and alcohol are. Then there was kind of a murmur through the crowd, and everyone looked up." Dad sighed jaggedly before he continued. It was the saddest, most defeated sound I ever heard my father make.

"One of the search parties was coming out the front door. The fireman in front was carrying a body. He'd taken his coat off and laid it across his arms, so I couldn't see much, but I could tell it was a person—I could make out the shape of a head beneath the coat, and I saw feet hanging out the other end." Dad rubbed his bloodshot eyes. "He looked so tiny, we all thought he had a child in his arms."

"Who did it?" I asked too suddenly.

"Maybe nobody did it," said Mom. "Maybe it was an accident. One of those furnaces blew up before, you remember that? When all the windows along Sixty broke?"

"No, he's right, it was somebody." Dad looked at me a little curiously. "And we know who. Mack Sanders lost his ball cap running away. His name was written inside of it. And Guthrie Kruer's truck was stalled at the iron bridge.

Sheriff Kohl already checked the trailer they both live in. It's empty and all their guns are gone."

"Guthrie Kruer and Mack Sanders killed Don Strange?" I asked.

"That's right."

It caught me off guard to hear the last name of my best friend like that. Not that it was that big of a coincidence; the hills were filled with Kruers, along with a few other key German surnames like Huber and Stemler. Since they were all robustly Catholic and had millions of kids, you pretty much had to be in the family to understand exactly how they were all interrelated. Their allegiances to each other showed in weird, subtle ways. I knew Tom's family, for example, drove their cars all the way to Floyd Knobs for repairs because some Kruer cousin owned a garage out there.

Guthrie Kruer had established himself that last December as something of a minor local celebrity. Like about half the adult male population of Borden, Kruer was a volunteer fireman. Acting loosely in that capacity, he had once climbed to the top of the Borden Casket Company's water tower to free a turkey buzzard that had gotten snagged in the tower's Christmas lights. The bird was scared shitless and squawking pitifully as Guthrie Kruer approached it—we were all certain the bird would knock him to his death with its giant dark wings. A *Courier-Journal* photographer happened to be passing through town that day, on his way back from a school board meeting in Salem, and he saw the crowd gathered and snapped a dramatic photo that appeared on the front page of the Louisville paper the next morning: a small man standing gracefully at the top of the rounded water tower, his arms

outstretched for balance, the giant bird mirroring him as it spread its wings gratefully and flew away. Tom tried to explain to me at the time exactly how they were related to each other, the gossamer-thin line of blood that connected them back to the different shipments of Kruers that came over from Bavaria in centuries past. The story was confusing even to him and he finally gave up and just identified Guthrie Kruer as his "cousin," which satisfied us both.

Mack Sanders, on the other hand, was an outsider. Even though he had lived in Borden as long as I could remember, I was always aware of the fact that he came from somewhere else—I think it was Tell City. He had no family in the area. I guess most people in Borden were like me, in that when I heard the name Mack Sanders, the thing that leapt immediately to mind was that the boy had just one nut. The only other thing I knew about Mack Sanders was that Guthrie Kruer was his best friend.

"Where are they now?"

"They must have grabbed somebody else's truck," said Dad. "Or maybe they hitchhiked. I'm sure they're in Louisville by now, probably headed south." It was a keystone of our local philosophy that all things evil either came from Louisville or ended up there.

I knew better. I pictured them creeping along the edge of the woods, just inside the trees, to the truck where they'd staged it at the iron bridge. It was a good choice—few people drove on that section of road in daylight and nobody drove at night, when you couldn't see to dodge the gaping holes in the bridge's planking. I pictured them there, panicked, turning the key over and over, within earshot of the sirens and maybe even the voices on the

picket line. I was sure they had parked the truck there, ready to flee to Louisville, just like Dad suspected. When it wouldn't start, they did just what I would have done. They grabbed their guns and took off into the woods. They would live off whatever fish, rabbit, and squirrel they could catch, and maybe a can or two of Dinty Moore Beef Stew if they'd really been thinking ahead when they loaded up the truck. They were killers, and I hated them for murdering Don Strange. I wanted them found and punished. But something bloomed alongside the rage as I imagined them, two best friends living off the land, tending a campfire, checking snares, and cleaning their guns. It was such a strong feeling, and so unexpected, that it took me a second to recognize it. I was jealous.

"I thought that fireman was carrying you," said Dad suddenly. He looked up from his coffee, directly at me. Every line in his face was darkened, as if ash from the explosion had set into his wrinkles, exaggerating his age. "For one split second, I was absolutely sure of it. I couldn't figure out why in the hell you would be down at the plant in the middle of the night."

He stifled a sob with a drink of coffee. Mom rubbed his shoulders.

Everything changed after that.

Four

The hunt was on for the "bombers," as everyone called them, and we finally had a story on our hands big enough to demand coverage from the Louisville TV stations. On their morning news broadcasts, all three channels showed footage of the roadblocks manned by the state troopers until dawn, the abandoned pickup truck that belonged to Guthrie Kruer, the scorched hole in the factory wall, and, finally, a close up of the grimy ball cap picked up on factory grounds after the explosion. On the front, it read LOCAL 1096, and on the inside, in boyish ballpoint pen, it read M SANDERS.

Activity was at such a fever pitch that morning that Tom and I had trouble deciding which aspect of the manhunt we wanted to personally witness. Reverend Nichols had announced he would host a revival meeting so that we all might repent, and lots of kids had gone down to watch the volunteers set up the huge tent down by the river. The sheriffs of both Floyd and Harrison counties pitched in with their helicopters, and the choppers were taking off and landing in the Little League field, throwing up massive clouds of brown dust we saw from on top of Cabin Hill.

We decided in the end to go see the psychic from

Louisville who had shown up to help the investigation. We made our way to the modest crowd that surrounded her at the edge of factory property, in the front, in view of the picket line. She was a tall woman with frizzy gray hair and a flowing black dress. She delayed her vision for a few minutes so the crowd could grow to an acceptable size. She then asked for silence, took the famous ball cap from an embarrassed-looking deputy, and held it in one hand with her eyes tightly closed. After inhaling deeply, she pointed to the northeast, exactly opposite the direction we'd seen the bombers run. She handed out business cards while we applauded.

After that, Tom and I decided to walk back to the cave to retrieve our bikes. The thrill of the psychic soon passed as we found ourselves alone in the quiet woods. Men had been pouring into the forest all day looking for the killers; we'd watched them enter in droves. But just a few steps into the woods Tom and I felt profoundly alone. It seemed the wilderness had no trouble completely absorbing all the fugitives, the search parties, and the curious. The sudden hush and the slower pace of travel on foot made us reflective.

"When did you find out about Mr. Strange?" I asked.

"The phone rang. Not long after we got back. The union was calling everybody, telling them about the explosion and an emergency meeting tomorrow. At the institute."

"Did your dad say anything?"

"Nah. And I didn't ask. He wasn't even talking to Mom about it. After the phone call, he just sat on the porch until the sun came up."

"He said it was all talk last night."

"I guess he was wrong about that."

"Is he going to talk to the sheriff?"

Tom shot me a look. "Why would he talk to the sheriff?"

"Because . . ."

"What about you?" he said a little sharply. "Is your dad talking to the sheriff?"

"Why would he?"

Tom shrugged. "Because he's a manager? I don't know. He's probably in charge of the plant now. And it seems like your mom is always talking to the sheriff. Aren't they friends or something?"

I felt my cheeks turning red. "I guess. They do talk a lot. Sometimes Dad gets mad, they talk so much."

"He's probably jealous," said Tom.

"My mom wouldn't do anything like that!" The thought of those midnight phone calls burned at the back of my mind. My overreaction lightened Tom's mood instantly.

"I didn't say your mom's *doing* anything," he said, laughing, "but that doesn't mean your dad's not jealous. Think about it. The sheriff with his badge and his gun, your mom gives him all this attention—of course your old man gets up tight about it. Think . . . what if you were going with Taffy and she was always talking to some other guy, always telling you how cool he was?"

"Going with Taffy?" It took me a second to spit it out. Tom grinned at how completely he had rattled me.

"I'm just screwing with you."

"Fuck off," I said. I tried to get the conversation back on track—I really wanted to hear Tom's thoughts on the matter. "But if Mom and Dad are married, and Mom's

not . . . I guess I don't understand why it would bother my dad at all when she talks to the sheriff." Or why it bothered me so much.

Tom gave me the shrug I was used to seeing. It was a shrug that said: *I've explained it as best I can. You'll have to figure it for yourself.* I wanted to believe what Tom was saying, but I couldn't forget that Tom didn't know the entire story. I considered telling him about Sheriff Kohl's phone calls, but stopped myself for fear of what conclusion he might draw.

"You think they're out here somewhere?" I asked after a few quiet minutes of walking.

"Who? Sanders and Kruer?"

"Yeah."

"No doubt."

"How can you be so sure?"

"We saw them running into these woods, right? And they haven't caught them yet. That means they're still out here."

"My dad says they're in Louisville. Maybe they hitchhiked or took another truck."

"What truck? Nobody got their truck stolen. And they couldn't go hitchhiking with all those guns. Nope, they're out here."

"Maybe we should tell somebody what we saw. We saw them run away, right? We're eyewitnesses and we should tell the sheriff." It was something that had been nagging at me, a guilty act that tied me to Don Strange's death.

"No way. What could we tell them? We saw Sanders and Kruer run into the woods? They already know that. If

we go to the sheriff, we'll just get ourselves in a shitload of trouble. It won't help anybody."

"I guess they'll get caught then. Every deputy in Clark County is tromping through the woods."

Tom laughed. "There's a million places they could hide. What if it was us? My cousin grew up out here just like us, and he could stay hid from a dozen fat-ass deputies just like we could."

"What about Sanders?"

Tom scowled. "I don't know. Sanders is crazy, and if they get caught it'll be because of him. But I still think they could stay out here a long, long time."

"I'm not so sure."

At that moment, a helicopter flew right over us. They'd gotten close before, but this time the noise swelled to a painful level as it flew directly overhead, seemingly just a few feet above the treetops. Tom ran ahead and began jumping up and down and waving his arms, the throbbing noise of rotors deafening as it passed. "Here we are! Here we are! It's us, the bombers! I did it!" The downdraft from the chopper violently kicked up the dead leaves left over from last fall, and enough dust that we had to shut our eyes tight. For all the noise and the wind, we barely saw it pass above the thick foliage, like a small dark cloud passing quickly in front of the sun.

"See? They'll never find 'em," said Tom when the noise had faded enough to speak, winded from his theatrics. "A chopper couldn't see 'em through the trees if they wanted to get caught. I don't know why they're even bothering. They'll have better luck with the fortune-teller, at least

until October." The brown, papery leaves floated slowly back to earth in a cloud around Tom. He put his hands on his hips, thoughtfully taking in the scene.

"Let's find 'em," he said.

"What do you mean?"

"Let's me and you find 'em. You know we can." He was smiling, already caught up in the idea.

I thought it over. I wanted to see the killers of Don Strange in jail. Guthrie Kruer was Tom's kin, not mine, and while I felt a strong loyalty to Tom, I felt no second-hand loyalty to his cousin. I didn't have an extended family. Don Strange was as close as I got, a presence in my home and in my life for as long as I could remember. He hired my father at the plant a million years ago, and he gave me a two-dollar bill the day he died. If we found Sanders and Kruer, I could tell Sheriff Kohl, he could arrest them and make everything right again.

Tom's motives were undoubtedly different. He certainly didn't want to deliver his cousin into the hands of law enforcement. Maybe he thought he could somehow help Guthrie Kruer. If Tom was acting in part out of loyalty to his cousin, however, and I was acting out of the same kind of feelings for Don Strange, I think we shared a bigger motivation in common. Finding two fugitives in the woods just sounded like a cool thing to do. It was exciting, secret, and dangerous, a kick-ass adventure we'd embark on without giving much thought to consequences, a cave we'd enter without any idea of where it might lead.

"Okay," I said. Tom looked pleasantly surprised. "Let's find them." I suddenly felt and smelled that cool ribbon of cave air, and noticed for the first time that Tom

was carrying a flashlight. I realized with a start that our hunt for Sanders and Kruer might already be in progress.

We walked quickly to the cleared ground in front of the cave entrance, where our bikes were neatly parked. "There's still time to watch the helicopters if we hurry back," I said. Tom was standing at the edge of the clearing, alertly studying the scene.

"Let's go," I said.

Tom kept staring at me and the bikes, waiting for me to catch on. I finally did.

We hadn't left our bikes standing up. We had left them well hidden in the brush. Now here they were, leaning on their kickstands in plain sight. I looked at the bike tracks in the dirt, following Tom's eyes. Barely visible, a set of footprints led right from the bikes to the the cave. Tom ran to the entrance, but I hesitated.

"What?" he said.

"Maybe we shouldn't go in there."

"You think Sanders and Kruer moved our bikes?"

"Somebody moved them. Maybe they were going to ride them out of here when they heard us talking."

"I thought you wanted to find them."

"I do. I just think we need to . . . think this through."

"Let's find out who moved our bikes." He was utterly unconcerned that two fugitives might be waiting for us inside the cave, nerves shot and guns loaded.

We walked through the main chamber and slid down through the first chute. We got to the hole that Tom had dug out the day before, and without hesitating Tom slid through it feetfirst. I didn't have time to argue. Tom had the

only flashlight. I climbed into the hole, and tried to slow my fall, remembering the scary drop from the day before. I was able to slow myself a little at first, but as soon as my feet came out of the hole, swinging in the empty air, my groping hands lost their grip. My fingertips slid smoothly down the end and I fell once again through the air and landed squarely on my ass, precisely in the same spot as the day before. When I shook my head to clear the stars, Tom was already probing the darkness with his flashlight.

I got up and ran over to him. "Do you see them?"

He didn't try to answer my question. "Where are you?" he yelled. The question echoed through the chamber, and down the tunnels we hadn't yet explored. "Don't worry!" His voice was playful, neither threatening nor frightened.

The sounds of our breathing and the underwater stream blended together into a steady rush in the darkness. Then, from an unseen corner of the cave, came a hiss, like air escaping from a punctured bike tire. From the same corner, a glow swelled until the entire chamber was visible to us for the first time. The room was even bigger than I thought, filled with more towering formations than I thought, but I couldn't take it all in right away. Instead, I just squinted at the center of the glow, where high above us sitting on a small stone ledge, dangling her scrawny legs and holding a Coleman lantern, sat Taffy Judd.

"Hi Andy." She surprised me by sounding so at ease. Although I did still carry a small scar below my ear from her lunch box, I had otherwise always thought of Taffy as quiet, cautious, and a little mysterious. In the cave, she seemed almost bouncy. She looped the handle of the lantern around her wrist, turned to the wall, and scurried straight down.

Although there were no perceptible handholds, she moved as agilely as a cat. She walked over to us.

"Sorry I was hiding," she said. "I thought you were my dad."

Tom and I stared openmouthed and wondered how to begin the conversation.

"Have you been down here before?" asked Tom. The answer was obvious.

"Lots of times. I could tell someone had been down here yesterday, I found your bikes. I also saw where you dug out the hole a little to get in here."

"Fell flat on my ass through that hole," I said. "Twice."

Taffy laughed. "Yeah, I saw," she said. "You don't have to do it that way." She put down the lantern and walked over to the wall where we'd come in.

She scurried up the wall, again without the benefit of any visible handholds or protrusions. She put two hands up to the lip of the chute from where I had plummeted, which overhung the wall slightly, and pulled herself up and in, athletically and gracefully. "Come over here and look," she said.

When we were closer, she climbed down slowly, taking her time so Tom and I could see where she placed her hands and her feet. When her arms were over her head, her Pink Floyd T-shirt raised to show her belly, making me gulp. Tom teasingly elbowed me, but I wasn't about to turn away. After having her repeat the descent a few more times than necessary, Tom and I were able to imitate her path, and in a few minutes we were zipping up and down the wall and even improvising slight modifications to the route. Taffy knew how to get around every inch of that cave, a tribute to both the

clear bright light of her lantern and the many hours she must have spent down there practicing.

"Hey, watch this," said Tom, trying to cross the wall horizontally from the chute to the ledge where we had first seen Taffy. He moved slowly but surely across the wall, his arms straining. It seemed as he got close that he was holding up his entire body with just his fingertips. When he made it to the ledge he pulled himself up, exhausted.

"Cool!" she said, clapping her hands. "I've never done that!" I felt a twinge of jealousy, and started searching the walls for an impressive maneuver of my own.

We all stopped cold as a noise rolled to us from what seemed like a very faraway normal world. The low voice was so deep and powerful that it almost sounded like the cave itself was growling at us. *"Taffy . . . Get your ass up here!"*

Taffy ran to the lantern in the center of the cave, I followed, and Tom scurried down from the ledge. In his rush he fell the last five feet or so and landed with a grunt—I hoped Taffy had noticed his misstep. He ran to us just as Taffy was turning down the lantern almost completely, until the room-filling sphere of light shrunk to a bright orange marble right in the middle of us, one that barely illuminated our six hands around it.

"It's my dad," whispered Taffy. "He's been on a tear since the strike. I come down here when I have to, to get away from him."

"Taffy!" we heard again, closer this time, right up against the hole. *"Get your ass up here!"* I embarrassed myself by cringing.

"Don't worry," whispered Taffy, laying her hand on my

arm. "He can't fit his fat ass down here. But I better go now." To my dismay, she removed her hand and headed toward the crevice we'd almost gotten trapped in, taking the muted lantern with her.

"You can get to Squire Boone Cavern through there," Tom said, trying to be helpful.

"I know," she said.

"We almost got stuck down there for good," I said. "Be careful."

"It's wider on this end," she said, without turning around as she walked to the far corner of the room, confirming Tom's theory from the previous day. "You can almost walk to Squire Boone without bumping your head this way. Bye, Tom. Bye, Andy." I tried to convince myself that there was some special, suggestive emphasis in her pronunciation of my name. The small orange light bounced through the crevice and disappeared. A few feet inside, she turned her lantern back up, and the crevice suddenly turned into a jagged bright band across the black cave wall, like a horizontal bolt of lightning frozen in a photograph. Tom and I watched the light slowly fade as she got farther away from both us and her scary father, who continued to rant above us.

Tom and I waited silently in the dark until the yelling stopped. After waiting a while longer, Tom turned his flashlight on and we slowly climbed out, using our new knowledge of the cave, ready to drop back down the hole if there was any sign of him. But he was gone. He had left behind a large oval puddle of piss, in the middle of which floated a bent cigarette butt. He had apparently walked right through it on his way out, leaving a set of giant wet

footprints in the dirt. "Even a dog knows better than that," Tom said.

At the first chute, Tom carefully placed his flashlight back in its hiding place behind the stalagmite, turning to verify it was completely hidden as we exited. Outside, squinting at the sunlight and immediately starting to sweat in the humidity, we saw to our relief that Orpod Judd was long gone. The only trace of Taffy's father was that both our bikes had been knocked roughly to the ground.

We were all more or less acquainted with our little town's history. It was originally named New Providence, after the capital of Rhode Island, not the biblical concept. It still today shows up as New Providence on some Indiana maps. The town took its modern name from William W. Borden, a self-taught geologist and farmer's son from the area who went west, to Leadville, Colorado, during the Gold Rush and was one of the lucky few to actually make his fortune there, cleverly exploiting silver claims that had been neglected by wild-eyed gold seekers. He sold his interest in the mining company after just two years in Leadville, and returned to Indiana a millionaire, with more than enough money to "carry out certain ideas for the advancement of learning and the benefit of my fellow man, which I had for some time entertained." That according to my personal copy of Borden's *Personal Reminiscences*, published in 1901.

The "certain ideas" of Professor Borden, as he was by then known, were remarkably progressive for his time and place. He founded the Borden Institute in 1884, a school chartered to provide the farm children of the area an

advanced education at little or no cost. This was a generation even before the casket company, when the area was widely known as "the strawberry district" and offered few opportunities beyond a life of backbreaking labor with hoe and plow. Not only did Borden's institute teach Cicero, Virgil, "public declamation," and, of course, geology, it taught these things to both boys and girls. It was as if Professor Borden knew that someday his achievements would be evaluated by the steely eyes of my feminist mother. The curriculum, while advanced and demanding, was loosely structured, allowing students to progress at their own pace and define their own courses of study, radical concepts all in 1884.

The good professor lived until 1906, pouring his money and his heart into the school that became so famous and beloved that the town changed its name in his honor. Thousands of Hoosier farm kids benefited from his generosity. The experiment couldn't continue, however, without his leadership and his money. Shortly after his death, his priceless geological collections were given to the Smithsonian, and the school closed.

The Borden estate donated his land and buildings to the public school system. The grand Victorian mansion that had housed the institute stood abandoned at the edge of the Borden Elementary School's parking lot, looking uncomfortable next to its brick-and-steel descendant. Other than the high school and the factory, the institute remained the biggest building in town. Public meetings were often held in the institute's ornate first-floor auditorium, when the town's two voting booths were shoved in a corner and covered with sheets. I don't think William Borden

would have been surprised that his institute couldn't outlive him—it was a bold, almost outlandish experiment to provide a free college-level education to the hill kids of our rural counties. But I think Borden would have been happy to see that his building was still at the center of town life, and witness to much of our drama, as it was the day after Don Strange's death, when Local 1096 called an emergency meeting at the institute, and Tom and I snuck in to listen.

The meeting was scheduled to begin at nine P.M., which was a problem for me: too late to be allowed out of the house, too early to sneak out. To top it off, my parents were still jumpy and protective because of the "bombing," and they were well aware of the union meeting that night. They didn't want me anywhere near it, so there was no way I was going to get down the hill by telling the unvarnished truth. I had to use an excuse I had been saving for extraordinary circumstances.

I waited until our regular game of Authors to ask. It was Dad's favorite game and one he insisted on playing around the kitchen table after dinner whenever our schedules permitted. The game was similar to Go Fish, but it was played with special cards that each represented one of four books written by thirteen different authors. In other words, instead of attempting to collect all four jacks, or all four twos, you collected *A Child's Garden of Verses*, *Treasure Island*, *Dr. Jekyll and Mr. Hyde*, and *Kidnapped.* Thus, over the course of my childhood, I memorized forever the names and watercolor portraits of thirteen authors and their fifty-two great works of English literature.

"Can I stay out late tonight?" I asked between hands.

"Why?" my dad asked in a tone that sounded very close to "no" already.

"Tom and I want to watch the Perseid meteor shower." This got his attention. He laid his cards flat down on the table. I knew that my sudden interest in astronomy sounded unlikely, but it also sounded scholarly enough for my parents to get their hopes up. Still, I saw the seeds of suspicion in my father's eyes as he peered at me from across the table. I tried to stay calm. I was attempting to bullshit a true space groupie about a meteor shower.

"You want to watch the Perseid?" he asked.

"Yessir," I said. "It's a clear night and this is the peak time of year to watch them." I paused. "It's very interesting." My mom now placed her cards on the table to better assist Dad in his evaluation.

"This is something you've taken a recent interest in?" he asked.

"We talked about it in school before summer break," I said, "and I marked it on my calendar. I've been reading about meteors ever since, and now I'd like to actually see one."

"I see," said my father. "So you've made a study of this."

"Yes," I said. "Meteors are cool."

Dad and Mom looked at each other, and I wondered if I had laid it on too thick. I still had my chief advantage intact. Dad really wanted to believe me.

"Yes, they are cool," my father said, not yet convinced. "Tell me, since you've been looking into it, what are meteors made out of?"

"Most are made out of stone," I said, regurgitating the

information I had reviewed in the junior *Britannica* just before coming downstairs. "Some are made out of iron and nickel."

My father nodded his head, impressed, unable now to keep a hopeful smile from flickering to life. But the logical, skeptical half of his brain still needed convincing.

"So, if you found a rock in the middle of the woods tomorrow that you suspected was a meteor, could you know for sure? How could you prove it came from outer space?"

"If I found it in the woods, it wouldn't be a meteor, it'd be a meteorite." He nodded approvingly. "You could look for the spherical chondrules in the rock, which don't show up in earth rocks." This was good, but I extracted one final piece of trivia from the *Britannica* that had lodged on the precarious edge of my short-term memory. "And, if it was an iron-nickel meteorite, the metallic crystals would be arranged in the Widmanstatten pattern."

"Widmanstatten pattern?" my father said. I thought he was going to cry he looked so happy.

"Look to the northwestern sky," he told me as I left.

I rode my bike down Cabin Hill Road, the setting sun shimmering behind me, and up to Tom, who was waiting beneath one of the towering tulip poplars outside the front entrance of the institute.

"How'd you get down here?" I asked him, proud of my meteorite fiction and wanting to share it.

"I rode down with my dad." He gestured toward his father's truck. An early load of firewood poked out from under the green tarp that covered it. Of course, I thought. Tom's family didn't think of union meetings as dangerous

gatherings to be avoided, saving him the trouble of fabricating a lie.

In fact there were dozens of spectators milling around the outside of the institute. Union wives socialized on the lawn in jeans and pro-union T-shirts. Other locals who lived nearby had wandered over, as they probably always did whenever something big enough to require the use of the institute's auditorium was going on. Many had shown up to witness the rumored arrival of representatives from "the National," high-level union men spoken of in tones both reverent and apprehensive. For a second, my heart raced as I thought I saw Taffy's blond hair in the crowd, but in an instant, I knew it wasn't her: the girl I saw was too graceless to be Taffy, who could move like a cat and disappear in a crowd like a rabbit in a field. Seconds later, when I saw her dad arrive, I gave up all hope of seeing her.

Orpod Judd glared at Tom and me as he walked by, his watery eyes appraising me so intently that I had to look away. In the middle of that jovial crowd, he was noticeably alone, given wide clearance by his union brothers on an evening when brotherhood was on conspicuous display. Judd was fat, but the fat seemed to disguise a body that was still strong despite the years of abuse and encroaching disintegration. His head slowly turned to watch us as he followed the crowd inside, a movement that reminded me of the snake I had shared a pipe with the night before. Like the snake, Judd seemed to be a purely physical being, without thoughts deeper than attacking threats and surviving. I had never spoken to Orpod Judd, but from the way he glowered I thought he must know me, aware of my connection to Taffy and the cave in some instinctive or

supernatural way. Then it occurred to me that he recognized my bike. I breathed a sigh of relief when he disappeared inside the doorway.

None of us on the lawn could see anything that was actually happening inside the building, as security was being enforced at the door by two burly but friendly-looking strikers who were checking the union cards of each person going inside. Tom and I watched as a self-important *Courier-Journal* reporter tried to bluster his way past, to no avail. He left in a huff as the men at the door looked embarrassed by the commotion.

"We'll never get in through the front door," said Tom.

Especially since one of us is the son of a manager, I thought.

It pissed me off. A big event was taking place inside the institute, in our town, and I didn't like being excluded, as I was now in all things having to do with the union. I was as determined to get inside the institute as I was opposed to family secrets. I wanted to hear what the union had to say about the death of Don Strange and those responsible. And if hanging out with Tom all my life had taught me anything, it was this: you can usually get yourself from one place to another if you want to get there bad enough.

Tom was examining the building with a critical eye. "Let's go around back."

I rode around slowly, following Tom, the tread of my bike tires crunching on the dusty gravel of the driveway. In back we saw a number of potential entrances, narrow doors that looked like they had been designed for servants back during the institute's glory days. I wondered who waited

inside those doors now. Guards with guns? Cops? I was constantly being warned by those around me that I had an overactive imagination, and I tried to keep it in check, but the fact was that men who belonged to this group had killed a man, and the criminals were still at large. I worried that my staid German neighbors had imaginations that were not active enough. Disaster had already struck in Borden, and I saw no reason why it couldn't again. Everyone but Tom and me seemed to have accepted on faith that Sanders and Kruer were gone, the trouble they caused a tragic but fleeting event, a lightning strike. I feared it might be more like a drought, something that could linger and worsen indefinitely.

Tom walked up to one of the small back doors and tugged on the knob. To my shock, the door swung open, and we looked right at the wide back of a man in a blue work shirt and jeans. Past him several other men stood in a relaxed circle inside a large, old-fashioned, institutional kitchen. It took the man just a second to feel the breeze at his back. When he turned around and saw us, he attempted to hide the dewy can of Falls City beer in his hand.

"You run along now," he said, his eyes darting guiltily from Tom to me and back, his free hand reaching to shut the door quickly. He certainly wasn't a guard or a cop—he was a regular dude sneaking a beer and a cigarette while locked safely away from a reproachful and possibly Baptist wife. Still, he might as well have been an armed sentry as far as Tom and I were concerned. The other back door opened into the same kitchen, no doubt, in view of the same men, who had every reason to keep us clear of their impromptu stag party.

"Hell's bells," said Tom. He scratched his chin and searched the building for another point of vulnerability.

My eyes followed his to a low roof that provided a small area of shelter for one of the narrow back doors, this one at the very back corner of the building. I imagined it as a haven for a uniformed deliveryman in a pouring rain a hundred years ago. Above the small roof was a second-floor window. This was a tactic we knew well—my porch roof was the starting point for many of our recent adventures. We ambled over for a better look.

"How can we get up there?" I asked. In keeping with the grand scale of the institute, the door was tall and the small roof above it seemed out of reach.

Tom jumped at the roof with his hands up in the air. Even with his considerable athleticism, it was futile.

"Can you lift me?" he asked.

"Then how will I get up there?"

"I'll pull you up after me."

It seemed risky. It was not yet dark, and just on the other side of the building were a dozen or so folks who could saunter around the corner at any second and catch us in the act. Opening a back door was innocent enough. A manager's son scaling the building to get to a second-floor window so that he could eavesdrop on a closed union meeting would be harder to explain. Tom either didn't think about those possibilities or didn't care.

I positioned myself with my back to the brick wall, and interlaced my fingers in front of me so that Tom could use them as a step. He stepped into my hands with one foot, and then deftly put the other foot on my shoulder. He continued his climb as he reached up to grab the edge of the

small roof, which was now just slightly higher than his shoulders. I felt his full weight for just a moment, then he pulled himself up and swung his legs onto the roof. The whole maneuver took just seconds.

He lay on his stomach, and extended his arms to me. They were out of reach. When I jumped, our fingertips brushed, but we could not connect solidly enough for him to pull me up. Tom scooted out farther over the edge, to the point where if I did manage to grab his hands, I was pretty sure I would pull him off. We heard clapping and whistling from the front of the building, as some heroes of the union arrived. I pictured the beer drinkers in the kitchen hurriedly finishing their brews before the official business of the evening began.

"What now?" I whispered.

"Keep trying," Tom said, scooting out farther.

"It's not going to work," I said. "Go on in by yourself."

Tom thought it over for a minute. "Bring your bike over here," he said.

I wheeled my bike directly under the roof, and stood it up on its kickstand.

"Climb up and stand on the seat," he said.

"Stand on the seat?" It seemed like some kind of circus trick.

"Just climb up real quick, it'll just take a second, then I can reach out and grab you."

I decided to give it a try, just to humor Tom, because I thought there was no chance of it working. I put my feet on the pedals, facing away from the handlebars, and then, with my arms outstretched for balance, stepped onto the bike seat. I stood like that for a full second or two, and it was

only because I hadn't expected it to work that I wasn't prepared to grab Tom's outstretched hands. I jumped clear of the bike as I lost my balance. I readied for another try, this time with every intention of making it up to the small roof.

Feet in the pedals, feet on the seat—I was up. I grasped Tom's forearms, and he grabbed mine, a perfect linkup, and he hauled me quickly onto the roof. My bike fell over with a clatter as my feet left the seat. Suddenly we were both on the small roof, with barely enough room to stand.

Tom turned to the window and began trying to open it—it occurred to me that it might have been a good idea to try that before devoting so much effort to getting us both on the roof. While it was locked in some way, the window frames were so old that the small lock just tore away from the crumbly wood, and the window opened with a screech. Tom jumped in and I followed, closing the window behind me, verifying that no adult on the ground was staring up in horror at us as we broke into the building.

We jumped down from the sill quickly to get out of the sight of anyone outside, kicking up a dry cloud of dust as we landed. It didn't take long for our eyes to adjust—it was still not completely dark out, and the room was full of large windows. What we saw amazed us.

It seemed that the Smithsonian had not taken all of Professor Borden's collections. The built-in cabinets lining the walls were crammed with leather-bound books, intricately carved wooden boxes, and a full complement of antique lab equipment: beakers, tubes, and delicate-looking scales. In addition, the room held three parallel rows of large, ornate lab tables. On top of every one stood stuffed and mounted animals. The professor seemed to have had a

particular fondness for exotic rodents, all of them posed by the taxidermist with snarling faces to better expose their long, sharp teeth. Most spectacularly, on the walls above the cabinets, were mounted a score of antique swords and knives, a row of them completely circling the large room. Far, far away, I heard the bang of a gavel and a muted baritone cheer.

"Holy shit," whispered Tom.

"Look at all this stuff." It was difficult to decide where to begin.

First I walked carefully to what appeared to be the room's only door, hoping I could lock it. I was afraid that at any minute someone would burst through it and roust us before we had a chance to take even a brief inventory. Wary of squeaks, I stepped carefully across the dusty wood floor, taking note as I passed of the crates and drawers I wanted to open later, when there was more time, if there was ever enough time. Next to the door, which I was disappointed to see held no lock, I found a glass-enclosed cabinet containing a number of artifacts relating to the institute itself. I got the impression that at some point decades earlier, a local historian had created the small display to inform visitors about the history of the Borden Institute.

A photograph of William Borden himself was at the center. He had a heavy beard and the comfortable smile of a wealthy man who knew exactly how lucky he was. Another document on display seemed to be an old bulletin for prospective students: *The building is new and is one of the finest in the State. It is finely finished and well furnished. A fine Stereopticon has lately been added by Prof. Borden, with views of a great number of places of historic*

interest in this and other countries. The bulletin was signed by the principal of the institute, Francis M. Stalker. One of our five named roads in Borden was Stalker Street, and now I knew why.

Next to the bulletin I found Borden's autobiography, *Personal Reminiscences.* I flipped through the first few pages, and scanned the part of the book that described his childhood in New Providence. The old philanthropist wrote that three major events from his youth were "indelibly impressed" on his mind. The first was the cholera epidemic of 1832. A friend of his had to quit school in order to help his father build coffins, a foreshadowing of what would become the town's main enterprise. The second event was a plague of gray squirrels on a biblical scale in 1833, requiring organized squirrel hunts that slaughtered upward of three thousand of the animals every day: perhaps the origin of the good professor's interest in stuffed rodents. The migrating squirrels were so insensible to danger that they allowed themselves to be killed with clubs. The final event was a spectacular meteor shower in 1834 of such intensity that sleeping people were awakened by the great light. One witness proclaimed, "Oh, my God, the world is on fire!" Borden went on to write, "Never did rain fall as thick as meteors fell toward the earth that day."

I was shocked at the coincidence, since a meteor shower had been my pretense for getting out of the house that night. "Look at this!" I called to Tom. He didn't respond.

I looked across the room to see that he had hastily stacked two crates onto one of the lab tables, and from that wobbly perch was attempting to pull a sword from its mount near the ceiling.

I hurried over. "What are you doing?"

At that moment he freed the sword with a grunt, lurched backward, and regained his balance atop the teetering crate, barely avoiding the fall that would have impaled one or both of us. He carefully climbed down to the floor, sword in hand.

"Look at this thing," he said, awe in his voice. The blade was large and straight, and sharp on both sides. The flange above the grip was slightly gilded, but most of the gold had worn or faded away. The metal had darkened in some places, as if it had been exposed to smoke, but the entire length of it was surprisingly smooth and unpitted—I wondered if that was an indicator of the quality of the steel. A small yellowing tag dangled from the handle, identifying it in old-fashioned script: *Sword, Probably German, 1525–1550.*

"Feel." Tom handed it to me.

It was surprisingly light, weighing no more than my Springfield M6. Although I had never held a sword before, I could tell that it was superbly balanced at the grip—the thing begged to be swung through the air. Also like my M6, the German sword was almost completely unornamented, having been designed purely to serve its function. I assumed that function had been to hack apart invading godless hordes. It took my breath away.

"I'm keeping it," said Tom as he took it back, already knowing I would object.

"You can't do that," I said, although my less scrupulous self was already scanning the walls for the sword I would most like to steal. A curved blade in the corner, like something Sinbad might use, caught my eye.

"Why not?" said Tom. "We keep stuff we find all the time."

"It's different when you take something that's been lost, or left out," I said. "This is a museum! This would be stealing." I heard an agitated rumble from the crowd below. Someone must have said something controversial. Tom and I didn't care. If Jesus Christ himself were addressing Local 1096, I'm not sure we could have torn ourselves away from all that medieval weaponry.

"This ain't a museum," said Tom. "This is no different from finding something in the woods. Locking stuff up in this room was the same as throwing it away."

"This stuff belongs to someone."

"I thought he left everything to the people of Borden," said Tom, throwing me off by demonstrating a knowledge of William Borden. "This stuff is sitting here because everyone has forgotten about it."

"It doesn't belong to us," I said. "And this isn't like digging up potatoes in some field or stealing melons. That thing is really valuable—taking it would be stealing."

"I'll bet Professor Borden would want me to have it."

"Where are you going to keep it?" I asked, thinking I had found my trump card. As hard as it would be for me to hide a gigantic four-hundred-year-old German sword from my parents, it would be impossible for Tom in that army barracks he called a bedroom. "Why don't you leave it here until we figure out what to do with it?"

Tom mulled it over. "Shit, I did want to go looking for Sanders and Kruer tonight."

"You did?" That was news to me.

"Yeah . . . you said you wanted to, remember?"

"I just didn't know we were doing it tonight."

"Every time we're in the woods, we're going to be looking for them." I could tell he briefly considered stalking them with sword in hand, but thought better of it. "That'll have to wait. I'm taking this thing and hiding it in the cave."

I had to admit that was a good hiding place—no one knew the caves of the area as well, and the thing would actually probably be preserved better in an arid cave than in the musty second floor of the Borden Institute. I thought of my imaginary archaeologist finding the old German sword in the future, an object whose presence in a Clark County cave would be even harder to explain than Tom's shorts and shoes.

Suddenly the door burst open into the room. Tom and I instinctively ducked down, like rabbits in a bramble. I knew we hadn't been seen, we were that quick. But I wondered if someone had heard us walking around up there, or arguing, and were now searching for us. If so, it wouldn't take long to find us.

The intruders shut the door slowly, and then crossed the room, to the windows, one row of tables in front of us. We saw their frayed bell-bottom jeans and work boots as they walked by.

The man in front walked right to the window where we had come in. He opened it a crack.

"This'll do just fine," he said. I recognized the voice. It was Ray Arnold, the man who'd fought with Tom's dad the night before. I heard the metallic clink of a Zippo lighter opening, and then a few seconds later the sickly sweet smell of Clark County weed drifted through the old classroom.

Tom and I looked at each other with some relief. They weren't up there to bust us; they were there to spark up. If we jumped up and yelled "boo!" they'd probably run out of the room. Tom and I carefully leaned back so we could sit against the tables and wait the potheads out. Tom had the sword lying across his crossed legs.

"This is better than listening to that bullshit downstairs, ain't it?" Ray exhaled loudly. "Jesus Christ, I am sick of it." Tom carefully stuck his head around the corner to get a better look, and I did the same.

It was the first time I'd seen a grown man after a genuine ass-kicking. Ray Arnold didn't quite have a black eye, not the perfectly round, perfectly black, comic-book variety, anyway. Half his face was dark red, however, almost as if it had been scraped badly on the asphalt. I noticed, too, in the way that he put his Zippo back in his pocket, that his fingers appeared to be hurting, as if maybe he'd gotten in a few good licks of his own. He was as wild-eyed as he sounded, with long thin hair and a ragged mustache that twitched when he spoke. With him was Lonnie Vogel, a stocky maintenance man at the plant who also grew Christmas trees on his family farm to make a few extra bucks during the holidays—we got our Scotch pine from him every year. Lonnie delicately took the joint back from Ray Arnold.

"We need to be careful," said Lonnie. "If we drop this thing in here the whole place will burn to the ground in about five seconds."

They both chuckled at that.

"So help me," said Ray, "if one more of those dipshits calls me his brother, I am going to kill him."

"Yep," said Lonnie with a sigh, clearly preferring that they not waste a good joint talking about the strike.

"They ain't my brothers," Ray continued. "Truthfully, most of 'em are assholes. I might cross the line just to piss 'em off. Just to piss off that dickhead George Kruer."

Tom and I shot each other looks. Tom was grinning.

"You're not serious," said Lonnie, releasing a lungful of smoke.

Ray thought it over. "I didn't want this strike. And I've never told no one no different."

"You can't cross the line."

"Look, man, I've got a hungry baby at home and a wife who won't get off my ass. I was going along with this bullshit, thinking we might get a raise after a week or two, but now they're killing folks. Hell, I liked Don Strange!"

"I did, too," said Lonnie thoughtfully.

"Now they're killing folks, and no raise we get is ever going to make up for the money we're losing on strike, and I am sick of it."

"So you're just going to walk across that line by yourself."

"I wouldn't be by myself," said Ray. "I guarantee you that. I ain't the only sorry asshole in Borden who needs a paycheck. I'd like to see George Kruer's face when I take a whole shift back into the plant. You'd follow me across, wouldn't you?"

Lonnie Vogel thought long and hard, so long I thought he might have forgotten Ray's question. "I don't know, Ray," he said finally. "My dad would kill me if I ever crossed a picket line."

Ray Arnold thought it over. "That's true. Your old man

would shit. Well, I'm sure somebody would come with me. I can't be the only one who sees how retarded this whole thing is."

There was thunderous applause downstairs, and a chant began: *Ten ninety-six! Ten ninety-six!*

Ray started whispering in rhythm: "Ten ninety-six! We're all a bunch of pricks!"

They both giggled hysterically, as they finished up the last of Ray's small joint. "Thanks, dude," said Lonnie. "That was good."

Ray sighed theatrically. "Let's go downstairs and see what we just agreed to." They tromped out of the room, considerably less carefully than when they came in. Ray pulled the door shut behind him as he exited.

Tom and I stood up. A thin layer of reefer haze floated at chest height.

"I'm keeping it," he said, picking up the argument where we'd left it.

We stared at each other a moment, Tom knowing full well that he always won these debates. A new chant began downstairs that we couldn't make out. Combined with Ray and Lonnie's departure, it led me to think the meeting was reaching a climax. We had to make our move soon, whatever it was.

"We need to go," I said. I ached for the Sinbad sword on the wall, but knew I couldn't bring myself to steal it, anymore than I could prevent Tom from taking his.

"Then let's go," he said, leading the way across the room with sword extended.

We got to the window, and I let Tom go out first. I followed, and carefully closed the window behind me, taking

one last look at all the treasure I was leaving behind. The sun had gone down, which was good news for Tom now that he was officially committing grand theft. Tom knelt down on the small roof. Leaning as far as he could over the edge, he dropped the sword straight down. It stuck in the dirt cleanly right by my bike's front tire, its weight driving the point into the gravel driveway. Tom jumped down after it, hanging briefly on the roof's edge by his fingertips before dropping down with a grunt. From above, I watched him pull the sword from the ground like young King Arthur.

I dropped down beside him. Tom was positively glowing.

"How are you going to get that thing home?" I asked.

"I'll hide it in the back of my dad's truck. I'll take it out tonight and hide it in the woods, take it to the cave when I get a chance. Next time, though, we're goin' lookin' for them."

"I still don't think you should have taken anything from a museum," I said self-righteously.

Tom laughed. "Well, you did." He pointed at my hands.

And I had. Without realizing it, I had taken the copy of Borden's *Personal Reminiscences.* So we were both thieves.

Tom ran over to his dad's truck and shoved the sword under the tarp just as the doors of the institute burst open and union men began rolling out, smiling and lighting one another's cigarettes. We turned to face them, trying to look casual.

"What'd you decide?" Tom asked two of the strikers as they passed.

"We're all sorry about Don Strange," said one of them. "We're buying flowers out of the strike fund."

"And we're staying on strike until hell freezes over," said the other. Those strikers close enough to hear him cheered.

I rode my bike home with the book shoved up my pants leg. My father was waiting for me in the living room, lying on the couch and reading *Chesapeake.* I could tell the second I walked in, from the quiet and from the general sense of emptiness, that Mom was not home, perhaps instead at one of her feminist gatherings in Louisville, or on a secret errand for the sheriff.

Dad greeted me with an eager smile. "Did you see any?"

For a second, I had absolutely no idea what he was talking about. Then it all came back to me, along with the fear that my stolen book was about to fall out of my pants leg, and that Dad would be able to smell the fine bouquet of Ray's weed coming off my clothes. He waited for an answer.

"They were falling like rain," I said.

Numerous historic preservation groups tried to save the institute, but in the end its own grand scale worked against it, making it prohibitively expensive to renovate, and too big to be of any real practical use in our small town. Despite the fact that the building had been on the National Register of Historic Places since 1973, it was condemned by the state fire marshal. Since it was so close to the grammar school, local officials finally decided to demolish the building in 1983, calling it a safety hazard to the romping schoolchildren nearby. I stood in the parking lot and watched them destroy it the day before leaving for college.

In all, William Borden's building had lasted ninety-nine years, which I think to a geologist would seem like just the blink of an eye. What remained of Professor Borden's collections were carefully inventoried by the preservationists, crated up, and sent three hundred miles away, to the Field Museum in Chicago. So, looking back, I think Tom was right. I'm glad at least one of those swords is still in Borden, and yes, I think Professor Borden would be happy about it, too.

Five

They buried Don Strange the next morning. I sweated in the front yard in my blue JCPenney sport coat and clip-on tie as my parents finished getting ready inside. Tires crunched on the gravel of Cabin Hill Road, a sound soon followed by Tom's father driving past in his blue Dodge truck. I automatically lifted my hand to wave, and he briefly made eye contact with me and waved back. His eyes went quickly back to the road. My father was on the front porch in his suit by then, looking out at me with an expression I couldn't decipher.

The service was at St. Mary of the Knobs Catholic Church, a center of community life I had been to many times, even though I wasn't Catholic. I'd attended weekly meetings in their parish hall during my brief hitch with the Cub Scouts. We went to their Strawberry Festival every March, where my dad and I would eat shortcake and Mom would buy a raffle ticket for a quilt made by the Knights of Columbus ladies' auxiliary. I'd even been to a wedding inside the church once, the only wedding I had ever seen, when a man my dad worked with invited us the summer before.

My father had complained that local law enforcement

would never challenge the strikers. Now we had state troopers at our funerals, observing the mourners from their black-and-white Crown Vic a respectful distance away. Inside the church, Don Strange lay on pillowy white satin inside a gleaming walnut casket, finally trying out one of the products he had been constructing his entire life. The walnut, it occurred to me, had sprung from southern Indiana dirt, and would now return to it, just like Mr. Strange.

The crowd in the church was arranged into two halves, in a way that reminded me of the bride's side and the groom's side in that wedding I had been to. In this case, plant management and Borden's small merchant class sat on one side of the church. The strikers sat on the other much more crowded side. The strikers looked as uncomfortable as I did in their suits, and I noticed that most of them, like Tom's dad, came alone, leaving their families at home, making that side of the church overwhelmingly adult and male. I wondered if it was because they anticipated danger in some way, although I doubted that, because any inkling of danger and my mother wouldn't have let me within a hundred miles of the church. Maybe they didn't want their families to see Mr. Strange laid out like that, the rosary wrapped around his clasped dead hands.

Sprinkled randomly among us, oblivious to the seating protocol of our two rival camps, were Mr. Strange's relatives and friends from out of town. There were two svelte daughters from the swank suburbs east of Louisville, jarringly beautiful women in black dresses and wide hats. There were crying grandchildren, old casket company associates, an aging army buddy in an American Legion hat, and a young grandnephew in a white navy uniform.

An unseen organ announced the start of the service with a startling minor chord. A smoldering censor swinging in front of them, a column of priests, deacons, and altar boys marched into the church, singing hymns in a mournful baritone, sending chills up and down my spine. In my fourteen years, I had been exposed just enough to the Catholic religion to become completely fascinated by it. When the priest began the mass from the front of the church, I noticed that the strikers more or less all crossed themselves in unison, while many on the management side of the church did not. Mr. Strange had labored in the mill room for a decade or so before working his way into management, and it appeared that at least as far as his faith was concerned, he had more in common with the rank and file than he did with management. Old stained-glass windows along each side of the church depicted the church's numerous patron saints in various stages of martyrdom, and a small plaque at the bottom of each thanked a familiar family name for their generosity a century earlier: Kruer, Stemler, Huber, and so on.

I was impressed with the studied impassiveness of the priest. Our preacher down at Blue River Christian Church always seemed like he was trying to sell us salvation with amplitude and clever sermons. To hold our interest, he had to play the opposing trump cards of eternal bliss and eternal damnation. The Catholic priest, in contrast, was stern and removed in a way that seemed confident to me, as he wearily executed the rites of his church. He wasn't trying to convince me of anything—he had two thousand years of tradition on his side. If you don't believe any of this, he seemed to be telling us, that's your problem. "What right

have you to recite my statutes?" he intoned. "To take my covenant on your lips, when you detest my teaching and thrust my words behind you?" I turned my head slightly from side to side, trying to identify to whom the priest was addressing the accusation.

When it came time for communion, the labor side of the church filed out of their pews smartly, while we had to step awkwardly aside to let those few Catholics on our side pass by into the aisle. I watched them all walk right up to the priest, who was directly in front of Mr. Strange's casket, and accept the Eucharist. About half the mourners, I noticed, looked inside Mr. Strange's casket as they passed. They glanced into it quickly, as if they weren't supposed to, and maybe they weren't. I didn't know what the rules were. I just knew that for the first and only time that day, I was glad to be in the Protestant minority. I knew I would not have been able to avoid peering inside the casket if I walked up there, and I knew doing so would give me nightmares for weeks. We stepped outside for the burial.

The cemetery was right next to the church. To get to Mr. Strange's grave, we had to walk through the older sections, where the epitaphs were written entirely in German. At Mr. Strange's grave, a row of chairs and a small Caterpillar backhoe awaited us. A green tent had been set up with enough room for Mr. Strange's closest relatives to sit in the shade. Behind it, the gravedigger snuck a cigarette and waited for his cue. Graveside, the priest pointed out to the crowd that Mr. Strange was being buried right next to Mavis, his beloved wife, who had died fifteen years earlier. After a few comments more they lowered Mr. Strange into

the ground, and the service was over. Dad took a few minutes to shake hands with some of the old-timers who had shown up for the funeral. All of them wanted to talk about the strike. My father did not.

The strikers stood around the outside of the church smoking, their jackets on their shoulders or hung on low tree branches, ties loosened, sweat beading on their foreheads. I realized that I was accustomed to seeing these men exhausted, either plodding into the factory at dawn, or treading across the parking lot at the end of a shift, covered in varnish, sawdust, and fatigue. Seeing them this way, large groups of them rested and idle, was a slightly scary revelation. They all quieted as we passed. Normally my father was the kind of guy who would start a twenty-minute conversation with the guy bagging his groceries. Upon seeing someone from the plant, he usually rejoiced and gossiped like he had found a long-lost cousin. After the funeral he hustled Mom and me as rapidly as he could to our car with his eyes straight ahead.

We were almost to the car, passing a small knot of strikers, when just two feet in front of us Tom's dad turned around and started walking toward the church, toward us. There was no way to tactfully avoid him; he and Dad almost collided. I could tell by the way Dad stiffened that it was exactly the encounter he had wanted to avoid.

"Howdy, George," said my mom and dad simultaneously.

"Howdy," he said back, trying harder than my father to hide his discomfort. Even so, he looked haggard, more genuinely mournful than his cronies, who turned discreetly to see how the conversation was going. "Sad day," he said.

"Yes, it is," said my dad. He was stubbornly refusing to take the conversational bait. In normal times he would have been halfway through the shitting-in-the-paddock anecdote.

"I've known Don all my life," said George Kruer, trying to fill the void. "I just . . . I just never thought something like this would happen here."

"I guess there are evil people everywhere," said my dad. George Kruer raised an eyebrow at that, allowing my dad a second to qualify his statement or tone it down. But he didn't.

"Nobody wanted this to happen," responded Mr. Kruer. He was defensive, but I thought I detected the slightest note of guilt in his voice, too.

"Looks like somebody did."

Mom stepped in, trying to bring us back around to the kind of weightless declarations that normally filled the air after a funeral. "We'll all miss him, very much."

"The plant won't be the same without him," said George.

My dad just nodded and stared past him, refusing to allow the conversation a peaceful death. Finally, Kruer turned uncomfortably around, abandoning whatever chore he had inside the church, returning instead to the safety of his union pals. We finished our short walk to the car.

When we got in, my father turned the key and sighed loudly. I suddenly realized how draining the funeral had been for him. Mother patted his knee sympathetically.

"They've got a lot of nerve showing up here like that, don't they?" he said.

My mother removed her hand quickly and looked out the window.

"Come on, it's not like Don died of a heart attack," my dad responded.

"Stop." Mom was offended. "This doesn't have anything to do with the strike. Most of these men have known Don Strange since they were boys."

"Nothing to do with the strike?" My father started to prepare a more detailed rebuttal, but thought better of it, and drove us home in silence.

I always slipped into kind of a trance in the backseat of Dad's smooth Buick back then, especially when the air-conditioning was cranked up on a sweltering day. The thought of Don Strange's death, the image of that gleaming casket sinking slowly into the ground, pushed me further into a kind of melancholy fog. I was staring out my window when we turned down our driveway, looking down the barely visible path Tom and I ran on the night of the explosion. Dad pulled up to the house and kept the car running for just a moment longer than normal, a change in rhythm that dragged me out of my trance. When I looked up, Dad was staring straight ahead, his hands clenching the steering wheel. Mom was crying softly for the first time that day, her hands up to her mouth.

YOUR NEXT had been painted in large brown letters on our garage door.

Sheriff Kohl came up immediately. Once he arrived, he sat in the driveway for just a few seconds in the brown Crown Vic, writing studiously in a small notepad. He reviewed his notes with a furrowed brow, then exited the car as we watched.

He was tall and slim in a way that for some reason reminded me of cowboys. The gun on his belt suited him: a .357 Colt Python with a royal blue barrel and a grip of dark, polished walnut, a serious gun for a serious man. His uniform was immaculate, all the way down to where the cuffs of his perfectly creased pants broke against the tops of his shiny brown shoes. Sheriff Kohl had a way of always looking equally concerned, whether he was arresting a drunk driver, handing out Halloween candy at city hall, or singing "I Saw the Light" from the main stage of the Strawberry Festival. Sheriff Kohl looked good, and he looked like a lawman, both of which helped him win reelection, term after term.

He and Dad shook hands formally. Kohl shook his head sadly as Dad showed him the garage door. "That's a real shame, Gus," he said. He spoke as if it were the result of some unpreventable natural disaster.

"I appreciate your coming up here so fast."

"You know I came as soon as I heard," replied the sheriff. "And when you and I are done, I'm going to start making calls. We'll make a list of who wasn't at the funeral and who wasn't on the picket line. We'll question everyone in town if we have to."

"I know you will, Sheriff," said my father, nodding his head. "Here, I want to show you something."

He took the sheriff to the shed out back where a half-used can of varnish sat open on the step. Wadded up inside was my basketball net, which the perpetrator had taken down and used to smear the ungrammatical threat on the door.

"I noticed the net was down when we pulled up," said my father.

"That's great, Gus. Nice observation." The sheriff meticulously wrote the information down as if it were the clue of the decade. It dawned on me that the two men were treating each other with a kind of exaggerated courtesy, as if to prove to each other that there was no problem between them, or to prove who was the bigger man. The three of us walked silently back down to the driveway.

I had waited patiently, but now it seemed like the sheriff was wrapping things up, and I thought the important question, the only question, had not been asked. I blurted it out.

"Did the bombers do it?" I asked.

Dad and the sheriff stopped and looked at me, both with very similar startled looks on their faces. It was as if they had no idea what I was talking about.

"The bombers?" I said again. I pointed into the woods by the driveway. The sheriff and my dad were looking at me as if I were inquiring about the odds of a unicorn galloping out of Hoosier National Forest.

The sheriff spoke first. "Son, I don't believe we have to worry about them. They're long gone."

"Why do we think that?" I asked. "Didn't you find their truck here in town?"

"I've got no reason to think they would want to stick around," the sheriff said. "There's other ways they could have got to Louisville."

"Like what?"

My dad stepped in. "They could have got a ride. Hitchhiked. Maybe they had another car nobody knew about."

"Well, who else could have done this?" I asked, pointing at the garage door.

The sheriff rubbed his forehead. "Son, unfortunately, there's more than one man in this town right now who might have done something this stupid. But I intend to catch him." He actually reached out and tousled my hair.

We continued our walk to the sheriff's car. I was just about to speak up again about the likelihood of the bombers lurking in our woods when the sheriff surprised all of us. Instead of heading back to his Crown Vic, he turned and walked up to the front of the house where my mom had been standing, maintaining her distance. He bounded up the steps while my mom dropped her hands to her front in a startled gesture. Sheriff Kohl took her limp right hand in his.

"I am so sorry about this, Cricket," he said. She bit her lip and looked to the ground, trying to avoid any more crying.

Sheriff Kohl left, and my parents spent the rest of the day avoiding each other, no easy trick in that small house. I thought about what Tom had said right before we discovered Taffy in the cave, how my dad might be jealous of the sheriff, just because my mom admired him and because he was the sheriff, a man with a badge and a gun who could do things my dad never could. Like arrest the man who made her cry. For the first time, it sort of made sense to me.

During the extended silence, I had lots of time to think. Of course I still didn't even consider telling Mom and Dad about what Tom and I had seen the night of the explosion. But I still didn't think that night was some isolated incident

that Tom and I could just walk away from, like our other close calls and near misses. Maybe it had implications that were still rippling toward us.

Starting at ten P.M., I watched the normally forbidden *Fantasy Island* alone in the family room, while Mom sewed buttons onto a small pile of shirts in the kitchen and Dad read Michener in bed, unable to sleep until their fight was resolved. Mom didn't normally let me watch the show because she thought it licentious. Dad opposed it purely on intellectual grounds. But they were at opposite ends of the house, like boxers in their corners, leaving me to my own devices in the center of the ring. When the telephone rang, I easily got to it first.

"Hello?"

"Hello, Andy?'

"Yessir," I said, not recognizing the voice.

"This is Sheriff Kohl—"

"Did you find who painted on our garage door?" I interrupted.

"Well, not yet." He cleared his throat during an extended pause. "Andy, I need to speak to your mother."

"Oh . . ." I said, the realization coming over me as Mom and Dad made their way to the phone. It was one of those calls. Mom stood at my elbow.

I handed the phone to her. "Sheriff Kohl," I said. "He doesn't know who painted on our garage door."

She took the phone. "Yes, Sheriff, this is Cricket." She listened for a few minutes with her back to me. "Yes . . . Sure enough . . . Oh my." She shook her head seriously. "I'll be right there."

Within minutes she was stepping into her shoes by the back door and running a brush through her hair while Dad and I watched.

"I'll get back as soon as I can," she said, the first words she had said to my father since her conversation with Sheriff Kohl hours earlier. She sounded apologetic.

"Take as long as you need," my father said. They hugged before she left.

As she drove down Cabin Hill Road, I turned to my dad.

"You know I can't say," he told me. "Don't even ask."

Later, I tried to stay awake but Mom still hadn't returned home by the time I drifted off into a restless sleep filled with questions.

When I awoke the next morning Mom was back, scrubbing the threat on the garage door into an unrecognizable brown smear with 409 and a bristle brush. I rode away on my bike and met Tom down on the picket line.

"What happened?" he said. I wondered how much he knew.

"Somebody wrote on our garage door."

"What'd they write?"

"'You're next.' Except they misspelled 'you're.'"

"Shit," he said. "Who do you think did it?"

"I've got an idea."

Tom scowled. "What do you mean by that?"

"You're the one who thinks they're out in the woods still. Maybe they snuck up to our house during the funeral and did it."

"They're out there trying to lay low. It'd be retarded to

come out of the woods to write some stupid threat on your garage. And besides, my cousin doesn't have anything against your dad."

"Did he have anything against Don Strange?"

Tom was getting pissed. "There's plenty of other dudes in this town who would write that."

"That's pretty much what the sheriff said." We stared at each other for a second. Like most good friends, I suppose, we sensed whenever we reached a line we couldn't cross together. We stopped ourselves from going further. We shrugged, and let the argument pass.

We cruised around the outside of the strikers, a bigger group than normal that included some wives and other townspeople still hungry for news about the biggest thing to hit Borden since the '37 flood. The blast damage wasn't visible from the front of the plant, but Mr. Strange's death and the giant hole in the factory were part of every conversation.

"Maybe the company did it," said an old man with a lazy eye. "For the insurance money! Make us look bad!" Everyone around him agreed halfheartedly that it was a possibility.

"Well, they must be geniuses then," said a young man with bushy Peter Frampton hair and bell-bottom Levi's. "Because it sure makes us look like shit." Several laughed bitterly. The picket line no longer had the genial small-town friendliness of a 4-H fair. With the barely concealed tension and smoldering resentment, it felt more like an auction at a foreclosed farm.

Looking back now, I realize that many of the families must have been running out of money about then—we had

passed the two-week point in the strike, when the final paycheck had run through its normal lifespan. Hamburger was being stretched with cornflakes and crackers. Gardens were being cultivated with more than the usual vigor. The men on the picket line were looking ahead to September's bills and wondering how they would pay them.

I think some of the men were also afraid of something more fundamental than getting their pickups repossessed. Before the explosion, the strikers seemed powerful to me, with the confidence of men in firm possession of the moral upper hand. They were just trying to get their fair share, they often said, and I believed them completely. The exorbitant retail prices of the coffins they manufactured had been a popular topic of conversation around the fire drum, and multiplying those prices by the number of coffins manufactured per day astounded me just as it astounded them. To deny the laborers who made it all possible a thirty-cent per hour raise seemed not just cheap, it seemed irrational. Surely, we all thought, it was just a matter of time before the owners came to their senses, met the demands, and everybody got back to work.

Now, with Mr. Strange's death and the giant hole in the back wall of the factory, the moral clarity on the picket line had been muddied. The factory workers I knew were God-fearing, law-abiding men. From the beginning, the strike had conflicted with their congenital inclinations to obey authority and work to exhaustion every day. These men had awoken one day to discover that they were allied with at least a few who would set explosions and kill people. It was a troubling revelation to those who had voted for the strike

swept up in a wave of righteous indignation. And, of course, somewhere out there were the men who had actually killed Don Strange. They had their own reasons for being afraid, like prison and eternal damnation.

"Look," said Tom. He pointed across Highway 60 to where a state trooper cruiser from the Seymour post was parked, two grim-looking out-of-towners with crew cuts sitting inside. It seemed to confirm that the picketers were now thought of as dangerous men.

Unlike the strikers, I was heartened to see that the troopers had not left after Don Strange's funeral. Like my father, I had come to doubt that local law enforcement was willing or able to protect Borden from itself during the strike. The writing on our garage door was a direct threat that I knew my dad wasn't laughing off, even if he had laughed off my theory that the bombers might have done it. The night after the funeral, I heard him checking all our door locks before he went to sleep, a new addition to his ten-thirty routine. I felt incredibly vulnerable as I lay there that night in my bedroom, endangered by the walls and windows that my parents thought would protect us. I knew all too well that the house gave anyone on the outside the advantage, the ability to approach us from any direction without being heard or seen. I seriously considered asking my parents if I could sleep outside until the strike was over, where I at least had a chance of detecting an intruder's approach: a stick cracking, whispered voices carrying on the wind, careless silhouettes crossing a ridge. From the outside, I could evade intruders or stalk them if I wanted to, my M6 cleaned and ready. Of course, Mom and Dad would never

allow it. I looked at the two bored troopers with their crew cuts and half-closed eyes, and tried to believe they could somehow protect us.

Almost as the thought popped into my head, reinforcements arrived on a yellow school bus.

Where the name of the school would normally be were painted the words SHIVELY SECURITY. The tires seemed thicker and knobbier than normal. The windows looked modified, too, tinted and strengthened, and closed tight despite the heat. The bus pulled right up to the front gate, stopping with a hiss from its air brakes. There was a dramatic pause. Then, with a squeak just as innocent as if it were getting ready to discharge a gaggle of first graders, the door swung open.

A huge man stepped down the stairs of the bus, turning sideways to fit. He was wearing black canvas pants and a bulletproof vest that accentuated the size of his barrel chest. Under the vest he wore a black sleeveless T-shirt that showed off his beefy arms. On one shoulder was tattooed the logo of the United States Marine Corps, the eagle and the globe. As he exited, he turned, and I saw Asian script tattooed on the other. His pants were tucked into shiny black combat boots. While he was unarmed, there was something unmistakably military in his bearing. He had a blond flattop and a freckled, incongruously boyish face that looked out of place atop that huge body. The strikers, like me, watched him, rapt.

Without acknowledging any of us, he walked to the padlocked gate, pulled a single tiny key from his front pocket, and unlocked it. He pulled the chain through the hasp, and pushed the gate open. Like everything at the

factory, the gate was exquisitely well-maintained and oiled; it swung open without a sound. He waved his arm dramatically at the unseen bus driver.

"*Move it!*" he barked, making all of us jump. The bus's brakes squeaked, and it slowly rolled inside as he waited at the gate.

Once the bus was safely on plant property, the blond soldier closed the gate behind it. He did not relock it. Instead, he casually threw the chain and the padlock on the grass beside the driveway in a way that almost seemed arrogant, as if he were saying to us that it would no longer be necessary to lock up now that he had arrived.

The bus rolled to a stop in the center of the vast, empty front parking lot, not far from the empty barrels where Tom and I had hidden. The passengers inside began filing out. All of them were dressed like the blond man, but there was something about them that seemed less authentic. It was the difference between my unadorned M6 and the stickers and meaningless painting on the BB gun I had owned before. That's not to say these guys weren't heavily armed. Every other man getting off the bus was carrying some kind of pump-action shotgun.

"Is that a Remington 870?" someone behind me asked about the security force's gun of choice. Some of the men stepping off the bus actually had bandoliers of shells crossing their chests. A small group of strikers pressed against the fence and soon they were all chattering about the guns on the other side.

"Looks like a Wingmaster to me."

His friend squinted in concentration. "Nah, it's a Mossberg 500."

"How can you tell?"

"My daddy shot a Mossberg all his life—I'd know that gun a mile away."

"Randall, get over here!" A short man with a handlebar mustache sauntered up to the fence.

"Randall, are those Mossbergs or Remingtons?"

Both men stepped aside deferentially so that Randall, apparently the shotgun expert in the group, could step up to the fence.

"You can't tell for sure from here," said Randall after a moment. "But I'd guess they're Remingtons."

"Why's that?"

"I don't expect these boys economize on their guns."

"We'll just have to wait until they get closer to be sure," said the Mossberg advocate. And by the end of the evening, I knew, the gun-loving men of Borden would have identified and evaluated every piece of armament inside the fence.

Unlike their leader, the rest of the guards did glance over at us as they got off the bus. They looked at the strikers, with their faded work shirts and scruffy beards, with complete disdain. The soldiers, or whatever they were, gathered around the bus until their leader, who was walking briskly toward them from the gate, shouted something. They quickly formed into two columns. When he got in front of them, he gave a brief talk that I strained my ears unsuccessfully to hear. He shouted another order, and the men ran to the bus and began to unload box after box of equipment, rolls of canvas, and plastic trunks full of supplies.

I looked at Tom to see if he was as impressed as I was. Silently, he mouthed "*Thugs.*"

The rest of the crowd on the picket line was coming to the same realization, muttering to each other about the latest development, so there was a short delay before we realized that the bus was not completely done unloading passengers. Stepping off quickly, in work boots and jeans, were a group of men who looked vaguely familiar. They walked hunched over, almost jogging, from the bus to the front door of the factory with their backs to us.

"Holy shit," said a man behind me, the first to realize what we were seeing.

"*Turn around you cowards!*" said another, and by now the whole picket line was up against the fence.

"*Scabs!*" many in the crowd shouted at once. They tried to count them as they ran through the door.

"I don't believe it," said another man behind me.

"*Assholes!*" someone yelled when it seemed as if the last man had hurried off the bus into the safety of the factory walls.

A few seconds passed, and then the last scab stepped dramatically off the bus. Unlike the rest, he was in no hurry to rush inside and he made no effort to keep his back to the picket line. He had on crisp new bell-bottom jeans and a short-sleeved work shirt that was almost completely unbuttoned, showing off his skinny, hairless chest. He turned and faced us with a huge grin on his face. Most of the redness on the side of his face was gone. It was Ray Arnold.

"*Ray, you pussy!*" someone shouted.

Ray beamed. In his posturing, in being the sole focus of our attention from the other side of a fence, and even in his skinniness, Ray strongly reminded me of the scenes I had

seen of British rock stars getting off airplanes in front of a mob of delirious fans.

As the insults reached their crescendo, Ray, still smiling, raised both hands with a flourish, and happily flipped us all off with both middle fingers.

Despite their anger, about half the crowd couldn't help but laugh.

The thugs and the scabs fell into a routine over the next few days. Four of the thugs strolled around the outside of the plant, in two pairs, at all times. One carried a shotgun. The other wore a wide, army-green web belt that held a baton, mace, and a radio that crackled constantly with military jargon. They never spoke to the strikers, never responded to the occasional insult that was thrown their way. Except for the blond man, they all looked vaguely alike, so it was hard to detect exactly when the guard changed, but it seemed like they worked a six-hour shift, more or less, just like the picketers on the other side of the fence. When they were off watch, they disappeared into the plant. Dad told me they had set up a barracks inside, eating in the cafeteria, showering in the locker room, and sleeping on rows of cots that had been set up in the now-empty receiving area. Despite my pleas, he would not take me to see it.

Dad fell into a routine, too, returning to the plant every morning, piecing together coffins with the small crew of scabs who were now clocking in and receiving paychecks once again. The scabs rolled through the gate every morning behind the tinted windows of the Shively Security bus, and went home at night the same way. Exactly how many

scabs there were was a matter of some secrecy. "About a dozen" was all my dad would tell me. According to gossip on the picket line, the number was growing by about one scab every three days. If anyone was more than five minutes tardy for the morning shift on the picket line, it was automatically assumed that he was on the scab bus, and all of his traitorous tendencies were discussed at length, at least until he showed up at the line rubbing his eyes and apologizing for oversleeping.

Despite the predictions of the strikers, Dad and his small crew of scabs somehow managed to finish some caskets. "We're getting 'em done!" he announced excitedly at dinner. The very act of production seemed to cheer him. "More than I thought, even with that small group. With so few men in there, there's no screwing around, everybody's dead serious. It's slow, but all the lights are on, the ovens are running, and by God, we're makin' boxes!" Dad pounded his fist on the table in excitement. The scabs may have been dead serious but Dad was darn near giddy. "The teamsters won't cross the line to pick them up, but I'll find a driver."

The happy optimism in my dad's voice was still in my ears when I rode up to the picket line the next morning. It was pleasantly cool for August, and the morning fog had not completely burned off. The men on the line were burning the first cigarette of the day and passing around a thermos of coffee, treating the start of their shift on the picket line exactly like the start of a workday. The scabs had arrived on their bus at dawn, greeted by some perfunctory jeering, but their appearance each morning had already assumed the status of just part of the daily routine.

Few strikers paid any attention when the empty flatbed truck pulled around to the back of the factory. A few trucks had come and gone, some removing equipment damaged by the explosion. The truck parked out of sight for about two hours, by which time Tom and I, like everyone else on the line, had completely forgotten about it.

When it pulled back out from behind the plant, to our shock, it was loaded with coffins, each snugly secured in its shipping container, the logos oriented neatly in the same direction. We rapidly counted the boxes as the truck rolled up, arriving at a consensus total of thirty-six.

"How'd they do it?" everyone was asking. There was genuine confusion all around. I believe every single person on that line thought it impossible to build a coffin without their individual presence on the line, much less the full group. That the company could without them produce any coffins, much less a full truckload, violated a fundamental tenet of the strike.

"There were some raw boxes in the warehouse," someone answered. "Still, they would have to trim them up, completely finish them. That would be the hard part."

"There must be more guys in there than we thought," somebody said angrily, "there's no way fifteen guys could finish thirty-six caskets in this much time."

"It looks like you're wrong about that."

The heavily laden truck pulled up to Highway 60, and waited for a break in traffic. There was a momentary surge in hope as the truck sputtered and stalled. They watched breathlessly to see if there would be some kind of divine, mechanical intervention to strike that Kenworth dead and halt the progress of the scab caskets. Without

even getting out of the cab, however, the driver turned the key, restarted the engine, and pulled smoothly onto Highway 60. We heard him shift through his gears as he accelerated down the highway, on to a distributor's warehouse on Dutchman's Lane in Louisville. I knew that because Dad had exuded about the details of the shipment the night before.

The picket line lapsed into complete, despondent silence.

While the thugs seemed to be more or less restricted to plant property, Tom and I saw the blond thug in Miller's on his first afternoon in Borden. Needing a break from the scorching heat, Tom and I pooled our spare change and determined that we had enough between us to split a can of Big Red at the store. More important than the cold drink itself, being actual paying customers meant that the bitchy Miller girls would have to allow us to hang out and enjoy their air-conditioning for a few minutes, a luxury neither of us had at home. The store advertised its AC on its main sign, a cartoon of a fan blowing on an ice cube, right next to the cartoon of the store's famous five-hundred-pound wheel of cheese, a smiling rat gazing at it lustfully. Despite the folksy friendliness that the signs promised travelers up and down Highway 60, the Miller girls—Patsy, Loretta, and Maybelle—were the nastiest people in Borden. Vern Miller, their father and the store's third-generation owner, had very successfully raised his little girls to believe that they were Borden royalty, superior to the mere factory workers and farmers who surrounded them. They wore rabbit fur coats in the winter and spent

their summers at the family condo in Destin, Florida. They became frustrated to learn as adults that despite their innate superiority, they could not leave Borden, but were required to stay and run the store. They lived for running off local kids who lingered too long, lest they suck up the air-conditioning and sully the atmosphere of the store for the tourists on their way back to Louisville.

To their credit, the place was an authentic general store. You could buy anything in there from mantles for your Coleman lantern, to a gallon of milk, to a tiny jar of Testor's blue paint for your model airplane. Miller's, along with the hardware store next door, pretty much made up Borden's entire retail economy, so maybe the Miller girls were even a little crankier than normal, as they felt the financial pinch of the strike. Or maybe they could sense that Tom and I had only enough money for one can of soda between us. Or maybe they'd heard that my mom bought her groceries at the Kroger's in New Albany. In any case, as Tom and I walked in the door and gratefully sucked in a breath of that artificially cold air, we were greeted by an unusually venomous stare from Patsy Miller at the cash register. We ignored her, and casually strolled through the store, past the giant wheel of cheese on its wooden spool, back to the lit coolers where we could begin our slow, deliberative soda-selection process.

To my surprise, Taffy Judd was also back there, at the cooler, staring longingly at the soda. It was the first time we'd seen her since the cave.

"Hey Taffy," Tom and I both said, startling her. She turned to face us with a slight smile.

"Hey Tom. Hey Andy," she said quietly. She went back

to staring at the dewy rows of icy soda cans: A&W, Welch's Grape, Orange Crush, and Big Red, each too cold to hold more than a minute with bare hands. Taffy seemed like a different person than the girl we'd seen in the cave, confident, laughing, climbing those walls with dazzling agility. Here, she seemed just like I remembered her at school: small, a little tired, a little sad. And beautiful.

"Thirsty?" I asked her, after I failed to come up with anything more clever.

"You bet," whispered Taffy.

Patsy Miller yelled at us from the register. "You kids get out of here if you don't got no money. I ain't a babysitter."

"We got money," said Tom.

"What about you? You've been back there twenty minutes, little girl."

"We've got money," I said, trying to match Tom's defiant tone.

"Let me see it."

We stepped forward, reaching in our pockets. We pulled out our grimy nickels and dimes, and displayed them for Patsy in the center of our sweaty palms.

Patsy grunted in acknowledgment. She then looked back at Taffy. "What about you, sugar? I know you don't have any money, do you?"

Taffy glared at Patsy, studiously avoided looking at Tom and me, and then walked briskly to the door. Patsy watched her triumphantly. Taffy slammed her hands into the door as she left, making it fly open and ring the attached bell crazily.

"You best not break that door!" screamed Patsy. "You don't have enough money for a Coke, I know you don't have enough to fix that door!"

As Patsy screamed, and before the bell had even stopped ringing, a shadow filled the doorway. I thought for just a moment that Taffy might be coming back to tell Patsy what she could do with her ice-cold Coke cans. But the shadow grew and grew, until it was replaced by a towering, huge man. It was the blond guy, the chief thug.

"Hello, boys," he said with a smile. Tom and I stared openmouthed. "Ma'am," he said nodding at Patsy, who gave him an enormously pleased and surprised smile in return, her anger at Taffy evaporating before our eyes. As she started moving around nervously behind the register, I swear I thought she was looking for a pen so she could get his autograph.

He seemed bigger than the other men I knew: I thought as he walked by the blushing Patsy that he would bang his head on the overhead racks of cigarettes. He was scary. Not because he was a stranger—strangers came into Miller's all the time, tourists looking for local color. At least those people, though, had the courtesy to act uncomfortable or perhaps even charmed by the simple hill folks of the area. This guy was neither uncomfortable nor charmed. He picked up a pound of baloney, a loaf of bread, and a cold six-pack of RC Cola with the ease of a man who might just do it every day for the rest of his life. He took his food to the register. Patsy, as I suspected, was not content to just bag his baloney and give him his change.

"And how are you this mornin'?" she asked once she regained the power of speech.

"Just fine, ma'am," he said, waiting for her to take the five-dollar bill from his fingers. "How are you?"

"We're so glad you're here." Patsy lowered her voice to

a stage whisper. "It's about time somebody taught those yahoos a lesson."

The thug again offered her his money without comment, but Patsy wasn't done yet. She was certain she'd found a fellow traveler in her hatred of Borden natives, and she wasn't about to let him go without some commiseration.

"The unions are ruining the country, I believe."

"That could be, yes, ma'am." His halfhearted agreement seemed just an attempt to bring the conversation to a close. But Patsy was just getting started.

"The Teamsters? Known communists. Longshoremen? Known communists. Autoworkers? I tell my little girl: you see this spool of thread? It costs fifteen cents. If we give everybody more money for making it than they deserve, then the spool of thread will cost a dollar. 'Momma, nobody can pay a dollar for a spool of thread,' she tells me." Patsy cackled at her daughter's precociousness.

"Yes, ma'am."

"So we're real glad you're here." Patsy actually clasped his hand in both of hers, like a grateful flood victim greeting a national guardsman. Her voice dropped to where we could barely hear her, although I sensed that she intentionally maintained it just high enough for us to make out her words. "You teach those rednecks a lesson."

"I'm not here to teach anyone a lesson," said the thug, escaping from her grasp, still smiling tightly. "I'm just here to protect company property."

Patsy cackled again and winked. "Of course you are," she said knowingly. "Of course you are!" She finally gave the man his change.

Tom and I had worked our way over to the door by the time he finally made his escape from Patsy. I read "Solinski" on his nametag as he passed.

"You boys stay out of trouble, okay?" he said. He flashed a pointy-toothed smile and winked at us as he left. Through the door, I watched him stride to catch up with Taffy, who was walking dejectedly down the road. He twisted off a can of RC from his six-pack and gave it to her.

When Tom and I returned to the picket line, the people of Borden were once again abuzz with excitement. The WAVE 3 Action News Team had arrived in a van painted gloriously with NBC's peacock logo. The Action News Team was unloading their equipment, while Borden's own Dieter Sajko did the same: six fat, tired-looking bloodhounds he had in the back of his ancient Ford Bronco. It seemed a little late for hounds to pick up the trail, and I suspected the event was being staged solely for the benefit of the news crew.

Sajko lived at the edge of town in a ramshackle converted barn. He somehow eked out a living raising bloodhounds and grinding tree stumps around the county. Sajko must have known in advance that his performance was to be televised—he was wearing an uncharacteristically clean shirt and what looked like a new straw hat. Sheriff Kohl stood to the side and nodded approvingly as Sajko tried to coax his dogs into at least looking like they gave a shit. Sajko took the notorious Mack Sanders ball cap from the sheriff, rubbed it in the muzzles of his confused-looking dogs, and then took off running with them into the woods beyond the bean field in front of the plant. It was

exactly the opposite direction that Tom and I had seen the "bombers" go—I thought Sajko might be taking his cue from the psychic. The scruffiest-looking member of the news crew trotted after them with a bulky camera on his shoulder, and Tom and I followed on our bikes.

The hounds briefly got into the spirit of things, howling dramatically as they ran in front of Sajko. Their enthusiasm didn't last long. The hounds ran to the edge of Muddy Fork, the nearest body of water. There they sat down, exhausted and gasping for breath, and lapping occasionally from the creek when they could muster the energy.

Dieter Sajko stepped between his hounds and the television camera. "They gone," he declared. "Lost the scent on the water. Probably gone to Lou-a-vul."

The sheriff and his deputies nodded soberly in agreement at Dieter and the small crowd that had caught up with us. I hoped the dogs were right, but I couldn't forget that image of the men running in the opposite direction, and I couldn't stop thinking about the threat scrawled on our garage door. The cameraman knelt down and put his camera on the ground, to get a low angle shot of the panting hounds.

Tom and I turned our bikes around and easily beat the crowd back to the picket line, which was now largely deserted. Inside the fence, I saw that the thugs were ignoring the running of the hounds. Solinski had a large topographical map laid out on a picnic table, the site of summer lunches and smoke breaks during happier days. Two of his RC cans were holding down the corners. Solinski was pointing out coordinates and drawing lines for his men. I could tell even from a distance that it wasn't a map of

Louisville: the large blue band of the Ohio River snaked around the very bottom edge of it. It was a map of Clark County. Solinski didn't believe Sajko's lazy dogs any more than Tom and I did.

That night after dinner had been cleaned up and the Sanka had brewed, Dad shuffled and dealt our well-worn deck of Authors cards.

"I'm feeling lucky tonight," said Dad, sorting his hand.

"*The Alhambra*?" I asked Mom.

"No," she said. I drew a useless *Pendennis* off the pile.

"*The Scarlet Letter*?" Dad asked me. I slid it across the table.

"Yes!" he said, as he happily laid out Hawthorne's four major works on the table.

"How'd they do it?" I asked suddenly. Dad looked at Mom, and I could tell that not only did he know exactly what my vague question meant, but that they had anticipated and planned for it. One of the many things I didn't like about being an only child was that it was nearly impossible for me to surprise my parents.

"How'd they do what?" Dad asked, buying time.

"The explosion at the factory," I said, pretending to sort my cards. "How'd they make it blow up?"

My father looked to my mother again, confirming the strategy they had decided earlier about what and how much to tell me.

"Do you remember the finishing ovens?" my father asked. "Where the caskets roll between coats?"

I nodded. That was in my father's area of the plant, the area I knew the best. The coffins rolled single file on a belt

through the paint booths, which applied each coat of prime, color, and finish. Then the caskets crept slowly through the warm ovens at a precisely calculated temperature, and rolled out the other side with the color more firmly affixed. Or something like that. My father had been largely unsuccessful in his attempts to interest me in the complexities of finishing fine wood coffins. Even so, I did distinctly remember the ovens. While I grew up in a town where virtually everybody paid their bills with money made from the sale of expensive wooden caskets, there was something spooky to me about that unending column of them rolling slowly through a glowing oven.

My father continued. "They lit a candle at one end of the finish line. Then, they blew out the pilot light on the oven, and turned up the throttle valve on the gas all the way. The place filled up with a cloud of natural gas, and when the cloud reached the candle, it ignited, and exploded." He paused, took a breath, then continued to explain to me how Don Strange died.

"Don was standing outside his office when it exploded. Maybe he heard something. Maybe he smelled gas. Maybe he was just getting ready to leave."

"So what actually killed him?" I asked.

"The explosion."

"No, I mean, how? Was he burned up? Did something go through his head?"

My mother was horrified. "Andy, don't be morbid."

"No, it's okay," said my father. "It was the explosion. The blast threw him across the finish room, into a concrete wall. Broke almost every bone in his body. It was enough to kill him five times over."

I pretended to focus on the unaffiliated array of Alcotts, Twains, and Sir Walter Scotts in my hand, and not on the image of tiny Don Strange helplessly flying across the finishing room and slamming into a hard wall.

"They'll pay for what they did. Sooner or later," my father said. "Although I would have thought they could catch at least one of them by now, Sanders or Kruer."

"How do you know they'll get caught? How can you be so sure?" I wanted to know it was certain; if there was no doubt, then I was all freed from any responsibility to come forward and tell the authorities what Tom and I had seen.

"Wherever they end up, somebody will rat them out," my mom said quickly.

I was mystified by her reaction. "Don't we want them caught?"

"Of course we do. I just don't like the way people are lining up to turn them in." Her Kentucky accent had sharpened in the same way it did when she spoke about Phyllis Schlafly.

My father sighed. "They'll get caught without anybody's help—they've hardly proven themselves master criminals."

"Maybe," my mom said.

"They found Mack's ball cap at the factory. With his *name* written in it. Plus, several people came forward and said Sanders was making a lot of crazy threats at the union meeting that very night."

"Like I said. Union people around here are pretty quick to turn on one of their own." I wanted her to elaborate on her own upbringing, where people presumably knew how to throw a proper strike.

"Well, God bless the people around here for that," said my father. "There are folks on our picket line who don't cotton to murder and arson."

"God bless them?" my mother asked.

"God bless them."

We went back to our card game.

Six

During the night, the phone rang and woke me from a deep sleep. I heard Mom hurriedly get ready and drive away, presumably to help Sheriff Kohl again with one of his secret midnight requests. It occurred to me as I drifted back to sleep that the frequency of the sheriff's calls was increasing as the strike went on.

That call was a hazy memory when a metallic pounding woke me the next morning. Through my window, I saw Mom out by the road hammering a small blue sign on a metal stake into the ground. I pulled on my shorts, rubbed my eyes, and walked out front to see what she was advocating. It looked almost like one of the pro-strike signs that dotted the lawns throughout town. It wasn't. When I got closer, I read in red and white letters: ERA—VOTE YES!

"I thought that already passed." I remembered her celebrating something similar years before, and a mention of the amendment in school.

"Not just yet."

"What's ERA gonna make us do?"

"It says you can't deny me my rights because I'm a woman."

I thought it over. "Are you sure that's not the law already?"

"It passed Congress in seventy-two. Now thirty-eight states have to ratify it for it to be part of the Constitution."

"How many states have passed it?"

"Thirty-five."

"How about Indiana?" I asked.

"Indiana was the last one, number thirty-five, two years ago."

"If Indiana already passed it, why put the sign up?"

"Moral support. And because we're running out of time—1982 is the deadline."

"Cool," I said. "You've got three years to get three states. That shouldn't be too hard."

"You wouldn't think," she said, giving the sign a final whack.

We walked back toward the house together. The sign was largely a symbolic gesture, I knew, even apart from Indiana's fait accompli. Only the Kruers lived between us and the end of Cabin Hill Road: few registered voters would pass and be influenced by my mom's efforts. Mom had put a similar sign in the yard years before, at some other key point in the amendment's legislative life. Of the few folks who drove by it, some asked Dad why our house was for sale.

Dad was furiously chopping through shrubs next to the house, in the center of a green cloud of unwanted foliage. Since the strike began, our yard had achieved a kind of glory, more edged, fertilized, and weeded than it had ever been before. Mom exchanged her hammer for a hoe

and began hacking between the rows of our vegetable garden. I suppose she imagined recalcitrant state legislators as she worked. I volunteered to pluck the ravenous worms from the tomato plants, avoiding their sharp horns and the green slime they oozed in panic as I dropped them to their doom in a small bucket of water. It felt good to be out in the heat working together. I was so intent on my chores that Mom saw Tom walk up the driveway before I did.

"Hello, Mrs. Gray," he said. He was shirtless, as usual, with a fishing pole in his hand and his M6 rifle slung behind his back. He gave me a quick, sly look, and I knew why he was there. We were going searching for the fugitives.

"Hi, Tommy," she said, smiling. While Tom's dad and mine might have been on opposite sides of our little labor war, neither family made any attempt at curtailing our friendship. Neither family was capable of that kind of cruelty, for one thing. For another, it would have been futile, short of locking us both in our rooms. And we had well-traveled escape routes for that eventuality as well. In any case, my parents genuinely liked Tom and had no interest in keeping us separated. And they had no idea, of course, that we were looking for something bigger than bass and squirrel.

"Can Andy go fishing?" Tom asked my mom. Dad had worked his way over to us. He was wiping sweat from his brow with one hand, holding hedge clippers with the other.

"How are you, young man?" he asked.

"Fine, sir."

"Your folks?"

"They're real good," Tom said automatically. "I thought Andy and me would go fishing."

"Must be some big fish you're after." He grinned and pointed at the gun. Tom shrugged and smiled back. I ran up to my room and got my gun and my fishing pole, and ran up alongside Tom, now identically equipped.

"Look at these two," my father said.

"Can I go?" I asked.

"Certainly," said my father. "Be careful. Be home for supper."

Mom and Dad watched us walk off, and I could tell that the scene gave them profound pleasure.

The guns slung across our backs were our prized possessions, and we often took them along with us in the woods, when both our meager budgets and our parents allowed us the use of live ammunition. Tom and I had both received the guns the previous Christmas. Up to that point, I had spent that holiday season in a funk, depressed again about the low population inside the Gray house. Starting at about Thanksgiving, I imagined generations bumping into each other in the tiny front rooms all over Borden, the folks repeating themselves to be heard over the noise. Our house was so quiet on Christmas mornings that we could hear the high-pitched whining of my dad's electronic flash recharging between photographs. Tom's house was so crowded that two of his younger siblings had to eat Christmas dinner on an ironing board in the living room, because the dining room table, the kitchen table, and two card tables weren't quite big enough for the whole clan. I always longed for that: a huge family with stupid traditions, family

recipes, black sheep, and crazy uncles. The feeling was especially strong during the holidays. But Mom's family was a mystery, and my father was an only child, like me. Crowded, chaotic Christmas mornings were something I'd never have.

Adding to my gloom was the giant foil-wrapped Hershey Kiss I'd been unable to give Taffy for Christmas. Right before school let out, I'd lingered in Miller's for thirty minutes until the store was completely empty except for me and Patsy. Then I snatched the kiss off the shelf, hurriedly picked a card, and rushed to the register, eager to complete the transaction before any of my friends could wander in and bust me. Patsy sensed my discomfort and took her time counting my quarters and dimes, but I was able to leave the store unseen. I imagined myself giving it to Taffy at school the next day, the look on her face as she accepted the gift, the resumption of the romance that had been interrupted by a misunderstanding over a shared sandwich with Theresa Gettelfinger.

But Taffy didn't show up for school the next day, or the next day, and then we were on Christmas break. I'd been unable to muster the nerve necessary to deliver the present to her home. The kiss was hidden in my top dresser drawer, making me think about Taffy every time I got a pair of socks, all of which soon smelled vaguely of chocolate. My parents must have sensed my moodiness when they decided to get me the best Christmas present of my life.

When I came downstairs Christmas morning, the gun was leaning unwrapped against the fireplace, so casually that it took me a few minutes to notice it. It was, in its own way, fairly nondescript, all black metal without a piece of

wood on it. As soon as I spotted it, I grabbed it and read the Springfield Armory name and logo etched into the side, two crossed cannons in a circle. On the other side was SPRINGFIELD ARMORY M6 SURVIVAL. As Mom and Dad watched, I broke the weapon down, looking at every part from every angle, memorizing the curves and colors of each component, and especially the way everything fit together in a meaningful, logical way. It's hard to explain how strongly I wanted to know immediately everything about that gun. A few years later, in a sweltering Indiana University dorm room, I would study a creased photograph of my first love with the same kind of devotion.

The gun was a Springfield M6 Scout. It was entirely made of metal, including the stock—the whole thing had a blocky, utilitarian look. It had two barrels, over and under, a .22 rifle barrel over a slightly larger .410 shotgun. I had seen double-barrel guns before, but always with two barrels of the same caliber. I associated the configuration with old-fashioned guns, museum pieces or heirlooms manufactured before pump-action or semiautomatic mechanisms, when it took two barrels to get two shots off quickly. My gun was clearly no antique, however, as indicated by the complete lack of wood or ornamentation in its manufacture. A knurled knob moved the firing pin on the hammer to one of two positions: the lower position for the shotgun, the top for the .22. The front sight was also selectable, a small "l" of metal that could be flipped up to a small "v" for the shotgun, or a tiny "o" peep sight for the rifle, both of which were labeled as such with tiny, almost microscopic numbers. While it was obviously not a Daisy BB gun, it wasn't all that much bigger: thirty-two inches long and

just four and a half pounds, according to the "Your New M6 Scout" operator's manual that I rapidly memorized. The strangest thing about the gun's appearance was that it lacked a trigger. In its place was a kind of squeeze bar. A black nylon sling ran from the very back of the stock to the end of the barrel.

The gun was designed to be compact. It broke open in the middle to load, and in the same way it could be folded almost completely in half. In the buttstock was a waterproof storage compartment for storing ammunition: a single row of nineteen holes, fifteen for .22 shells, and four larger ones for .410 shotgun shells. I owned a Crossman pellet gun, and a BB gun, too, both designed to mimic the look of real guns as closely as possible. But here was the real thing, right in front of me, and it was all mine. I could scarcely believe my luck.

"You be careful with that," my father said. "Like they taught you."

Dad was referring to the gun-safety class Tom and I had taken side by side the summer before, the summer of '78. At the time we were a little curious about why our fathers had enrolled us. We'd both been shooting our fathers' guns for years, under their careful supervision, and a respect for firearms and an intimate knowledge of the damage they could cause was a part of our lives. Like Tom, I had already felt the exhilaration and the shame of a well-placed shot, killing my first rabbit with the Crossman pellet gun, gingerly examining the limp, bleeding carcass to confirm what I had done. (We were both so bothered by the experience that we independently asked clergymen for solace. Tom's priest told him killing the rabbit wasn't a

sin because the rabbit didn't have a soul. Reverend Nichols told me it was okay because God gave man dominion over the animals.) We didn't think some class had anything to teach us about the power of guns. Nonetheless, Tom and I weren't going to argue with an opportunity to hold and shoot our fathers' guns for a week.

For the class, I used my father's lever-action .22 Marlin rifle, and Tom shot his dad's old Remington. The class was held in the cinder-block "clubhouse" of the Georgetown Conservation Club, and was filled with city kids from New Albany and Jeffersonville, most of them wearing amber-lensed shooting glasses and pristine Cabela's vests. On the first day, when we stood to introduce ourselves one by one, the kids snickered at Tom and me, either at our presidential names or our hillbilly accents. We had to wait through three days of classroom training before we could show them up. We might talk funny up in the hills, they would learn, but we could shoot like Sergeant York.

The safety classes were excruciatingly thorough and repetitive—to this day I can recite the three fundamental rules for safe gun handling verbatim: *ALWAYS keep the gun pointed in a safe direction. ALWAYS keep your finger off the trigger until ready to shoot. ALWAYS keep the gun unloaded until ready to use.* We were motivated to study by our knowledge that a passing grade on the written test was required before we could go out on the range. The firing point was in sight and in earshot, just outside the windows of the classroom where we vowed repeatedly to Know Our Target and What Is Beyond. The occasional pop-pop-pop from outside was a tantalizing incentive to study hard.

All but two of our classmates passed the written test. One of those who failed was a chunky loudmouth from Clarksville who had told us all at every turn that he already knew everything about guns and didn't need the class; he surprised us by crying in humiliation when the instructors announced his failure. The other washout was a nervous, skinny youngster from Georgetown. Throughout the course he had asked the instructors earnest and specific questions about the potential for self-inflicted wounds on the range. When they announced that he had failed the written test and would not be shooting, he let out a heartfelt sigh of relief.

The instructors then marched the rest of us out on the range where Tom and I immediately asserted our superiority. We were naturals. The rules the other kids had to think about individually with each shot—focus on the front sight, breathe, relax, aim, squeeze-the-trigger-don't-jerk-it—came automatically to us. While the other kids were learning to their surprise how loud a real gunshot is, and how sharply a little .22 rifle can kick you in the shoulder, Tom and I actually thought about the wind direction and the inch of angle the bullet dropped on its way downrange to the paper bull's-eye. I could actually see my bullet leave the barrel and the arc it traced as it flew downrange. When I told the instructors, they said it wasn't possible, but Tom said he could see it, too. The instructors soon took a special interest in the two of us, as we punched holes in the centers of ever more distant targets while our classmates struggled to keep their rounds out of the dirt.

At the end of the week, the instructors pitted Tom and me against each other in a friendly shooting competition

as the other kids watched jealously. We shot targets at a variety of ranges from a standing, sitting, and prone position. Tom actually outshot me by a little, but I won the prize for best overall score in the class by virtue of my higher grade on the written test. I received as my reward a certificate that pronounced me to be an "Eagle of the Indiana Wilderness," and a new box of .22 shells, both of which were displayed proudly on my dresser during the six months between the class and Christmas day, the day I discovered why dad had enrolled me in a gun safety class to begin with.

"Can I show Tom?" I asked, when I finally regained the power of speech that Christmas morning.

"Sure," said my father. "Go on." He grinned in a way that told me the surprise wasn't quite over.

"Bundle up," my mother said.

I found my coat, hat, and gloves in record time, shoved my box of shells in my pocket, and then walked as quickly as I could (the safety rules prohibited running with a weapon) up my driveway and down Cabin Hill Road. About halfway down the road, I saw Tom coming my way, with an identical gun in his hands. We found out later that his father had found them both at a gun show at the fairgrounds in Louisville, and quickly identified them as ideal first guns for us both. Our fathers had carefully coordinated the gifts, after agreeing on the gun safety class and evaluating our maturity and readiness for gun ownership.

Tom and I spent the rest of Christmas morning blasting away icicles that hung from tree branches—they exploded with a satisfying noise and sparkle. When we paused to reload or talk, we heard all around us the distant, jubilant

firing of other men and boys with their Christmas-morning guns.

Yes, these were real guns, and we were shooting real ammunition, unsupervised, at will, all over the countryside. We were not inside any city limits, and there were no laws that prevented two kids like us from shooting icicles, Dr Pepper cans, or any other inanimate object for as long as our ammunition held out. Out in the country you heard people shooting all year long, the blast of shotguns and the high-pitched crack of powerful rifles. It was not any more surprising to find empty red and yellow plastic shotgun shells on a path in the woods than it was to find acorns. At thirteen, my age that Christmas morning, I was far from the first of my classmates to own a real gun. Every boy I knew had a hunting license before he had a driver's license, and most had killed their first deer before their first kiss.

The M6 was not designed for marksmanship. In our hands, however, after shooting thousands of rounds through spring and summer, Tom and I became dead-eyed experts. We knew exactly what the little gun was capable of doing, and within those limits, we could command the weapon perfectly. We designed ever more challenging targets and scenarios for ourselves. When the Coke can on the fence post became too easy, we switched to a small tuna can, which we soon after hung on a string from a tree limb, learning to shoot it dead center as it swung in the breeze. By the time school let out, we were shooting the string.

For our everyday shooting, we bought boxes of shells at Miller's, whenever we had a few dollars from a birthday or a mowed lawn. The ammo secured in the buttstock's

storage compartment, however, was sacred, to be saved for an "emergency," that situation Tom and I fantasized about in which we'd need the little gun to save our lives. Most often these fantasies involved invading communist hordes swarming across Clark County. While Tom and I certainly had nothing resembling formal military training, countless shots in every corner of the valley, an intimate knowledge of the landscape, and our vivid imaginations taught us well the value of high ground and interlocking fields of fire. I like to think we might have given an invading horde a pretty good fight.

For the .22 shells in the storage compartment, we chose the Winchester .22LR. That decision was made easy because that was pretty much the best .22 round we could buy in Borden, although we had heard about a .22 centerfire round that was more accurate. That was far too exotic to be found on the shelf at Miller's. In addition, we practiced constantly with the inexpensive rimfire rounds, and thought it wise to have a familiar rifle round at the ready when the Commies finally came over the hill.

The decision as to what shotgun shells to store in the buttstock was more complicated. A wide variety of things can be fired from a shotgun, one of the reasons it is the most practical of guns. The options we studied included shrieking noisemakers, flechette rounds that shot tiny steel darts, and flamethrower rounds that shot pure fire about twenty feet. After an exhaustive evaluation of our options, Tom and I finally picked up three flare rounds at a gun show at the Holiday Inn in New Albany. That we paid four dollars for each was an indication of how badly we wanted the flares. This gave us one to store in each of our

guns, and a third to shoot, to try it out and see what it looked like. On a cool spring night, after flipping a coin to see who would get the honor, I shot the third flare round from my M6 into the sky. It exploded above our heads with a pop and a blinding red starburst that burned intensely for seven seconds, just as the box advertised. Ever since, we had each kept three regular rounds of .410 birdshot stored in our guns, along with the flare round, a compact, portable fireworks display that forever tempted us.

Tom stared into the woods more intently than normal as we walked, fishing rods in our hands and guns across our backs. We were actually going to fish, we hadn't been lying about that. But from now on, just as Tom had said that night at the museum, every walk in the woods would also be a search for Sanders and Kruer. He studied the path for any sign of them as we walked to Silver Creek, walking a half step slower than normal and peering through the trees. My thoughts about the bombers were vivid at night, when I remembered the dark silhouettes of them running in front of the fireball, or their somehow menacing black-and-white yearbook photos reproduced in the newspaper. When I was trying to fall asleep, Sanders and Kruer represented everything that was dangerous and out of control in my town. But out there in the bright sunlight, with Tom and my Springfield beside me, I tried to get into the spirit of the hunt without feeling any real fear, or even excitement. The woods seemed utterly, completely normal. Actually finding a couple of killers out there just seemed too unbelievable to be frightening.

After a while, Tom began scratching his head and

clearing his throat as we walked, and I got the feeling he had something to tell me.

"Did you hear about Taffy Judd?" he finally asked.

"No. What?" I was certain she was lost in a cave.

"She's gone," said Tom, the regret clear in his voice. "Her mother and sister, too. Their dad was beating the shit out of all of them last night, all liquored up. Taffy ran down the road to Miller's in the middle of the night with a broken arm and called the sheriff on the pay phone. Dad heard it all on his police radio—says that drunk might have killed them all if Taffy hadn't got away."

"Shit," I said, picturing poor Taffy running down the dark road, her arm at a funny angle, wincing as she put a nickel in the phone with her good arm. I was relieved beyond words that she hadn't died in the cave. At the same time, I was sickened by the thought of her brutal father hitting her. I knew Taffy could get away from him, especially if he was slowed down by cheap booze. If she got hurt, I knew it had to be because she was trying to protect her sister and mother. And now she was gone.

"I guess their dad beat them up all the time," said Tom.

"He did?"

"That's what Dad said, said it like everybody in town knew about it. He said Judd spent so much money on booze that their mom had to get food from the church."

"I guess that's why Taffy didn't talk much in school," I mumbled.

"How's that? Because she was hungry?"

"And she was probably worried all the time, about what her dad was going to do to them every night when

he got home from Kirtley's, or wherever he got liquored up."

"The cave was probably the safest place she could go," said Tom, and I realized it was true, despite the fact that I was so worried about her getting hurt down there.

"Where are they now?"

"Their dad's in jail. No tellin' where the rest of them ended up. Maybe she's got family somewhere. I hope."

"Yeah," I said. People rarely left Borden, at least for any period of time longer than an army enlistment contract. So it took a few seconds for me to comprehend that I might not ever see her again. And I didn't even have a picture to remember her by.

"Shit," I said. We'd stopped walking. Tom stared at the ground sympathetically, hands on hips.

"I'm sorry, man."

I shrugged, trying to fight off the gloom, or at least put on a brave front. I was surprised at the force of my sadness, the feeling of loss. I could tell by the careful way Tom was handling the situation that he wasn't surprised by my reaction.

"She'll be back," Tom said unconvincingly.

"Sure." We resumed walking.

Tom and I pushed through the weeds to a wide spot in Silver Creek where we'd had some recent luck with bluegill and small but tasty channel catfish. It was a popular spot among knowledgeable locals, so I was relieved to see that Tom and I had it to ourselves, at least for the moment. I really didn't feel like talking to anyone. The creek was pinched and fast moving at both ends of the pool, but the

water where we fished was wide and deep—the pool was roughly in the shape of a giant eye. We leaned our guns on a fallen tree that ran along the bank, a natural bench, dug some grubs up from under a rotten log with our hands, dropped our baited hooks in the water, and waited. The sweltering heat didn't encourage conversation.

After a time, Tom reeled in out of sheer boredom, and got his line snagged on some floating weeds. He pulled hard, trying hard to free the hook from a variety of angles, because neither of us had brought along any spare tackle. Finally, with his rod bent almost completely over on itself, the line snapped.

"Well, shit."

We both turned and started looking into the tree branches behind us, looking for any hooks that had been snagged and abandoned by fishermen before us. It was amazing what some guys would leave behind just because they didn't feel like climbing a tree.

With nothing visible close by, Tom began walking along the bank, looking in the weeds and along the water's edge for anything remotely usable, even an old rusty hook that might be sharpened on a rock.

"Here we go," he said, about halfway to the end of the pool. He was leaning down almost to the dirt, where a length of fishing line was running from a small tree near the shore into the water. Tom tugged it, hoping that a hook in relatively good condition would be at the other end.

As he pulled, the whole thing came out of the water. It ran all the way across the creek, where it was tied to a branch on the opposite shore. A dozen leaders baited with red worms dangled from it on swivels at neatly spaced

intervals. On two of them, tiny bluegills shimmered in the sunlight, twitching and fighting to escape.

I put my pole down and ran over to look. "What the hell?"

"It's a trot line," he said, excited. "That's smart—fishes all day for you, you just come haul them in at night! You lay low, don't have to worry about anybody seeing you out here."

"Do you think . . ."

Tom was grinning wildly. "Who else could it be?"

"We can't be sure, anybody could have made this thing . . ."

"Let me ask you something, Andy. We've been fishing here a long time, right? Years and years? Have you ever seen anything like this before?"

I had to shake my head. "Still . . ."

"Well, if we watch this thing long enough, I guess we'll find out who it belongs to. We need to come back at night. Goddamn, a trot line—what a great idea." He unsnapped the nearest leader, and let the line go. It dropped back into the water until only a few inches of it were visible again, the short distance from the waterline to the baby tree. "Holy shit, that is cool."

We walked back over to our log. Tom grabbed his pole in a kind of happy daze, convinced we had found our first concrete evidence of the bombers. He tied on the leader and cast it into the pool, still using the red worm that the bombers, or whoever, had used. He stared across the water contemplating the possibilities. The complete lack of action made it easy to get lost in thought. We fished silently and fruitlessly for an hour, listening for any sign of

the bombers, glancing occasionally at what we could see of the trot line. Soon, I was again pretending to concentrate on my line while thinking only of Taffy.

"Look at that," Tom said, after a long period of quiet. I saw what he was talking about, a big, slow hit on the surface of the water, right in the center of the eye, the large ripples expanding outward. The waves weren't the frantic work of a bass snapping its hungry lips at a fly, but something big and lumbering.

"Was it a turtle?"

"I think it was a carp," Tom said. "A huge one."

We both reeled in our hooks and threw them in the general direction of the fish, to no avail. Then it hit the surface again, and this time we could actually make out the gaping white mouth. Its pale whiskers broke the surface, and just below we could make out the body, widening and disappearing into the deep. It was a monster.

"How'd that hog get in here?" I asked.

"Probably came down the creek as a baby," said Tom. "Grew up to where he was trapped in this pool by his size."

The activity of the big fish on the surface stopped, it having either filled its stomach or heard our voices.

We tried again tossing our hooks in front of it, hoping at least to provoke the fish into rising to the surface again so we could take another look at it. Already I was losing the image in my mind, forgetting the actual size of the thing. I was about to give up when Tom suggested a new course of action.

"Let's jump in and look at it," he said.

"What?" I had been fishing my whole life, and no one had ever before suggested just jumping into the water and taking a look around. It was the kind of original thinking that made Tom both fun and a little unsettling to hang out with.

"I'm serious," Tom said. "The water's pretty clear. The pool's not that big across. Let's jump in and see if we can see it." He was standing on the log, waiting for me to follow his lead. As was so often the case, Tom's idea was so far out in left field that I couldn't even formulate a rebuttal. The heat also made the idea of jumping into the cool water sorely tempting. I removed my shoes, stood up on the log, and on the count of three, we jumped in together.

I sank slowly to the bottom with my eyes closed. The cold of the water quickly soaked through my shorts. The current pushed me downstream with surprising force, pressing me into a sideways lean. When my feet hit the gravelly bottom, something tiny and hard scurried to escape from under my heel. I opened my eyes.

The water was clearer than I'd expected. Rays of sunlight hit the smooth surface about two feet above our heads, and broke into sparkles that danced across the muddy bottom. Weeds grew around the edges of the pool and swayed with the current, and I could see all the way to the steep walls of the far bank. Dancing bubbles marked where the swift water of Silver Creek tumbled into the pool, the trot line invisible in the turbulence. And directly across from us hovered the enormous carp.

It was huge, at least twenty-five pounds. Its large, mirrorlike scales reflected the sunlight with a greenish glow. It stared at us, swinging its big, flat tail calmly from side

to side. Its large lips were turned downward in a mild frown. The fish was unhappy to share his pool with us, but seemed to recognize that we couldn't last down there for long. We stared at each other until my lungs burned. As my breath finally ran out, the carp's mouth opened slightly, allowing a perfectly spherical bubble to follow me as I pushed up and shot to the surface.

Tom popped up right after me. We both gasped for breath.

"I can't believe it," I said. "Did you see the size of that thing?" Tom didn't respond, and I turned to see what had his attention.

Calmly sitting on our log, his booted feet dangling nearly to the water, was Solinski, the head thug. Solinksi was inspecting Tom's rifle, and mine was across his lap.

I was too stunned to move—I wouldn't have been more surprised if I saw Solinski sitting on Tom's living room couch. Tom was already climbing out of the water and heading toward him, seething.

"Hello, boys," said Solinski with a smile, wholly unthreatened by Tom's outrage.

Tom grabbed his gun away, so Solinski picked up mine and resumed his inspection.

"An M6," he said. "I'll be damned. I've never seen one before."

I was out of the water and standing by him, but I didn't have the nerve to snatch it away like Tom had. I just stood there and dripped.

"Did you know these were designed for air force bomber pilots?" he said. "So that when they crashed in Siberia or

whatever, they could hunt their food and chase away the polar bears for a few days. That's why they've got this squeeze bar instead of a trigger," he said, pointing at it. "So you can shoot it with mittens."

"Yeah, we know," said Tom. He was so emphatic that I am sure Solinksi could tell he was bullshitting. In fact, I had always thought the small gun was designed for kids. Solinski's information made the gun seem even cooler, and I was grateful to him for that.

"I saw you two in the store, remember?" asked Solinski.

"No," said Tom. Now he was just being obnoxious.

"What are you doing here?" I asked. I didn't mean it to sound confrontational. I really wanted to know.

"I've been out here a lot. Walking around, getting to know the area, enjoying the scenery. I should ask you what you're doing here," he said, in an equally friendly tone. "You're the ones trespassing on Borden Casket Company property." It was true, and Tom and I both knew it. The company owned vast tracts throughout the county. Every now and then we'd stumble upon and ignore an orange-lettered sign in the middle of the woods that read YOU ARE NOW TRESSPASSING ON BORDEN CASKET COMPANY PROPERTY. Since none of the land was fenced, and since the property lines ran helter-skelter throughout the valley, the company had always let the locals hunt and fish, just as they always had. As long as they didn't damage any of the company's slow-growing assets, nobody seemed to mind.

"Are you here to run us off?" I asked. Tom remained sullen, inching slowly toward the trailhead at the edge of the woods.

"Not at all," said Solinski. "I'm just out here taking a walk through the woods."

"You're looking for Sanders and Kruer," said Tom.

Solinski looked each of us over carefully, then shrugged. "They're in Louisville, haven't you heard?"

We didn't say anything.

"Personally, I don't know about that," continued Solinski. "If it was me, looking at the map, I would have headed this way—into the hills. Especially if I grew up around here and knew people around here. Knew these hills. Like you two."

I smiled in spite of myself, proud to have my expertise acknowledged.

"Have you seen anything?" Solinski asked, leaning close to me. "Campfires? Tents?" I was consciously fighting the urge to glance in the direction of the trot line when Tom jumped in.

"You'll be the last guy we tell," he said, practically shouting.

Solinski laughed a bit, but then turned serious. "Let me tell you two something," he said, clearly addressing his comments to Tom more than me. "They aren't heroes. Those are bad men. They killed a guy—one of your own. If you do see them, I don't care if you tell me. I don't even care if you tell the cops. But tell someone. Okay?"

"Okay," I said. Tom glowered and didn't say anything.

Solinski resumed his inspection of my gun. He found the latch for the buttstock storage compartment and popped it open.

"This is great," he said. "A .22 and a .410. You guys must be the envy of the neighborhood." The word "neighborhood" marked Solinski as an outsider. Borden was too small

to have neighborhoods. I appreciated the compliment nonetheless.

I shrugged my shoulders with false modesty. "It's a good smallbore," I said. "Rabbit and squirrel."

"Screw that," said Solinski. "A .22 is the most deadly caliber, did you know that?"

I shook my head.

"Bigger bullets, they have enough energy and momentum to go right through the human body. If they don't hit anything important, they'll just pass right through, leave a big hole but pretty much no other damage."

"Huh," I said. Solinski sounded like he knew what he was talking about.

"A .22, though, once it penetrates, it won't have enough energy to come out the other side. It'll just rattle around inside the body, pretty much turning everything inside to soup."

Solinski saw the metal cap of the flare round and pulled it out with two big fingers.

"A flare?" he asked, smiling.

I grinned and nodded.

"I didn't even know they made those for .410. That's really cool."

I nodded again—I thought so, too. "It's small," I said.

"Trust me," said Solinski, "if you shoot that thing at night, people will see it. I've seen flares save lives, plenty of times, getting guys out of really tough spots."

"Where was that?" I asked. Tom was pacing around the trailhead, annoyed with me for extending the conversation, but I was dying to hear where Solinski had seen flares save lives. I was pretty sure I knew the answer, but

I wanted to hear him say it. In my little hometown in 1979, there were plenty of young men walking around with tattoos like Solinski's, but none of them ever wanted to tell me anything about it.

"Vietnam," he said, confirming my theory. "Sometimes they'd send us into the bush to rescue downed pilots. If we got close, or if things got too hot, the pilots would shoot flares from their .45s so we could find 'em in a hurry. They'd shoot those things up, and everybody would go running toward it. On both sides." I followed his eyes upward, half expecting his memory to conjure up a burst of light in the sky. "What color is it?" He asked suddenly, like he wanted to change the subject.

It took me just a moment to understand what he was asking. "Red," I answered.

"Well, if I ever see a red flare out here, I'll come running for you."

I was embarrassed at how comforting I found that. I nodded my head quickly.

"We need to go," said Tom impatiently.

Solinski handed my gun back to me. "Here you go. Those things are cool. You be careful with them."

"Yessir," I said.

"We need to go," Tom said again. I started walking to him at the head of the path.

"Do you guys really know how to shoot those things?" asked Solinski. There was no mistaking the note of playful taunting in his voice. I looked at Tom. After the briefest of pauses, Tom walked to the water's edge, breaking down and loading both chambers of his gun as he did. I did the same. We stood on each side of Solinski.

I wanted to impress Solinski with my marksmanship. I hurriedly scanned Silver Creek and the opposite bank for a target that would be sufficiently showy.

I was in luck. In the far side of the pool, drifting with the swift current, a small snapping turtle passed by. Just its head stuck out of the water, a target roughly the size and shape of my thumb. It moved fast in the water, from left to right.

I pulled the selector up, from the safe position to the .22. I raised the gun to my shoulder, got the picture in the small circle of the rifle sight, and led the turtle, all in one motion. I squeezed the trigger and blew the turtle's head clean off. It exploded into a puff of green and red mist that lingered over the surface of the water.

"Jesus Christ," said Solinski, sucking in his breath in surprise. My gunshot echoed across the valley.

The crack of my rifle flushed out three bats from whatever small cave they were sleeping in across the creek. They came flying directly at us, panicked enough by the noise to venture out into broad daylight.

Tom raised his gun. Bats, we had long since determined, were the hardest of all God's creatures to shoot. Unlike a duck or a goose, or my turtle, they didn't travel in cooperative straight lines. Bats, especially bats crazed by fear, flew in unpredictable swooping zigzags.

Tom pulled the trigger on his gun, unleashing a tight cone of birdshot into the sky. There was a small explosion of black dust as lead pellets shredded one of the bat's wings. It fell straight down and landed on the surface of the water with a satisfying slap, and began floating quickly downstream. Without taking the gun off his shoulder, Tom

pulled the selector up to the .22 position, and changed his stance infinitesimally to accommodate the different shot. To fire the shotgun, he'd held it loosely against his body, allowing it to swing with the moving target. To shoot the rifle, he turned rigid, his entire frame a stable supporting tower for his weapon. He shot the dead bat out of the water with a perfectly aimed .22 bullet. Its carcass cartwheeled out of the water and landed with a splat on the mud of the far bank. Tom and I lowered our smoking rifles and looked at Solinski.

"Goddamn," he said, as the three rapid shots rang in our ears. There was real wonder in his voice. "You boys can shoot."

Tom allowed himself a smile at the praise, even coming as it did from the head thug.

"We need to go," Tom said again.

"Why were you such a jerk?" I asked as we walked.

Tom shrugged. "I don't like him. I don't like any of them."

"Why?" I asked.

Tom was starting to scowl, the way he always did when I asked my third or fourth question about the same thing. "Those guys are trying to bust the union," Tom said.

"What's that mean?"

"My dad just wants to do his job, and they won't let him."

"I just don't know why you had to be such a dick."

"Did you hear what I just said?" he said. "They're fucking with my dad's job!"

"But your dad went out on strike, right? They didn't fire him." Tom didn't respond. "And, come to think of it, isn't Solinski just doing his job?"

Tom stopped walking. He seemed a little apologetic. "It's confusing," he said.

"It really is."

"I don't understand everything about why they went on strike, or why the company won't just give them what they want. Dad's tried to explain it to me a million times, and there's a lot of it I just don't get."

"Same here." I was glad to hear that he shared some of my confusion.

"But I do understand one thing," said Tom.

I waited. "What's that?"

"I know what side I'm on."

We walked thoughtfully, as I digested this key difference between us.

As we neared the edge of our property, five cleared acres unprotected by the thick canopy of leaves, the light became brighter and the air became incrementally warmer and more humid. The gray gravel band of Cabin Hill Road was visible through the trees.

"You want to eat supper at my house?" asked Tom as we walked.

"Sure," I said. I loved the chaos of family meals at Tom's. He was the oldest of six uncontrollably energetic kids, all of whom, boy and girl, looked exactly alike except for height. The last time I'd been there for dinner, after we'd eaten, Tom yelled "Hop on Pop!" and the entire mob of them jumped on his dad at once, knocking him out of his

chair. They tried to keep him pinned to the ground as he hurled shrieking, laughing kids across the room, while Tom's mother ordered them all to stop and hit whatever heads came in range with a wooden serving spoon. It was somewhat of a contrast to our postdinner game of Authors.

"We only have Kool-Aid to drink right now," said Tom as we walked. "Kool-Aid and water. The milk is just for breakfast and for the baby."

"Okay . . ." I said. It seemed like a strange thing to point out, but I could tell Tom attached importance to it.

"Saving money," he continued. "Mom says no Coke until the strike's over."

"That's a good idea." I liked Kool-Aid, anyway. "I'll tell my mom she should do that, too."

Tom laughed and stopped walking. It was one of those times he was absolutely mystified by how dense I could be. "You don't need to save money," he said. "Your dad is still getting paid. He's been getting paid this whole time."

Once again, Tom's knowledge of the strike left me in the dark. "Even when the plant was completely shut down?" I asked.

"Because he's management," Tom explained patiently.

"Well, I guess it's sort of fair. My dad didn't want the strike."

"Neither did my dad. He voted against it. Thought they could work everything out with the plant open. But he still won't get any money until they go back to work."

"Your dad was against the strike? But that night we heard him talking—"

"I know," said Tom, interrupting me.

"Was it because one of the bombers is a Kruer? Is that why your dad got in a fight with Ray down there?"

Tom shrugged.

"Or was it because they're all in the union together?"

"Maybe," said Tom. "It's confusing." I knew this time he meant that it was confusing only to me.

I was mulling it all over when we heard a branch crack behind us. We stopped moving and looked at each other silently. There was a large rustle off the path, a movement of the leaves and litter of the forest floor out of harmony with the gentler rhythms caused by the small breeze all around us. Another stick broke, farther off—there was acceleration in the movement, acceleration in a direction directly away from us. And it wasn't a deer. Even the biggest bucks were more graceful than that. I'd seen panicked record-setters sprint right by my face without breaking a twig.

"Let's go," whispered Tom, pivoting toward the noise.

"Do you think it's Solinski?"

"It could be. But he'd be crazy to sneak up on us like that after seeing how we can shoot."

"Sanders and Kruer?"

I could tell he was trying not to get his hopes up. "Could be Judd. Could be a lot of things. Let's go find out."

I hesitated. "We can't."

"Why not?"

"Whoever it was, he was following us. Or maybe we just crossed his path and scared him. But either way, he knows we're here now. We need to be the ones sneaking up to do this right. Plus . . ."

"What?"

I hated to be the one to say it. "It's suppertime. We have to get home."

"Goddamn it." Tom sighed in frustration, and ran his fingers through his hair, reluctant to give up the hunt so easily. "You're right," he said finally. "Okay. Let's get home, eat supper. We'll go find 'em tonight."

Seven

I verified both chambers of my gun were empty, put it on safe, and carefully laid it on the gun rack in my room below my encyclopedias. My father had been known to spot-check the gun to make sure that it was both clean and safe, especially when he could smell the tang of a recently fired weapon wafting from my room. Before heading back downstairs, I pulled down the red "F" volume of my encyclopedia and scanned the article about fish. Carp, I learned, can live up to forty years. That lonely hog in Silver Creek may be down there still. I ran downstairs.

"Can I eat supper at Tom's?" I asked my mom.

She looked me over. "Put a decent shirt on," she ordered.

I paraded by my mom in three shirts of gradually increasing quality until she finally granted her approval.

"Have a good time," she said. "Don't be a pig." Tom was waiting outside. By the time we got to his house, my stomach was growling from hunger.

Tom lived in a big log cabin at the very end of the graded portion of Cabin Hill Road. The road turned into an old logging road at that point, really just two ruts through the forest, before reconnecting with the Buffalo

Trace about two miles into the woods. While our house sat in the middle of about five cleared, neatly mown acres, Tom's log house was in the middle of the trees, looking almost as if it had sprung from the soil itself. The Kruers saw spectacular amounts of wildlife from their front porch, owing to the fact that one time, long ago, their hilltop had been an orchard. Gnarled, feral apple trees, along with abundant wild persimmons, carpeted the forest floor with fruit irresistible to deer, fox, and raccoons. An excitable family of flying squirrels lived in their rafters, and Tom's dad would sometimes pound on the wall with his fist to initiate an aerobatic display. Tom's father had built most of their home with his own hands, and much of the lumber came from trees he had cleared on the property. We stepped up to the porch, passing by what looked like a half-buried bathtub on end, home to a blue-and-white plaster statue of the Virgin Mary. A Wiffle ball was jammed between Mary's head and the edge of the tub.

The house had three tiny bedrooms upstairs: one for Tom's parents, one for the two girls, and one for the four boys, who slept in two sets of bunk beds. The land around the house had been in Tom's family forever. Above their fireplace, Tom's dad had constructed a mantel out of a thick timber he had salvaged from the crumbling remains of his great-grandfather's cabin on the edge of the property. On one of the timbers GW KRUER had been carved deeply into the wood by his namesake a century before.

The second I walked in I could smell dinner—a giant crock of beans and hamhocks that had simmered all day. Tom's mother was pulling a black iron skillet of corn bread from the oven when she saw us.

"Well, look who it is!" she said.

"Andy Jackson!" said Tom's dad, coming into the kitchen to see us. He was a naturally good-looking guy, his hair always neat and in place, and a smile that was the result of good genes and not orthodontia. Like my father, he looked more rested than I was used to seeing him, and at the same time a little manic, as if the surplus energy was starting to fight its way out. I was sure he was thinking about the last time we'd seen each other, the tense conversation with my father after Don Strange's funeral, and was trying to compensate for that unpleasantness. Of course, like me, he had secret memories of the night of Don Strange's death, and I'm sure he was also trying to compensate for that. "You gonna help us eat these beans?" he practically shouted.

"Yessir," I said. "I'm starving."

"Good, good, good!" he said, punching me hard on the shoulder. We found our way to the table, as the rest of the clan rattled downstairs, shouting, fighting, and laughing as they came. A fat, slumbering baby was placed next to Mr. Kruer at the head of the table, and he would occasionally give the bassinet a gentle poke with his toe to rock her as we ate.

I saw no signs of financial strain beyond my glass of peach Kool-Aid, though I diligently searched the kitchen for differences between labor and management. Our houses certainly were dramatically different. Local folklore had it that the farmer who built our house had modeled it on his daughter's dollhouse—it did have more gingerbread trim and a more steeply pitched roof than was typical in the area. I saw no overt pro-union posters or anything like that

in Tom's house—although I remembered his dad did have a faded Local 1096 sticker on the bumper of his truck. Another difference: hunting trophies—deer, bass, and turkey—hung in an arc over the Kruers' fireplace. My mom didn't allow dead animals on the wall and we never used the fireplace. When I asked why once, after a winter evening at Tom's, she said that anyone who had ever depended on game for food and wood for heat found it hard to get pleasure from such things. "It's the same reason I don't put an outhouse in the front yard and plant daisies around it," she told me.

"Have some more." Tom's dad ladled more beans into my bowl. "You're practically family."

"Thank you," I replied, as much for the family comment as for the food.

Tom's mother correctly interpreted my gratitude. "Oh, being a Kruer is no big deal," she said. "Look how many of them there are!"

I laughed, but that was really it, the biggest difference between our two houses: the number of nieces, nephews, and cousins pictured on the walls. Weddings, confirmations, baptisms, and first communions were commemorated on every inch of available wall space, interchangeable German faces and forced smiles looking back at me in their stiff sport coats and wide clip-on ties, usually with a dour Catholic priest close by in the frame. At my house, one whole side of the family was a secret, which by itself kept the number of family photos down. But even on my dad's side, the families tended to be small. Tom was one of six kids. Tom's dad was the youngest of ten, and had slept in a sleeping bag in the middle of their small living room until

his oldest brother got married, moved out, and started cranking out kids of his own. Tom's mother was a Huber, one of the biggest clans around. I remembered my dad saying once that "Grays are custom made; Hubers are mass produced." I concluded that there was some kind of complicated link between unionism, Catholicism, and large, devoted families.

"Are you looking forward to high school?" Mr. Kruer asked me as I worked my way through my third bowl of beans.

I rolled my eyes, making him laugh.

"But you do so good in school!" said Mrs. Kruer. "Aren't you proud of yourself? I always see you on the honor roll in the *Banner-Gazette*."

"I guess so," I said. In fact, schoolwork was something I put absolutely no effort into, and consequently took little pride in. They might as well have asked me if I was proud of last month's lunar eclipse.

"He's humble," said Mr. Kruer. "He's smart in school. Just like his daddy was."

"Thank you," I mumbled, looking down at my bowl. The rest of the kids quickly took up the conversation, rapidly increasing the volume, as if they sensed my embarrassment at the praise and wanted to help me out. The noise built steadily until one of the sisters called one of the brothers a "dumb-ass." After an infinitesimal moment of silence came a tidal wave of yelled accusations and counteraccusations. At that point, all of the siblings except Tom and the sleeping baby accepted Mrs. Kruer's invitation to leave the table. They clamored upstairs where the argument continued.

"Good riddance," said George Kruer as the kitchen went suddenly quiet. "Now, Andy, weren't you telling us how smart you are?"

"Leave the boy alone," said Mrs. Kruer as he and Tom laughed.

"All right, all right," said Mr. Kruer. He held up an empty coffee cup. "Momma, is there any . . ."

He stopped in mid-request.

We followed his eyes to the front window. A rattling truck with two unaligned headlights passed the house. The truck slowed at the foot of the Kruers' driveway, and then the struggling engine gunned and then it continued on to where the road ended, just out of our sight. Since Tom's house was the last on the dead-end road, it was something we paid some attention to, but it was not quite unusual enough to be alarming, especially in the summertime. Sometimes hunters parked back there. More often it was kids looking for an isolated place to make out, drink beer, or smoke a joint. I knew if enough time passed without seeing that truck heading the other direction, Tom's dad would walk back there to investigate with a .38 tucked in his belt.

The silence at the dinner table was broken when Tom's dad stood up, backed two steps away from the table, and farted explosively.

"Good Lord, George," said Tom's mom, her mouth open in horror. Tom was laughing so hard he had to put his forehead down on the table.

"I thought it was okay as long as I wasn't at the table," said Mr. Kruer, his arms stretched out apologetically. "Isn't that the rule?" He tapped the pack of Swisher Sweets in his shirt pocket and pointed at the back door.

"Yes, please," said his wife. "Go outside and be disgusting."

"You're the one who made beans," he said. He quickly exited out the back door, a huge Cheshire cat grin on his face.

"Andy," said Mrs. Kruer, "do me a favor and don't tell your momma and daddy what it's really like over here."

I couldn't think of a polite response, so I finished what remained of my beans, wiping the bowl clean with a chunk of corn bread. At that point, I decided I'd better honor my mother's request that I not make a pig of myself. I started to move toward Mrs. Kruer at the sink with my bowl in hand.

"Thank you for dinner, Mrs. Kruer."

"Sit yourself down," she said, rejecting my attempt to help clean up. "I've got six kids to help me clean up this mess." It did not appear to me that any of them intended to help her. It sounded more like they were upstairs destroying the cabin's entire second story.

"Well, I better get going, then," I said.

She wiped her hands on the dish towel and pulled me into a close hug. She smelled pleasantly of smoked ham.

"Thanks again," I said.

"Tom, walk him home," she ordered. Tom started to get up.

"No, that's okay," I said. "Really." I was actually looking forward to a few minutes of silence, a little solitude. A couple of hours in Tom's frenetic house sometimes did that to me. At the door, Tom and I gave each other a quick look to confirm that we'd see each other later that night.

I walked alone up the Kruers' long, dark, gravel drive-

way to Cabin Hill Road, a good quarter-mile hike in itself. I turned right, toward my house. I could have walked in a quicker, straighter route over a well-traveled path in the woods, but I didn't feel like stumbling onto the source of that earlier mysterious noise Tom and I had heard, whether it was Solinski, the fugitives, Taffy's dad, or some other supernatural horror. At least not without Tom or my M6 at hand. The gravel road looked blue in the moonlight. I kicked the bigger rocks with the tip of my shoe as I walked, seeing how far and how straight I could send them down the road.

I heard the truck coming back the other way before I saw it. The roar made it sound a lot faster than it was; in fact, it was crawling toward me in a slow-moving cloud of yellow light and acrid smoke. I could have turned and hustled back to the Kruers, but, not for the last time, fear of looking like a pussy kept me standing in harm's way.

The rider was leaning out the passenger-side window to speak to me as the truck pulled alongside. He was wearing a flannel shirt with the sleeves ripped off. A sloppy homemade purple tattoo of a skull grinned at me from his shoulder. All I could see of the driver was the red tip of his cigarette glowing in the darkness of the cab's interior. A double gun rack in the rear window held a twenty-gauge shotgun above a large carpenter's level.

"How you doin', boy?" the passenger said out the window with exaggerated friendliness. He had hazy, drunk eyes and the sour smell of liquor rolled out of the cab.

"Just fine," I said. The truck sputtered like it was about to die, but then coughed itself back to life. It backfired. I jumped, making the man giggle.

"Hey, ain't you Mr. Gus Gray's boy?" he asked when the truck quieted back down. A drunken smile exposed gums stained by years of chaw.

"Why?" I asked. Something in the way he emphasized the word "mister" made me hesitate.

"Come on now," he said. "You're Gray's boy, ain't you?"

I was about to tell him that in fact I was, when George Kruer appeared suddenly at my side.

"Can I help you with something?" he said in a loud voice, a cigar clinched in his perfect teeth. He put his arm around my shoulders and pulled me close.

"We're looking for Gus Gray's house," said the passenger again, dropping the fake smile and glowering defensively at us now. "We know he lives up here somewheres. We just want to tell him somethin'."

"All right," said Tom's dad. "I'm Gus Gray. Now what the fuck do you want?"

The driver spoke for the first time. "That ain't Gus Gray," he growled. He then gunned the truck, and without another word they jerked away from us as loud as a rocket, backfiring and throwing gravel behind them each time the engine caught and propelled them down the road.

A few seconds later we heard the truck's roar subside. I can't say I was completely surprised when I heard a shotgun blast, followed by the roar of the truck driving into the distance.

George Kruer and I ran down the road. Our mailbox had been obliterated; the white post stood headless. My dad and mom were already standing there inspecting the damage by the time we ran up. Dad saw me run up.

"Get inside!" he shouted.

"I was at the Kruers . . ."

"Goddamn it, go inside!" Dad had the same look in his eyes he had the night of the tornado—mortal danger swirled in the air and he didn't want my participation; he wanted me locked safely away. I tried to sputter out what had happened as he pulled me by the elbow down the driveway.

Sheriff Kohl drove up. I broke free from Dad, and stepped aside to put the cruiser between us. As he stepped back, Dad seemed to notice for the first time that George Kruer was there, too, looking at the ground sheepishly.

Kohl rolled to a stop and stepped slowly out of his car. He stared at the splintered remains of our mailbox.

"Good Lord." He looked at Dad. "Did you see them?"

"No. We didn't see anything."

"I saw them," I said. All eyes swung to me. "I talked to them."

I told my story: the conversation with the men and how George Kruer heroically ran them off. Mom's jaw dropped. Kruer concurred tersely and then walked home.

The sheriff broadcasted my description of the truck on his radio, and just a few minutes later his deputy radioed back to report that he had arrested the men as they pushed their stalled truck across the railroad tracks at the bottom of the hill. We found out later that one of them, the driver, was in fact a dues-paying member of Local 1096, and worked for my dad in the finish room. My dad said he couldn't remember anything he'd ever done to piss the man off. The other was just a troublemaker from out in the county who did just enough construction work to keep himself in Sterling Beer and Levi Garrett tobacco. In addition to being charged with

destroying our mailbox and drunk driving, the sheriff charged them with the vandalism to our garage door. They denied everything except the drunk driving.

My parents sent me upstairs when the sheriff left. They did their best to keep their voices low.

"My God," my father said downstairs. I heard the fear in his voice, the recognition of the escalation: first the garage door, now a gunshot. At the same time, now that the immediate crisis had passed, I knew he would try to explain in that engineer's calm way why the world was still a rational place. Once at King's Island in Cincinnati, Dad and I rode the tallest wooden roller coaster in the world, both of us crammed into the same small car. The entire time, while I laughed and screamed, he talked of vector addition and potential energy, newtons and ergs. The funny thing was, he enjoyed the ride every bit as much as I did. It was just the way he saw the world, and his role in our family: to analyze, to study, to strip situations of their drama. It was Mom's role to resist.

"They painted a threat on our garage door! Two crazy men were threatening Andy!"

"I know . . . I know."

"With a couple of loaded guns in their truck and a fifth of whiskey in their bellies!"

Dad paused. "Sure enough, you mix enough whiskey and gunpowder together with those rednecks and a lot of bad things can happen."

"Thank God for Sheriff Kohl. He caught them in two minutes."

At my mom's mention of the sheriff, something shifted

in Dad's voice. "Well, if he'd been doing his job right, maybe he would've stopped them before they even got up here."

"What do you mean by that?"

"If you let these people set cars on fire in the middle of a state highway, I guess we shouldn't act surprised when they think they can drive up and down Cabin Hill Road looking for trouble and get away with it."

"*These people?*"

"Yes, *these people.* People who blow things up. The people who killed Don Strange. The people who are up here shooting our mailbox while Sheriff Kohl is calling bingo down at the Mason's Lodge, or whatever the hell he was doing."

"I'm grateful Sheriff Kohl is in this town, or I do believe everything would be worse. I am sure of it."

"Cricket, I am proud of you for helping him out, especially these last few weeks, I truly am." I wondered what he meant by that. I was certain it had something to do with the midnight phone calls.

"But?"

"But I swear sometimes I get tired of living in Sheriff Kohl's campaign headquarters. The fact is, if there was law and order in this town the way there ought to be, Sheriff Kohl wouldn't have to ride up here and save the day."

"I think it was George Kruer who saved the day," she responded. "If he hadn't come up when he did . . ."

"What?" my father barked. He was angry that others had rescued me, a job that belonged to him: George Kruer pretending to be my father. "Are you saying Kruer saved Andy's life?" He made it sound like the most ridiculous idea in the world.

"I'm saying it's a possibility. There are a lot of angry, desperate people out there right now."

"And is that my fault? What would you have me do about it?" His language always took a turn for the formal when he got defensive, a habit that infuriated my mother.

"First, you can stop the stupid jealousy."

My father threw his hands in the air in frustration and walked away just as I came down the stairs.

For the next few minutes the tension was stifling. My parents weren't exactly fighting any longer, but they were battling. In the kitchen, Mom slammed drawers and cabinet doors as she furiously neatened. Dad turned the volume of the television up louder than the level they had agreed upon after years of complicated marital negotiations.

I sat next to Dad and watched President Carter on the eleven o'clock news. To my shock, the president was actually in southern Indiana—he was making a surprise visit to the river town of English, in Crawford County, which had been stricken by floods. I couldn't believe the president would stop by English, which flooded each and every year, and not come up to Borden where a real crisis brewed.

"Look at that," I said, wanting Dad's opinion on why the president had chosen their tragedy over ours. "English."

"Godforsaken place," my dad grunted.

"Why do you think . . ." I started to ask. I gave up, though, as Mom roared into the family room behind the vacuum cleaner, and not even Dad's extra volume could compete. He pretended to watch the news unaffected, but I went up to my room.

I read about the labor movement in my red *Britannica*. There was information about CIO organizer John L.

Lewis, a name I vaguely remembered my mother referring to reverently. There was a definition of picketing that didn't sound the least bit familiar: *workers march up and down in front of the company building carrying signs telling the public that the employer is "unfair" to them.* All told, the article was about as exciting and as useful to me as the information on Labrador, Canada, that followed it, and explained little of the drama in my town or in my home. I fell asleep trying to discern the difference between a business agent and an organizer.

Tom tapped on my window. I'd been sleeping lightly, knowing he was coming. I stood up and listened for a moment, verifying that no one else was awake. I slipped out quietly and followed him down the porch.

"I think your dad saved my ass," I whispered as we crossed the yard.

"I knew something happened, he was gone so long, then he comes home and mumbles to my mom for an hour in the kitchen. What happened?"

"Two rednecks shot up our mailbox," I said. "But they were talking to me before that, when your dad came up and ran them off."

"Shit! What do you think would have happened if he hadn't showed up?"

I thought it over. "I don't know. I don't know if they would've shot me."

"They wouldn't have shot you," said Tom. He thought I was bragging to say so.

"They were pretty drunk. Maybe they would have beat

me up, if they would have found out who I was before your dad got there."

"How would they find out who you were?" said Tom.

I wasn't about to confess that I was going to tell them myself, a tactical mistake I could not imagine him ever making. "I don't know," I said. We crossed the threshold from mowed grass into primeval forest. The sounds of domesticated animals, lowing cows and lonely hounds, faded as we entered a world of wild noises: crickets, cicadas, and swarms of the undiscovered and unidentifiable.

We soon approached the bend where we'd heard the branch snap. We stopped talking and began watching our steps, avoiding any noise that would give us away. I heard Silver Creek gurgling in the distance when Tom turned off the path.

I knew suddenly where he was leading us. Tom had mentally drawn a line through the noises we'd heard in the woods as they raced away from us, and that line led down the hill to an odd rock formation we had always called "the fort." We stopped talking as we got close, walking slowly and flat-footed to remain quiet. I started paying close attention to my breath, and to every twig in the path, achieving a kind of silence I only could at night. Tom, just in front of me, did the same, absolutely noiseless as we approached the fort. I saw it in front of me. Actually I saw it by not seeing it, a darkness near the ground where it obscured the silhouette of the trees beyond. We'd been to the fort a thousand times, but as the hair stood up on my neck, I realized that I had always before avoided it in the dark.

The fort was a large circle of huge rectangular stones

standing on end that had been a centerpiece of our childhood war gaming. The whole formation was about fifty yards in diameter. The interior of the fort was sunken, lower than the surrounding ground. From the outside, the dark, mossy rock walls of the fort were only a couple of feet high. From the inside, they were as high as ten feet. This made the fort a place of supreme natural cover. From the outside, you could barely see it. From inside, you had the perfect hiding spot, a place where you could stand completely upright and not be seen outside the circle. Years ago, Tom and I had discovered that we could stand at opposite ends of the circle whispering, and the sound would be amplified as if we were standing right next to each other. It was a weird place, a place that compelled you to think about things like human sacrifice and primitive religion. Once Tom and I snuck up on four sweaty day hikers from Louisville in the fort, as they stood in the middle of the circle and contemplated their "discovery." When Tom and I jumped down from the wall, they all yelped and nearly jumped right out of their pricey-looking backpacks. And that was in broad daylight.

Because of the low ground inside, one theory held that the fort was a remnant of a cave that had collapsed in on itself. The more popular explanation, and the one that Tom and I always chose to believe, was that the fort had been constructed centuries before Christopher Columbus by a Welsh prince named Madoc.

Most versions of the legend went something like this: a thousand years ago or so, Madoc, the illegitimate son of a Welsh king, left Wales and discovered the New World with a group of colonists. Putting ashore around what would be

called Mobile Bay, Alabama, Madoc and his crew made their way inland, leaving a string of crude fortifications along the way. They stopped to make their permanent home near the Ohio River. By the time the next batch of Europeans arrived, three or four centuries later, the Welshmen had been completely assimilated by the Indians and the land, although the European explorers were surprised to discover Indians who fished from basketlike boats reminiscent of old Wales. In 1803, Meriwether Lewis and William Clark began their famous expedition in southern Indiana, where Silver Creek meets the Ohio, in my county, a county named for William Clark's brother. Two years into their journey, Lewis and Clark were stunned to discover on the plains a dying tribe of fair-haired Indians who spoke a language that sounded eerily like Welsh.

Like so many things hidden in our woods, scholars dismissed the legend of Madoc, always explaining away the evidence as it would occasionally come to light. During the construction of the Big Four Bridge across the Ohio River in 1888, a leather bag of ancient Roman coins was discovered buried in the murk. In 1968, a helmet with Welsh inscriptions was discovered during the development of a shopping mall in Clarksville. The coins, said the professors, must have been lost by a collector. The helmet was fake. And our fort, as creepy and geometric as Stonehenge, was a sinkhole.

Tom scampered off the path onto the gentle slope that led to the wall of the fort, hunched over to stay low. I followed him. Tom got to the wall slightly before I did, and what he saw surprised him so much it stood him up straight.

"Oh, shit." he said. I reached his side and looked down. Inside the bowl of the fort was a neat camp: a Coleman two-man dome tent, two nylon jungle hammocks slung between some slight trees, and a campfire that we hadn't seen until we were on the wall.

"Shit."

Someone grabbed my elbow. An instant later, someone lunged at Tom noisily and did the same to him, as he tried to jerk away.

"Hello, boys," said the one grabbing Tom. Without even looking, I knew with absolute certainty that the one grabbing my arm was Guthrie Kruer. Only a local could have snuck up on me like that.

As they pushed us down into the fort, I took stock of the guns spread throughout their camp. There was a .22 Winchester rifle with a nice scope leaning on a tree. Next to that was an expensive twelve-gauge shotgun designed for turkey hunting, every inch of it camouflaged with green splotches in an attempt to gain an advantage over the tricky birds. On a tree stump next to the tent lay a shiny stainless-steel .38 Colt revolver. I was terrified, but not by the guns themselves. It would have been far stranger for Tom and I to come upon adults wandering around in the woods without guns. What alarmed me more was what the men had planned for dinner. A sizable box turtle had been placed on its back near the fire so it couldn't get away, its leathery legs moving helplessly in the air. Next to it was a scrawny but neatly cleaned rabbit crucified on a spit made of twigs. It was a puny thing, something no normal person would have bothered to shoot, much less eat. That wasn't the scary part. As every Borden boy knew, until the first

week of November, rabbits were out of season. Sanders and Kruer were killers and fugitives, I already knew, but that scrawny, contraband rabbit was to me an ultimate sign of lawlessness and desperation.

Kruer positioned me with surprising gentleness next to the campfire, then walked over to the tree stump, pushed the Colt revolver aside, and wearily sat down. Sanders, who had Tom, shoved him beside me, and placed his hands on his hips in an attempt to look authoritative.

"What are you boys doin' out here?" he said loudly. "Shootin' and carryin' on?" Tom and I didn't have our guns with us. It confirmed that he must have been the one watching us earlier that afternoon, the source of the mysterious noise.

"Nothin'," I said, with as much bravado as I could muster. Tom didn't say anything. My mind was running a thousand miles an hour, as I calculated the best escape route from the camp, the best way over the wall of the fort, the best way to run from this mess. There was one rock I knew, behind us, that had some indentations that might serve as toeholds in a pinch. I wondered how fast I could fly up and over it with a running start. If I made the slightest move, no matter how crazy, I knew Tom would follow me. My muscles tense, I stood on the balls of my feet, ready to do the same for him.

"Well, as you young men know," he continued, "this here is Borden Casket Company property, and you boys are *trespassing*!" He jabbed his finger at the smudged BCC company logo on his dirty jacket, which I hadn't noticed up to that point. "We're guards for the company."

I didn't look at Tom, but if I hadn't been so scared I

would have laughed. I wanted to tell Sanders that I'd seen the actual guards hired by the company, and that they had a more stringent dress code. He continued.

"We're security guards, and I might just have the police come out here and take you boys to jail."

"Go ahead," I said. "I'll tell them you're poaching rabbit."

As Sanders stepped closer, Tom punched my side in warning, which surprised me—he was usually the first to challenge anyone in authority, as he had earlier in the day with Solinski. This seemed to be one of those rare times when he sensed real danger. Sanders got in my face, and everything about him, including his breath, smelled like campfire smoke. It was as if he were about to burst into flames himself.

"Don't sass me, you little shit," he said, poking me in the chest. My instincts told me that I was about to get the shit kicked out of me. I leaned back slightly, ready to bolt. Just in time, Kruer came off his tree stump and calmly pulled his partner back. He shook his head as he regained his composure, and returned to the script he had apparently prepared for our little meeting.

"Well, you seem like good boys," he said, incongruously just seconds after calling me a little shit. Sanders seemed to think we actually bought into the charade, that there might be two guards out there camping in the woods. There was something tangibly off about him. I would recognize it later in life as a characteristic of real craziness, the inability to keep track of even the reality inside your own head. He cleared his throat and spit a gob far into the darkness. Kruer looked on, completely miserable at the

spectacle. "I'll tell you what I can do. Just leave, don't come back here, and don't tell anyone about our little talk. If you do that, then I won't have to get the police involved. Okay?" He gave us a lupine smile.

"Sure," I said, the relief obvious in my voice. I wanted nothing more than to get away. Tom and I started to back slowly away from the fire.

"Hey," said Kruer quietly. "Are those twenty-twos? Can you spare some?" He had heard the shells jingling together in Tom's pocket. Surprising me, Tom reached in his pocket, pulled out the small handful of shells, and walked over so he could drop them in his hand. He gave Tom a weak smile in return, and closed his fingers around the gift.

Tom and I continued walking out of the fort with fake assuredness. We climbed up the rock I had been thinking of; my toes did fit neatly into the crevices I had remembered. We could have scooted up it in a hurry had that been necessary. As soon as we climbed to the top of the wall, Tom turned and shouted back at the men.

"You don't want to eat that turtle," Tom yelled.

"Why not?" yelled Sanders with a smirk. "Haven't you ever heard of turtle soup?"

"Those box turtles eat poison mushrooms," said Tom. "The poison builds up in the meat. It don't hurt them, but it'll kill you."

"What?" His smirk faded.

"It's true," said Kruer, who had returned to his seat on the tree stump.

"Well, why didn't you tell me before? I was about to eat the motherfucker!" In his anger, Sanders actually lunged for the .38, snatching it off the stump. We all were startled.

It was not the action of someone who had grown up around guns, someone who was familiar with the damage they could cause and the very narrow set of problems they were designed to solve. I think it was the disbelief in all our stares, including Kruer's, which caused Sanders to drop the gun to his side, although in his jitteriness he scared me still, as he unconsciously tapped the cocked gun against his thigh and muttered nonsensically into the darkness.

Kruer ignored him and gently put the turtle on its feet. It marched calmly into the darkness.

Tom and I also made our escape.

Exhilaration flooded my system, as it always did in the aftermath of one of our close scrapes.

"Can you believe that?" Tom said as we ran. "Can you believe we really found them?"

"So what do we do now?" I asked.

Tom pretended not to hear me, refusing to allow me to interfere with his jubilation.

Eight

The next morning, I rode my bike down Cabin Hill to the picket line. Tom eagerly waved me over as I approached. Two of the strikers were causing a ruckus by heatedly arguing over the communal radio, a dusty thing liberated from someone's workstation in the factory. It now sat between them, on an overturned steel drum on the shoulder of Highway 60. When the strike began, the spirit of solidarity was so strong on the picket line that no one could have imagined a fistfight between two strikers. Now it appeared that fully half the crowd was cheering for one.

On one side of the radio was Johnny Steinert, a popular, recent graduate of the high school. He'd been a four-year starter on the basketball team, where his height made up for skinny limbs that seemed to be almost devoid of muscle. Upon graduation, Johnny had taken over a spot in the paint room. Johnny's mom, we all knew, had died of cancer when he was a baby, and no one ever mentioned Johnny without saying what a good job Johnny's dad had done in raising him, and what a good boy Johnny had turned out to be. He wore a CAT hat and a faded IU T-shirt commemorating Coach Knight's perfect season three years before. His curly blond hair stuck out wildly

from around the cap, making him look like a slightly roughed-up Roger Daltrey. Johnny was holding his hands over the radio, theatrically refusing to allow anyone to change the station. "My Sharona" by the Knack was the song causing all the trouble.

Johnny's adversary was Russ Knable, who glared at Johnny with hands on hips and close, dark eyes set deep in a fleshy face. Russ's blue work shirt stretched over the kind of beer belly that, while big, looked as hard as sculpted marble. He and Orpod Judd competed for the title of meanest drunk in Borden. Russ did, however, seem to represent the majority as he demanded that the radio be returned to the bland voice of Milton Metz prattling endlessly on WHAS 840 AM about the heat and the upcoming state fair. I suppose if these men had wanted to listen to music, they would have preferred something from Nashville. To be honest, though, they were sober people who even in good times rarely allowed themselves something as frivolous as music, even if it was sung by somebody respectable, like Porter Wagoner or George Jones. They listened to music at church. The rest of the week they preferred weather and news.

"Hey," I said, riding up next to Tom as the volume of the argument began to overtake the music.

"Hey," he said back. We were right at the edge of the strikers, and I could tell Tom was evaluating how much he could say without pulling back away from the crowd. He was almost jittery he wanted to talk about it so badly. "Let's go back there right now," he finally said to me with a raised eyebrow.

"Shit no," I replied. I didn't even want to think about it.

I'd been up all night trying to decide whether to tell my parents about the encounter, but it seemed like too much to reveal all at once: *Tom and I sneak out of the house periodically in the middle of the night. We witnessed the plant explosion. We've located the men who killed Don Strange.* Try as I might, I just couldn't figure out how I would begin the conversation. I knew it would be difficult to just forget everything I knew about Mack Sanders and Guthrie Kruer, maybe the most difficult thing I had ever done. But I had decided to give it a shot.

"Why not? Come on!" said Tom.

I shook my head again. I can't say I was surprised that Tom wanted to go back to the fort, but his urgency hit me like a punch in the stomach. I felt like I wasn't living up to the responsibility of being Tom Kruer's best friend. As bad as that felt, it wasn't going to get me back to the fort. From the crucified rabbit to the smoky breath of Mack Sanders, there was absolutely nothing there I wanted to experience again.

"We don't even have to talk to them," said Tom. "Let's just go spy on them, check 'em out, see what they're doing."

"I ain't going back," I said quietly.

"Come on!"

"No way."

Out of the corner of my eye, as I tried to think of a way to make Tom drop the subject, I saw thugs moving in formation inside the fence. The entire force was coming out of the plant in kind of a trot, jogging deliberately toward the main gate. There was a rustle of lawn chairs as the picketers turned their attention from the fight over the

radio to their approach. For the moment, rock 'n' roll won the day, as the Knack continued belting out their hit from tinny speakers. The thugs assembled in two rows, one on each side of the driveway just inside the gate.

"We can go tonight," whispered Tom. "After dark. How about it?"

I had no intention of actually saying a word about Sanders and Kruer to anybody, but I felt an almost physical need to make Tom shut up about them. "Maybe we should tell someone where they are," I said. "Maybe I should tell my dad. Or the sheriff."

Tom's face fell in an expression of complete betrayal. I wasn't sure if it was because Guthrie Kruer shared his last name, or because they all shared a union, or because Sanders and Kruer were the most remarkable discovery yet that we'd made in the woods: telling anyone about them would be like standing up in front of our class and talking about the secret passage we'd crawled through to Squire Boone Caverns. Tom wanted to explore our new discovery in secret, map its every corner. I wanted to forget about it and never go back.

"I won't tell anyone," I recanted quickly. "I promise. But I'm not going back." Tom was shaking his head, still speechless from my threat to snitch.

We heard shouted orders inside the fence in Solinski's commanding, raspy voice. The thugs came to attention. Solinski then strode between the two columns to the gate and opened it, reminding me again that he arrogantly kept the thing unlocked. Solinski didn't look at the strikers as he walked up. They had to pay attention to him, he seemed to be saying, not the other way around. Most of

the strikers were now on their feet to get a better look at whatever was going down. The state troopers in their cruiser, I noticed, on the other side of Highway 60, were also craning their necks for a better view. Whatever Solinksi was up to, they weren't in on it.

"Clear the driveway!" Solinski suddenly shouted in our direction, startling us all. The strikers had gotten into the habit of drifting from the shoulder of Highway 60—public property—and onto the driveway—BCC private property—during the day, after the daily delivery of scabs in their armored Shively Security bus. The strikers always grudgingly moved back again to the shoulder before the end of the shift so that the bus could leave amid a course of halfhearted jeers. It seemed Solinski was expecting midday visitors.

At first, some of the strikers actually stepped obediently aside in response to Solinski's command. They were a group of men raised to respect authority and follow orders. Then they remembered who was giving the order, and quickly got back into character.

"Screw that," mumbled Russ Knable. His adrenaline was already jacked up from the battle with Johnny, and he happily took the lead in the confrontation with Solinski. He strolled with exaggerated ease to the center of the driveway, and crossed his short, muscular arms against his chest. A couple of his friends moved reluctantly behind him in support.

"Step aside," said Solinski. "You're on company property."

Russ looked around at his comrades with an eyebrow raised before turning back to face Solinski. "Fuck you,

Sarge," he said. A ripple of nervous laughter went through the picketers.

"Move or I'll move you."

"Goddamn that would make me happy," said Russ, and you could tell he meant it. He spread his feet slightly and clenched his fists.

Solinski stood patiently for a few seconds. He seemed to be waiting for Knable to make the first move, certain that he would. Sure enough, Russ suddenly stepped forward, fists up, eyes wide, more alert than I'd ever seen him, every inch the savvy bar fighter as he took small steps to move in close, surprisingly deft for his size. Knable feinted to his left, and Solinski responded, turning just a tiny bit. Russ ducked his head and went inside, as he had to because of Solinski's much larger reach, and punched Solinski hard in the ribs. Knable turned his whole body as he struck, efficiently putting his considerable weight behind the punch. Solinski grunted in pain.

But Solinski turned, too, anticipating the punch, stepping back with it, neutralizing some of its power, although I thought it would have leveled most men. Even as he moved backward Solinski was pulling a short black billy club from a loop on his belt. When Knable stepped forward to deliver the next punch, Solinski raised the club in the air, and smashed it down across his face.

Even after the bloodshed and death that would end that summer, it remained the single most violent act I ever witnessed. It sounded like a wooden bat being dropped on a concrete driveway. In movies, people are always hit directly on the top of the head, a blow that delivers them into unconsciousness as neatly as a dose of anesthetic. This was

much less hygienic. Solinski's club crossed Knable's face diagonally. He immediately buckled in pain, dark blood and snot pouring from his mouth and nose in a thick stream onto the asphalt, like hot oil from an engine after the plug has been pulled. A large tooth poked up from the center of the expanding puddle of fluids. His right eye immediately swelled shut and turned purple. He kept his feet for a second before his knees quivered and he crumpled to the ground, his two hands cupped in front of his face as if he thought he could retain anything he caught. The two state troopers were now frantically running across the highway, their own clubs drawn, dodging the cars that were slowing down to take a look. Through the waves of heat that were rolling off the asphalt, it looked like they were swimming toward us.

Club still in hand, Solinski eyed the two strikers who had joined Knable in the driveway. They immediately abandoned the fight to pull their badly hurt friend onto the shoulder. The state troopers arrived, and the stunned silence of the crowd changed instantly to vocal outrage.

"Did you see that?" they shouted, pointing frantically at Solinski. "Did you see that?" Johnny Steinert, one of the few calm people in the crowd, was on the shoulder, holding Knable's head with one hand and a wadded up T-shirt over his nose with the other. Dark blood was still pouring from his face into the grass. I fought a strange urge to explain to Solinski what he'd done, what a horrible mistake he'd made.

Solinski was inching backward toward the gate, facing the crowd warily, while the state troopers tried unsuccessfully to calm everybody down. Behind Solinski, the

two rows of thugs stood stone-faced. Someone heaved a glass Coke bottle at Solinski; he jabbed it out of the air with his club, smashing it to the ground. I saw two men sprinting to the pay phone at Miller's, whether to call in reinforcements or an ambulance I didn't know. Because of the military discipline on their side of the fence, and the accelerating chaos on ours, the cops found themselves naturally aligned against the strikers. The two overmatched troopers tried to back the crowd away from the driveway, along roughly the same boundaries that Solinski had tried to enforce. As they pushed back on the surging crowd, one of the troopers talked into a radio, and I saw in his eyes real fear that the situation was cartwheeling out of control. I felt the same fear. I began eyeing routes through and around the crowd, should an escape become necessary. The noise from the crowd rose to a menacing high buzz, but Solinski stood his ground. A full pint of Early Times zipped by his head. He deftly turned to dodge it. It crashed behind him at the feet of the other thugs, and the smell of cheap whiskey floated through the air.

Suddenly, a car turned into the driveway. It was a shiny brown Buick, with two somber old men in the front seat, their eyes looking straight ahead. One of the whitewalled front tires crunched over Knable's tooth and the puddle of his blood. The car drove slowly through the two rows of Solinski's thugs, and he closed the gate behind them. He marched his troops back into the factory without another look in our direction.

"Who is that?" I said to no one in particular.

"The owners, I believe," one of the strikers said bitterly. "Looked like Dubois County plates. They used to

come here about once a year, stand up on a workbench, tell us what a great job we're doing." Russ Knable recovered enough to begin blubbering in pain through his smashed, swollen lips.

The Buick, now safely inside the guarded, gated confines of plant property, cruised slowly across the deserted parking lot, the bloody front tire leaving a dark, glossy tread mark with each rotation. Standing in the middle of the lot to greet the visitors, holding a clipboard and wearing a short-sleeved dress shirt, was my father.

Without saying a word to Tom or anyone else, I turned and rode my bike as fast as I could, terrified that someone on the picket line might discover who I really was, outside the gates, beyond Solinski's protection.

Tom caught up with me about a mile down the path. I hadn't known where I was going, but Tom somehow had.

"I didn't even see you leave," he said.

I shrugged.

"That was a bad scene down there."

"Yeah."

"You want to . . ."

I glared at him, just waiting for him to ask if I wanted to go back to the fort.

"Not that," he said. "You want to go see the sword? I hid it in the cave."

Maybe because of my thoughts about Taffy, I had actually started to think of the cave as a kind of refuge. And no matter what was going on in my head, a centuries-old German sword was still pretty cool. I didn't say anything to Tom one way or another, but as he took the lead and

started riding toward the cave, I followed. We stood up our bikes outside the cave and walked inside.

In the first room, in the middle of the floor, sat Taffy's glowing lantern.

We walked right up to it. My spirits soared as I thought for a second that maybe she was back in town. "Taffy!" I shouted. I was so happy that I didn't even notice the smell of Pall Malls and cheap whiskey until it was too late.

It grew dark again as he moved behind us, between us and the entrance.

"Which one of you is her boyfriend?" slurred Orpod Judd.

Tom and I both jumped backward.

"You're her boyfriends, aren't you? I recognize your bikes, you little shits."

Tom and I backed up against the hole. We were planning, I thought, on grabbing a hidden flashlight and heading down to the chute, where we knew Taffy's dad couldn't follow. I was ready to go. It's funny how fast my perspective had changed. A few days before I had vowed never to go through that crevice again. Now it was my escape route.

"Now, where is she?" he asked. "I'm sure she called her *boyfriend,* I'm sure her *boyfriend* knows where she is. Which one of you is going to tell me where I can find that bitch mother of hers?" His words came out a little breathlessly. "I knew you'd come back."

Suddenly Tom moved backward, and I moved with him. He reached behind us to grab the flashlight behind the stalagmite so we could jump down through the hole and escape. Taffy's dad gave a phlegmy laugh.

"You looking for this?" he said. He pointed the beam of the flashlight to Tom's arm, rooting around in the hiding place behind the stalagmite. We both turned to look at him.

With a kind of animal quickness, as soon as we were facing him, Judd hurled the flashlight at us, end over end. Tom moved his head just in time, as it smashed into the stalagmite and broke into a million pieces. Tom continued to root around frantically behind the stalagmite, reaching as far back as he could.

"Oh, I found that, too," Judd said, smirking. Tom stopped. "Yeah, I found your big sword, pretty cool. Were you planning on using that on me? I wish I would've left it there."

Tom abandoned the stalagmite, and lunged for the lantern. But the cave was too small. Orpod Judd just took one step forward and waited.

"Come on, you little dick," he said. "I'm gonna teach Taffy's boyfriend a lesson."

Instead of diving to grab the lantern, Tom took one long step forward and kicked it as hard as he could. It hit Judd right in the gut, breaking and spilling fuel on his shoes. I don't think it hurt him, he was pretty well anesthetized, but he was definitely surprised, and his brain did have a hard time processing the new information in the dark. Tom backed up and I followed him through the second chamber and down into the blackness of the chute.

It was a more controlled descent this time, because of what Taffy had taught us, even though this time we were in a world of absolute darkness, the kind of total blackness contained only in caves. Taffy's dad yelled at us from above.

"I'm gonna get you, boyfriend! I'll be waiting right here. And when you see Taffy and that mother of hers, tell her I'm gonna get them, too!"

I wasn't worried at all about Taffy's dad coming down there. I was amazed he could fit through a normal doorway, much less the small hole we'd dug for ourselves. But I wondered how long we would have to sit in the darkness.

A small rock fell on my head.

"Ow," I said.

"I got you, didn't I, boyfriend!" Judd cackled and threw a handful of rocks after us.

I thought I saw a vague outline of Tom to my left, but when he spoke, he was actually on my right. "Move over here," he said.

I scooted over, and just as I did a huge rock rolled through, and from the sound, it split in two as it landed and rolled away in pieces. We listened silently as rocks of various sizes tumbled through the chute and onto the floor.

"How long?" I whispered.

"He'll wear out soon enough," said Tom. "He doesn't have any light now, either. And I get the feeling with all the crazy shit in his head, he's not going to want to stay in the dark for long."

Sure enough, the rocks gradually stopped falling down. We kept waiting, and I actually began to hallucinate fully formed shapes in the darkness. I saw the outlines of cars, bedroom furniture, and Halloween pumpkins. When I turned my head, they stayed right there. I heard Tom breathing next to me, and I thought if that stopped, the one real sensory input I had left, I would surely go crazy.

"Let's try it," Tom said finally.

We both stood, and felt along the wall until we found the handholds we had learned just once before. It actually felt good to be pressed up against the solid wall of rock, something so real and unmoving. I continued up, occasionally feeling Tom's shoes brushing against my face.

Once we got our heads into the chute, we could see a little light. The chute was half filled with rocks and dirt, almost as if Orpod Judd had tried to fill it in after us, trapping us forever, and then gave up because it took too much effort. Tom looked around for a good long time before climbing out, making sure Judd wasn't lurking in some corner. He reached behind the stalagmite.

"Goddamn it," he said. "That asshole took my sword."

When I got home, the Buick with Jasper plates was in the driveway. I pictured the owners driving back out through the gate with Dad in the backseat, an image I found somehow humiliating. I vividly imagined them driving slowly and silently through the protective cordon of Solinski's men as the strikers watched them with pure hate in their eyes. I snuck in the back door of our house, just catching a look at the backs of their heads before sneaking up the stairs.

They were Ross and Worth Habig, heirs to the company, part of a large third generation of Habigs who divided up the ownership. My father told me once that he remembered Daddy Habig from way back when, "intimidating but fair," he said, but it had been a generation since anyone with the name Habig had actually worked in the plant, or had done anything to help turn a tree into a

coffin. I learned, as I eavesdropped on the steps, that the brothers had insisted against my father's recommendation on not only seeing the damage at the plant firsthand, but on driving right through the front gate and the picket line.

"I told you there'd be trouble," my dad said. "We should have gone around back."

"And what, Gus? Walk into the plant through a hole in the back wall?" There was silence before Ross Habig continued. "I appreciate your concerns, Gus, believe me I do, but I'll be damned if I'm going to sneak into the factory that my granddaddy built, the factory that I own."

"Well, we should have at least told the police to be prepared."

"I don't trust those yokels," said Ross. My dad sighed in exasperation. The state police were complete strangers from the Seymour post. The Habigs saw anyone from south of Indianapolis as potentially complicit.

"I understand why you didn't want to go around back," said my dad, though I knew he'd been tactfully sneaking inside in just that way every morning. "I just didn't want trouble. Now Knable is all smashed up, the police are involved . . ."

The other Habig spoke up. "Let them investigate. Knable threw the first punch. You can still use force to defend yourself in this state. At least for now you can." I heard in his voice the same kind of prideful indignation that I heard from the strikers. Their voices dropped to a murmur, and from where I sat on the top of the stairs I could not for a time make out their words. Soon enough, though, emotions surged and I could hear them again.

"Come on, Ross," I heard my father say. "This company's been in your family a hundred years."

"You know, I'm not the only owner," said Ross Habig. "*We're* not the only owners. We've got two sisters and another brother, each of whom owns just as much of this company as we do. Between us, we've got fourteen kids—they're all owners, too, even the little ones. At our last stockholders' meeting, it occurred to my siblings that they're getting a three percent return on their stake in this plant. They can beat that by selling out and putting their money somewhere else. Anywhere else."

"They want to sell the plant and what . . ." my father said. "Put their money in the stock market?" He made it sound like they planned on becoming drug dealers.

"They don't feel any loyalty to this place," said the other brother, the quiet one. "They don't even live in Indiana. They just see a tiny profit that keeps getting tinier, every year. Some of them have wanted to cash out for years, but we've been able to fight that off—barely. When my father was alive he used to stand up at every stockholders' meeting, give the revenue numbers, and practically dare anyone to bring up the idea of selling out. None of them ever did." I'd seen portraits of their ancestors in the front office, each with a tiny brass light illuminating a frowning man in an old-fashioned black suit. It didn't surprise me to hear that the children and grandchildren had been afraid to present these men with a plan to liquidate their life's work.

Ross Habig continued. "Since my father died, they've really started pushing for it. This strike, and the money

we're going to lose because of it, is just the excuse they need. There's a meeting in Indy in September. If the strike is still going on, we're going to have a massive loss on the books—our first full-year loss since the Depression. I'm not sure we'll be able to hold them off."

"My daddy used to tell me about how they'd time the strikes to coincide with deer season," my dad said. I could hear the forced smile in his voice, another attempt to put everything in a less threatening perspective, just as he had with my mother the night our mailbox was beheaded. "We've had labor problems before."

"They've never killed one of our plant managers before," said Ross Habig.

That pretty much ended the conversation.

As I lay down in bed that night, I prayed I wouldn't see Tom Kruer at my window. Or Orpod Judd, or the fugitives, the sad, bleeding ghost of Don Strange, or any of the other terrifying specters in my life. I prayed to Jesus Christ that Solinski or Sheriff Kohl would find the fugitives, which would relieve me of any responsibility I had to rat them out. Just to cover all the bases, I even tried to fake my way through a Catholic prayer, to the Blessed Virgin Mary, asking for those same things. I felt guilty about it, guilty for wanting to betray Tom, guilty for not telling my mom and dad what I knew, guilty about Don Strange's unavenged murder. And when the tapping on the window came, I did pretend to be asleep for a little while, until the tapping came again, more urgently, and I finally went to the window.

"Come on," Tom said when I finally slid it open. "We're going to get my sword back."

We approached the single-wide trailer from a backyard, if you could call it that, that had been stripped bare both by a complete lack of care and by the dozen or so dogs who slept, trampled, and shit on the premises. The dogs who weren't sound asleep cowered from us as we approached, as if accustomed to frequent, random beatings. What few touches of hominess there were made it that much more depressing, as they reminded me of how hard it must have been for Taffy to try and live her life there. A small clay flowerpot with a smiley face finger-painted upon it, cracked in two by the back door. A sandbox devoid of sand was at the end of the driveway, filled with stagnant water and floating beer cans. A rope swung from a tree limb, its swing nowhere in sight.

Blue light from a television flickered through the small window by the back door. Tom approached, peaked in, and waved me over.

Through the smeared glass, we saw an unconscious Orpod Judd sprawled across a decaying recliner on which the stains had become indistinguishable from the faded pattern of the upholstery. He was wearing only his underwear, over which his sizable belly rolled. A beer bottle was in his hand, and two were on the floor. *Billy Jack* was wrapping up on the WDRB late movie as he drunkenly dozed.

Close behind him were three nearly empty bookshelves. On the lowest was a collection of commemorative Derby glasses. On the second shelf was a small, cheap-looking

revolver and an ashtray. On the top shelf, reflecting the light of the TV, was Tom's sword.

Tom tugged at the back door. I doubted it was locked, but like everything else at the trailer the door was in such poor repair that it wouldn't operate properly. He tugged harder but gave up for fear he would make a noise and wake up Judd. We ran around the side.

At the very end of these trailers, I knew, was the "master bedroom," which was perhaps a slightly presumptuous term for it. The bedroom did have its own door, and even a window, which Tom found was cracked open against the heat. He pushed it open more, and although it squeaked, it was too far from the living room, the TV was too loud, and Orpod Judd was too drunk to be awoken. Tom pulled himself in, and I followed.

The bedroom stank of cigarettes and body odor. The mattress was bare and the lone, stained pillow had no case. Near the bed, several cigarettes had been rubbed out directly on the worn carpet. I wondered how much of the squalor had occurred during the short time Orpod Judd had lived there alone, and how much was a result of the crazed night he broke Taffy's arm. Tom began slinking out, toward the living room.

The floor of the mobile home, like others I had been in, creaked in a way that reminded me of a boat at sea. The hallway that divided the master bedroom from the rest of the trailer was narrow; Tom and I had to skulk single file into the living room as the song "One Tin Soldier" marked the end of the movie.

I stopped at the entry to the living room as Tom continued in, drawn to the sword like a magnet. There was a

cluster of framed family photos atop the TV. One caught my eye: Taffy in a pink dress, maybe a year younger, smiling brightly at the camera and tilting her head in response to the command of the unseen photographer. I slowly lifted the photo up, careful not to knock any of the others down, as Tom inched his way closer to Orpod's recliner.

Something about being there in the same room with Orpod Judd excited me in a dangerous way; I wanted to hurt him for what he had done to Taffy, and there he was, completely vulnerable. Even so, he was still scary; I don't think it was just the tiny cramped room that made him look big. Tom walked within inches of Judd's giant, dirty big toe sticking through its torn sock. He kept his eyes on Judd the entire time, even as he went behind him to the bookshelf. After verifying that Judd remained unconscious, Tom turned, rose up on his toes, and grabbed the sword by the handle.

At that moment, the theme song and the credits for *Billy Jack* ended, and, after a pause, the television began emitting a loud, steady hum to go along with the colored bars of its test pattern. It was just enough to wake Orpod Judd up.

His eyes fluttered open. Tom was frozen behind him, his hand on the sword, but Judd was facing me. I turned to run, but he was quick, and my feet got tangled for an instant in a dirty T-shirt crumpled on the floor. Even seriously drunk, Judd knew what he was doing—it was not the first time he had chased a quick, agile kid through the trailer. He didn't try to grab me, from which I could have twisted away. Instead, he hit me full-speed with the bulk of his big body, sending me flying into the door of the

master bedroom and onto the floor. When I opened my eyes, he was on top of me. I was vaguely aware that I still held Taffy's picture.

"Hey, look who it is." He panted heavily, his breath sour. "Taffy's boyfriend." His eyes were unfocused. A smile crossed his dimpled face. I was rolling, twisting, trying to get away, but he was stronger than me, and he just kept pushing me back and forth with his bearlike left hand, keeping his other hand raised, waiting for a good shot with a weird kind of patience. "I thought you might try to get in here."

When he finally hit me, it was with the practiced violence of a hunter gutting a deer, or a fisherman cutting the head off of a bluegill: it was something he had done many, many times before. I also noticed that he was slapping me with his meaty hand open, not with a fist. Maybe he'd learned that a slap left fewer marks; maybe he thought he'd be more likely to make solid contact with an open hand than with a fist.

Pain exploded on the right side of my face as he made contact. He hit me so hard my whole body hurt, right down to my toes.

"How'd you like that?" He was breathless, not with the exertion, but with excitement. "You seen Taffy lately? How 'bout that mom of hers?" He slapped me again, harder, on the same side of my face. I was struggling, but the fight was going out of me. I covered my face with my arm and just hoped that he would wear himself out.

I felt a shadow come over us, and when I opened my eyes, I saw that Judd felt it, too, although he didn't want

to turn away from me to see the cause. The sword came down right where his thick neck met his shoulder. Tom did not decapitate Orpod Judd, but he would have had the tip of the sword not caught the low ceiling of the living room, tearing off an asbestos ceiling tile as he swung it down. Even with that loss of velocity Tom hurt Judd badly. Blood shot from his shoulder, some of it falling on my face and into my mouth. Even badly hurt and surprised, Judd still had the animal skills to take a shot at Tom. He rolled off of me and against the wall, and tried to pull Tom's legs out from under him with a sweeping motion of his long caveman arm. Tom jumped over him sword in hand, helped me to my feet, and in seconds we were out the bedroom window and back in the woods.

In the darkness outside, it was impossible to tell how bad I looked. I could feel that my face was swollen, and with my tongue I felt a couple of loose teeth. My face stung, but I knew I would live. My far bigger problem was how I was going to explain the injuries to my mother and father. There was no way I was going to hide something like this. Before Tom and I separated at my house, we talked it over, and decided reluctantly that there was only one plausible way to explain it when that moment arrived.

In my room I stared at Taffy's photo for a good ten minutes before hiding it in my nightstand drawer, a place of honor it retained through many years and many nightstands in dorms and apartments throughout the Midwest. I fought the temptation to turn on my light for a better look. The glass was broken and the photo was creased down the middle, but all told the picture had made it out

of that trailer in better shape than I. I went to sleep profoundly happy for that.

Mom came in to check on me at some point during the night, and saw the bright, bloody faceprint on my pillow. "Son, tell me right now who did this to you," she said, shaking me awake.

"What?" I said through swollen lips, in one futile, final effort to pretend it was no big deal.

"Come take a look at yourself." She hustled me into the bathroom to look in the mirror. Dad shuffled in behind me in his pj's, rubbing his eyes, curious about the commotion.

The visible damage had gotten worse during my few hours in bed. My face was redder, the worst parts were purple, and I had developed a full-blown black eye, with tiny lines of blood inside my eye to go along with it. Everything was swollen. I had to admit, along with my mother, that I looked horrible. My only regret was that school was out and I couldn't show it off to my friends.

"Who did this?" my mother demanded again.

"Good Lord," my father said, as it all came into focus. Mom turned me around. She was so mad I thought she would blacken the other eye.

"Tell me right now."

I waited, hoping I wouldn't have to use the plan Tom and I had devised, but as we had determined, there was no other believable option. And we certainly weren't going to start telling the truth.

"Tom did it," I said. "We got in a fight after we left the picket line and he kicked my ass."

Mom gasped. Dad scratched his head, aware, even

though the story made perfect sense, that there was some other story out there, somewhere.

The next day at lunch, as I painfully sipped iced tea through a straw, Dad told Mom something funny he'd heard at the plant.

"Sheriff Kohl was down at the plant today, told me a heck of a story. Orpod Judd called the police in the middle of the night, said he'd been attacked." Dad was smiling broadly.

"I'm sure he was stinking drunk," said Mom, as I stared down at my BLT.

"You're right about that. He said the bombers broke into his trailer and robbed him."

"The bombers?"

"That's what he said. And he did have some nasty wound to his neck apparently, looked like it needed stitches, but he refused to go to the clinic. Just wanted to talk about the robbery, file a report, asked for the name of the Casket Company's insurance agent. He actually thought that somehow the company's insurance should pay for it. That's why Kohl was telling me about it."

"What on earth could there be in that trailer worth stealing?"

"That's the really funny part," said Dad. "He said they'd stolen an antique sword from him, worth, in Judd's estimation, five thousand dollars. Cut him with it and ran. Of course he had no receipt or anything proving he ever owned such a thing."

"A sword? Mercy." Mom and Dad both laughed. "How does the sheriff think he got the cut to his neck?"

"He's not sure, and it was a nasty wound, apparently. Figures Judd just did something stupid while he was drunk. It wouldn't be the first time."

"Lord knows."

The conversation then thankfully turned to the high price of gasoline, and I was able to breathe again.

I thought it over in my room after hurriedly finishing my sandwich. Judd had probably wanted to get his loss on the record, stupidly reasoning there might be some insurance company somewhere that might compensate him for the loss of something he had never owned. Perhaps Judd blamed the bombers because he didn't want to admit he was waylaid by a couple of kids, and didn't know exactly who we were, making it harder, in his dense mind, to file an insurance claim. On the other hand, I thought, maybe he didn't tell the sheriff because he knew exactly who we were, and wanted to take care of us himself.

I was, of course, banned from seeing Tom. Mom and Dad decided not to call Tom's parents, as Tom and I had anticipated, not wanting to humiliate me further after my ass-kicking nor complicate matters further with our neighbors. While they never asked me directly, they were certain that the fight had something to do with the strike, a manager's kid versus a striker's kid, superimposing their struggle over ours. I passed the day watching game shows and reading the same library books over and over.

The most surprising part of my exile from the woods was how much I enjoyed it. I didn't have Tom pulling me toward the fugitives, the cave, or Orpod Judd. I discovered that I liked being out of danger, safe in my house,

with just Bob Barker and my parents to keep me company. There had been a notion in my mind since we saw George Kruer fighting at the picket line, a notion that I should not be keeping all these secrets, and that things would continue to get worse until I unburdened myself. That thought grew steadily, all day, nurtured by indoor lighting and my mom's home cooking.

That night, after dinner, my father tried to broach the subject of my fight with Tom during our game of Authors. He was not a man who believed in silently mulling over one's problems.

"Everything okay?" he asked.

"Sure," I said. I managed to get the word out pretty well, my lips had deflated back down to only slightly over their normal size.

"Haven't seen this much of you around the house since the blizzard," Dad said, as Mom pretended to contemplate her cards.

I shrugged again. "It's been kind of nice, really. *Huckleberry Finn*?"

"How's Tom been doing?" he asked. "I mean, before . . ."

"Okay," I said. I tried to think of something else to say on the matter. "They're drinking Kool-Aid because of the strike."

There was an awful silence. "It's okay," I backtracked. "They like Kool-Aid."

My dad grimaced and placed his hand on my mom's knee. It was her turn.

"*The Pickwick Papers*?" she asked me, clearing her throat.

"Nope."

"The strike will be over soon," she said. "And everything will get back to normal." It felt good to hear the certainty in her voice.

"Do you think they'll ever catch Sanders and Kruer?" I asked. My observant, caring parents immediately detected the hopefulness in the question, and they nearly guessed right about why I would ask such a crazy thing.

"Is that what's bothering you, boy?" my father asked, relief pouring into his voice.

"I wouldn't mind seeing them caught, I guess."

"They wouldn't hurt you," said Mom.

My father shot her a quick look before turning a sympathetic grin back on me. "Those dumb-asses are probably two hundred miles away from here by now!" My mother reflexively elbowed him in the ribs upon hearing the cuss word, but Dad continued jubilantly. "The sheriff sent dogs into the woods and everything! They're long gone! Don't you worry about them!"

"I guess," I said quietly.

"Your father's right," my mom said. "If they were out there, somebody around here would surely rat them out."

My father walked upstairs with me on my way to bed. With each step, I considered telling him everything: about Kruer and Sanders, about Orpod Judd, about the night Don Strange died. The lies were piling up so high that I could no longer find my way around them. I loved Dad, believed to the core of my being in his reasonable nature. The man had an engineer's passion for order and process, and I had no doubt that in the black-and-white rule book of the world, I was supposed to tell someone that I knew

where two killers were bivouacked in the woods. As I felt him walking close behind me on the steps, at the end of a long, boring, enjoyable day, I had a hard time believing that disclosing everything to him would be so bad.

But it would betray Tom. My own mother, it seemed, would also regard me as a rat. I had heard the expression "get it off your chest" before, and now I really knew what it meant—the secrets weighed on me with a physical force, slowing my steps and making it hard for me to breathe. Maybe being away from Tom a full day had somehow weakened my resistance. I had to tell Dad everything, and even if my best friend and my mother disagreed, I could at least take comfort in Dad's approval.

"'Night, Andy," my dad said, rubbing my back as I lay down.

"'Night." Cicadas chirped outside the window. A muted pulse of heat lightning briefly illuminated my father's serious face.

Dad continued to sit on the edge of my bed, sensing that I needed to talk more.

"Are we against the strikers?" I asked.

He sighed. "That's complicated. You know I'm management, so most of those guys on the picket line see me as the enemy. But I don't wish those men any harm. Fate has put us on opposite sides of this thing. May God let it end soon."

"Why are you management?" I asked. "You went to high school with Tom's dad, right? How did you two end up on different sides?"

My dad shrugged and thought it over. "I guess part of it's because I have a college degree," he said. "There

aren't too many of those around here, so that's why they made me a manager when I came back from Purdue."

"Why do you have a degree?" I asked. I wanted to reduce the differences all the way down, all the way back to something solid and irreducible.

Dad thought about it. "It's hard to say. My parents always wanted me to go to college, although I suppose a lot of parents feel that way. I did well in high school. I guess I probably did okay on some standardized test somewhere along the line, got into college prep classes. Some luck, I guess. Some hard work."

"So," I said, going back to my original question, "we're against the strikers?" I needed clear-cut affirmation from him before I ratted out Kruer and Sanders.

"I want the strike to end, yes. I never wanted a strike to begin with. So yes, I guess I am against the strike." His emphasis of the word "I" once again cheated me of the clear green light I was looking for so desperately.

"Are you talking about Mom?" I asked. "Is she for the strikers?"

My dad laughed. "That, my boy, is a perceptive question."

"She does sometimes seem like she's pulling for them on the line."

There was a long silence before my father spoke again. "Let me tell you a story," my father finally said. "You know your mom's from Kentucky, right?"

I immediately went on full alert, ready to seize whatever details of my mom's life were about to fly my way.

"Well, she grew up in coal country, in Harlan County. But for a long time, her daddy didn't work in the mines—and let

me tell you, they were miserably poor. Did you know she never celebrated Christmas or her birthday until she was a teenager?"

I shook my head. I had no idea.

"That's when her daddy got on at the mine. Everything changed for the better. They got plumbing, Coca-Cola once in a while, a dress or two from an actual store. As far as her daddy was concerned, and he reminded them of this every night, they owed it all to the union. Suddenly they had meat on the table that they didn't have to shoot themselves. And when her momma or daddy would say grace over that meal, they would thank Jesus Christ, John L. Lewis, and the United Mine Workers for everything they were about to receive."

"Wow," I said. I was used to the details of my mom's life dripping in slowly, my knowledge accumulating like a stalactite, a few loose molecules at a time. Now the facts were coming in a torrent, and I was frantically trying to stack them up in my mind, lest I forget something. "So, Mom likes the strikers?"

"She grew up in a time and a place that was ferociously pro-union. She felt, with a lot of justification, that the union lifted her family out of poverty. They even paid for her college, did you know that?"

"No," I said.

"She won a UMW scholarship, that's how she was able to go to Purdue. So it's very hard for her to objectively look at both sides of something like this."

"Is that why she never talks about her family?" I asked. "Are they mad because you're not in the union?"

My dad sighed. "You're close." I could tell he was trying

to decide again whether to tell me something. "What the hell," he sighed. "You need to find this out sooner or later." He paused before continuing.

"Your mother has a brother named Russell." My father didn't even pause for that bombshell. "Russell was determined to get out of the mines, get out of Harlan County, so when he turned eighteen—he's four years older than your mom—he moved up this way, got a good job as a welder at Jeffboat. A union job."

"Okay," I said. Jeffboat was on the Ohio River in Jeffersonville, not all that far from us.

"Anyway, Russell got married, had kids, was raising this nice little family when Jeffboat went on strike. They went on strike all the time down there, and lordy, it is shitty work. But anyway, for some reason—maybe he needed the money, maybe he's stubborn like your mom and didn't like those union boys telling him what to do—Russell crossed the picket line."

"What's that mean?" I asked.

"He went to work during the strike. Walked right by the picket line, went inside, clocked in, and started welding."

"So he was a scab?"

My dad grimaced at my use of the word. "I'm sure they called him that—and a lot worse, too. Anyway, your grandpa, your mother's father, the proud United Mine Worker, found out about it, and he never spoke to his son again. He couldn't forgive Russell for crossing that picket line. That man had grandkids he never saw."

"So Mom was mad at her dad?" I asked.

"She was mad at them both. She was mad at her dad for swearing off Russell. But she was mad at Russell, too,

for crossing the picket line and starting all the trouble. Her mom had a stroke and died while this was going on, and your mom believes all the stress and the heartache had a lot to do with it."

"So they never spoke again?" I asked.

"Your grandpa and Russell never spoke again. Your mom tried with them both, here and again. She talked to her dad on the phone sometimes, went to see Russell's babies once. It was just too hard for everybody, too much damage had been done. So I think this strike has just dragged a lot of that stuff to the surface, stuff she tries hard not to think about most times. It's been real tough on her."

"Okay," I said. I knew how hard it was to try and forget things you didn't want to think about—I had definitely not mastered the art myself, and wondered if my mom was any better at it after a lifetime of practice. The story my father had just told me was careening through my mind. I pictured a band of unknown cousins cavorting around Jeffersonville. It was so much more information than I had ever known about my mother, an entire set of her secrets revealed. There were others, of course. I considered asking Dad about the sheriff's midnight phone calls.

"You can see from your mother that something like this strike can really tear people apart," he continued.

"Yeah," I said. "It can." I thought about Taffy, and her disappearance from Borden.

"So whatever is going on," he continued, "I hope you and Tom stay friends."

"We will!" I said. I hadn't even considered the alternative. I knew my father was basing the statement on the

fight he thought we had, but just hearing the words scared me. I considered our friendship to be so permanent, part of the bedrock of my world, I hadn't even considered myself capable of endangering it.

"Okay, okay," my father said, surprised at the strength of my reaction. "It's just . . . you had this fight . . ." He gestured toward my wounded face.

"It's just a fight," I said. "We're not even mad anymore."

Dad sighed. "I know, but your mom lost family because of a strike, right?"

"Right."

"And I've lost a friend because of this strike, right?" His voice cracked slightly. The scent of Old Spice and pipe tobacco seemed to waft through the air.

"Right," I said quietly.

"So I don't want you to lose a friend, too, okay?"

"Okay."

"That would be one of the worst things to come of this strike, if you lost a friend as good as Tom."

So it was settled.

My dad closed my bedroom door behind him as he left. Over the next three hours, I watched the shadows of the trees move on my wall as the waning moon crossed the sky. When I heard the tapping on my window, I slid it open, and drifted noiselessly with Tom into the southern Indiana night.

Being away from Tom and the woods all day had heightened my awareness and my appreciation of it all. I loved the way the ground felt beneath my feet, firm and yet giving slightly with each step. I loved the almost inaudible

groan of the old trees as they swayed in the slight breeze. The night was clear but very dark, the moon just a tiny sliver of white. Tomorrow, I knew, it would be gone completely and the night would be black. I felt quick on my feet in the blue darkness, with my legs strong after the day's rest, and my shoes almost bounced off the path I knew by heart. Tom stopped after a while and pulled his backpack from a fragrant thicket of honeysuckle. I saw as he stepped into it that the pack was loaded down.

"What's in there?"

"Food," he grunted, as he adjusted the straps. I heard the clanking of cans and the crinkling of cellophane.

"For Sanders and Kruer?"

"They must be starving." Tom stopped talking as we stepped over a log across the path. He wanted them to stay in our woods, I sensed, forever if possible, which was why he was bringing them the food. Tom wanted to keep and nurture them, like the wounded bald eagle we fed hamburger and watched die for two weeks the previous fall.

We walked the rest of the way to the fort.

Tom was clearly making no effort to sneak up on Sanders and Kruer. We walked right down the main path, the one I am sure they were monitoring in some manner. Tom's cargo made a racket in his backpack the entire time. I knew from experience that on a still night like that, our approach could probably be heard a half mile away.

We climbed over the fort's rough limestone wall. No one was in camp, but the fire was still smoldering, recently extinguished. We climbed down the wall and walked to the center of the camp. All the guns were gone. I knew they

had fled at the sound of our approach, and were now observing us from somewhere in the darkness. With a chill, I discovered what it felt like to be watched through a gun sight.

"It's us!" Tom yelled. "Don't worry!"

Slowly the two fugitives drifted up to the walls of the fort from opposite directions. Guthrie Kruer looked down at us a little puzzled. After he took us in, I followed his concerned eyes to the other side of the circle, to the scarecrowlike silhouette of his friend.

Mack Sanders looked even crazier than before. He had a long gun dangling at the end of each jittery arm. Dark circles outlined his eyes, and he looked like he hadn't slept in days. His face was dirty and lean. His eyes darted from Guthrie to Tom to me, as if he suspected a conspiracy between the three of us. He recklessly threw his guns down into the fort, making me cringe as they hit the ground, certain they would fire randomly, sending a ricocheting bullet right to us just as the curved walls of the fort focused sound. When they didn't go off, Sanders slithered down the wall, picked the abused guns back up and walked toward us. Guthrie had slipped down the other side but I hadn't even noticed.

Tom threw off his pack as they got close. He dumped all the food into a pile like a kid evaluating his haul on Halloween night. There were cans of Campbell's soup, two packs of American cheese slices, Tootsie Pops, a box of Captain Crunch, and more. Mack Sanders stepped up to the pile, dropped his guns again, and lunged at a pack of hot dogs. Up close, I noticed that both guns were safe, a precaution I was certain Kruer was responsible for. Although

the embers of the fire were still glowing behind them, Sanders tore into the pack with his teeth and began eating the hot dogs raw. With two whole dogs in his mouth, he handed the pack to Guthrie, who began feasting on them with equal gusto. Tom grinned, extraordinarily pleased with himself.

The fugitives ate an apple apiece and a half box of Little Debbie oatmeal cream pies before even sitting down. When they did, Tom, without an invitation, sat beside Guthrie at the fire. That left a seat next to Sanders for me. The mood had relaxed slightly. We all tried to coax the fire back to life, blowing on it and poking it with sticks.

"Well, looks like somebody got their ass kicked," said Sanders, noticing my face as the firelight grew. "Ha!" I couldn't help but stare. Every part of him was in motion, his skinny legs that he couldn't seem to get in a comfortable position, his twitching eyebrows, his hands with which he kept rubbing his face. He was giggling to himself as he ate, so crumbs occasionally spilled from his mouth and down the front of his shirt.

"Thanks. For the food," Guthrie said, as he finally took a break from gorging himself.

"No sweat," said Tom.

"How'd you know we need food?" said Mack, still challenging us, still suspicious. Tom shrugged in response.

"You know who we are, don't you?" asked Guthrie.

"You're the fugitives," I said. "The bombers."

Tom spoke up: "You're my cousin."

Guthrie turned to Mack. "We have got to get out of here. Right now. They know who we are and where we are. There's no time left."

"We'll leave," said Sanders, never taking his eyes off Tom and me, a tight smile on his face. "When the time is right."

"When's the time going to be right?" asked Guthrie.

"We need something before we go and you know it," said Mack. "Just like we talked about. Precautions!"

"Shit," whispered Guthrie.

"I need you boys to bring us some more shells," announced Sanders, ignoring his partner. "Can you do that? Tomorrow night. The big stuff this time. Twelve-gauge buckshot, as much as you can bring us. How about it?"

Tom looked to Guthrie before answering, just as I looked to Tom. Sanders studied Guthrie's response to us. There seemed to be some complex, silent set of understandings at work, and I was the only one not taking part. "Sure," said Tom carefully. "We'll bring you some buckshot." Guthrie dropped his head in disappointment.

"Good," said Sanders. "Then we can get out of here and we'll all be happy."

We were quiet for a while as Sanders went back to eating. For a time, the hush was interrupted only by the now crackling fire and the sound of Sanders chomping on corn chips and his occasional unprompted giggle. Finally, Guthrie took it upon himself to break the silence. "What grade are you boys in?" he asked. His voice was scratchy from a week of breathing in campfire smoke.

"Going in ninth," I said.

"Cool, high school," he said a little wistfully. "Who's the principal these days?"

"Mr. Nevels," Tom and I both said.

"The old driver's ed teacher?" said Guthrie, nodding his

head. "He's a dick." We all laughed at that, even Sanders, who hadn't gone to our little school. It dawned on me that in the big scheme of things, these guys weren't all that much older than us. In the light of the small fire, with their faint but recognizable familial resemblance, it was almost hard to tell Tom and Guthrie apart. We all popped open cans of A&W root beer. It was warm, but felt good on my throat, dry from the hike and the fire.

Tom belched as he finished his root beer. "I've got to piss," he said.

"Me, too," said Guthrie. "I'll show you where, cousin." He led Tom down a faint path leading from the fire to a slight, crumbly break in the wall of the fort. They had apparently established a regular location for the call of nature, presumably downwind and far from any paths regularly traveled by hunters, hikers, or fishermen. I thought about the path they were taking—a walk in that direction would take you to the general area of the cave entrance. That made me realize that the crevice we crawled through might be directly below the fort, which kind of made geologic sense, if I was willing to consider the sinkhole theory, and evidence that contradicted the legend of Prince Madoc.

"My buddy there wants to take off right now, doesn't he?" Sanders spoke suddenly, snapping me back into the present. I realized with a start that it was just me and him alone by the fire. He smiled.

"Yeah."

"We can't do that. Not right now."

"Why not?" I asked.

"Outside these woods, they're all looking for us, right? How far you think we'd get in broad daylight?" His words

tumbled out, as if he couldn't control them once he began talking.

"Go at night," I said, eager to help him escape. I knew from experience how one could disappear into the woods after sundown.

"Can't do that, either," he said. "Those asshole thugs keep patrolling these woods at night between us and the highway; we'd never get past 'em."

"Go to Kentucky," I said.

He snorted. "How am I supposed to do that? You think anyone would notice me and Guthrie walking across the Kennedy Bridge?"

There was another way, I thought, but for some reason I stopped myself from telling him. I looked down at the fire instead. The silence grew unbearable. I could only think of two things to talk about with Mack Sanders, and one of them was the killing of Don Strange. I decided to talk about the other one.

"What was it like?" I asked.

Sanders cleared his throat and spit. "You mean settin' the explosion?" he said proudly. "Awesome."

"No," I said. "Losin' a nut."

"Oh," he said. He stopped short, and then wagged his tongue in an attempt to look devilish. "The bitches like it," he bragged. "You know what I mean?"

"No," I said. "Why do they like it?"

He shrugged. "No, I'm just messin' with you. You can't really even tell without looking close. The doctor says it shouldn't affect anything, as far as having kids or anything. Said that's why the good Lord give us two." He shrugged again.

Some more silence passed. "How bad did it hurt?" I asked.

"It hurt," he said. "How do you think it felt?"

"What did they do with the one that got torn off?" It was a part of the story I'd always been curious about.

"What is wrong with you?"

"I don't know," I said. "I'm just curious."

"Seriously, what the fuck is wrong with you? Asking me about my nuts. You want to see?" He stood up with his hands poised on his zipper.

I stared down at the ground, mortified with embarrassment. "No!" I said. "I was just curious."

"Seriously, I'll show you if you're that goddamn curious, you homo."

"I'm sorry!" I was ready to run off if he unzipped.

Sanders stopped suddenly, perhaps moved by my genuine terror or by his own memories of that day. He sat down heavily again on his log. He sighed and for a while we just watched the fire burn. He lapsed into a kind of stillness I hadn't seen from him before, all his kinetic energy turned potential, his eyes half closed in thought. I hoped he would remain calm until Kruer and Tom returned. They'd been gone a long while and I wondered what they were talking about.

"We didn't mean to kill Strange," Sanders muttered, still looking somberly into the fire. "Now we can't ever go back. We didn't know he was in there. I liked that old man." A huge mosquito landed on his cheek, stabbed him, and began sucking his blood. Sanders didn't react.

"Why'd you do it?" I asked.

He thought it over for a moment, but it seemed like he couldn't find words strong enough to express his feelings.

"Because . . ." he said, his brow furrowed, staring hard at the fire. "Because I hate that place." He spat a sizable goober onto the top of a smoldering log, and waited until it completely sizzled away before he spoke again, mumbling so softly I could barely hear him.

"We didn't know he was there. We just wanted to shake things up, maybe give those assholes something to think about. What the hell was he doing in there that time of night, anyway?" Flames curled around the log as Sanders wallowed in regret. I felt again like I had to say something.

"My dad says Mr. Strange would go in at all hours."

"Your dad works at the plant?" Sanders snapped back to life, energized by a piece of information his predatory instincts recognized as significant. He slapped at the mosquito, and a teardrop of blood ran down his cheek.

I had said too much. I nodded my head to answer his question, trying to look unshaken.

"Where at? What part of the plant?" He was smiling broadly, pressing me now, pushing his way through the crevice to which I had led him.

"Finish room," I mumbled. A log popped.

"Me too!" he said with sudden, artificial enthusiasm. "What's his name?"

I stammered.

He leaned in close. "Come on, man, what's your dad's name?"

I was fumbling for an answer when Tom and Guthrie came running back into camp. "Put out the fire!" whispered Guthrie. Mack hesitated for just a second, looking at me, wanting to continue the interrogation. He then lunged for an old five-gallon bucket that they had filled with creek

water and placed next to the fire. He doused it, placing us in total, smoky darkness.

"What's going on?" whispered Mack as we headed to the wall of the fort. Both Sanders and Kruer brought rifles with them.

"Voices," said Guthrie. "The thugs again. Closer this time."

By then we heard them. Men shouting, small branches snapping, larger ones being pushed out of the way. They certainly weren't trying to be sneaky. A marching band wouldn't have made more noise. Sanders shouldered his rifle, using the rock wall of the fort for support. He was trying to impress us, I could tell, but his awkwardness with the weapon had the opposite effect. When he raised the gun, his cheek was too close to the stock, an uncomfortable and potentially painful stance an experienced shooter would have avoided. His index finger probed the trigger guard for the safety, but he finally had to take the rifle off his shoulder to locate it. Sanders clearly didn't know anything about his gun, and he didn't even know enough to be embarrassed by that.

Flashlights came into view, the beams swinging casually back and forth. They were coming directly from the highway, following the wide, easy path that ran to Silver Creek, a path kept clear and flat by a regular parade of fishermen and day hikers. The bulk of the group was walking together up front in a jovial mob. We heard their voices, which were lighthearted: laughter sprinkled with occasional good-natured bitching.

Behind them, a tall silhouette walked alone and trained his flashlight with more deliberation. A few times, the

beam pointed right at us, although we knew from that distance no one could see us, especially hunkered down as we were behind the fort's limestone wall. Even though the fire was out, I worried about a log popping, giving us away. The lone thug hesitated, almost as if he sensed that we were near. He grew frustrated with the noise coming from his teammates in front.

"Shut the fuck up!" he shouted ahead. They instantly quieted. No one challenged his authority, although it was clear from their continued, casual pace that no one else really expected to find anything of interest during their midnight hike. I knew the voice. Of course it was Solinski.

They continued to walk down the path. Although they were no longer talking, their careless footsteps continued to make an unholy racket. Soon, they all passed from view, and the sound faded in the distance.

"Solinski," I whispered.

"We have got to get out of here!" Guthrie hissed to Sanders. "They're getting closer every night."

"We will," said Sanders, his sharp teeth flashing in the moonlight. "Tomorrow night, after our little buddies here come back with what we need."

"Goddamn," whispered Guthrie.

"Go on," Sanders said to us. "You kids go on and get home. We'll see you tomorrow."

"With the shells?" said Tom.

He paused for just a second. "Right, with the shells."

"Guthrie told me about the bird," Tom said, after we had hiked a safe distance away.

"The bird?" I asked.

"The bird, the bird," Tom said. "The buzzard he rescued from the water tower."

"Oh," I said.

"He couldn't stand the sound," Tom said. "That's why he went up there. Said he couldn't believe nobody planned on doing anything. All the other firemen were just standing around down there in the parking lot, listening to the thing squawk, waiting for it to die."

"I remember," I said. "It was freezing cold, right before Christmas. There wasn't a place in the valley you could go without hearing it."

"Guthrie said after a few minutes, he decided he had to climb up there—he seriously thought the sound of it was going to drive him crazy."

"It didn't even sound like a bird."

"He said he just had to climb up the tower and make it stop."

"Save it?" I asked.

"Save it or kill it."

We both thought that over as we crawled over and under a series of trunks and limbs that had been lying across the path most of our lives.

"How about you?" Tom asked suddenly. "What did you and Sanders talk about? When I went with Guthrie to piss?"

"Sanders said he doesn't want to leave," I said.

"Really?"

"Said they'll be seen by the cops in the daytime, or caught by the thugs at night," I said.

Tom thought that over. "Then I wonder how come he'll be ready to leave tomorrow if we just give him a box of

buckshot," he said. "Surely he's not planning on shooting his way out of here."

"I don't know," I said. "That's a good question."

Tom mulled it over in the deepest, smartest part of his brain, the part of my brain I didn't have full access to. I knew he continued to work on the problem even as he asked me his next question.

"Did Sanders say anything else? What else did you talk about while you two were alone?"

I thought about Sanders closing in, circling me, on the verge of discovering the identity of my father.

"Nothing," I lied. "What else did you and Guthrie talk about?"

"Nothing," he said.

Nine

I slept soundly that night, deeper than I'd slept in days. I had a dream where I could jump miles into the air. I had to grab the skinny top branches of trees as I passed to avoid flying into space. I looked down as I hung on, and saw Tom, Guthrie, and Sanders sitting around the fire inside the fort without me. They looked around for me, but none of them thought to look straight up, where I was safely hidden in the treetops. Beyond the fort I saw the cave entrance, a small black void tucked into the thick foliage. The Buffalo Trace snaked in and out of view, in curves that I suddenly realized were not at all random, as they appeared from the ground, but in fact led the buffalo herds efficiently through the hilly topography, around the biggest crags and across the few level plateaus. In the middle of the eye-shaped pool in Silver Creek, the giant, lonely carp came to the surface for a gulp of air, his mirrored scales reflecting the moonlight.

I woke disappointed, unable to fly. The elation of my dream evaporated, making room for the dense, heavy dread that kept me earthbound. I still knew the location of Don Strange's killers, and I still was supposed to meet them one more time, to deliver whatever buckshot shells

Tom could lay his hands on. I didn't want to get out of bed. Doing so would put me one step closer to a reunion with Mack Sanders.

I suddenly realized that it was the unfamiliar sound of male voices arguing downstairs that had awoken me. Sunlight streamed in my window, telling me that I'd slept late. I looked out and saw Mr. Kruer's truck in the driveway. I slipped out my bedroom door and halfway down the stairs to listen.

"We're trying to get by on twenty dollars a week from the strike fund," said Tom's dad bitterly. "That was a week's worth of groceries for us." There was a note of desperation in his voice, something I was sure he wouldn't have allowed himself in front of Tom. Or me.

I saw my dad hesitantly reach for his wallet. George Kruer waved his hand in disgust.

"I didn't come here for your money, Gus," he said. "Just tell Andy that Tom can't come out. He's grounded until he decides to tell me what he did with all that food, and until he comes up with the money to pay for it." He walked out the front door and stomped down the porch steps.

Dad sighed, his hand still on his wallet. He spotted me on the steps.

"Come on down here, buddy," he said wearily. I did. My mother had found her way into the front room, dressed to go somewhere. She was wearing new jeans and a shirt that was old but freshly ironed. She had earrings in as well, a rarity. They were the kind of clothes she'd wear to help paint the church or to assemble gift baskets for the poor: old but not too old, nice but not too nice.

"What on earth did Tom do with all those groceries?" asked Dad.

I shrugged, choosing to remain silent rather than lie.

"Sounds like Tom's dad doesn't even know you two were in a fight. Doesn't know you weren't together at all yesterday."

I shrugged again.

"Do you two have a friend who needs food? We can help if you let us know."

My silence hurt Dad's feelings deeply. He knew that I had secrets, of course, that fact didn't bother him by itself. I spent days on end in the woods with my best friend, and he realized that we had built up whole volumes of stories together that he would never know. This was different, though. He was asking me something directly, and I was refusing to tell him. It was a new kind of conversation for us, and neither one of us knew quite how to handle it.

"Well, whatever you've been doing, you're not doing it today," he said, when it became clear that I wasn't going to volunteer any more information. "Tom's grounded, and so are you, until you boys find a way to get along with each other, and pay for all that food."

My parents watched me closely, and I did my best to hide my true feelings about the punishment: unbridled relief. I couldn't leave the house and neither could Tom. I didn't ever want to see Mack Sanders again, I didn't want to satisfy his mysterious need for buckshot, and I didn't want him to ask me again what my father did at the plant. Tom getting grounded was the best thing that could possibly happen to me. My parents were suspicious, I saw, and curious, but they couldn't quite put the pieces together, and

were in the process of writing off the whole grocery theft as one of those illogical acts of mischief that could never be completely explained. I walked upstairs fighting the urge to clap my hands.

My father drove away soon after that, some plant business to attend to. A few minutes later, Mom knocked on my bedroom door and walked in.

"Put on something respectable," she said. "You're coming with me."

"What are we doing?" I asked.

"It's a secret," she said seriously. I started to laugh. "No, really," she said. "It's secret. I wouldn't bring you if I didn't have to, but there's no way I'm going to leave you here alone with all this craziness going on. Have I got your attention?" she asked.

I nodded.

"You have to promise me that you won't tell anyone what you see today."

"Not even Dad?" I said.

"He knows all about it."

"Can you at least tell me where we're going?"

She hesitated. "Jeffersonville."

The yards got smaller with each mile as we drove toward the city on Highway 60. The undefined property lines around the houses in Borden gave way to the large fenced yards in Sellersburg, and finally to the small industrial city of Jeffersonville, where dreary split-levels and duplexes sat next to each other on identical rectangular lots, each surrounded by chain link to protect the

integrity of a microscopic yard. I was certain that from one of those front yards I could hurl a baseball over three complete houses. I tried to imagine what it would be like to live within those kinds of constraints, and I couldn't. On some blocks, black kids ran around, much less fascinated by me than I was by them. Each time Mom slowed the car for a red light or a stop sign, my heart raced, certain that I was about to pull into the driveway of my secret cousins. I hoped there were dozens.

My mother steadfastly refused to tell me why we were going to Jeffersonville. My wildest hopes were confirmed, however, when we passed by Jeffboat, her brother's employer according to Dad, and THE WORLD'S LARGEST INLAND SHIPBUILDER, according to their huge sign. I saw the skeletons of giant coal barges inside the fence as laborers crawled like ants along their ribs, showers of sparks occasionally flying from their welding rods. Green glimpses of the Ohio and the Louisville riverfront skyline flashed between buildings: Kingfish, the Galt House, the ornate Belknap Hardware warehouses. I tried to spot the *Belle of Louisville,* the steam-powered paddle wheeler that took tourists up and down the river.

Rolling past the shipyard, we entered Jeffersonville's oldest neighborhood, a row of old mansions facing the river, homes that had once belonged to riverboat captains back when captains were treated like astronauts, the masters of the most expensive and powerful technology of the day. Conspicuous wrought-iron balconies and widow's walks seemed to indicate that many of the captains had grown fond of New Orleans's architecture during their long voyages downriver. Some of the mansions

showed every day of their age, with peeling paint and bowed roofs. Others had been lovingly restored to their full glory.

We pulled into the driveway of a house that was somewhere in between. While some of the paint was peeling, and many of the shingles needed replacing, there was a solid-looking new front door, and a freshly planted flower bed around an unlabeled mailbox. New young trees had been planted in the yard, tiny seedlings in a neat row along the street. There was a gate at the end of the driveway, too, the only one I'd seen on the street, and that excited me more. I wondered why my cousins would need it. Was Uncle Russell still in danger because he crossed that picket line all those years ago? My mother put the car in park, and turned to face me.

"Promise me again that you'll never tell anyone about this place," she said.

"I promise."

"It's incredibly important that you keep this a secret," she said.

I nodded my head, so excited I could no longer speak.

My mother left the car running and got out. I was surprised to see that she had her own key to the padlock on the gate. No one came out to greet us. After she pushed the gate open, she pulled the car through, got out, and then relocked the gate behind us.

Mom held my hand as we walked to the front door, a move that would normally have mortified me, but seemed somehow appropriate given the seriousness of what we were about to do. I wondered how my cousins would see me, what we would talk about. Could they come out to

Borden sometime and run around with me and Tom? Surely they would now that we knew each other, all the time probably. Tom and I could teach them how to shoot and fish, and they could teach us whatever it is that city kids know how to do. I wondered if one of the johnboats tied up at the pier across the street belonged to them.

A sophisticated-looking intercom box was installed near the front door. Mom pushed a button, got an immediate response from within, and said her name. After a slight delay, I heard the clicking and sliding of a series of locks and latches being undone.

The door came open and a ruddy, solid-looking woman hugged my mother dramatically in the foyer. She had the straight hair, no makeup, and earnest face that were the telltale characteristics of my mother's feminist friends. "Hello, sister," she said. But I knew she wasn't the kind of sister I was looking for.

"You must be Andrew," she said to me as she released my mother from her clinch.

"Andy," I said, trying to look beyond her into the house. It was almost devoid of furniture. It was unmistakably old, but the place had a fresh-scrubbed, dust-free cleanliness to it.

"Andy, we're glad you could come."

We walked inside.

Past the front room, we entered a spacious kitchen. Two women sat silently at a card table and smoked, a communal pack of Parliaments and a Bic between them. One had a relatively fresh black eye, an eye that was still vibrantly bloodshot from the blow. Neither woman said

anything to us as we walked in. They didn't have the swaggering, theatrical toughness of my mother's friends on their way to a protest march. When my mom went out of the house without makeup, she had to announce to us that she was making a political statement, because her skin was so fair on its own we could never tell otherwise. The women at the card table had bags under their eyes, wrinkles, and hair that had been brushed back just enough to keep it out of the way of their smoking. They wore baggy T-shirts, old jeans, and house slippers. Their tough stares looked completely earned to me as they looked up, knowingly evaluated the fading wounds on my face, and then dismissed me with taps of their cigarettes on the edge of the clay ashtray. My mother nodded at them.

She then enthusiastically grabbed a yellow bucket from under the sink and a large green sponge—in her eagerness, she seemed to have almost forgotten that I was in the room. She talked with the woman who had answered the door about what she was going to accomplish that day: clean and line the cupboards, and cook a turkey noodle casserole before leaving. I had noticed this internal conflict before in my mother, the battle between her studied feminism and her native southern genius for cooking and cleaning. She was a virtuoso in the kitchen, as well as a tireless scrubber and organizer. While she reminded my father frequently that she shouldn't be required to do all the cooking, she couldn't even let him toast his own Pop-Tart, so painful was it for her to watch him fumble around in the kitchen. As she turned on the faucet and began running steaming water into the bucket, she suddenly remembered that she had to do something

with me. Our hostess recognized the problem at the same time.

"I'll take him upstairs, with the other kids," she said. She put a hand on my shoulder and we walked together up a creaking grand staircase.

She led me to a cavernous room on the third floor, and then with a pat on my shoulder abandoned me. A few toys were scattered across the vast floor. An old chandelier hung from the middle of the high ceiling, a chandelier so old that it had actually used candles for light—a telltale black smear on the ceiling above it reminded me of the Indian fire pits we'd seen in caves. The chandelier, the vast size of the room, and the smooth wood floor made me think it might have been a ballroom in its glory days, with musicians in the corner and an armada of steamboats moored just outside the window. Some modern educational posters had been tacked to the wall: the letters of the alphabet, Spanish numbers *uno* through *diez*, cartoonish portraits of the thirty-nine presidents.

There were three other kids in the room, looking just as out of place as the posters. One was a little blond girl who turned toward me with a big pretty smile. A slightly chunky boy in the middle of the room ignored me as he energetically rolled Matchbox cars across the floor and into the far wall. The third girl, the oldest, had her arm in a cast and straight straw-colored hair that fell across her face. She looked down at the floor. Even if she hadn't been wearing the Pink Floyd T-shirt, I would have recognized her immediately. I'd spent hours studying her photograph.

"Hi, Taffy," I said.

She didn't say anything back.

"What's your name?" asked the little girl. She seemed excited to have company. I realized that the pretty, cheerful little girl was Taffy's younger sister—she looked just like her.

"Andy," I said. "Andy Jackson Gray. What's your name?"

"Becky."

"Becky Judd, right?"

"We're not supposed to say," she said, still cheerful. I couldn't take my eyes off Taffy and her stark white plaster cast. The other boy, ignoring us all, was now trying to roll a car into the one he had already crashed across the room, a difficult shot from that distance. "Why are you here?" Becky asked.

I was still trying to figure that out myself. "My mom's downstairs cleaning," I said, as close as I could come to an explanation.

"So your mom's a helper," Becky said brightly.

"Sure. Why are you here?"

"We're here because my daddy smacks us."

Taffy glared at her sister, the first I'd seen of her face, and then looked back at the ground, bright shame in her eyes. "We're not supposed to talk about it, Becky." She almost whispered.

"I can talk about it if I want," she replied. They stared at each other, the other boy crashed his cars, and I continued to wonder where my mother had brought me.

After a while I thought I heard a steam whistle in the distance, and walked over to the window to take a look while the sisters continued their stare down. The tall window reminded me of the one Tom and I had climbed through at the Borden Institute. It was slightly warped

with age, with tiny bubbles entrained inside the glass. I hoped to catch a glimpse of the *Belle* outside, taking a sightseeing cruise past the house. Taffy walked up and stood beside me, making my heart race. Her good elbow rubbed against my arm.

"We're not supposed to stand by the window like that," said Becky, in the background and as chipper as ever.

"Why's that?" I asked.

"It's a rule." She paused. "Because if my daddy's out there driving around looking for us, he might see us in the window and come in here and kill everybody."

I heard a strange wet tapping sound, like raindrops on mud, and looked over to Taffy. She was crying silently. The tapping was the sound of fat tears falling on her cast. I had never in my life wanted to do something so badly while feeling so completely clueless about what to do. So I stood there, for what seemed like hours, staring out the window, trying to think of something useful to say.

Gradually, Taffy stopped crying. When it seemed it might be okay, I got down on the floor and started playing cars with Becky and the boy. I kept low and away from the big front windows, telling myself that it was just to keep Becky happy, and not because I was afraid of Orpod Judd. Occasionally a car would pass the house, and I breathed easier whenever it continued on down the road.

I spent the rest of the day with them in the ballroom. After a while, Taffy joined in, sniffling slightly, but ready. She soon became just as friendly and outgoing as her sister. We joined the boy in his game, trying to crash Matchbox cars together from gradually increasing distances, each of us winning a round in turn. When we got tired of that, we

slid across the wood floor in our sock feet, pretending to skate and surf as we whooped and hollered and crashed into each other, all of us being careful not to run into Taffy's wounded arm. I was at an age when I still had a big time playing with toys and pretending, even though I couldn't possibly act that way with most of my friends. The rest of the afternoon flew by.

Just as the warm orange sun began going down, we heard the steam whistle again and all of us went to the window, all of us for a moment forgetting the rule and the danger.

This time we saw it. *The Belle of Louisville* came paddling into view, its red stern wheel propelling it slowly upstream, churning the muddy water behind it to the muted tune of its steam calliope.

"Look at that," I said. We watched for a few minutes.

"Cool," said Taffy, brushing her long straight hair out of her face with her left hand. But she wasn't looking out the window. She was looking at me. I was more paralyzed than when I'd been trapped in the cave.

She suddenly leaned over and kissed me on the cheek, as I watched the sun set and the big steamboat move imperceptibly upstream. With girlfriends later, in high school, college, and the real life after, I would sometimes try to slow the moment down, as I wish I could have that day in Jeffersonville. I wish I would have taken stock of every detail that made it perfect, the old ballroom, the way calliope music always sounds sad, Taffy's hair falling in front of her face. A more perceptive girlfriend in Bloomington, sensing my remoteness, once begged me so earnestly to tell my

story that I almost gave in. But I have inherited my mother's great ability to keep secrets.

"Andy!" she called from downstairs. "Stop playing, time to go!"

"See you around," I said to Taffy with a scratchy voice.

"Yeah," she said, "see you around, Andy."

Mom called me again and I went downstairs, feeling Taffy's eyes on my back as I went.

Mom was putting a large casserole in the oven when I got to the kitchen, and then she stood and clapped her hands in a way that announced the completion of our day. The two other women were still at the card table, still smoking, still silent. I tried briefly to figure out which was Taffy's mom, based on my memory of a family photo in the Judd home. Cigarette butts had mounded in the center of the big clay ashtray. They didn't say a word as we left.

"Did you have a good time with the kids upstairs?" my mom asked in the car. "You seem out of sorts."

"It was okay. Didn't those women even say thank you?" I asked quickly, wanting to change the subject and knowing that Mom was a stickler for common courtesies.

"They've got plenty of other things to worry about," she said. "I go in there now and again so they can get a decent meal without having to say please or thank you to anybody."

"How did Taffy get here?"

"The sheriff called me the night it happened. I went and picked them up at the Kohls' house, drove them to the hospital, then here."

"What was the car ride like?"

My mom took her eyes off the road briefly to look at me. "What do you think it was like?"

"Were you mad?" I asked.

"I was very, very sad."

"How did the sheriff even know about this place?"

"I told him about it," she said. "Before this shelter came along, there was nowhere for these poor people to go. Sheriff Kohl, he could put the men in jail for a night, maybe a weekend, but they'd always get out eventually."

"That is sad."

"Sheriff Kohl had to go see the same poor women, the same scared kids, over and over again. Sometimes every drunken weekend."

"Why don't they just leave?"

"These women don't have anywhere else to go," said my mother. "They truly don't. Anybody that took them in would be risking their own family's safety."

"So Sheriff Kohl asked for your help?" I asked.

"He came up to me three years ago and told me he wanted to do something to help these women, and asked me if I had any ideas. He was willing to try anything."

"Why did he ask you?"

"He'd seen the ERA signs, everyone in town knows about my politics. So I guess he thought, who else am I going to ask? And at first, I didn't have any help to offer. But I asked around, and I found a group of people who knew about this shelter. They agreed to let me bring women and kids from Borden here."

"I'll bet Sheriff Kohl was glad to hear about this place."

"Overjoyed. He even kicks in part of the jail's food

budget when we've got somebody here, to help make ends meet."

"That's cool," I said.

"He's a good man," my mom said. "He's not doing it for political reasons—no one in Borden knows about it. The only vote he gets out of this deal is mine."

"Has Sheriff Kohl ever been out here to see what it's like?"

"He has no idea where it is. No one in Borden does. Except me," she said. "And now you."

I thought about the kiss and fought the urge to rub my cheek. "Now that I know about this place, can I come back? To help?"

A slight smile crossed her lips. "We'll see."

When I got in Mom's car that morning, I thought I knew what the details of my fourteenth summer's final, dramatic chapter would be: rescued from a final rendezvous with Sanders, done with the fugitives forever, I would finally get to meet the cool, rambunctious, extended family I was entitled to. Turns out I was wrong on all counts.

Ten

I guess it was silly to think that getting grounded would keep Tom in his room all night. It's not as if in normal times we had parental permission to climb out our windows in the middle of the night and run off into the woods. I thought that we were done with Sanders and Kruer because I badly wanted to think that, and I still believed it when I lay down to go to sleep that night. The tapping on the window surprised me when it came.

I slid the window open. "What are you doing?"

Tom looked surprised by the question. "Let's go."

"I thought you were grounded." I heard the silliness of it myself.

"Come on, let's go," he said, impatient.

"To take them the buckshot?"

"To help Guthrie Kruer."

"Maybe we shouldn't go back," I said. "They killed Don Strange." Tom noticed that I was echoing the words of Solinski, and it pissed him off.

"Are you coming or not?" he asked after a long pause.

"No," I said finally. "I'm all done with it." I could tell it didn't completely surprise him. That hurt me more than anything.

"But you'll keep it all a secret, right?" he asked. "Everything?"

I thought it over. "I'll keep it a secret," I said. "On one condition."

"What's that?" He was fuming now.

"I don't want to know any more about it. Leave me completely out of it from now on."

Now it was Tom's turn to look hurt. "Okay," he said. "It's a deal. You keep this a secret, and you won't hear another word." He actually stuck out his hand and we shook on it, a formality we had never before thought necessary in our commitments to each other. As he was leaving he turned around. "You should have just pretended to be asleep if you didn't want to come out."

He climbed silently off my porch. The night was moonless and dark, but I could still see him as he quickly crossed our yard, until he disappeared into the woods like a puff of smoke.

For hours, I lay there with my window open and thought it all over. I worried about my father's warning, about losing a friend because of the strike. Taffy was in a shelter, and I might not ever see her again. I worried about Tom, alone in the woods with two killers. I worried about the plant moving to Mexico and how Tom would ever pay his dad back for all those groceries. I don't know how much time passed. With no moon in the sky or shadows on my walls it was impossible to judge. I just know it was very late when I first heard the dull pop of distant gunshots.

I jumped out of my bed, leapt into my jeans and sneakers, flew through the window and off the porch, and

started running down the trace. With my arms extended for balance as I crossed the old fallen tree across the gap, I hardly slowed down. I heard random shots all the way, louder as I ran, but as I got deeper into the woods, I heard also crazed screaming between shots. I ran up to the edge of the fort.

"Where are you, Guthrie!" Sanders screamed into the empty fort. He kicked the tent into a heap. I was surprised and confused. And stupid, I suppose. Without really thinking about it, I just climbed down into the fort. In a way, I felt a kind of kinship with Sanders. Both of us just wanted to know what the hell was going on.

"What the hell?" he said as he saw me coming down the wall. He looked absolutely skeletal, his crazed eyes bulging out of his head.

"It's me," I said.

He smiled in a way that said: *now I've got this all figured out.* I walked right into the middle of the fort, right to Sanders. The neat camp was wrecked, as if without Guthrie present the forces of chaos had immediately taken over. I could see no sign of Tom—or Guthrie. Mack had the camouflaged turkey gun in hand. I could smell gunpowder thick in the air; the discharge gases had pooled inside the fort on the windless night.

"It is you," he said. "I'll be damned." He had calmed suddenly, like I'd seen once before, his eyes half closed and his arms hanging loosely as he muttered.

"Where's Tom?" I asked. Mack smiled again. Then he swung the gun like a baseball bat, hitting me squarely in the temple.

* * *

I came to, but it was so dark, and I was so groggy, I couldn't even tell what direction I was facing. My hands were tied painfully tight behind my back. I rolled over, putting my face right into something hairy and foul. I lifted my head high enough to see I had rolled right onto the crusty pelt of the poached rabbit we'd seen on that first night, now stiff with age and half buried in leaves. I rolled the other direction, and found myself looking up directly into the deranged face of Mack Sanders.

"Wake up, sleepyhead," he said. "I want to finish this before anyone notices you're gone."

I noticed for the first time the dark, jagged scar across the palm of his hand, where he had grabbed the chain in panic the day his nut was ripped off. "Finish what?" I mumbled.

Sanders ignored me. "You never did answer me the other night. What's your daddy's name?"

"What?" I asked. Panic swept the cobwebs from my head. Sanders pulled a glowing stick from the fire that still burned near where the tent had stood.

"You heard me. What's your daddy's name?"

"George Kruer," I sputtered.

He scratched his chin theatrically, as if thinking it over. "Bullshit," he said, and jammed the sharp, glowing end of the stick into my neck. Everything went white as I screamed in pain. The sound bounced right back at us from the curved walls of the fort, and I heard the scream, even in my pain, like it belonged to someone else. When I stopped, he was leaning over me, his face just inches away. "The other little asshole is Guthrie's cousin. Now, tell me again, what's your daddy's name?" he whispered.

"Gus Gray," I whimpered.

He exploded. "*I knew it!*"

"No," I said. "It's not what you think . . ."

"I knew we never should have trusted you little shits!"

"No . . ."

"*Shut up!*" he screamed. He was pacing around me, pulling fingers through his dirty hair.

"Did you know that I'm the one that wrote on your garage door?" he said after calming himself down slightly. He laughed loudly. "Snuck up there when I knew everybody would be at the funeral. What a joke! Your daddy was my manager! And you were right here, sittin' on a log right next to me."

"I didn't . . ."

"Next question," he snapped. "What did you guys do with Guthrie? Is he sittin' in the sheriff's office right now, drinkin' coffee and rattin' me out?"

I must have looked genuinely confused enough to buy myself a few seconds. "He's gone?"

"That's right, shithead, like you didn't know. We were waiting here to take you little assholes hostage. Guthrie was being such a big pussy about the whole thing, I gave in when he said he wanted to wait for a moonless night, which sounded like typical hillbilly bullshit to me. Then he up and disappears while we're waiting for you. Went to take a piss and never came back."

"Hostage?"

"You little assholes were going to be our insurance policy. You think we really needed buckshot?"

I nodded.

"Guthrie said that you guys might be smart enough to

avoid coming back here. I think he hoped that was the case. I guess he was half right."

Sanders threw the stick back into the fire in disgust. He had his back to me, and was uncharacteristically quiet. I watched him walk away from the fire, out of my view. I struggled against the twine around my wrists, but it was too tight. When Sanders came back into the dim orange light, he was carrying the turkey gun again, chambering a shell. A little bit of my blood and hair were stuck to the barrel.

"I don't know anything!" I screamed. "I don't know where they are!"

"How many people have you told about our spot here?" he asked.

"No one!" I said. "I promised I wouldn't!"

"The hell you wouldn't!" he shouted.

"Take me hostage! I can get you out of here."

His eyes showed a glimmer of hope, but he heard something, either in his own broken mind or in the still air, that made him abandon any hope of escape.

"Guthrie's probably tellin' 'em all now it was all my idea. They're on their way now. I think I can hear 'em!"

He was ranting, but when he paused, I actually thought I heard them, too, the sound of men tromping through the woods in a hurry, without trying to be quiet. I knew they were too far away to help me but I tried anyway.

"*Help!*" I screamed.

"It's too late for both of us, little man."

I imagined Solinski at the front of the group hearing my scream, running my way. I just didn't have time. I

tried to roll away from Mack, but bound up as I was, he just stepped over me and I rolled right into his booted foot. He laughed at my hopelessness as he straddled me. He pointed the turkey gun at my face, and smiled. I saw his finger strain against the trigger, and I saw the surprise in his eyes when it didn't move. He took his eyes off me for just a second and lifted the gun to locate the thumb safety.

That's when I sat straight up and rammed my head as hard as I could into his one nut.

Sanders fell over clutching his crotch and I struggled to my feet, my hands still tied tight behind me. I ran to the far edge of the fort, where I had on that first night climbed the stone with toeholds that I thought might have saved me. As Sanders groaned in pain and rose to his feet, I ran flat out at the wall as if sheer adrenaline, speed, and desire could propel me up and over, or as if I could jump to the stars like I did in my dream. I actually got a toehold with my first foot, and then a little higher with my second. For one brief second, my head rose above the level of the wall. Flashlights bobbed in the distance, moving fast, but much too far away. My momentum spent, unable to climb farther with my hands tied, I fell straight back down into the fort, on my back with a thud, right at Sanders's feet.

"Nice try, my man. Really. Nice try." He chambered a shell in the turkey gun, fingering the safety, ready to shoot this time. I was looking right into the barrel.

"Don't do it," I said.

He actually thought it over for a moment. "What have I got to lose?" he asked. He squinted and prepared to shoot.

Over his shoulder, I saw movement on the dark wall of the fort. A rifle swung into place, then froze as the shooter took aim. After a flash and a crack, a .22 caliber bullet penetrated Mack's head, rattled around, and turned everything inside to soup.

At some point in the middle of the night it had all come together for my father. All the information had been collecting there in his unconscious mind, where the engineer's brain went to work on it, assembling and rearranging the pieces until it all finally made sense: my questions about Sanders and Kruer, my concerns about where our loyalty belonged, even Tom's missing groceries. Maybe it was the distant sound of Sanders' crazy gunshots that finally made it all crystallize for him—my dad would say all his life he didn't know exactly what woke him up. Whatever it was, he ran into my room, saw I was missing, saw the window I'd left open, and grabbed my M6 off the rack because it was close by and seemed more potentially useful than an encyclopedia. He shouted to my mom to call the sheriff, forgetting that she wasn't there, she was back at the shelter helping out the battered women of southern Indiana on an overnight shift. He ran downstairs, and then into the woods, following the path he'd seen Tom and I take so many times, and maybe even remembered from his own youth.

He ran down the Buffalo Trace, where he heard me scream as Sanders jammed the burning stick into my neck. He followed the sounds to the fort, then crawled to the edge of the limestone wall. He chambered a shell from the buttstock. He put Sanders in his sights, from about

fifty yards away, out of breath and in shock at the scene, with only the unsteady light of a dying campfire to see by. Dad then inhaled gently, focused on the front sight, held his breath, softly squeezed the trigger, and put a .22 rimfire bullet precisely in the middle of Mack's skull.

That was the best shot I ever saw.

Dad slid down the wall of the fort and pulled the corpse off of me. He helped me stand. As he pulled the twine off my hands, Solinski appeared at the edge of the opposite wall.

"Is he okay?" shouted Solinski. Two of his flunkies were at his side, out of breath, handguns drawn. Solinski himself was in better shape, breathing hard but not panting, his .45 still in its holster on his hip.

Dad looked me over again, then right into my eyes before responding to Solinski. "I think he's fine, praise the Lord." Solinski bounded down the wall like a deer and came to my side. His eyes fell to the throbbing burn wound on my neck. It enraged him. He looked down at the dead body of Sanders and for a moment I thought he was going to kick it.

"Where's Kruer?" he asked me.

I misunderstood—I thought he was asking about Tom.

My father knew what he meant. "Where's Guthrie Kruer?" he asked.

Still in shock, I looked slowly around the camp, and their eyes followed mine, as if we might see him hiding somewhere in the debris. They stepped closer, a little breathless, desperate to hear from me exactly what was going on.

And, in an instant of certainty, I did know exactly where Kruer was. I knew just as clearly that my father, and maybe

even Solinski, were good men. My father had just saved my life, and I believed Solinski would have done the same. I tried to remember why I should keep the truth a secret, why telling these two men the location of a killer would be some kind of betrayal. I pictured in my mind what I knew had happened, and my eyes drifted to the path that led out of the camp, to the spot where Guthrie had gone to piss, to where Tom had waited for him. Tom had hidden in the dark for hours, waiting for his chance. When his cousin had finally appeared, Tom had stepped out of the bushes, and had helped Guthrie, and only Guthrie, escape. I had never more clearly thought Tom's thoughts, felt how he felt while hunched over in the darkness, listening to the gnats whine in his ears, waiting to see Guthrie and show him a path out of the valley that only the two of us, and Taffy, knew. I raised my hand to point, ready to explain everything to Solinksi and my father.

At that moment they both raised their eyes to the heavens in wonder, their faces illuminated by a beautiful bright crimson light that glowed brilliantly for precisely seven seconds.

Solinski took off toward the flare. My father and I followed, trailed by Solinski's lumbering men.

We found Tom sitting calmly on a large limestone outcropping along the trace. His M6 was leaning against the rock, some smoke still curling out of the barrel. He was alone.

"Tom, are you okay?" asked my father.

"Yessir."

"Where's the other one?" barked Solinski. "Where's

Kruer?" His team huffed and puffed their way up next to him. Tom shrugged in response. Even in the dark, I saw the bright orange clay on his boots.

"What happened, boy?" Dad put his hands on Tom's shoulders. "Why'd you shoot the flare?"

Tom paused before responding.

"I got lost," he said.

At that, my father stepped back and looked at Tom, and then at me, and shook his head. Somewhere beneath our feet, I knew, Kruer was running or crawling through the cave, through the wide end of the crevice, to Squire Boone Caverns; through the Christmas Tree Room, perhaps slowing briefly to pay his respects as he passed the dusty casket. Then across the shallow stream where the eyeless fish swam, to the door set loosely in the rock, to the fishing boat with the good oars and the Kentucky sticker, across the muddy Ohio, to freedom.

They never found him.

By the time Sheriff Kohl showed up, just as dawn was breaking, Tom and I had been next to each other on that rock just long enough to get our stories straight. We'd been able to speak when Dad turned to Solinksi to mutter about the night's events, or when the two of them jogged into the woods a few yards to investigate a noise. We'd whispered the outline back and forth until we'd constructed a version of the night's events that was, if not entirely believable, at least possible.

"We snuck out to go frog gigging," Tom told Sheriff Kohl. There were in fact several of the three-tined spears throughout the camp. I noticed that even at this odd hour,

after a decent hike into the woods, Kohl's uniform was still immaculate, the creases of his pants crisp. There was a single bur clinging to his knee, and I had to fight the urge to pick it off for him.

"Mack Sanders snuck up on us and grabbed me," I said.

"And I ran away to get help," said Tom.

There was a long pause. "And that's when you got lost?" asked the sheriff.

Tom nodded his head. The sheriff turned to me, perhaps more hopeful that I might reveal the whole truth. "And you never saw Guthrie Kruer?"

"Never did," Tom and I said together.

The sheriff scratched his head, unwilling to push me too hard for some reason, perhaps because of the strange dynamics between him and my dad. He would come out to the house a few times in the coming weeks, and to Tom's, to question us separately, but the frog gigging story held, and after a while nobody saw any productive reason to tear it apart, even if nobody quite believed it.

"Well," said Sheriff Kohl, looking at the eastern edge of the woods, just starting to turn pink. "We should get you home, Tom, I am sure your parents are in a panic."

Tom slid off the rock, picked up his gun, and started walking in front of the group down the trace.

"You sure you know the way?" asked Sheriff Kohl. Tom didn't turn around.

My father was promoted to plant manager soon after. After a few touchy meetings with the Habigs, the strike ended with a thirty-cent-per-hour across-the-board pay raise. Their main demand met, the union declared the

strike an unqualified victory. Solinski and his men left in their souped-up bus on the same dewy Monday morning that the school buses of Borden swung back into service.

Tom and I began high school surprised to find ourselves segregated from each other. I was placed in Borden's modest college prep program while Tom sailed through regular classes. I don't know what classes Taffy would have been in; she was gone. That first morning of school I began my lifelong habit of scanning crowds for her straw-colored hair and Pink Floyd T-shirt, to no avail. When I asked Mom about her absence, she said that was pretty typical, people in those situations have to get away while they still can, and no she didn't know how to find Taffy and wouldn't tell me if she did. My banged-up face was still impressive enough to entertain my classmates, all of whom wanted to hear the story from me. The wounds from Orpod Judd and Mack Sanders had faded around the edges and blended together, and the only story I ever told anyone was the story of frog gigging, Sanders, and the fort. While that story was a lie and Sanders was dead, however, Orpod Judd was still very much alive, and still always lurking at the back of my mind.

I would see him sometimes, fat and mean, strutting through town like he was proud of what he had done. I tried to convince myself again that he didn't know or had forgotten who I was, but I never could quite believe it. I was bigger, too, as high school went on, no longer the scrawny fourteen-year-old he'd beaten down in his trailer. But once someone gets the better of you like that, I learned, it's very hard to unlearn the fear.

Judd was cunning, never doing anything that we could take to Sheriff Kohl. There were petty harassments: slashed tires, silent phone calls in the middle of the night, all our pumpkins smashed in the garden once while we were at church. Nothing I could prove, nothing I even bothered to say to anyone other than Tom, because I knew no one else would believe that Orpod Judd was still after me.

One of the last times I saw Judd was my junior year of high school, when he threw me into a rack of potato chips inside Miller's. I was in there with Tom, looking to spend a ten-dollar windfall I had gotten from winning a speech contest at the library. Tom and I were big by then, probably fifty pounds heavier than when he'd chased us through his trailer two years earlier, both of us finally starting to put on muscle and height that I suppose would have been attractive to a coach, had Borden High School been big enough to have a football team. Whatever our size, Judd had surprise and ruthlessness on his side. He came up fast behind us, before we could see him, and threw a hip into me so hard I fell and knocked down the entire rack of chips. Startled, on my back, I could smell Cheetos as I watched Tom force Judd back away from me.

Loretta Miller yelled from the register: "Andy Gray, your daddy is gettin' a bill for all those snacks!" I suppose she knew she'd never get a dime from Judd.

A small crowd gathered. Past Tom, Judd extended one of those long caveman arms with a "What, me?" smirk on his face, as if it were all just an accident. I refused his hand, and he skipped out of the store without a word, as I

got to my feet and brushed crumbs off my legs. It was another warning shot from Judd, I knew, a reminder that we still had a score to settle. Without his wife and two daughters to beat up, I was sure Tom and I were the focus of his most violent fantasies. Just as he had the night we stole back the sword, he was just pawing at me, putting me in position, waiting for his shot.

Soon after the incident at Miller's, Orpod Judd set his truck on fire in his driveway, and tried to collect from the good folks at State Farm. The insurance company was reluctant to pay—it seems Judd watched the truck burn down to its wheels from a lawn chair before doing anything, and then called the agent to ask about his coverage before calling the fire department or the sheriff. Judd was drinking more and more, and his natural atavistic strength seemed to be bleeding away. Everyone knew that Orpod Judd's story would not end happily. I found myself looking at it as a kind of race, where I was just trying to stay out of Judd's way until the clock ran out and he finally went to jail, or walked in front of a truck, or set himself on fire.

On an October Saturday, at the beginning of my senior year of high school and as the leaves reached their full glory, Dad appeared in my doorway. I was lying on my bed, staring into space, thinking about nothing. Abject idleness was the one aspect of adolescence that my father could not tolerate.

"Let's hike to the tomb," he said, clapping his hands. "Scare up some morels." I stepped into my boots.

The hike to Captain Frank's Tomb was one of our old favorites, especially in the fall when the white morel

mushrooms stood out starkly against the brown blanket of leaves. It was not a long hike, but it was just vigorous enough, traversing up one of the steepest sections along the banks of the Ohio.

We walked slowly along, keeping our eyes low, enjoying the cool fall air and the scenery, the green band of the Ohio just visible through the trees behind us as we climbed. Although I'd been on these mushroom hunts with my dad countless times, he still carefully inspected every mushroom I plucked before dropping it into our bulging paper sack, verifying that it was indeed a morel and not one of its deadly look-alike cousins. Before long, we'd arrived at the tomb, our spot to rest and take inventory before hiking back home.

The tomb looked like an undersized stone picnic shelter, a small version of what you might see in the state forest, with the unusual addition of a limestone throne inside. Just outside the structure were the remains of several campfires, confirmation that many before us had made the same pilgrimage. Captain Frank had been a prosperous turn-of-the-century steamboat captain who retired at the height of the paddlewheel era, when the riverfront was crowded with the mansions of men who'd made fortunes on the river. Captain Frank loved the Ohio so much that in his will, he arranged to be interred sitting down and facing the river. He constructed himself a tomb on a bluff not all that far from where Tom and I had made our hurried exit from Squire Boone Caverns. Inside the crypt he made a stone chair, where he was seated in death, watching the boats for all eternity through a small opening in the wall.

It seemed like a good idea at the time, but in fact the crypt was so bizarre that it became a kind of tourist attraction, with people hiking out from town for a peek in the window to see the good captain's rotting corpse, and to knock chips off the walls for souvenirs. Soon enough, Captain Frank's scandalized family tore down one wall of the tomb and had him moved to a more respectable gravesite, one in which he'd be buried lying down and facing heavenward like a good, normal Christian. But the vacant tomb remained, its front wall knocked down, the rest intact.

"You remember the first time I brought you up here? When you were seven?" My dad was catching his breath and smiling. He'd laid out all our mushrooms on the ground in a row, in order of size.

"You bet." He'd suggested to me then that I sit on the chair in the tomb as he told me the legend of the curse. Barges on the Ohio, I learned, shine their searchlights on the tomb as a show of respect when they pass that section of the river. As Dad told me this, we watched a searchlight crawl up the hill looking for the tomb.

"If you're sitting on the chair when the light hits it," Dad told me, just as the light reached the edge of the tomb, "you're cursed!"

"You jumped out of that chair so damn fast." He laughed hard at the memory. "God you were pissed at me."

"I just couldn't believe you'd let your only son get cursed."

"I was just trying to make sure my only son didn't grow up addled with superstition."

"Thanks. It worked."

In the distance, a barge came into view through the

trees. It slowly pushed downstream, fully loaded with coal. Its big yellow searchlight clicked on.

"So . . ." Dad said, "you want to have a seat?"

"No," I said.

"Me neither."

At home, Mom was thrilled with our harvest. We decided not to even wait for dinner, as she sliced the morels in half, dipped them in egg, coated them in crushed saltines, and fried them crisp in butter. She piled them high on a steaming platter while Dad and I waited, forks in hand.

That night, after a game of Authors, I got ready for bed still pleasantly stuffed from the fried morels. When I turned my light off, my eyes adjusted just enough as I walked to my bed that something outside caught my eye, a variation easy to detect in a landscape I'd seen a million times. I walked a step closer to the window.

It took a second more, as my eyes completely adjusted to the dark, to see it well. Someone was across Cabin Hill Road, hiding in the tall weeds that had gone brown already after the first hard frost. I waited a moment to be sure. It was a decent hiding space, tall weeds growing up in front of a ditch, it would have been the kind of place a duck hunter might choose as a natural blind if it were located next to water. The intruder lifted his head just slightly, to check out the house, and I was certain. It had to be Judd.

My breath caught. Judd hunkered back down, waiting—for what? It was already completely dark, I had spotted him only because of the moonlight. More likely, I decided, he was waiting for all the lights in our house to go off, so he could catch us all sleeping.

I didn't look but I could sense my M6 in its rack, the .22 shells lined up neatly inside the stock. I contemplated the shot. It wouldn't be easy, complicated as it was by the downward angle and the seventy-five yards or so between us. But I knew I could do it. Through the weeds I couldn't get a precise look at Judd, but would instead have to aim for the "center of mass," as they said in the shooting magazines. I would only get one shot, and it would have to be perfect. I imagined myself loading the single jewel-like shell in my gun, pulling the hammer up to the .22 position. I visualized myself cracking open the window, just enough to get the barrel through and the sights clear. Taking my time, setting up the shot. Exhale . . . pause . . . squeeze. I imagined the sound of the shot, and the half-second or so it would take the bullet to fly downrange, Judd hearing it but not having time to react, right before it slammed into him, hopefully in his chest or his neck, a head shot probably being too much to hope for. I pictured him falling forward, through the weeds, his hiding space revealed, his blood bright on the dry, dusty gravel.

Dad appeared at my side. "What's up?" He'd come upstairs to say good night.

I pointed out my window toward the weeds, without taking my eyes off the target. Dad squinted, unable to see him at first. "What?" He was confused. "I don't see anything."

"Judd." I mouthed the word, my throat too dry to say it.

"What on earth are you talking about?"

Just then Judd broke from the weeds. He was still hunched over, in an attempt to be stealthy, but there was

too much open ground between him and the house. His long stringy hair flopping, hunched over as he ran, he looked even more like a caveman than normal. He was heading for a small maple tree, the last bit of cover between him and our house.

"What the hell? It is him," my father said.

I started walking around Dad, toward the gun rack.

"What?" said Dad.

I pointed at my M6.

"Good Lord, Son, that's not how we handle things here in civilization." Mom appeared in the doorway. "My dear," he said, "please call the sheriff." Dad then walked casually down the stairs, flipped on the porch light, and threw open the front door.

Through my window I watched Judd stop cold in his tracks.

"Mr. Judd, how are you this evening? Can I get you a cup of coffee?" All his life, this was my father's way of saying "you appear to be drunk."

Judd stood up straight, startled by my father's forthright greeting. He walked to the front door like he had legitimate business, and disappeared from view beneath the porch roof. "Mr. Gray, I have a matter I need to discuss with you." Judd was being humorously formal. In all his plans, I am sure, he had not expected to be invited inside for a cup of coffee. Even with that great effort, however, Judd could not control his slur, as he was seriously, dangerously drunk.

"What can I do for you?" Dad asked.

"I have reason to believe your boy knows the location of my children," said Judd. "I don't care about that bitch wife of mine, but a man's got a right to see his offspring."

"I can assure you no one here can tell you where your family is."

"And . . . I believe your son also knows the location of my sword."

"Your what?" I heard suppressed laughter in Dad's voice.

"Those little shits broke in my trailer and stole my sword," said Judd. He had exhausted his supply of fake cordiality. I couldn't believe my dad was down there trying to talk to him like a normal human being.

"I have no idea what you're talking about."

"Your boy knows what I'm talkin' about, why don't you let me talk to him?" I heard movement on the porch, the shuffling of feet, like he was trying to get by my dad into the house.

"Mr. Judd, I think you better get on home," my father said, still completely affable. There was a tone in my dad's voice that I identified, to my surprise, as pity. "I'll talk to Andy, and you and I can discuss this over a cup of coffee, tomorrow in my office."

"I ain't going home till someone tells me where my kids are at. A man's got a right to see his offspring!"

Dad sighed. "I really think you ought to go now."

There was suddenly another shuffle, louder, and I looked again at the gun on my wall. Then Dad and Judd both appeared back in view, as Dad steamrolled him backward. Judd was big and strong, I knew, but so, I realized with some surprise, was my dad. Dad was just manhandling Judd backward, not trying to do any fancy moves, just steadily forcing the man across the front porch. Judd hit the railing, and Dad gave a final shove, cracking the railing and

forcing Judd to flip over it backward, where he landed hard in our perfectly trimmed evergreen bushes. Partially upside down, Judd waved his arms as he struggled to overcome the fulsome bush and his own disorientation to get to his feet. With his feet in the air, I saw a knife sticking out of Judd's boot. Even so, he was so diminished in that position that it didn't shock me entirely when Dad actually leaned over the rail and offered a helping hand. Judd finally pulled himself upright into kind of a squatting position over the bush.

Before Judd could accept Dad's hand, the sheriff pulled up, lights spinning but with no siren. Judd hung his head in despair, no doubt tabulating the many terms of probation and parole he had just violated. Kohl trotted up to the porch and quickly cuffed him, deftly removed his boot knife and dropped it on the ground, and then led him to the backseat of his cruiser. I could tell by the way Judd carefully ducked his head as he slipped into the backseat that it was not the first time he'd executed that move. With Judd safely locked in the back of the car, Kohl came back up to talk to my dad. Mom and I made our way downstairs.

"What did Mr. Judd want?" the sheriff was asking my dad. "Besides trouble?" They were handing Judd's knife back and forth as they talked, examining with a critical eye the sheath, its metal boot clip, and the sharpness of the edge.

"Bunch of drunken nonsense," my dad said. "Thinks we know where his kids are." He didn't say anything about the sword.

"You want me to charge him with assault? Destruction

of property?" The sheriff waved his hand over the broken porch railing.

"No." Dad scoffed, shaking his head.

"You sure? He did have a knife."

"Just let him sleep it off," said Dad. "I don't need to see the man put in prison for being a stupid drunk."

The next morning I walked out to see where Judd had been hiding in the weeds across Cabin Hill Road. I wanted to see the spot he'd chosen, how well he'd picked his ground. Up close, it wasn't a great blind, with thin weeds to the front and no cover at all on the other three sides. The grass was still flattened where Judd had been sitting, watching our house, my window. Something caught my eye in the weeds as I kicked around. I bent to pick it up. It was a black Zippo lighter. I flipped it open and spun a flame to life with one crunch of the knurled brass wheel.

I knew right away I wouldn't tell Dad about the lighter. He would say it didn't mean Judd was going to burn our house down, and that I couldn't even know for certain that the lighter belonged to Judd. And it certainly wouldn't change his conviction that his way of handling Judd had been right, and mine wrong. I shut the lighter and threw it as far as I could into the woods.

Judd didn't take my dad up on his offer for a conversation over coffee. In fact, he never showed up for work at the factory again. He did, however, find a credulous insurance agent two days later, took out a $20,000 insurance policy on his trailer, and then set it on fire with Coleman camp fuel. He was promptly tried and thrown in prison for insurance fraud. Of all the strange endings in Borden, perhaps the

oddest to me is that when Orpod Judd finally got put behind bars, it was for a white-collar crime.

For our last two years of high school, Tom took the long bus ride every day to Prosser, a vocational school in Clarksville, for their Manufacturing Technology Program. The events of 1979 had definitely changed us both, and our lives were on somewhat divergent paths, but we were by no means done having adventures together in those deep woods, and we continued to spend the summers and weekends hunting, fishing, and getting ourselves in and out of serious trouble.

The story of Guthrie Kruer entered town lore, taking its place alongside the legends of William Borden and Prince Madoc. Folks periodically spotted the bloodthirsty Guthrie running through the woods like Bigfoot, and kids scared each other to death with stories of the crazed fugitive by the campfire, in parked cars, and on stormy nights. Variations of the legend became plentiful. Some argued that Sanders and Kruer were innocent of blowing up the plant and killing Don Strange. The most plausible alternative offered was Orpod Judd, because of his known tendency to set things afire. Even today, some say Sanders and Kruer are both still alive, and some say they're both dead. That particular story seemed like it might be proven true during my sophomore year of college, when a group of local cavers found a skeleton crouched inside a tiny anteroom in Marengo Cave, a skeleton that was presumed to be that of the long-lost Guthrie Kruer. It was carefully removed to the University of Louisville, where scientists determined that the small, brown bones belonged not to

Tom's cousin but to a one-thousand-year-old Hopewell Indian woman.

My father's rescue of me also became part of Borden mythology, and he was constantly invited to brag about his marksmanship, invitations he always politely declined. He never allowed pride in that remarkable shot to overcome the profound fear he had felt at that moment when he saw me in an ancient Welsh fort with a gun in my face. He and Mother carefully monitored me for signs of post-traumatic stress, but the pink, arrow-shaped mark on my neck appears to be the sole lasting scar of the episode. That, and I can't stand the smell of wood smoke, something that I guess is almost universally regarded as pleasant.

Reminders of the strike around town became rare. The hole in the back of the factory was repaired, and within a year the brown paint had faded and evened out to the point that no one could tell precisely where the breach had occurred. I'd see Russ Knable around town sometimes, when he wasn't working, and I'd have to fight the urge to stare at a face that seemed somehow misaligned. The Little League field where helicopters had taken off and landed the day after the explosion was renamed Strange Field. A brass plaque with Mr. Strange's name and lifespan was bolted to the dugout wall while two fidgety T-ball teams lined up along the baselines to pay their respects. Like most of the important things in Borden, the strike was rarely talked about because everybody already knew everything about it.

After high school, I determined that I would not be able to make a living using marksmanship, my sole natural talent. I got a degree in business instead, while Tom got a

good job at the factory, as mill room supervisor. We stayed closely in touch through college, hunting a couple of times a year, and fishing whenever we could. I sometimes asked him if he'd heard anything about Taffy, if she'd found her way back to Borden after her dad finally got put away. There was never a trace of her, not even a rumor.

Tom kept his promise. He never told me the details about the night he helped Guthrie Kruer escape, and he never told me if he knows where Kruer is right now. And I kept my promise. I never told anyone, not even my parents, what I knew about Kruer and Sanders. I've tried a few times to sort out in my mind the legal issues involved, harboring fugitives and lying to the police, just to start. In truth, I've never really worried about that part of it. I'll keep my secret because it's not really mine to give away. And because I know Tom has never doubted me for a moment.

The summer I graduated from IU, Tom married Shelly Stemler, and I was right up there at the front of St. Mary of the Knobs with him, the only person in the front half of the church, including the priest, who wasn't a blood relative of either the bride or groom. As the only non-Catholic in the bunch, I had to step awkwardly aside as the rest of the wedding party took communion. While I waited, I saw Don Strange's grave through the window, a stained-glass depiction of a suffering saint.

After college, I swapped my redneck for a trader's red jacket, and took a job at the Merc in Chicago, where I participated in huge, abstract financial transactions related vaguely to the price of milk. As a mental exercise, I try sometimes to calculate the effect my actions are having on

the shelves of Miller's General Store. I ride a train home at night to a condo that's pure big-city sophistication, without a Mason jar or lard bucket in sight, although my M6 is tucked deep inside my closet, in violation of a dozen gun laws, city and state. I just can't bring myself to get rid of the thing.

I've hung on to that kiss from Taffy as well, and the lingering feeling that we both were cheated out of something special. I still scan crowds for her, as my eye-rolling friends will attest, especially in bars where beer and seventies rock are both being served in overly generous quantities. It is not a completely insane notion. Lots of Indiana kids attracted to bright lights and skyscrapers end up in Chicago, and I have, once or twice, actually spotted other Borden expatriates walking down Rush Street, or in the bleachers at Wrigley. But I never see Taffy. I've tried to just be grateful for what I have, the photograph and the kiss. But I know now what I think Taffy completely realized at the time. It was a kiss good-bye.

A few times a year I make the long drive back from Chicago to Borden to see Mom and Dad, and Tom's growing family—he's up to four kids now. I like to drop by his place unannounced, so they don't make a big deal of getting the kids scrubbed clean and dressed up. I like walking over from my parents' house and just watching for a few seconds before they all spot me, the scruffy, shirtless boys shooting arrows into hay bales, the tomboy daughters trapping lizards in Mason jars. Tom always meets me on the front porch with a smile and a firm handshake, looking more like his dad every time I see him.

Shelly, like my mother, has a strict no-dead-animals-in-the-living-room policy, but a few reminders of those eventful days are still visible in their home. Tom keeps his dad's union card in a small frame right by his high school diploma. On the same wall is a picture of Tom and me together on our dirt bikes just before the strike, shirtless, smiling, and bushy-haired, the Borden Institute looming in the background. The most striking memento of that summer is proudly displayed over the fireplace, above a mantel crowded with framed photographs of sons and daughters in white celebrating the holy sacraments. On wrought-iron hooks, looking not at all out of place, hangs an ancient German sword.

Acknowledgments

I have thanked two friends in this section of all my previous books: Doug Bennett of New Albany, Indiana, and Professor Tom Buchanan, of the University of Tennessee at Chattanooga. In this case, I am especially grateful to Tom, for running around with me in the woods of southern Indiana when we were kids, for encouraging me always as a writer, and for on more than one occasion pulling me out of a cave.

Also, of course, thanks to my parents, Ken and Laura Tucker, two of the world's great readers, and my wife, Susie Tucker, for always having faith in me and this book.

A huge thanks to all the folks in the publishing business who helped see this through. Frank Scatoni and Jennifer de la Fuente of Venture Literary, for taking a chance on this book and helping it through the first few revisions. Most of all, thanks to Peter Wolverton of Thomas Dunne Books, who tirelessly worked with me to make this book better. I am lucky to have worked with you.

CONTENTS

CONTENTS

INTRODUCTION

Women have always done things. They have run businesses, faced danger, been creative and generally got up and gone out into the world since time began. Active, exciting, adventurous, working women are not new phenomena; women weren't just the helpmates of men, suddenly coming out of their shells after the Second World War. Since pre-history women have been a driving force in society. This quiz book is my attempt to show the wide diversity of things women have done. To put them back in their rightful place, at the forefront of the world.

The original idea for this quiz book came about while I was a teacher. As someone committed to promoting equal opportunities it became obvious that many books and worksheets I had available to me for use in the classroom made little or no reference to the achievements of women. I began to try to counteract this by developing my own materials. From this evolved almost an obsession to discover the practical and real contributions women have made in all aspects of life and at all times. This was not easy, but as my quest continued I moved away from simply producing classroom material to collecting and collating a huge amount of information about women. What to do with this collection was my next question. It was from here that the idea for *The Women's Quiz Book* emerged.

I then found as the quiz book progressed that, although I had lots of facts about women, it became more and more apparent that some women's achievements, if not hidden from history, are certainly well disguised. This is especially so for non-white and working-class women. The inevitable biases in the book reflect not only my own interests but the difficulty of unearthing material about certain groups of women. In addition, in order to give any readers who have been enthused—and wish to find out more about specific women's achievements–access to the facts, I have used as references only those books that are available in the local library. I have included an extensive bibliography at the end of this book as a useful starting point for the quest!

As knowledge about women seems to be kept secret most of the time it tends not to be generally part of society's frame of reference. I have, therefore, divided each quiz category into 'easier', 'medium' and 'hard', the placing of each question depending on my own general knowledge and the ease with which I could guess the answer (if it's not Newcastle, try Manchester!).

I hope you enjoy this book, and find it as stimulating as I did to find out how Dawn Fraser celebrated her swimming victory, who became the first black female millionaire, how the screen name of Joan Crawford was chosen, why Moll Cutpurse was such a good pickpocket, and the countless other trivial (and not so trivial) facts about famous (and not so famous) women.

Finally, my thanks to the many people who have helped in any way and offered their support–especially my partner David, whose proof-reading skills were put to good use, and my sister-in-law Judith, who valiantly came to my aid in the panic over the *Archers* questions.

HERSTORY QUIZ 1

1 Why did diarist Anne Frank (1930–45) have to hide during the Second World War?

2 What was Helen Sharman the first British person to do?

3 Whom did British theosophist Annie Besant help in 1888?

4 In the days when men were allowed to beat their wives, how thick a stick could they use?

5 In 18th-century Britain, what did Mary Read and Anne Bonny do for a living?

6 On her return from the Crimean War, for what did Florence Nightingale ask the British Government?

7 Why did four of the American delegates at the 1840 World's Anti-Slavery Convention have to sit behind a curtain?

8 In 1867, what did Britain's male teachers suggest authorities could reduce in order to be able to give them, the men, additional allowances?

9 After whom were the first trousers for women named?

10 Of which British religious movement was Catherine Booth the co-founder?

11 Why was Ida B. Wells forced to leave a first-class railway coach, in the US in 1884?

12 What did Britain's Elizabeth Fry want to reform?

13 What right did British women over 30 years old win in 1918?

14 What nationality was British Member of Parliament Nancy Astor?

15 Which British peace camp held its 10th anniversary on 5th September 1991?

1 HERSTORY ANSWERS

1 *She was a Jew*

2 *She was the first Briton to become a cosmonaut and go into space*

3 *The 'Bryant and May' Match Girls*

4 *No thicker than his own thumb*

5 *They were pirates*

6 *A training school for nurses*

7 *They were women*

8 *They suggested the salaries of school-mistresses should be reduced*

9 *American Amelia Bloomer*

10 *The Salvation Army*

11 *She was black*

12 *Prisons*

13 *The right to vote*

14 *American*

15 *Greenham Common Peace Camp*

1 In which year did divorce first become available to women in Britain?
2 What was the result of the first report of Britain's *Commission on the Employment of Children in Mines and Manufactories* in 1842?
3 What was the stated object of the Queen's College for Women, founded in London in the 19th century?
4 What did Member of Parliament Eric Forth wear around his neck during the House of Commons debate on Clare Short's so-called 'Page Three Bill' (anti-pornography in the tabloid press) in the late 1980s?
5 The statue of which First World War heroine faces London's National Portrait Gallery?
6 How did Britain's Women's Farming Union celebrate its 10th anniversary?
7 What sparked the revolution overthrowing the Russian Empire's monarchy?
8 In 1991, black women made up 2 per cent of the British population. What percentage of the prison population did they make up?
9 Whom did playwright Aphra Behn (1640–89) go to Antwerp to spy on during the Anglo-Dutch war?
10 What did British politician Linda Chalker lose on April 9th 1992?
11 In 1811 Hester Stanhope lost all her possessions in a shipwreck. What kind of clothes did she decide to wear for the rest of her life (spent in Syria)?
12 What did British women teachers and civil servants get in 1955?
13 How many years did Judith Ward spend in prison after being wrongly convicted of the IRA bombing on the M62 motorway?
14 How old was Native American Pocahontas in 1607 when she saved the life of Captain John Smith?
15 In 1992, which post in the British Cabinet was given to Member of Parliament Gillian Shephard?

1 HERSTORY ANSWERS

medium

1. *1857*
2. *All women and boys under 10 were forbidden from working underground*
3. *To teach 'all branches of female knowledge'*
4. *A topless female torso on a gold chain*
5. *Edith Cavell*
6. *With the production of a cookery book*
7. *The 1917 Women's Day march in Petersburg*
8. *24 per cent*
9. *British exiles*
10. *Her seat in the House of Commons*
11. *Men's clothes*
12. *Equal pay*
13. *18*
14. *10*
15. *Employment Secretary*

1 When did the 'Women in Black' begin their regular (every Wednesday) anti-war vigil in Belgrade, Serbia?

2 Who closed Maria Montessori's schools in 1934?

3 In the 19th century, what two reasons did employers give for being happy to employ women workers?

4 What did American Linda Essex find in 1993?

5 Of which armed service was American Reverend Alice M Henderson the first female chaplain?

6 In which year did Nancy Astor, Member of Parliament for Plymouth South, resign from Parliament?

7 Which Goddess is honoured in Rome each year on 1st March with the Feast of Matronalia?

8 What Chinese innovation is the Goddess of Thunder, Lei-zi, also credited with?

9 In which year was Britain's Sex Discrimination Act of 1975 updated?

10 In which year did Susan Lawrence become the first female chair of the British Labour Party?

11 Which 'first' can be claimed by Lady Tweedsmuir, in the House of Commons in 1949?

12 What gardening skill was Jane Loudon (1807–1858), gardener and writer, the first woman to tackle?

13 In 1928 Louisa Lumsden was awarded her Master of Arts degree in Classics from Cambridge University. In which year had she actually passed the exams?

14 In 1346, when the Scots attacked the English at the Battle of Neville's Cross, County Durham, who raised the army that defeated them?

15 Which hotel in Llangollen, North Wales was officially opened by Angela Rippon on 15th June 1987?

HERSTORY ANSWERS

1 *October 1991*

2 *Mussolini*

3 *Women were seen as cheap and docile*

4 *Her 23rd husband*

5 *The Army*

6 *1945*

7 *Juno*

8 *The breeding of silk worms*

9 *1986*

10 *1928*

11 *She was the first pregnant woman in the House*

12 *Pruning*

13 *1873*

14 *Philippa of Hainault*

15 *The Wishing Well Hotel*

BRITISH ENTERTAINMENT QUIZ 2

easier

1 In the 1950s and 1960s, who were children encouraged to watch TV with?

2 Which bar has Betty Turpin worked behind for over 22 years?

3 Which comedy duo consists of Sue Ryding and Maggie Fox?

4 What kind of 'ending' has the book (and film of the same name) by Joan Smith?

5 In 1992, 19,193 people changed Glenda Jackson's career. How?

6 Which British actress played Bobbie in the film version of *The Railway Children*?

7 Which television prison drama series starred Googie Withers?

8 Valerie Singleton was a presenter on which children's TV programme?

9 Which star of *After Henry* and guest at *Fawlty Towers* died in May 1992?

10 Vanessa Kirkpatrick presents which local TV news?

11 Who is not only an alternative comedian and but also the *Red Dwarf* computer?

12 Elizabeth and Shula are sisters in which radio soap?

13 Who starred as V. I. Warshawski in Radio 4's adaptation of *Killing Orders* by Sara Paretsky?

14 At the beginning of which children's programme would Julia Lang ask 'Are you sitting comfortably? Then I'll begin'?

15 In which children's TV programme would you find Ermintrude the cow?

BRITISH ENTERTAINMENT ANSWERS

1 Watch With Mother
2 *The Rovers Return, on* Coronation Street
3 *Lip Service*
4 *Masculine* (A Masculine Ending*)*
5 *They voted her in as a (Labour) Member of Parliament*
6 *Jenny Agutter*
7 Within These Walls
8 Blue Peter
9 *Joan Sanderson*
10 Granada News
11 *Hatty Haybridge*
12 The Archers
13 *Kathleen Turner*
14 Listen with Mother
15 The Magic Roundabout

1 For which regional television station did Wincey Willis begin reporting the weather in 1981?

2 Who became the first black woman Radio 1 DJ (in 1970)?

3 Who set up and fronted the first all-woman dance band?

4 On which American sitcom, created by Susan Harris, was the ITV sitcom *Brighton Belles* based?

5 What is the aim of the Clean Break Theatre Company?

6 Of which BBC crime-fighting series was Geraldine McClelland producer?

7 Which former Avenger now plays Laura in *The Upper Hand?*

8 Who toured Britain with *Margaret III, parts 2 and 3* in 1990?

9 For which two Second World War series was Jill Hyem a scriptwriter?

10 Which soap opera did Joanna Lumley appear in, as Elaine Perkins, in July 1973?

11 For which long-running Radio 4 soap is Vanessa Whitburn the producer?

12 Which *Second Thoughts* actress also stars in the BBC sitcom *2 Point 4 Children*?

13 Of which BBC consumer affairs programme did Anne Robinson take over as presenter in September 1993?

14 Which ITV soap, set in the countryside, is produced by Morag Bain?

15 Who played Mrs de Winter in the 1940 stage version of Daphne Du Maurier's book, *Rebecca*?

BRITISH ENTERTAINMENT ANSWERS

1. *Tyne Tees Television*
2. *The Rankin' Miss P*
3. *Ivy Benson (1913–93)*
4. The Golden Girls
5. *To take theatre into prisons*
6. Crimewatch UK
7. *Honor Blackman*
8. *Lip Service*
9. Tenko *and* Wish me Luck
10. Coronation Street
11. The Archers
12. *Belinda Lang*
13. Watchdog
14. Emmerdale
15. *Dame Celia Johnson*

1 What reason did Lynsey de Paul give for revealing the details of her affair with Sean Connery to a Sunday paper in 1993?

2 Of what movement in the theatre was Annie Horniman a founder?

3 What was the documentary *Women Like Us* about?

4 Where did the Amber Film workshop make their film about the lives of Estate women in 1991?

5 When Sarah Siddons (1755–1831) played the part of Lady Macbeth for the first time in 1785, how long before the first night did she start learning her lines?

6 What was Audrey Russell (1907–89) the first woman to be employed as, by the BBC Radio Newsreel during the Second World War?

7 What was unusual about the Royal Victoria Coffee and Music Hall, opened by Emma Cons in 1880?

8 Which theatre in Manchester was founded by Annie Horniman?

9 What did the BBC do with the three-minute version of *Beatrix Potter's Peter Rabbit*, by the comedy duo Lip Service, which was played on Radio 2's *Pick of the Week*?

10 Who played the lead role in *When I was a girl I used to scream and shout* when it was first on in the West End?

11 Which British actress played the mother of the children in the Bette Davis film *Nanny*?

12 Which service is portrayed in the Second World War film *The Gentle Sex* (1943)?

13 Which regular *Watch with Mother* programme was written by Louise Cochrane and produced by Freda Lingstrom?

14 What was the stage name of Irish ballerina Edris Stannus (b. 1898)?

15 What did Gillian Taylforth train as before becoming an actress?

1. *She objected to him saying that any woman should, or could, ever deserve a slap in the face*
2. *Repertory*
3. *Older lesbians*
4. *Meadowell Estate, North Shields*
5. *The night before*
6. *War correspondent*
7. *It did not sell alcoholic drinks*
8. *Gaiety Theatre*
9. *They burned the tape*
10. *Geraldine McKenna*
11. *Wendy Craig*
12. *ATS (Auxiliary Territorial Service)*
13. Rag, Tag and Bobtail
14. *Ninette de Valois*
15. *Secretary*

1 What is the title of the only published work by author Anna Sewell (1820–78)?

2 Who was the youngest Brontë sister, born in 1820?

3 Which book by Maggie Redding was published in Britain in 1984 and featured the character Daffodil Mulligan?

4 Whose first novel, later made into a film in Britain, was entitled *Union Street* and was published in 1982?

5 During the 1870s and 1880s, of which art movement was Marie Spartalia (1843–1927) an adherent?

6 Who is the detective in *She Came Too Late* and *She Came in a Flash* by Mary Wings?

7 Under which other name does novelist Catherine Cookson write?

8 Which novel by Anita Brookner tells the story of Edith Hope, author of romantic novels, on her exile to Lake Geneva?

9 Which radical women's magazine issued its first edition in July 1972 and its last in March 1993?

10 Which New Zealand-born writer of detective novels founded the British Commonwealth Theatre Company in 1950?

11 Who wrote *Orlando* (1928)?

12 What is the title of the first book written by Germaine Greer, published in 1970?

13 Which British writer and illustrator of children's books lived at Hill Top Farm, Sawery, Cumbria (Lake District)?

14 On what subject is Emily Post (1873–1960) most well remembered for writing about?

15 On which poem by Christina Rossetti did artist Margaret Agnes Pope base the design and creation of a stained glass window in 1905?

1 Black Beauty (The Autobiography of a Horse, Translated from the Original Equine) *(1877)*

2 *Anne*

3 The Life and Times of Daffodil Mulligan

4 *Pat Barker*

5 *Pre-Raphaelite Movement*

6 *Emma Victor*

7 *Catherine Marchant*

8 Hotel du Lac *(1985)*

9 Spare Rib

10 *Ngaio Marsh (1899–1982)*

11 *Virginia Woolf*

12 The Female Eunuch

13 *Beatrix Potter*

14 *Etiquette*

15 'Goblin Market'

1 What was the family relationship between novelists Edith Somerville (1858–1949) and Violet Martin (1862–1915), who wrote and illustrated *Some Experiences of an Irish RM* (1899) and other books together?

2 Which literary competition did novelist, poet and short story writer Muriel Spark (b. 1918) win in 1951?

3 On which Brontë sister was the character Helen Burns in Jane Eyre (written by Charlotte Brontë) based?

4 What is the book *The Yellow Wallpaper* (1892) a description of?

5 What working title did Jane Austen use for the book that was published as *Sense and Sensibility*?

6 Which New Zealand author's three-volume autobiography was made into a film entitled *Angel at My Table*?

7 In which famous London cemetery was poet Christina Rossetti buried in 1894?

8 In the 19th century, what were female students at London's Royal Academy of Art schools not allowed to draw?

9 Who wrote *The Color Purple*?

10 In what year is *Bodies of Glass* , written by Marge Piercy, set?

11 Which 20th-century American artist lived at Ghost Ranch, near Abiquiu?

12 What was the pseudonym of author Mary Ann Evans (1819–80)?

13 What sex did Simone de Beauvoir write about?

14 Wendy Henry became editor of Britain's *News of the World* in 1987. On which British tabloid paper did she work before this?

15 Under what name does Professor of English at Columbia University, Carolyn G. Heilbrun, write her detective novels featuring Kate Fansler?

3 LITERATURE & ART ANSWERS

medium

1 *They were (second) cousins*

2 *The* Observer *Short Story Prize*

3 *Maria Brontë*

4 *A woman's mental breakdown*

5 Elinor and Marianne

6 *Janet Frame*

7 *Highgate Cemetery*

8 *A nude human body*

9 *Alice Walker*

10 2061

11 *Georgia O'Keeffe*

12 *George Eliot*

13 The Second Sex

14 *The* Sun

15 *Amanda Cross*

1 For how long did the brother of Palestinian poet Fadwa Tuqan condemn her to stay inside the family home as a punishment for having had a romance?

2 Who wrote *The Vindication of the Rights of Women* in 1792?

3 What kind of writer was Englishwoman Julian of Norwich?

4 Of which art movement was Eleanor F. Brickdale a well-known member?

5 Which writing technique did May Sinclair (1863–1946) explore and develop?

6 Julia Margaret Cameron was a prolific artist. In which medium?

7 In which year did male grammarians of the time get an Act of British Parliament passed which legally insisted 'he' should stand for 'she'?

8 What is the subject of playwright, poet and novelist Aphra Behn's (1640–89) poem *'The Disappointment'*?

9 Who said 'to be a woman is a rather splendid thing'?

10 Which American hymn was written by Julia Ward Howe in 1861?

11 Who won the Pulitzer Prize in 1950 for her book of poems entitled *Annie Allen*?

12 Where can you find the two stone heads representing Isis and Thames, sculpted by Ann Damer in 1785?

13 What is the title of Dorothy Bryant's only mystery novel starring Jessie Posey?

14 What kind of artist was Mary Edmonia Lewis (1846–1890), creator of the works *Death of Cleopatra* and *Forever Free*?

15 How does Mrs Huntingdon (in *The Tenant of Wildfell Hall* by Ann Brontë) earn her living?

LITERATURE & ART ANSWERS

1 *For the rest of her life*
2 *Mary Wollstonecraft*
3 *A spiritual writer*
4 *Pre-Raphaelite movement*
5 *The stream-of-consciousness technique*
6 *Photography*
7 *1850*
8 *Male impotence*
9 *(Novelist and short story writer) Naomi Mitchison*
10 'Battle Hymn of the [American] Republic'
11 *Gwendolyn Brooks (b. 1917)*
12 *Henley Bridge, London*
13 Killing Wonder
14 *Sculptor*
15 *As a landscape painter*

1 What were Britain's Oldham Blues and Lancaster Belles?

2 Which is the most popular indoor sport for women?

3 What did Sonam Sherpa train as in Nepal?

4 Charlotte Dod won the British Open Amateur in 1904. What sport was she champion of before taking up golf?

5 Which Channel was New Yorker Gertrude Ederle the first woman to swim, on 6th August 1926?

6 Who was considered the first female tennis star?

7 In the 19th century, who was the first white woman to climb Mount Cameroon, Africa?

8 What sporting 'delivery' is Christina Willes usually credited with having invented in 1807?

9 In support of which issue did Billie Jean King call for a boycott of professional tennis tournaments in 1970? NAS 1996

10 Where was Naomi James (b. 1949) the first woman to sail, on her own, in 1977?

11 In which combat sport did Jane Bridge become the first British World Champion in 1980?

12 When Fay Taylour (1908–1983) won the Australian Speedway Championship in 1929, being the first British person to do so, was she competing against men or women?

13 In the 19th century, what did Catherine Beecher suggest was the best form of exercise?

14 Which famous American basketball team hired Lynette Woodward in 1985?

15 What is the name of Britain's only 'fanzine' dedicated to women's soccer?

SPORTS ANSWERS

1 *Women's soccer teams*

2 *Swimming*

3 *A mountain-trekking guide*

4 *Tennis*

5 *The English Channel*

6 *Blanche Bingley*

7 *Mary Kingsley*

8 *Round-arm bowling (in cricket)*

9 *The difference between men's and women's prize money (women got less)*

10 *Around the world*

11 *Judo*

12 *The top men*

13 *Housework*

14 *The Harlem Globetrotters*

15 *Born Kicking*

1 Why was polo player Eleanor Sears sent off the field in 1909?

2 What was the title of the first British magazine devoted entirely to women's sports, published in 1901?

3 For which event did parachutist Jackie Smith (b. 1952) win a gold medal at the World Parachuting Championships at Zagreb with an unbeaten score of 10 out of 10?

4 Which ball game association did Audrey Beaton form for women in 1912?

5 When was the last time two British women met in the finals at Wimbledon?

6 What reason was given for women being supposedly unsuccessful at National Hunt racing?

7 Tennis star Elizabeth Ryan won 19 titles at Wimbledon. Which title did she never win?

8 Which former Wimbledon Ladies' Singles Champion presented Martina Navratilova with her Ladies' Singles Trophy in 1986?

9 In May 1993 Rebecca Stevens became the first British woman to climb to the top of Everest. When asked what kept her going, what was her reply?

10 Where was the Inaugural Women's Rugby World Cup held, in April 1991?

11 In the 1950s/60s, who was considered the fastest women's sprinter of all time?

12 In the 1933 British Golf Championship, how many clubs did Gloria Minoprio use?

13 In 18th-century England, Elizabeth Stokes excelled at which sport?

14 At what age did tennis champion Charlotte Dod win her first championship?

15 What was aviator Amelia Earhart's first aeroplane?

4 SPORTS ANSWERS

medium

1 *For wearing trousers*
2 Hockey Field
3 *The accuracy event*
4 *Ladies Lacrosse Association*
5 *1961*
6 *Their bottoms were 'the wrong shape'*
7 *The Ladies' Singles Championship*
8 *Kitty Godfree*
9 *'I didn't want to go back and have to do it again'*
10 *Cardiff, Wales*
11 *Wilma Rudolph*
12 *One (a cleek)*
13 *Boxing*
14 *15*
15 *A Kinner Canary*

1 Who owned the 1992 Grand National Winner Party Politics?

2 Why did the British National Women's Water Polo team have to pull out of the 1989 European Championship?

3 Who won Britain's first Women's Golf Championship in 1893?

4 Why were Spartan girls encouraged to take part in sports?

5 Which American won the Ladies' Singles Championship at Wimbledon in both 1957 and 1958?

6 Whom did female golfer Cecil Leitch beat at golf in 1910?

7 On 11th July 1788, who scored the first recorded century in cricket?

8 What was broadsword contestant Etta Hattan (stage name Jaguarina) billed as in the 19th century?

9 In what year was the All-England Women's Field Hockey Association formed?

10 Maud Watson won the first National Tennis Championships for Women at Wimbledon. How many more times did she win this competition?

11 Who became the first woman to swim 100 metres in less than one minute, in 1962?

12 In the middle of the 1986 bicycle race across the United States (3,107 miles), defending champion Sue Notorangelo paused. Why?

13 In which year did a Japanese woman, Junko Tabei, and a Tibetan woman, Phantong, reach the top of Everest via different routes?

14 20th-century aviator Bessie Coleman was born in America. Which country did she have to move to in order to learn to fly?

15 What was the prize won by Maud Watson, winner of the very first Ladies' Championship at Wimbledon in 1884?

SPORTS ANSWERS

1 *Patricia Thompson*
2 *Their grant from the Amateur Swimming Association had been cut*
3 *Lady Margaret Scott*
4 *To make them healthy mothers*
5 *Althea Gibson*
6 *Harold Hilton, former British Open Champion*
7 *Miss S. Norcross*
8 Ideal Amazon of the Age
9 *1895*
10 *Once, in 1885*
11 *Dawn Fraser*
12 *To save the life of an injured cameraman*
13 *1975*
14 *France*
15 *A silver flower basket (worth 20 guineas)*

1 In 1919 Nancy Astor became the second woman to be voted in as a Member of Parliament. What was she the first woman MP to do?

2 What was the original meaning of the word 'brewster'?

3 In which month is International Women's Week held each year?

4 How many women were included in the British Parliamentary Cabinet of 1992?

5 Who was Queen of Iceni in AD 60?

6 In 1989, 75 per cent of the UK's teachers were female. What percentage of these women were headteachers?

7 How did Betty Boothroyd make British history on 27th April 1992?

8 Which Queen had the motto *Semper Eadem* (Ever the Same)?

9 Which 'railroad' was former slave Harriet Tubman a 'conductor' on?

10 What did Winnie Mandela train as?

11 Under the UK's 1937 Factory Act, what was the maximum number of hours a woman could work in a week?

12 Which subject made Queen Victoria so furious she could not contain herself?

13 Of which British political party is Betty Boothroyd a member?

14 Who was Parthenope Nightingale's sister?

15 In 1894, women in South Australia and which other country were granted the vote?

HERSTORY ANSWERS

1 *Take her seat in the House of Commons (Constance Markiewicz was the first woman MP, but declined to take up her seat in the House)*

2 *A female brewer*

3 *March*

4 *Two: Gillian Shephard and Virginia Bottomley*

5 *Boudicca (Boadicea)*

6 *15 per cent*

7 *She became first female Speaker (moderator) in the House of Commons*

8 *Queen Elizabeth I*

9 *The Underground Railroad*

10 *A social worker*

11 *48 hours*

12 *Women's rights*

13 *The Labour Party*

14 *Florence Nightingale*

15 *New Zealand*

1 In 1992, which Member of Parliament became health secretary?

2 At the Earth Summit in Rio de Janiero (1992), who did Jane Fonda say should have more power so that the world would be a better place?

3 In the British Census of 1921, what percentage of professional women workers were either teachers or nurses?

4 What was the name of the space shuttle in which astronaut Sally Ride blasted off into space in June 1983?

5 In 19th-century America (Canterbury, Connecticut), what happened to Prudence Crandall when she opened a 'school for Negro girls'?

6 Which constituency voted Nancy Astor (1879–1964) in as their Member of Parliament in 1919?

7 Which theatre in Stratford-upon-Avon was designed by architect Elisabeth Scott (1898–1972) in 1927/28?

8 Which 19th-century fossil collector became such a tourist attraction that, on her death, her home town of Lyme Regis suffered financially?

9 What was Betty Keyser the only British woman to be employed as during the Second World War?

10 Which London employment bureau was started by Margery Hurst soon after the Second World War?

11 What did the London Society for Women's Suffrage change its name to in 1953?

12 In which country did Henrietta Dugdale (1826–1918) campaign for the vote and rights for women?

13 Whose profile was on the 1979 U.S. dollar coin?

14 In which African country was Sylvia Pankhurst (1882–1960) living when she died?

15 In 1993, out of 1,247 academic staff at Oxford University, how many were women?

HERSTORY ANSWERS

1 *Virginia Bottomley*

2 *Women*

3 *86 per cent*

4 *Challenger*

5 *She was arrested*

6 *Plymouth South*

7 *The new Shakespeare Theatre*

8 *Mary Anning (1799–1847)*

9 *Off-shore welder*

10 *Brook Street Bureau*

11 *Fawcett Society*

12 *Australia*

13 *Susan B. Anthony (1820–1906)*

14 *Ethiopia*

15 *176*

1 What was Labour Member of Parliament Helene Hayman the first woman to do in the House of Commons in 1976?

2 In which British northeastern town did one of the founders of the Salvation Army, Catherine Bramwell Booth, preach her first sermon?

3 On the streets of which city do the 'Women in Black' keep their anti-war vigil?

4 In 1975, Yvonne Pope became the first British woman to captain an airline flight crew. With which airline?

5 In 1209 when Agnes, referred to as 'Wife of Odo', was accused of witchcraft, in her trial by ordeal (which she survived) what was she forced to hold in her hand?

6 What does the American acronym WHISPER stand for?

7 What rights did Britain's *Infant's Custody Act* of 1839 give divorced mothers?

8 How old was Margery Newall Robb, survivor of the Titanic disaster, when she died in June 1992?

9 What did a series of Lectures for Ladies given in London in 1847 result in?

10 Which subject did Sophia Jex Black lecture in at London's Queen's College (1858)?

11 Which group of women workers staged the first strike ever to be held in Japan (in 1886)?

12 Who was proclaimed the Patron Saint of Spain in 1814?

13 During the Second World War, for how long did British Agent Violette Szabo, acting alone, keep over 400 German soldiers pinned down?

14 Why was Australian Grace Bussell (1860–1935) awarded the Royal Humane Society Medal for Bravery?

15 In 7th-century Africa, Yamina of Byzantine was captured in battle. How did she escape the usual fate of prisoners (to be made a slave)?

1 *Breastfeed her baby*

2 *Gateshead*

3 *Belgrade, Serbia*

4 *Dan Air*

5 *A red-hot iron*

6 *Women Hurt In Systems of Prostitution Engaged in Revolt*

7 *If they had not committed adultery they could have custody of their children under seven, with the right to access of their elder children at stated hours*

8 *103*

9 *The founding of Queen's College for Women, in London*

10 *Mathematics*

11 *Female silk workers*

12 *Teresa Cepeda*

13 *Two hours*

14 *For rescuing passengers from a sinking ship, in 1876*

15 *She deliberately leapt off her camel, breaking her neck*

ENTERTAINMENT QUIZ 6

1. Of whom did Dorothy Parker say, 'She ran the whole gamut of emotions from A to B'?
2 Whom (besides herself) does Sophia Loren play in the film *Sophia: Living and Loving*?
3 Who were the two stars of *Whatever Happened to Baby Jane* (1962)?
4 What did Grace Kelly 'dial for murder' in 1954?
5 On which Australian soap was Kylie Minogue a regular before changing her career?
6 In which Disney movie did the star of *Murder She Wrote*, Angela Lansbury, have a leading part?
7 Which 1931 film made Marlene Dietrich a star?
8 In which 1992 film does k.d. lang play a woman pretending to be a young man, called Kotz?
9 In the 1930s which actress said, 'It's hard to be funny when you have to be clean'?
10 Whom did film director Euzhan Palcy say women had more guts than?
11 In 1940, which film adaptation of a Daphne de Maurier book starred Joan Fontaine as the second wife?
12 Which British Queen does Bette Davis portray in *The Virgin Queen* (1955)?
13 What are the names of the four '*Golden Girls*'?
14 In early film making days, why did actresses who also directed refuse to be credited for their directing?
15 Who was the director of *Desperately Seeking Susan* (1985)?

1 *Katharine Hepburn*

2 *Her own mother*

3 *Bette Davis and Joan Crawford*

4 M (Dial M for Murder)

5 Neighbours

6 Bedknobs and Broomsticks

7 The Blue Angel

8 Salmonberries

9 *Mae West*

10 *Men*

11 Rebecca

12 *Elizabeth I*

13 *Rose, Dorothy, Blanche and Sophia*

14 *It would alienate the box office*

15 *Susan Seidelman*

1 In which Australian soap about a country hospital does Joyce Jacobs play Esmee Watson?

2 Which film starred the actresses Sally Field, Julia Roberts, Shirley McLaine, Olympia Dukakis, Daryl Hannah and Dolly Parton?

3 How did Joan Crawford get her high cheekbones?

4 Which 1960 Disney movie starred Hayley Mills?

5 Who played the pregnant heroine in *Rosemary's Baby* (1968)?

6 Who played *The French Lieutenant's Woman* in 1981? B1D

7 Who was the character played by actress Janine Turner in the TV series based in Alaska, *Northern Exposure*?

8 Who played Iris in the 1989 film of a Pat Barker novel, *Stanley and Iris*?

9 What was the title of k.d. lang's video, following her career over seven years, released in 1992?

10 Who starred with Ginger Rogers in the 1937 film *Stage Door*?

11 Which American comedy about women living together in Florida was created by Susan Harris?

12 In the 1916 film *God's Country and the Woman*, which three roles (in front of and behind the camera) were filled by Nell Shipman (1892–1970)?

13 Which English film actress was born in Brussels in 1929, and named Edda Hepburn van Heemshra?

14 Which famous actress, born in Puerto Rico, was christened Rosita Dolores Alverio?

15 Which film released in 1926 was based on an original story written by Adela Rogers St Johns, had a screenplay by Dorothy Arzner and was produced by Dorothy Davenport Reid?

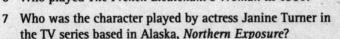

1 A Country Practice

2 Steel Magnolias

3 *By using make-up*

4 Pollyanna

5 *Mia Farrow*

6 *Meryl Streep*

7 *Maggie, a pilot in the air courier service*

8 *Jane Fonda*

9 The Harvest of Seven Years

10 *Katharine Hepburn*

11 Golden Girls

12 *Producer, director and actress*

13 *Audrey Hepburn*

14 *Rita Moreno*

15 The Red Kimono

1 Euzhan Palcy works in films. What as?

2 When Marilyn Monroe changed her name from Norma Jean Mortensen, where did she get Monroe from?

3 In 1934 how much was screenwriter Dorothy Parker paid a week by MGM?

4 How old was Ruth Gordon (1896–1985) when she won an Oscar for her role in *Rosemary's Baby*?

5 What kind of troupe did stuntwoman Helen Thurston (b. 1916) join when she was 16?

6 Anita Loos (1893–1981) wrote 105 film scripts between 1912 and 1915. How many were not made into films?

7 Which 1933 play, written by Zoë Akins, won Katharine Hepburn her first Academy Award in 1933?

8 In 1929 Elinor Glyn (1864–1943) directed the first talkie What was its title?

9 Who describes herself as 'one of the first women to do everything; write, sing, play, produce'?

10 In which psychological thriller does Goldie Hawn not play a scatty blonde?

11 How did Ann Turner make enough extra money to make her first feature film *Celia*?

12 Which film directed by Xavier Koller won the Academy Award for best foreign film in 1991?

13 Who was the first 'constructed' Hollywood star?

14 Where is *Brezhnev's Children* by Olwen Wymark set?

15 Who are the subjects of Derrah Cloud's play *The Stick Wife*?

1 *A director*

2 *It was her grandmother's married name*

3 *$5,200*

4 72

5 *A travelling acrobatic troupe*

6 *Four*

7 Morning Glory

8 Knowing Men

9 *Danielle Dax*

10 Deceived

11 *By filming horse races*

12 Journey of Hope

13 *Theda Bara*

14 *In a Soviet maternity ward*

15 *Wives of members of the Ku Klux Klan*

1 *A Pin to See the Peepshow* by F. Tennyson Jesse was originally published in 1934. Which publishing company republished it in 1979?

2 Whose lamb did Mrs Sarah Joseph Hale write a poem about?

3 Who was described by Virginia Woolf as 'the inventor of the female sentence'?

4 Where was Fanny Price brought up?

5 Who wrote *Frankenstein, or The Modern Prometheus*?

6 In *The Yellow Wallpaper* (1892), by Charlotte Perkins Gilman, what was nailed securely to the floor?

7 What other, more famous name, did British children's author Mary Pollock write under?

8 In which Agatha Christie mystery does Miss Jane Marple get Lucy Eyslebarrow to do the legwork for her?

9 Who wrote the poem *'Goblin Market'* in 1862?

10 What is the title of the sequel to Sherry Ashworth's novel *A Matter of Fat*?

11 In 1977, who created private-eye Sharon McCone of San Francisco?

12 Who were Acton, Currer and Ellis Bell?

13 What is the title of the anti-slavery novel written by Aphra Behn (1640–89) and published in 1688?

14 In 1863, on what issue was a vote taken and passed by London's Royal Academy of Arts?

15 Who wrote *The Diary of Anne Frank*?

LITERATURE & ART ANSWERS

1 *Virago Press Limited*
2 'Mary's little lamb'
3 *Dorothy Richardson*
4 *Mansfield Park*
5 *Mary Shelley*
6 *The bed*
7 *Enid Blyton*
8 4.50 from Paddington
9 *Christina Rossetti (1830–94)*
10 Personal Growth
11 *Marcia Muller*
12 *Anne, Charlotte and Emily Brontë*
13 Oronooko
14 *That women were no longer to be admitted to the Academy*
15 *Anne Frank*

1 Under what pseudonym did Marion Milner, writer and psychoanalyst, publish her autobiography *A Life of One's Own* in 1934?

2 In which prison is the woman in Nawal El Saadawi's novel *Woman at Point Zero* imprisoned?

3 In which year did Barbara Hepworth (1903–1975) hold her first one-woman exhibition?

4 About which subject was the first British film with an all-woman crew, *Betteshanger*?

5 Where were novelists Edith Somerville (1858–1949) and Violet Martin (1862–1915) educated?

6 Novelist and poet Stevie Smith (1902–71) wrote in her spare time. What was her regular paid job?

7 What part of Britain's northwest is represented in most of Sheila Fell's (1931–1979) paintings?

8 Who wrote *Lark Rise to Candleford*, published in 1938?

9 Whose two-volume autobiography is entitled *The Tamarisk Tree*?

10 What is the name of the Dame Elisabeth Frink sculpture in Paternoster Square, London?

11 In which country was African-American poet and former slave Phillis Wheatley (1753–84) born?

12 In which area did 19th-century artist Fanny Corbaux achieve great success, both monetarily and artistically?

13 In her first post as a governess, what action by Anne Brontë resulted in her being sacked?

14 For which British national broadsheet newspaper did Flora Shaw (1852–1929) become the first female foreign correspondent in 1892?

15 Which 19th-century pickpocket and receiver of stolen goods did Ellen Galford write the 'true history of', in 1984?

1 *Joanna Field*

2 *Qanatir Prison (the prison Nawal El Saadawi herself was imprisoned in, in 1981)*

3 *1928*

4 *The organization of miners' wives during the strike of 1972*

5 *Alexandra College, Dublin*

6 *She worked as a secretary for a firm of magazine publishers*

7 *Cumbria*

8 *Flora Thompson*

9 *Dora Russell's*

10 Shepherd with Three Lambs

11 *Senegal, West Africa*

12 *Portrait painting*

13 *She tied two of the children she was governess for to the leg of a table while she got on with her work*

14 The Times

15 Moll Cutpurse: Her True History

1 What is the title of the first-known autobiography, written by Margery Kempe (c.1373–1438) in approximately 1431–1438?
2 In which magazine did the first 'lonely hearts' column appear in 1798?
3 In 1940, aged 77, which African-American fighter against racism and sexism wrote her autobiography, calling it *A Colored Woman in a White World*?
4 What is the title of the only novel by African-American poet and political activist Frances Harper (1825–1911), written in 1892?
5 On whose life story is the novel *Jubilee* (1966) by African-American author Margaret Walker (b. 1915) based?
6 In which year did *The Female Spectator*–the first magazine edited by a woman (Eliza Haywood, c.1693–1756), for women–appear?
7 How long did it take Mary Wollstonecraft (1759–97) to write her book *The Vindication of the Rights of Woman*?
8 Which American University did writer Toni Morrison (b. 1931) graduate from in 1953?
9 What is the title of author Alice Walker's (b. 1944) first novel, published in 1970?
10 Which war is represented in the painting *The Roll Call* by Elizabeth Thompson?
11 For which British national and Northern broadsheet newspaper did Caroline Lejeune (1897–1973), the first woman film critic, write her reviews?
12 In which year was African-American poet Phillis Wheatley's (1753–84) first poem published?
13 Which British public collection of artwork contains the highest proportion of work by women artists?
14 Why did poet and playwright Margaret Cavendish, Duchess of Newcastle (1623–74), go to France in 1645?
15 Which two women artists were among the founder members of the British Royal Academy in 1768?

LITERATURE & ART ANSWERS

1 The Boke of Margery Kempe
2 Ladies' Monthly Museum
3 *Mary Church Terrell (1863–1954)*
4 Iola Leroy
5 *Her grandmother's*
6 *1745*
7 *6 weeks*
8 *Howard University, Washington, DC*
9 The Third Life of Grange Copeland
10 *The Crimean War*
11 The Manchester Guardian
12 *1770*
13 *The National Portrait Gallery*
14 *As Maid of Honour to Queen Henrietta Maria she followed her when she went into exile*
15 *Angelica Kauffmann and Mary Moser*

1 In which year did the British Football Association allow girls under 12 to play on school football (soccer) teams?

2 On 19 August 1993, in Stuttgart, for which track and field event did Britain's Sally Gunnell win a gold medal and at the same time set a new world record of 52.74 seconds?

3 In the 1976 transatlantic yacht race, who finished 13th overall?

4 Alison Fisher and Stacey Hillyard are British champions of which indoor sport?

5 Which sport was featured in the comic strip *Bess of Blacktown*?

6 In 1892, Lady Margaret Scott entered a Golf Championship at Cheltenham and won. Which sex were all her opponents?

7 In ancient Greece, who took part in the athletic festivals, called *Heraia*, at Olympia?

8 In 1805 an Englishwoman called Alicia raced against Francis Buckle, a professional jockey. Alicia rode side-saddle. Who won?

9 In 1985 the BBC television sports round-up of the year lasted 90 minutes. To the nearest five minutes, how long was given to coverage of sportswomen?

10 What was Amelia Earhart the first woman to do, in 1928?

11 When Californian Penny Dean set the record for swimming the English Channel on 29th July 1978, from which British port did she set off?

12 At the European Cup in 1967, why was Polish sprinter Eva Klobukowska stripped of her Olympic and other athletic medals?

13 How is Artemis, Greek Goddess of the Moon, represented in ancient art and literature?

14 Who was the first woman in the world to throw her javelin more than 250 feet?

15 What kind of horse races did Bilistiche of Magnesia win twice in the 3rd century BC at Oxrhynchus?

SPORTS ANSWERS

1 *1991*

2 *400 metres hurdles*

3 *Clare Francis*

4 *Snooker*

5 *Women's football (soccer)*

6 *Male*

7 *Young women*

8 *Alicia*

9 *3 minutes 45 seconds*

10 *Fly the Atlantic—as a passenger (and log-keeper)!*

11 *Dover*

12 *A sex test purported to reveal that she was not a woman*

13 *As a huntress*

14 *Fatima Whitbread*

15 *Four-horse chariot races*

1 When Amelia Earhart decided to pilot her own plane across the Atlantic in 1932, she hoped to land in France (Paris). In which country did she actually land? N N

2 Why did the German Bishops cancel a women's gymnastics festival in Neuburg an der Donau in 1927?

3 By 1987, how many Wimbledon titles had Billie Jean King won altogether?

4 When Gertrude Ederle swam the English Channel in 1926 she swam to Dover. From which French port did she set out?

5 What was Gertrude Bacon the first woman to do, in 1898?

6 In 1882 who partnered Lottie Dod and went on with her to win the Ladies' Doubles (tennis) Championship at the Northern Tournament in Manchester?

7 Which ball sport did Catherine of Aragon and Mary Queen of Scots both like to play?

8 In 1966, whom did Billie Jean King beat to win her first Wimbledon Singles title?

9 In which year was Britain's Women's Football Association formed?

10 What kind of plane was Lady Mary Bailey (1890–1960) the first woman to fly?

11 Who was the first female captain of a vessel in the Whitbread Round the World Event?

12 Who was the first American to win the British Women's Golf title?

13 Who owned 'Scorched Earth', the horse ridden by Muriel Tufnell at Britain's Kempton Park (who became the first female jockey officially to win a race)?

14 In 1988 Annie Bassett became the UK's first female General Manager of a football league team. Which team?

15 What kind of race did motor-racing champion Desiré Wilson become the first woman to win in 1980?

SPORTS ANSWERS

1 *Ireland*

2 *They feared male spectators might be present*

3 *20*

4 *Cap Gris-Nez*

5 *Make an ascent in a hot-air balloon*

6 *Her sister Ann*

7 *Golf*

8 *Maria Bueno*

9 *1969*

10 *A glider*

11 *Clare Francis (b. 1946)*

12 *Mildred 'Babe' (Zaharias) Didrikson*

13 *Her mother*

14 *Reading AFC*

15 *A Formula One race*

1 Which sport was Britain's Joyce Wethered a champion of?
2 From which country did the female gladiators at the games staged by Emperor Nero in AD 66 come from?
3 What did Ann Field, of Stoke Newington, London, challenge Elizabeth Stokes to in 1728?
4 How many consecutive national Singles titles did Ora Washington, star of the US All-Black Tennis Association, win between 1929 and 1935?
5 To whom did Amelia Earhart lose her altitude record?
6 How did Dawn Fraser celebrate being the first woman to swim 100 metres in less than one minute?
7 Why did American surgeon Piro Kramer decide to turn back as she was just about to reach the summit of Annapurna in 1978?
8 Who is the only athlete in history to hold the 5,000 metres, 10,000 metres, half-marathon and marathon world records simultaneously?
9 At the summit of which mountain in Peru did American climber Annie Peck plant a 'Votes for Women' sign in 1911?
10 In which year did the first recorded women's cricket match take place in Britain?
11 In 1967 women were still not officially allowed to enter for the Boston Marathon. How was Katherine Switzer able to enter the race officially that year and be given the number 261?
12 In 1982 England and Sweden reached the finals of the UEFA (United European Football Association) Cup for women. Who won the match?
13 What was British motor-racing champion Dorothy Levitt's top speed when she won the Brighton Sweepstake in 1905?
14 Which British tennis champion was runner-up in the 1957 table tennis World Championship?
15 What was the name of the first British rock-climbing club for women, set up in 1921 by Pat Kelly?

SPORTS ANSWERS

1 *Golf*

2 *Ethiopia*

3 *A boxing match*

4 *Seven*

5 *Ruth Nicholas*

6 *By getting drunk*

7 *She had frostbite in her (index) finger*

8 *Ingrid Kristiansen (of Norway)*

9 *Mount Coropuna*

10 *1745, on Gosden Common, near Guildford, England*

11 *She applied as K. Switzer and the organizers assumed she was a man*

12 *Sweden*

13 *79.75 mph*

14 *Ann Jones*

15 *The Pinnacle Club*

1 What do the initials EOC stand for?

2 In 1917, Madame C. J. Walker was part of a group visiting the White House to petition President Woodrow Wilson. What was the petition about?

3 Why did Deborah Sampson dress up as a man in 1782?

4 What have Sara Thornton, Kiranjit Ahluwalia and Amelia Rossiter in common?

5 What was the original meaning of the word spinster?

6 In which year did Boudicca lead her warriors against the Romans?

7 Which Frenchwoman, who met her death by being burned at the stake, was canonized a saint in 1920?

8 Novelist and Egyptologist Amelia Blandford Edwards left in her will provision for the establishment of a University Chair in a certain subject. Which one?

9 What was Elizabeth Southern, known as 'Old Demdike', who lived in Pendle, Lancashire (England) and died in 1612?

10 Which Queen's name is 'Jennifer' the Cornish form of?

11 Which British politician was known as 'Red Ellen'?

12 What did Marie Stopes campaign for in Britain?

13 What was the name of diarist Anne Frank's sister?

14 Which former slave, abolitionist and feminist is famous for asking 'Ain't I a woman'?

15 Christabel and Sylvia were two of British Suffragette Emmeline Pankhurst's three daughters. What was her third daughter called?

9 HERSTORY ANSWERS

1 *(British) Equal Opportunities Commission*

2 *Making lynching a Federal crime*

3 *To enlist in the (US) Army*

4 *They were all jailed for killing their violent husbands*

5 *A woman who earned her living by spinning*

6 AD 61

7 *Joan of Arc*

8 *Egyptology*

9 *A witch*

10 *Guinevere*

11 *Ellen Wilkinson (member of the Independent Labour Party)*

12 *Birth control*

13 *Margot*

14 *Sojourner Truth*

15 *Adela*

1 Which Nobel Prize was Jane Addams (1860–1935) the first woman to be awarded in 1931?
2 In which marches of the 1930s did the mother of Tory Member of Parliament Virginia Bottomley take part?
3 How many times was England's Queen Anne (1665–1714) pregnant during her marriage?
4 What caused the death of designer and businesswoman Laura Ashley in 1985?
5 Before becoming a nurse, how did British First World War heroine Edith Cavell (1865–1915) earn her living?
6 Of which country did Vigdis Finnbogadottir (b. 1930) become president in 1980?
7 Which three languages could American Helen Keller (1880–1986), blind and deaf from the age of 19 months, speak fluently?
8 What did Rosie Newman take colour photographs of during the Second World War?
9 In the US Census of which year was the husband no longer automatically defined as 'head of the household'?
10 Which city was the birthplace of Labour Member of Parliament Ellen Wilkinson (1891–1947), in which there is also a High School named after her?
11 The Aztec Goddess of Earth and Fire, Coatlicue, had a 'live skirt'. What was it made of?
12 Which large British grocery business was Daisy Hyams one of the leading lights of (when it started) and Managing Director of during the 1970s?
13 In 1964–66, what was Indira Gandhi (1917–84), Indian politician, Minister of?
14 By what nickname was American anarchist Emma Goldman (1869–1940) known?
15 Which medal was Odette Sansom, MBE (Member of the Order of the British Empire), awarded in August 1946 for the courage she showed while imprisoned as a British Agent during the Second World War?

HERSTORY ANSWERS

1 *Peace Prize*

2 *The Hunger Marches*

3 *18*

4 *She fell down the stairs at her home and died a week later from her injuries*

5 *As a governess*

6 *Iceland*

7 *English, German and French*

8 *London, immediately after the Blitz*

9 *1950*

10 *Manchester*

11 *Snakes*

12 *Tesco*

13 *Information and Broadcasting*

14 *'Red Emma'*

15 *The George Cross*

1 In 7th-century Africa, why did Kahina destroy her capital city, Baghaya?
2 What else got arrested and detained along with the members of the Women's Peace Vigil outside the UK Foreign Office in 1991?
3 What did Mary Elizabeth Lease (1853–1933) think the farmers of the US state of Kansas should raise instead of corn?
4 What did New Zealand-born aviator Jean Batten auction to raise money for her flying lessons?
5 Where did Beguine, Jutta of Huy, spend the last 40 years of her life until her death in 1228?
6 What was the physical attribute that made Moll Cutpurse (c. 1589–c. 1662) such a good pickpocket?
7 In the Second World War, to what did Special Operations Executive Virginia Hall give the codename 'Cuthbert'?
8 To which Goddess did Boudicca (AD 61) sacrifice any Roman women she captured?
9 As a member of the resistance in Belgium during the Second World War, what group was José de la Barre (now José Villiers) a member of?
10 In the 15th century, where did Bristol businesswoman Alice Chester export cloth to and import iron from?
11 In 1926, how did Miss Jeffryes of London earn her living?
12 What did most of the wives of British sailors do during the Napoleonic Wars?
13 In 1985, why was Briton Pauline Cutting risking her life in the Palestinian refugee camp of Bourj al Barajneh while it was under siege, with no electricity or running water and very little food?
14 In which church in Britain's Northwest was Salema Begum given sanctuary during her fight to live with her parents in the UK?
15 What was the result of the case Briton Helen Marshall took to the European Court of Justice in 1986?

9 HERSTORY ANSWERS

1 *So it would not fall into enemy hands*

2 *A giant white polystyrene (styrofoam) peace dove*

3 *Hell*

4 *Her piano*

5 *In a cell adjoining a leper house*

6 *She had an unusually long middle finger*

7 *Her artificial (brass) foot*

8 *Andraste ('She Who Is Invincible')*

9 *The aviation section of Service Zero*

10 *Spain and Flanders respectively*

11 *She was a shipping agent*

12 *Most of the women went with their husbands; during battles they would help tend the wounded*

13 *She was a surgeon and had work to do, no matter what the conditions*

14 *Chorlton Central Church*

15 *Women in public sector jobs could no longer be forced to retire at a younger age than men*

1 In 1954, what did *'little things'* mean to British singer Alma Cogan?

2 How many women are there in the UK group Two Nice Girls?

3 Who was *'Walkin' Back to Happiness'* in 1961?

4 Which Liverpudlian singer made a come-back on Britain's Top of the Pops TV programme in September, 1993 – 30 years after her first appearance?

5 What song did Judy Collins have a UK hit with seven times in 1971 and 1972?

6 Who had a number one hit in the UK in 1968 with *'Those Were The Days'*?

7 Which instrument does Suzi Quatro play?

8 What were Nancy Sinatra's boots *'made for'* in January 1966?

9 Which Brontë book did Kate Bush sing about in 1978?

10 By 1992, who had had more number one hits in the UK than any female star ever?

11 In which language did Mary Hopkin record many successful records at the beginning of her career?

12 Who had two records released in the UK in 1952 – *'Auf Wiedersehen Sweetheart'* and *'Yours'*, which sold a million copies each?

13 Which country singer sang of *'Walkin' after Midnight'*?

14 In the 19th century, why did male composers use female pseudonyms?

15 Nicole won the Eurovision Song Contest in 1982 – with which song?

MUSIC ANSWERS

1 *A Lot* ('Little Things Mean A Lot')

2 *Three*

3 *Helen Shapiro*

4 *Cilla Black*

5 'Amazing Grace'

6 *Mary Hopkin*

7 *Bass guitar*

8 *Walking* ('These Boots Were Made for Walking')

9 Wuthering Heights

10 *Madonna*

11 *Welsh*

12 *Vera Lynn*

13 *Patsy Cline*

14 *Because they were more likely to sell their work, as at the time there was a high demand for women's compositions*

15 'A Little Peace'

1 What was *'the only way'* for British singer Yazz in July, 1988?

2 Which song won Patsy Cline the Arthur Godfrey Talent Scouts Television Show in 1957?

3 Who was *'a big lass and a bonny lass and she likes her beer'*?

4 What was Joni Mitchell's only hit single in the UK?

5 What did Lita Roza ask the price of in March 1953?

6 Which British singer was born Mary O'Brien?

7 What was Diana Ross' first solo number one hit in the UK in 1971?

8 Which song did Shirley Bassey have a UK hit single with three times in 1960?

9 How many UK number one hits did Blondie have in 1980?

10 In which year did Odaline de la Martinez become the first woman to conduct a prom (prestigious concert)?

11 What was Shakespear's Sister's first top 10 hit in the UK?

12 Who won the Grammy Award for Best Rhythm and Blues Vocal Performance (Female) every year from 1967 to 1974?

13 Who did Suzi Quatro sing *'wouldn't like'* her in 1975?

14 Which singer is daughter of folk singer Peggy Seeger?

15 How many *'lonely days'* did Gisele McKenzie have a UK hit with three times in 1953?

10 MUSIC ANSWERS

1 *Up* ('The Only Way is Up')
2 'Walkin' After Midnight'
3 *Cushie Butterfield*
4 'Big Yellow Taxi'
5 *That doggie in the window* ('How Much Is that Doggie in the Window?')
6 *Dusty Springfield*
7 'I'm Still Waiting'
8 'With These Hands'
9 *Three*
10 *1984*
11 'You're History'
12 *Aretha Franklin*
13 *Your mamma* ('Your Mamma Won't Like Me')
14 *Kirsty MacColl*
15 *Seven* ('Seven Lonely Days')

1 What hand-held instrument does Zimbabwe's Stella Chiweshe play?

2 In which year did the British composer Rosalind Ellicott (b. 1857) die?

3 What was the pseudonym of British composer Helen Rhodes (1858–1936)?

4 In 1879, which student at London's Royal Academy of Music became the first woman to win the Mendelssohn Scholarship?

5 What annual event did Americans Boo Price and Lisa Vogel start in 1976?

6 Tata Bambo is a 'djely mousso' from Mali, West Africa. What kind of singer is she?

7 Which American singer was born Dione La Rue?

8 What did Mary Lou Williams do for Duke Ellington, Benny Goodman and Louis Armstrong?

9 Which song did Maggie Bell have twice in the UK charts in 1978?

10 In 1975, for which British singer were the Love Squad the backing group?

11 To what did British singer Leslie Wonderman change her name?

12 Which record did Whitney Houston keep at number one in the UK for 12 weeks in 1988?

13 How many times did Rose Marie have *'When I Leave My World Behind'* in the UK charts?

14 Who won Grammy awards for Best Solo Female Performance, Best Contemporary Rock 'n' Roll Vocal Performance and Best New Artist, all in one year, 1967?

15 Who cut the first record by a blues singer, called *That Thing Called Love*?

MUSIC ANSWERS

1 *Mbira (thumb piano)*
2 *1924*
3 *Guy d'Hardelot*
4 *Maude Valerie White*
5 *The Annual Michigan Womyn's Music Festival*
6 *A 'woman praise singer'*
7 *Dee Dee Sharp*
8 *She was their music arranger*
9 'Hazell'
10 *Linda Carr*
11 *Taylor Dayne*
12 'One Moment in Time'
13 *Three*
14 *Bobbie Gentry*
15 *Mamie Smith*

1 In which city in northeast England was Marie Hall (1844–1956), one of the greatest violinists of her day, born?

2 In which country was the secret annexe in which Anne Frank (1930–45) and her family lived until they were betrayed by an informer in 1944 and turned over to the Nazis?

3 In which UK city can you visit the Pankhurst Centre, former home of Emmeline Pankhurst and her daughters?

4 Where did the Brontë sisters go to school?

5 In which country was tennis champion Evonne Goolagong born?

6 Where was doctor/nurse and businesswoman Mary Seacole (1805–81) born?

7 In which country was the 'Inn of Eight Happinesses' set up by missionary Gladys Aylward (1930–70)?

8 Which Channel did Gertrude Ederle swim in 1926?

9 Where are the offices of the British EOC (Equal Opportunities Commission)?

10 In which three countries did novelist and journalist Vera Brittain (1893–1970) serve as a VAD (working with the Voluntary Ambulance Division) during the First World War?

11 Benazir Bhutto was president of which country?

12 In which British city was Member of Parliament Ellen Wilkinson born?

13 Where did 20,000 women march against their inclusion in the Pass Laws in October 1956?

14 In which Cornish town did sculptor Barbara Hepworth live after the Second World War?

15 In which street in London will you find the Silver Moon Women's Bookshop?

11 GEOGRAPHY ANSWERS

easier

1 *Newcastle upon Tyne*

2 *Holland (Amsterdam) (accept: The Netherlands)*

3 *Manchester*

4 *School for Daughters of Clergymen, Casterton*

5 *Australia*

6 *Kingston, Jamaica*

7 *China*

8 *The English Channel*

9 *Quay Street, Manchester*

10 *Malta, France and England*

11 *Pakistan*

12 *Manchester*

13 *Pretoria, South Africa*

14 *St Ives*

15 *Charing Cross Road*

1 In which concentration camp did Anne Frank (1930–45) die of typhus?

2 In 1860, where was The Nightingale Nursing School set up?

3 From which aerodrome did British aviator Amy Johnson set off for her successful solo flight from England to Australia?

4 How far did New Zealand-born nurse Louise Sutherland cycle without getting a single puncture?

5 British zoologist Jane Goodall (b. 1934) studied the chimpanzees of which country for over 30 years?

6 Which Scandinavian country has a women's university?

7 In which country will you find the feminist group Kareta?

8 Before becoming part of the UK Football Association in 1993, in which British city would you have found the Women's Football Association?

9 To which South African state was Winnie Mandela restricted in 1977?

10 For which Northern town was Ellen Wilkinson Member of Parliament until her death in 1947?

11 Which country did tennis champion Martina Navratilova defect from?

12 In 1775, novelist Jane Austen was born in which British county?

13 In which concentration camp was British Agent Violette Szabo when she was shot dead?

14 What is the name of the northern English town, now a city, where journalist Kate Adie was born?

15 In which county in Wales was singer Mary Hopkin born?

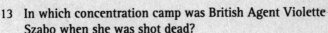

11 GEOGRAPHY ANSWERS

1 *Bergen-Belsen*
2 *St Thomas' Hospital, London*
3 *Croydon*
4 *Around the world*
5 *Tanzania*
6 *Norway*
7 *Croatia (Yugoslavia)*
8 *Manchester*
9 *Orange Free State*
10 *Jarrow*
11 *Czechoslovakia*
12 *Hampshire*
13 *Ravensbruck*
14 *Sunderland*
15 *Glamorgan (South Wales)*

1 In which country did British journalist Victoria Brittain work as a television foreign correspondent during the 1970s?

2 Where did playwright Aphra Behn (1640–89) go as a spy for Britain's King Charles II during the Anglo-Dutch War?

3 Where did Florence Nightingale spend three months training to be a nurse in 1851?

4 In AD 269, which African country was captured by the Syrian Queen Zenobia (d. 274)?

5 Where did Englishwoman Mary Carpenter open her first 'ragged school' in 1846?

6 Where was the Women's Peace Conference of 1915 held?

7 Where was South African Winnie Mandela exiled to in 1977?

8 From which British seaport did Ann Davison begin her successful single-handed Atlantic crossing in 1952?

9 Hatshepsut ruled which country in the 15th century BC?

10 Where did missionary Gladys Aylward (1903–70) set up her hospital after the Japanese bombed Yangcheng in 1938?

11 Of which African country was Helena empress in the 16th century?

12 Where was nurse and heroine Edith Cavell shot and killed on 12th October 1915?

13 Which city was ruled by the Syrian Queen Zenobia (d. 274)?

14 What is the name of the city which inspired Lucinda Denning to paint *Last Supper with Hats*?

15 In which country was Rhodesian author Doris Lessing (b. 1919) born?

11 GEOGRAPHY ANSWERS

hard

1 *Vietnam*
2 *Antwerp, Holland*
3 *Kaiserwerth Deaconesses' Institute, Germany*
4 *Egypt*
5 *Bristol*
6 *The Hague*
7 *Brandfort*
8 *Plymouth, England*
9 *Egypt*
10 *In a cave in a hillside (in China)*
11 *Ethiopia*
12 *Schaerbeck, Brussels*
13 *Palmyra*
14 *Florence (Italy)*
15 *Persia (present-day Iran)*

1 Why was Briton Elizabeth Garrett (1836–1917) stopped from attending lectures while at medical school?

2 Which disease caused Helen Keller's blindness and deafness?

3 In the UK, what is the recommended safe limit of units of alcohol per week for a woman?

4 Of 8,000 late abortions in a Bombay Hospital in 1991, how many were of female foetuses?

5 What did African-American Madame C. J. Walker create and sell which made her a millionaire?

6 What did Emmot Syddal, an inhabitant of Eyam, Derbyshire, die of in April 1666?

7 Who isolated the elements of Polonium and Radium?

8 Who was the world's first test-tube baby?

9 What did British scientist Dorothy Hodgkin (b. 1910) take the first x-ray photograph of in 1933?

10 Where have historians and archaeologists found evidence of ancient Egyptian women healers?

11 In the 18th century what animal product was used to give stays their shape?

12 Before it was decided only (male) university-trained doctors could look after the sick, who did?

13 After which British mathematician is Somerville College, Oxford, named?

14 In the 19th century, after qualifying as a surgeon where did Miranda Barry (1795–1865), dressed as a man, get a job?

15 In which country was astronomer Caroline Herschel (1750–1848) born?

SCIENCE ANSWERS

1 *Because she (the only woman at the lectures) got top marks in an exam*

2 *Scarlet fever*

3 *14 (= 7 pints of lager)*

4 *All but one*

5 *Skin and hair preparations for black women*

6 *The Black Death (accept: the plague)*

7 *Physicist Marie Curie (1867–1934)*

8 *Louise Brown (b. 1978)*

9 *Pepsin (a protein)*

10 *On paintings in tombs and objects found in Egyptian graves*

11 *Whalebone*

12 *Women*

13 *Mary Somerville (1780–1872)*

14 *In South Africa, as an army surgeon*

15 *Germany (Hanover)*

1 In which American city did four-year-old Laura Davies, from Manchester, have a liver and bowel transplant in June 1992?

2 What is an ectopic pregnancy?

3 What stopped the sunken Tudor ship *Mary Rose* from rotting away?

4 How did Elizabeth Garrett (1836–1917) get a licence to practise medicine?

5 Who were blamed for the spread of contagious diseases in the 19th century?

6 Why were women in Paris banned from practising medicine in the 13th century?

7 In which year was abortion made illegal in Britain?

8 During the Crimean War, who paid for doctor/nurse Mary Seacole to go to the Crimea and set up a hospital?

9 What did pitric acid do to women working in munitions factories during the First World War?

10 In the 19th century, where were male medical students told to look when examining women?

11 What did physicist Marie Curie die of in 1934 (at the age of 66)?

12 What kind of French wine was produced by wine-maker Nicole-Barbe Clicquot?

13 Who was the first scientist to be awarded two Nobel prizes?

14 What is Britain's Mary Archer an expert in?

15 Why was renowned mathematician Mary Somerville (1780–1872) not buried in Westminster Abbey?

SCIENCE ANSWERS

1 *Pittsburgh*

2 *A pregnancy where the fertilized egg implants outside the uterus–usually in the Fallopian tube*

3 *The mud it sank in*

4 *She sat and passed the Society of Apothecaries exam*

5 *Female prostitutes*

6 *In case they killed a man*

7 *1803*

8 *Mary Seacole herself*

9 *It turned their skin yellow*

10 *At the ceiling*

11 *Leukaemia*

12 *Champagne*

13 *Marie Curie (1867–1934)*

14 *Solar energy*

15 *A jealous Astronomer Royal refused to give his permission to allow her to be buried there*

SCIENCE QUIZ 12

1 What did 'Crazy Sally' (Sarah Mapp) set in 18th century England?

2 What form of transport did British nurses Maria Chisholm and Elsie Knocker use to carry medical supplies to the trenches in First World War?

3 In Victorian Britain, who was likely to suffer from 'phossy jaw'?

4 Which Egyptian Goddess was believed to protect pregnant women?

5 Who wrote *Diseases of Women* in the 11th century?

6 In 1991, what was the penalty for having an abortion if you were a woman living in Salt Lake City, Utah?

7 Which workers did American Sarah Boone help with her 'narrow ironing board' invention in 1892?

8 Which award did American Dr Harriet G. Jenkins receive from NASA?

9 Marie Curie won the Nobel prize twice. In 1911 she won it for Chemistry; what did she win it for in 1903?

10 In the 18th century, which American thought up the original idea for the mechanical cotton gin?

11 In AD 370, which two subjects did Alexandrian scholar Hypatia specialize in teaching?

12 What was the subject of the book published by botanist Margaret Getty in 1863?

13 Which British association for new technology was founded by Caroline Haslett in 1924?

14 How old were the human-like footprints discovered by anthropologist Mary Leakey in Tanzania's Olduvai Gorge in 1976?

15 In what subject does British TV presenter Judith Hann have a BSc?

12 SCIENCE ANSWERS

1 *Bones*
2 *Motorbike*
3 *Workers in match factories*
4 *Thueris*
5 *Trotula of Salerno (Italy)*
6 *Death*
7 *Dressmakers*
8 *Distinguished service medal*
9 *Physics*
10 *Catherine Greene (1755–1814)*
11 *Algebra and mechanics*
12 *British seaweed*
13 *Electrical Association for Women*
14 *3.5 million years*
15 *Zoology*

1 Whose statue on the banks of the River Thames at Westminster, London portrays her riding on a scythed chariot?

2 Which is the biggest women's organization in Britain?

3 Which concentration camp was British Agent Odette Sansom sent to in July 1944, after a year of torture?

4 What was Jane Wenham the last woman to be condemned to death for in 18th century Britain?

5 In the Middle Ages, how did Christine de Pisan earn her living after she was widowed?

6 What does FANY, founded in Britain in 1907, stand for?

7 After the passing of the (UK) Sex Discrimination Act of 1975, what did 'fireman' become?

8 On 2nd December 1955 what did American Rosa Parks refuse to give up to a white person?

9 How did the male business rivals of watch engraver Emma Cons destroy her business?

10 Which London Borough Council increased the rent for the Feminist Library from £1 per year to £16,000 per year?

11 In which year was Margaret Thatcher elected Leader of the British Conservative Party?

12 Before becoming a full-time suffragette, what was Annie Kenney's job?

13 In which year was Queen Elizabeth I born?

14 Whose gravestone in Westminster Abbey reads, 'Dyed April 16 AD 1689/Here lies proof that wit can never be Defence enough against mortality'

15 After the execution of Marie Antoinette during the French revolution, who made the wax model of her head?

HERSTORY ANSWERS

1 *Boudicca (Boadicea)*

2 *National Federation of Women's Institutes*

3 *Ravensbruck*

4 *Witchcraft*

5 *As a writer*

6 *First Aid Nursing Yeomanry*

7 *Firefighter*

8 *Her seat in the 'whites only' part of the bus (in Montgomery, Alabama)*

9 *They attacked the messengers she used to collect work and deliver it back to her customers*

10 *Southwark*

11 *1975*

12 *Mill-worker*

13 *1533*

14 *Aphra Behn's*

15 *Madame Marie Tussaud (1761–1850)*

1 Of which federation was American Margaret Sanger (1883–1966) founder?
2 When a prisoner in the Maison de Correction de Fresnes during the Second World War, why was Odette (Lise) Sansom punished in her first few days there by having to miss her main meal of the day (a bowl of soup)?
3 Who was Chair of the British Labour Party, 1981–82?
4 Why was Margaret Damer Dawson, founder of the Women Police Volunteers, sued along with some of her women police officers by London's Metropolitan Police in 1920?
5 Which Queen preceded Queen Elizabeth I to the British throne?
6 When was the women's peace camp at Greenham Common established?
7 Which British Prime Minister was taught by the Principal of Somerville College, Janet Vaughan, while at Oxford University?
8 In which year did female teachers eventually receive equal pay to male teachers?
9 In 1913 why were Gwyneth Bebb, Karin Costelloe, Maude Ingram and Lucy Nettlefold refused permission by the Law Society to sit their law exams?
10 When the London Society for Women's Suffrage changed its name to the Fawcett Society, who was this in honour of?
11 How many pupils did Briton Emily Davies (1830–1921) have when she opened her first women's college in 1869?
12 Why were Lilian Rolfe and Denise Bloche in France during the Second World War?
13 Where does the Chinese Goddess Heng E live, in the form of a toad?
14 What does the FI Group, founded by Stephanie (Steve) Shirley, do?
15 In which year did Betty Williams and Mairead Corrigan, from Northern Ireland, win the Nobel Peace Prize?

HERSTORY ANSWERS

1 *International Planned Parenthood Federation*

2 *For breaking a pane of glass in the window of her cell, in order to see the sky*

3 *(Dame) Judith Hart (b. 1924)*

4 *For 'impersonating' police officers*

5 *Queen Mary I*

6 *September 1981*

7 *Margaret Thatcher*

8 *1961*

9 *Because, according to common law at the time, women were incapable of carrying out a public function*

10 *Millicent Garrett Fawcett (1847–1929), a leader of the British suffragette movement*

11 *Five*

12 *They were wireless operators for the French Section of the SOE (Special Operations Executive)*

13 *On the moon*

14 *Designs, develops, builds and installs computer systems*

15 *1977*

1 Why might you want to keep yourself and young children away from the Greek Goddess Lamia?
2 At the end of the 18th century, how did Deborah Gooding earn her living?
3 Prior to the 19th century, dairying was always seen as part of a woman's work on the farm. What happened in 1843 to change this?
4 In 1924 Constance Wilkins made her living in the City of London by buying spices from abroad. At the time women were not allowed to be members of the Commercial Salesrooms, so how did she get round this problem?
5 During which war did Lady Sarah Wilson work in Mafeking as correspondent for the *Daily Mail*?
6 What code name did Noor Inayat Khan (1914–44) use when she was working in France as a wireless operator for the SOE (Special Operations Executive) during the Second World War?
7 Which was the first American state to give women the vote in 1869?
8 Who was the first woman in the world to gain her pilot's licence in March 1910?
9 What was the aim of the Women's Provident and Protective League, founded by Emma Paterson in London in 1874?
10 To which English City Council was Hannah Mitchell (1871–1956) elected in 1923?
11 In the early 18th century, at the age of 13, what job did Mary Read have which she found so boring she left to join the Navy (as a sailor boy)?
12 In which year was the UK's Rational Dress Society formed?
13 What did Tomyris, Queen of the Massagatae, do to the Persian Emperor Cyrus the Great when she defeated him in 528 BC?
14 As well as commanding five ships in the fleet of Xerxes in 480 BC, what other role did Queen Artemisia have?
15 Which Queen of Scotland was canonized in 1250?

1 *Because Lamia ('She Who Swallows Up') was believed not only to be a vampire but also an abductor of children*

2 *She ran an inn and the Essex-to-London coach route*

3 *It was stated in the Royal Commission on Women and Children in Agriculture (1843) that women were not suitable to dairying because of the skills, patience and strength such work demanded*

4 *She employed a (male) broker, who was allowed into the salesrooms*

5 *The Anglo-Boer War (1899–1902)*

6 *Madeleine*

7 *Wyoming*

8 *Raymonde de Laroche*

9 *To make sure that, in whichever trades women worked, there was a union they could join*

10 *Manchester City Council*

11 *Footboy*

12 *1881*

13 *Cut off his head*

14 *Naval Consultant*

15 *St Margaret (d. 1093)*

1 In *Eastenders*, who is Pauline Fowler's daughter?

2 In 1931 ballet dancer Marie Rambert founded the Ballet Club. What famous ballet troupe did it become in 1939?

3 When the Vic-Wells Ballet company was granted a Royal Charter in 1957 and became the Royal Ballet, where did it move to?

4 Which 20th-century feline musical was choreographed by Gillian Lynne?

5 Who played Rita in the film *Educating Rita*?

6 Who played Peggy in *Hi-de-Hi*?

7 What was Joanna Lumley's career before becoming an actress?

8 What is the name of the BBC travel programme presented by Penny Junor?

9 For which 1960s TV series was Lee Grant awarded two Emmys?

10 The screenplay for which film starring Maggie Smith was written by Jay Allen in 1969?

11 What is the title of the book, radio series, and TV comedy series by Sue Limb?

12 Who was star of the 1980s programme *Training Dogs the Woodhouse Way*?

13 In 1993 who said 'Men are fine. As a concept'?

14 In which TV sitcom does Nicola McAuliffe play surgeon Sheila Sabatini?

15 Which 1992 comedy series starring Jennifer Saunders and Joanna Lumley was written by Jennifer Saunders?

BRITISH ENTERTAINMENT ANSWERS

1 *Michelle Fowler*
2 *Ballet Rambert*
3 *Covent Garden*
4 Cats
5 *Julie Walters*
6 *Su Pollard*
7 *Model*
8 The Travel Show
9 Peyton Place
10 The Prime of Miss Jean Brodie
11 Up the Garden Path
12 *Barbara Woodhouse*
13 *Comedian Jo Brand*
14 Surgical Spirit
15 Absolutely Fabulous

1 What is the name of the character in *Emmerdale* played by Sheila Mercier?

2 In which long-running Agatha Christie play, in the West End, did Joan Sanderson act?

3 Who wrote the television sitcom *Screaming*?

4 Who was the small one in the *Big One*?

5 Who played the original *Liver Birds*?

6 Which black-and-white bird was Susan Stranks involved with for a long time?

7 Who starred in the 1992 musical *70, Girls, 70*?

8 In 1966 Cleo Sylvestre played a factory worker in *Coronation Street.* Which soap did she join in 1970?

9 On which BBC series looking at the technology of the future did Dana Purvis work as editor?

10 What is the name of the ITV morning word show produced by Christine Williams?

11 In *Crossroads,* what was Melanie Harper's relationship to Meg Richardson?

12 In 1993 which Radio 4 problem-solving gardening programme was produced by Amanda Mares?

13 In which television drama series, about the Second World War, did Claire Oberman play Kate Norris?

14 In 1993 which BBC series of travel programmes was produced by Rachel Hebditch?

15 Where were Ivy Benson and her All Girls' Band playing when they got their first booking by the BBC?

BRITISH ENTERTAINMENT ANSWERS

1. *Annie Sugden*
2. The Mousetrap
3. *Carla Lane*
4. *Sandi Toksvig*
5. *Nerys Hughes and Polly James*
6. Magpie
7. *Dora Bryan*
8. Crossroads
9. Tomorrow's World
10. Cross Wits
11. *Foster daughter*
12. Gardener's Question Time
13. Tenko
14. The Travel Show
15. *The Ritz Ballroom, Manchester*

1 How many women applied for the two posts for female TV announcers when they were advertised in 1936?
2 What was comedian and actress Josie Lawrence's mother's job?
3 Which Radio 4 Playhouse, by Pam Gem, was directed by Sue Dunderdale and starred Prunella Scales as Deborah Pedersen?
4 Which West End show did Gillian Lyn both choreograph and direct when it was taken to the former USSR?
5 Why was actress Lily Elsie (1886–1962) sacked while acting in *The Little Cherub* at the Prince of Wales Theatre?
6 In *The Happiest Days of Your Life* (1950) what did the games mistress, played by Joyce Grenfell, ask everyone to call her?
7 What was the title of Estela Bravo's documentary, first shown on Channel 4 on 1st June 1992?
8 Which ballet company did Ninette de Valois (b. 1898) run?
9 In the 18th century, when a farmworker earned about £26 a year, how much could actress Sarah Siddons (1755–1831) earn for one performance?
10 In which British city was actress Ellen Terry (1847–1928) born?
11 In which year did ballerina Margot Fonteyn make her debut with the Royal Ballet?
12 At which teacher training college in Britain's northwest did TV personality Rustie Lee work for a time, as Head of Catering?
13 At the beginning of the 20th century who was Britain's highest paid music hall star?
14 Which theatre company was founded in 1935 by producer Joan Tuckett?
15 Which theatre, owned by Emma Cons and run by her niece Lilian Baylis (1874–1937), was the first to house the National Theatre Company?

1. *1,222*
2. *Dinner lady*
3. Deborah's Daughter
4. Cabaret
5. *For kicking a football into the stalls*
6. *'Sausage'*
7. Miami–Havana
8. *The Vic-Wells Ballet, which became (in 1957) the Royal Ballet*
9. *Over £50*
10. *Coventry*
11. *1934*
12. *Padgate*
13. *Vesta Tilley (1864–1952)*
14. *Bristol Unity Players*
15. *The Old Vic*

1 What kind of tomatoes were sold at the Whistle Stop Café?

2 In which British woman's magazine does Zoe Fairbairns write a monthly page?

3 Who was the author of the highly successful book, *The Railway Children*, published in 1906?

4 Who published the first novel by Scottish author Alison Fell (b. 1944), *Every Move You Make*, in 1984?

5 Which 19th-century writing sisters lived at Howarth Parsonage, Yorkshire?

6 Which complete Jane Austen novel was not published until after her death?

7 Which novel by Ellen Galford describes the return of the Queen of ancient Briton, Albanna, in a time of strife to help her more modern-day subjects?

8 Which British novelist of South Tyneside was born in South Shields in 1906?

9 Which amateur detective made her last appearance in *Sleeping Murder*, by Agatha Christie?

10 Where was there 'something nasty in the woodshed'?

11 Which hymn, often sung in schools, was written by Mrs Alexander?

12 Over whom did Mary Wollstonecraft (1759–97) think women should have power?

13 What happened to *The Professor* by Charlotte Brontë when she first submitted it for publication?

14 In which year did Virginia Woolf kill herself?

15 What kind of devil did novelist Fay Weldon write about?

15 LITERATURE & ART ANSWERS

easier

1 *Fried green ones (*Fried Green Tomatoes at the Whistle Stop Café [1987] by Fannie Flagg)

2 Everywoman

3 *Edith Nesbit*

4 *Virago Press Ltd*

5 *The Brontës*

6 Lady Susan

7 Queendom Come *(1990)*

8 *Catherine Cookson*

9 *Miss Jane Marple*

10 Cold Comfort Farm

11 'All things bright and beautiful'

12 *Themselves*

13 *It was rejected*

14 *1941*

15 *A she-devil (in* The Life and Loves of a She-Devil, *1983)*

1 What kind of school was British novelist and journalist Antonia White (1899–1980) educated at and expelled from at the age of 14?
2 Before the 19th century, which word was commonly used in literature when the sex of a person was not known?
3 In 1621 why did Lady Mary Wroath write her first novel, *Urania*?
4 When poet and writer Irina Ratushinskaya was put in a Soviet labour camp, what was the name given to the area of the camp in which she lived?
5 What subject was Briton Evelyn Dunbar commissioned to paint as an official War Artist during the Second World War?
6 The singer and dancer Dorothy Dandridge (1923–65) was the first black woman to appear on the cover of a magazine. Which (American) magazine was it?
7 Which Scottish city is the setting for most of Joan Eardley's paintings?
8 In which language did Charlotte Brontë forbid her novel *Villette* (1853) to be published?
9 In which century did the poet Sappho live?
10 What was odd about the 'nude' male when female students at the Royal Academy of Arts schools were eventually allowed to draw one in 1893?
11 Whose poem *'The Spleen'* was published in 1701?
12 In 1984 Paulette Randall was the first black woman to have a play produced in London's West End. What was its title?
13 In 1798 the first lonely hearts column appeared in the *Ladies Monthly Museum*. What were most of the letters about?
14 In which British gallery does the self-portrait of artist Mary Beale (1632–99) hang?
15 Anne Conway (1631–79) wrote a very influential scientific text entitled *Principles of the Most Ancient and Modern Philosophy*. After her death why did readers of the book assume it was written by a man?

1 *A convent school (Convent of the Sacred Heart, Roehampton)*

2 *'They'*

3 *To keep herself out of debtors' prison*

4 *The Small Zone*

5 *Women's war work*

6 Life

7 *Glasgow*

8 *French*

9 *6th century BC*

10 *He wore a loin cloth*

11 *Anne Finch, Countess of Winchilsea (1661–1720)*

12 Fishing

13 *Women's dread of being 'spinsters'*

14 *National Portrait Gallery*

15 *Her name had been deliberately removed from the title page*

1 In which year was the Fawcett Society founded?

2 Why did Sarah Biffin (b. 1784), the famous British miniaturist, paint with the brush held in her mouth?

3 In a *Radio Times* interview in 1960, on which poet did Margaret Drabble say the character Jane Gray in her novel *The Waterfall* (1969) was partly based?

4 Who wrote *Reply to Sor Filotea de la Cruz*, a vindication of the right of women to intellectual emancipation, in 17th-century Mexico?

5 Hilda Doolittle's book *Her* was published in 1981. In which year was it written?

6 In the 19th century, which artist was given the name 'The rose and primrose painter' by the French?

7 Agnes Strickland (1796–1874) was famous for writing biographies. Why were her books so popular?

8 What was the title of the cookery book written by Eliza Acton in 1845 and dedicated to 'The Young Housekeepers of England'?

9 In which part of the US did the poet Anne Bradstreet (1612–72) live?

10 For what form of writing is the Japanese poet Kaga no Chiyo (1701–75) famous?

11 Which Finnish poet had a statue erected in her honour in Helsinki in 1949?

12 Who wrote *A Serious Proposal to the Ladies*, published anonymously in 1694?

13 Why was it impossible to see the first British actress officially to appear on stage, in 1660?

14 Under what pseudonym did Mary de la Rivière Manley (1663–1724) edit her national newspaper *The Female Tatler*?

15 Which German poet was co-winner, with S. Y. Agnon, of the Nobel Prize for Literature in 1966?

1 *1866*

2 *Because she was born without arms (or legs)*

3 *Sylvia Plath (1932–63)*

4 *Sor Juana Ines de la Cruz*

5 *1927*

6 *Mary Harrison (1788–1875)*

7 *She included a lot of gossip and domestic detail about the lives of the people she wrote about*

8 Modern Cookery for Private Families

9 *New England (Massachusetts)*

10 *Haiku*

11 *Larin Paraske (1833–1904)*

12 *Mary Astell (1668–1731)*

13 *Because her face was covered by a veil*

14 *Mrs Crackenthorpe*

15 *Nelly Sachs (1891–1969)*

1 In the 1904 Olympic Games women were allowed to enter only one event–archery. What was unusual about the contestants?

2 What was the aim of the sex tests at the original (ancient Greek) Olympic Games?

3 During the 1948 Olympics in London, what did the *Daily Graphic* insist was world-champion Fanny Blankers-Koen's 'greatest love next to racing'?

4 What nationality is champion runner Mary Decker Slaney?

5 Why could Lucy Morton – who set the first records for the 150 yards backstroke and 200 yards breast stroke – not compete in these events in the 1920 Olympics in Antwerp?

6 Which British honours were given to athlete Mary Peters in 1973 and 1990?

7 Who was the youngest contestant in the 1976 Montreal Olympics?

8 Why do women have to undergo sex tests at the modern Olympics?

9 In which Olympics did Briton Tessa Sanderson win her gold medal for the javelin throw?

10 Jennie Fletcher won two medals for swimming at the 1912 Olympics. Her bronze was for the 100 metres freestyle. For which event did she win gold?

11 Why did gymnast Elena Mukhina miss the 1980 Moscow Olympics?

12 Which former Communist country did gymnast Olga Korbut represent?

13 In which race at the 1984 Los Angeles Olympics did Zola Budd and Mary Decker have their disastrous meeting?

14 Which event, introduced in 1984, was Glynnis Nun of Australia the first woman to win, with 6,390 points?

15 What relation are Olympic gold-medal winners Tamara Press and Irina Press of the former Soviet Union?

16 THE OLYMPICS ANSWERS

1. *They were all American*
2. *They were specifically aimed at keeping women out*
3. *Housework*
4. *American*
5. *There were no such events for women then*
6. *The MBE* (Member of the Order of the British Empire) *and CBE* (Commander (of the Order) of the British Empire) *respectively*
7. *Sharron Davies (British swimmer)*
8. *In case they are men in disguise*
9. *1984 Los Angeles Olympics*
10. *4 x 100 metres freestyle relay*
11. *She was paralysed when she landed heavily on her neck during a routine floor exercise practice session three days before the Games began*
12. *Soviet Union*
13. *3,000 metre final*
14. *Heptathlon*
15. *Sisters*

1 What reason was given by the Olympic Committee for not allowing women to run the 3,000 metres at the 1980 Olympics in Moscow?

2 In the 1904 Olympic Games held in St. Louis, USA, women were allowed to enter only one event. Which?

3 Which is the only year there has been no female representing Great Britain in the diving event since it was first introduced in 1912?

4 Elizabeth Packer won the 800 metres (running) in the 1964 Olympics, with a record time of 2 minutes 1.1 seconds. How many times had she run this race before?

5 What were the Women's World Games held in Paris, France in 1922 originally going to be called?

6 In 1921 when the Olympic organizers continued to refuse to allow women to enter track and field events, what did Frenchwoman Alice Milliat do?

7 In the 1972 pentathlon, won by Mary Peters, what was the opening event?

8 How many children had Tatyana Kazankina when she ran the 3,000 metres and set a new world record in the 1984 Olympics?

9 When Mildred Didrikson and Jean Shirley both made record jumps of 5 feet 5 inches in the 1932 Olympics, how did the judges decide who should be awarded the gold medal and who the silver?

10 In which track and field event did Briton Mary Rand win gold at the 1964 Tokyo Olympics?

11 In which sport, as well as the shot-put, did Tamara Press of the former Soviet Union win gold in the 1964 Tokyo Olympics?

12 Who was captain of the British Olympic team at the 1968 Olympics in Mexico?

13 How many events, over how many days, does the heptathlon consist of?

14 In which race at the 1988 Seoul Olympics did British athlete Liz McColgan win silver with a time of 31:08.44?

15 Which country won the volleyball championships at the 1984 Los Angeles Olympics?

THE OLYMPICS ANSWERS

1 *The race was considered 'too strenuous for women'*

2 *Archery*

3 *1932*

4 *Seven*

5 *The Women's Olympics*

6 *She founded the FSFI* (Fédération Sportive Feminine Internationale), *which organized their own track and field events*

7 *100 metres hurdles*

8 *Two*

9 *They judged Mildred Didrikson's jump illegal, because of her style, and awarded her the silver and Jean the gold*

10 *Long jump*

11 *Discus throw*

12 *Mary Peters*

13 *Seven events over two days*

14 *10,000 metres*

15 *China*

1 At the 1988 Olympics at Seoul, who was the only Australian to win gold in a track and field event?

2 How old was Lorna Johnstone (UK) when she competed in the 1972 Olympic Dressage event?

3 Which event did British sisters Sheena and Vora Mackintosh both compete in at the 1952 Winter Olympics?

4 Who set the first world long-course record for the 100 metres backstroke in the 1956 Olympics?

5 In the Olympic Games at Paris in 1900, which two events were women allowed to compete in?

6 What was the name of the horse ridden by Jane Bullen when she won a gold medal for Britain for the three-day event (in the 1968 Olympics)?

7 In 1956 Judith Grinham (née Rowley) won a gold medal for Britain in the 100 metres backstroke. What was her time?

8 Who won the 400 metre hurdles when it was first introduced for women in 1984 at Los Angeles?

9 Which athletics event did American Wyomia Tyus win twice in a row, in 1964 at Tokyo and again in 1968 at Mexico?

10 Which country (now known by a different name) won all the distances – 500 metres, 1,000 metres, 1,500 metres and 3,000 metres – for speed skating in the 1984 Winter Olympics?

11 Ann Packer (GB) won the silver medal for the 400 metres in 1964 at Tokyo. For which race did she win the gold?

12 How many times has Britain won the 400 metres freestyle since its introduction in the 1912 Olympics?

13 In 1984, at Los Angeles, who tied with Nancy Hogshead (US) to win gold in the 100 metre freestyle, both with a time of 0:55.92?

14 Briton Priscilla Welch broke the British marathon record in the 1984 Olympics. What was her finishing position?

15 At the 1988 Olympics in Seoul, which two running events were won by Florence Griffith-Joyner (US)?

THE OLYMPICS ANSWERS

1 *Debbie Flintoff-King, 400 metre hurdles*

2 *70 years (and three days)*

3 *Alpine skiing*

4 *Judith Grinham (Britain)*

5 *Golf and tennis*

6 *'Our Nobby'*

7 *1 minute 12.9 seconds*

8 *Nawai El Moutawekel (Morocco)*

9 *100 metres*

10 *GDR (East Germany/the German Democratic Republic)*

11 *800 metres*

12 *Once, in 1912*

13 *Carrie Steinseifer (US)*

14 *Sixth*

15 *100 metres and 200 metres*

1 When is International Women's Day celebrated each year?

2 From which British political party did Sara Parkin resign in August 1992?

3 Which abbey in northern England was founded by Saint Hilda (614–80) in AD 657?

4 In which year was Britain's Family Allowance Act passed, which made child benefit payable directly to mothers?

5 Which chain of shops was started, and is run, by Anita Roddick, winner of the 1984 *UK Business Woman of the Year award*?

6 Which British intellectual society did Elizabeth Montagu, Elizabeth Carter and Hannah More all belong to in the 1760s?

7 What was the rallying call of American feminist Susan B. Anthony (1820–1906)?

8 In 1875 the UK Post Office introduced 'the marriage bar' for its female employees. What did this mean?

9 Why was British Quaker and scientist Kathleen Lonsdale (1903–71) imprisoned in 1939?

10 Who celebrated her Golden Jubilee in 1896?

11 Of which British union did Brenda Dean become general secretary in 1984?

12 On what grounds was the marriage of Marie Stopes (1880–1958) annulled in 1916 after five years?

13 Which Act of Parliament took away from women the ability to vote, by stressing voting was for males only?

14 What was Mother Theresa awarded in 1979?

15 Of which European country was Isabella the Second (1830–1904) Queen from 1833 to 1868?

HERSTORY ANSWERS

1 *8th March*

2 *The Green Party*

3 *Whitby Abbey*

4 *1945*

5 *Body Shop*

6 *Blue Stocking Society*

7 *'Failure is impossible'*

8 *Single women who married had to leave. Married women who were not widows were not appointed*

9 *As a pacifist she refused to sign up for war work*

10 *Queen Victoria*

11 *SOGAT (Society of Graphical and Allied Trades)*

12 *It had never been consummated*

13 1832 Reform Act

14 *Nobel Peace Prize*

15 *Spain*

1 What did the Family Endowment Society, founded by Eleanor Rathbone (1872–1946) in 1917, campaign for?
2 In which city in northwest England did Isabella Tipping run her successful linen drapers business until her death in 1598?
3 Which City of London stronghold allowed women to become members (and so share in the profits of the money they earned the company they worked for) rather than just being paid commission, on 25th March 1973?
4 Who became Chair of Britain's CND (Campaign for Nuclear Disarmament) in 1981?
5 In which year did women set up the Greenham Common Peace Camp, as a protest against Cruise Missiles being installed at the American Air Force base near Newbury, Berkshire?
6 Which British service did aviator Amy Johnson (1903–41) work for during the Second World War?
7 Which political figure, born in Derbyshire in 1871, called her autobiography *The Hard Way Up*?
8 Until 1871, when Angela Burdett was given a peerage, what had most women who were given a peerage done to earn one?
9 Who was the first British woman to sit and get her certificate as a Ground Engineer?
10 By the age of 51, how many times had American Linda Essex been married?
11 What did Russian women, in 1991, say democracy without women was?
12 In the House of Commons, at whom did Sam Galbraith MP bellow, 'You're not a real woman'?
13 Who founded the religious group known as the Sunnites?
14 'Standing, as I do, in the view of God and eternity I realize that patriotism is not enough.' Who said this as she was waiting to be executed by the Germans for helping British, French and Belgian soldiers escape German-occupied Belgium during the First World War?
15 What did Mary Tudor (1516–58) say would be lying in her heart when she was dead and buried? B 7P

HERSTORY ANSWERS

1 *State-funded Family Allowances*

2 *Manchester*

3 *The Stock Exchange*

4 *Joan Ruddock*

5 *1981*

6 *ATA (Air Transport Auxiliary)*

7 *Hannah Mitchell (1871–1956)*

8 *They had been a King's mistress*

9 *Amy Johnson (in 1929)*

10 *22 times*

11 *'Not democracy'*

12 *Member of Parliament Teresa Gorman*

13 *Abou-Bekr*

14 *Edith Cavell*

15 *Calais*

1 Why did Helen Oliver dress as a man in 1818?

2 For what reason was the General Secretary of Britain's NUFW (National Union of Factory Workers) dismissed in 1937?

3 What form of architecture was Lady Allen of Hurtwood (1897–1976) an expert in?

4 For which southern constituency was Elaine Burton (later Barness Burton) Member of Parliament from 1950–59?

5 Which Oxford college was founded in 1341 in honour of Philippa of Hainault?

6 In 1887 which poet was born in Scarborough, North Yorkshire, at Woodend, now the Woodend Museum of Natural History?

7 Ammit, a female demon believed to be a major figure in the Egyptian Day of Judgement, has a body made up of which three animals?

8 In which year did the last trial for witchcraft take place in England?

9 In 1918, Countess Markiewicz won a seat in the House of Commons. Why did she not take it up?

10 Which English feminist said, in 1871, 'Economics lie at the very root of practical morality'?

11 Who brought stability to Egypt in the 15th century BC?

12 As what did Briton Carrie Morrison qualify in 1922?

13 What happened to the British National Federation of Women Workers in 1920?

14 Member of Parliaments Edith Summerskill, Irene Ward and Lady Astor, among others, formed a parliamentary caucus in 1940 criticizing the Government for its failure to recruit women successfully throughout 1940–41. What was the caucus called?

15 What official post did Madame Blanchard hold under Napoleon?

17 HERSTORY ANSWERS

1 *So she could go to Glasgow and learn plastering*

2 *Sexual harassment of female clerical staff*

3 *She was a landscape architect*

4 *Coventry South*

5 *Queen's College, London*

6 *Edith Sitwell*

7 *Her head is that of a crocodile, her torso that of a predatory cat and her buttocks those of a hippopotamus*

8 *1712*

9 *As an Irish republican (in favour of Ireland's independence) she refused to take the Oath of allegiance to the British sovereign*

10 *Josephine Butler*

11 *Hatshepsut*

12 *A solicitor (accept: attorney)*

13 *It was absorbed by National Union of General Workers*

14 *Women Power Committee*

15 *Chief of Air Service*

1 Who did all the stunts in silent movie star Mabel Normand's films?

2 Which 1986 film starring Whoopie Goldberg was directed by Penny Marshall?

3 Who started as *'The Max Factor Girl'*, and in 1987 produced *Fatal Attraction*?

4 What award did Rita Moreno accept for her role in the 1961 film, *West Side Story*?

5 Who played housebound Leona Stevenson in *Sorry Wrong Number* (1948)?

6 Which 1967 film about two legendary gangsters was edited by Dede Allen?

7 For her part in which 1964 children's film did Julie Andrews win an Academy Award?

8 Why did Pearl White, star of the silent movies, cover her red hair with a blonde wig?

9 Who was the first blind and deaf person to star in and produce a movie, in 1918?

10 Whom did Helen Thurston (b. 1916) double for, teasing a leopard, in *Bringing up Baby* (1938)?

11 Which road movie starred Geena Davis and Susan Sarandon?

12 In the Australian soap, *Home and Away*, what is Sophie Simpson's baby daughter called?

13 In which 1939 film did Helen Thurston (b. 1916) double for Marlene Dietrich in a bar brawl?

14 Why was African-American singer Marian Anderson not allowed to sing at Constitution Hall, Washington, DC in 1939?

15 On whose life was the film *The Inn of the Sixth Happiness*, starring Ingrid Bergman, based?

18 ENTERTAINMENT ANSWERS

easier

1 *Mabel Normand herself (1894–1930)*

2 Jumping Jack Flash

3 *Sherry Lansing*

4 *Academy Award*

5 Barbara Stanwyck

6 Bonnie and Clyde

7 Mary Poppins

8 *It gave a better photographic effect*

9 *Helen Keller (1880–1968)*

10 *Katharine Hepburn*

11 Thelma and Louise

12 *Tamara Simpson*

13 Destry Rides Again

14 *Because she was black*

15 *Missionary Gladys Aylward (1903–70)*

1 Who played Googie Gomez in the 1976 play *The Ritz*?
2 Of which large film company was Dawn Steel president in 1987?
3 Which 1977 science-fiction blockbuster film was edited by Marcia Lucas?
4 When could cinema-goers first see *The Perils of Pauline* starring Pearl White?
5 Which movie serial starred Helen Holmes (1892–1950) as the weekly heroine?
6 What was the result of the Canadian TV policy to have equal numbers of females and males in their programmes?
7 Which 1945 film won Joan Crawford an Academy Award and rejuvenated her career?
8 Which American comedian and actress had a hit with her one-woman show *Without You I'm Nothing*?
9 Which early film star was described as 'one of the few great stars who was also a great producer'?
10 Who wrote, starred in and directed the 1971 film *Wanda*?
11 Where was the first International Festival of Women's Cinema held in 1972?
12 Which film star said, 'Any girl can be glamorous. All you have to do is stand still and look stupid'?
13 How many times was Ginger Rogers married?
14 When the comedy series *The Golden Girls* finished, what was the name of the comedy series three of the actresses went on to star in together?
15 Which 1971 TV series starred Shirley MacLaine?

1 *Rita Moreno*

2 *Columbia Pictures*

3 Star Wars

4 *1914*

5 Hazards of Helen

6 *Viewing figures increased*

7 Mildred Pierce

8 *Sandra Bernhard*

9 *Mary Pickford (1893–1979)*

10 *Barbara Loden (1932–80)*

11 *National Film Theatre, London*

12 *Hedy Lamarr*

13 *Five*

14 The Golden Palace

15 Shirley's World

1 For how much did Betty Grable have her legs insured?

2 In which year was Shirley MacLaine born?

3 In which European city is Chantal Akerman's film *Night and Day* (1992) set?

4 What issue is addressed in the film *Smooth Talk* (1985), directed by Joyce Chopra?

5 Who directed the first narrative film, *La Fée Aux Choux* (The Cabbage Fairy) in 1896?

6 What did film director Lois Weber (1882–1936) start her career as?

7 Which 1921 film, directed by Lois Weber (1882–1936), did a critic call 'a brilliant, lively fugue of urban vs. rural values'?

8 What did director Dorothy Arzner (1900–79) regularly threaten to do if she didn't get her own way when directing a film?

9 In which 1932 film was Sylvia Sidney's first starring role?

10 On which short story by Joyce Carol Oates is the 1985 film *Smooth Talk* based?

11 Who was the first performer to become a millionaire through acting?

12 Which 1971 film was based on an article in the American *Sunday Daily News* entitled 'Did Justice Triumph'?

13 How much was Elaine May paid to direct the box-office disaster *Ishtar* (1987)?

14 Mai Zetterling has achieved acclaim in which field of entertainment?

15 Who starred in the film *Hapki Do* and was described as the 'first lady of Kung Fu'?

ENTERTAINMENT ANSWERS

1 *$25,000*

2 *1934*

3 *Paris*

4 *A young girl's coming of age*

5 *Alice Guy Blaché*

6 *A street corner evangelist*

7 The Blot

8 *Quit*

9 Merrily We Go to Hell

10 *'Where are you going, where have you been?'*

11 *Mary Pickford (1893–1979)*

12 Wanda

13 *2 million dollars*

14 *Cinema*

15 *Angela Mao*

1 From whom did Shula inherit Glebe Cottage?

2 What was Peggy Woolley's maiden name?

3 For which paper does Jennifer Aldridge write a weekly page?

4 Where does Marjorie Antrobus live?

5 Who was Lucy Perks' mother?

6 Whom did actress Moir Leslie play when she was in *The Archers*?

7 Which of the Archers runs a riding stables?

8 After whom did Sharon name her baby?

9 Where did Peggy Archer make her home after leaving *The Bull* in 1972?

10 What enterprise did Jill Archer develop in 1992?

11 Who made the video for the twinning of a French town with Ambridge?

12 Where does Clarrie Grundy work part-time?

13 Who was trying to sell *The Bull* in 1993?

14 How did Grace Archer die in 1955?

15 Who was 'Miss Snowy' in 1986?

19 THE ARCHERS ANSWERS

1 *Her grandmother, Doris Archer*

2 *Perkins*

3 The Borchester Echo

4 *Nightingale Farm*

5 *Polly Perks*

6 *Sophie Barlow (student fashion designer)*

7 *Christine*

8 *Actress and singer Kylie Minogue*

9 *Blossom Hill Cottage*

10 *Bed-and-breakfast holidays at the farm*

11 *Linda Snell*

12 *At* The Bull *as a barmaid*

13 *Peggy Woolley*

14 *She died while trying to rescue a horse ('Midnight') from the stables, which were on fire*

15 *Elizabeth Archer, when she was selling ice-cream*

1 Which energetic TV presenter used her skills to renovate the village hall in 1993?

2 Which agricultural college did Ruth attend?

3 In which year did Marjorie Antrobus first appear in Ambridge?

4 Which 'A' level did Elizabeth Archer pass in 1986?

5 What was Jill Archer suffering from when she was rushed to hospital, after collapsing, in 1976?

6 In 1963, what did Jennifer Aldridge start training as?

7 What did Susan Carter win at the church fête in 1983?

8 What did Elizabeth Archer sell when she worked at *The Borchester Echo*?

9 Which university did Lucy Perks go to?

10 With whom did Ruth lodge when she first arrived in Ambridge as a student?

11 Who ran out of money in Bangkok when visiting Asia in 1979?

12 On which Channel Island does Peggy's daughter Lillian live?

13 Who was born with a hole in the heart?

14 Who changed the family newspaper from the *Express* to the *Guardian* in the early 1980s?

15 Why did Clarrie Grundy start buying and taking the labels off lots of unusual types of food in the summer of 1993?

19 THE ARCHERS ANSWERS

medium

1 *Anneka Rice*

2 *Harper Adams*

3 *1983*

4 *English*

5 *Thyroid deficiency*

6 *A teacher*

7 *A pig*

8 *Advertising space*

9 *Nottingham University*

10 *Marjorie Antrobus*

11 *Shula Archer*

12 *Guernsey*

13 *Elizabeth Archer*

14 *Pat Archer*

15 *She had been bitten by the competition bug*

1 In 1977 Caroline Bone arrived in *The Archers*. What was her job?

2 During the Second World War, which service was Peggy Woolley (then Peggy Perkins) in?

3 When Polly Perks won £1,000 on a Premium Bond in 1968, what did she do with the money?

4 On which children's radio programme was Patricia Gallimore (Pat Archer) a presenter for many years?

5 Hedli Niklaus plays Kathy Perks now. She has appeared twice before, once as Libby Jones, a milk recorder. What was her other appearance as?

6 What was Lesley Saweard's career before she got the role of Christine Archer?

7 Who originally played Christine Archer, before Lesley Saweard?

8 Who started a craft shop called *'Two Jays'* in 1978?

9 Why was actress Judy Bennett (Shula) sacked from her part as understudy in *The Chinese Prime Minister* at the Globe Theatre?

10 In 1958, what happened to Lillian Archer while she was skating?

11 What did aunt Laura Archer plan to do in 1972?

12 When did Jill Archer move into Brookfield?

13 In 1972, who had a nervous breakdown and fled to London when she could not cope with farm life?

14 What was Carol Tregorran found not guilty of in Felpersham in 1976?

15 Which member of the Royal family attended the NSPCC Gala Dinner at Grey Gables in 1984?

THE ARCHERS ANSWERS

1 *Temporary barmaid (at* The Bull*)*

2 *ATS (Auxiliary Territorial Service)*

3 *Used it as a deposit to buy the village shop*

4 Listen with Mother

5 *Eva Lenz, Home Farm's au pair girl*

6 *Teacher*

7 *Pamela Mant*

8 *Jill Archer and Jennifer Aldridge*

9 *She didn't have an Equity card*

10 *She fell through the ice on the village pond*

11 *She planned to buy 100 acres of Lakey Hill and use it as a caravan site*

12 *1970*

13 *Jill Archer*

14 *Shoplifting*

15 *Princess Margaret*

1 Who was Cassandra Austen's sister?

2 Under what pseudonym was *Jane Eyre* published in 1847?

3 Who is the book *Gertrude and Alice*, written by Diana Souhami, about?

4 What does the Fawcett Society work for?

5 Who wrote *The Woman on the Edge of Time*, published in Britain in 1979?

6 What was New Zealand writer Janet Frame awarded in the Queen's Birthday Honours list of 1983?

7 What is the title of the famous book on household management written by Isabella Beeton, published in 1861?

8 Whose friendship did Vera Brittain write *Testament of Friendship* (1946) as a tribute to?

9 Which play, based on an Agatha Christie book, has been running in London for longer than any other?

10 Who wrote *Goblin Market and Other Poems* in 1862?

11 What inspired Mary Shelley to write *Frankenstein, or The Modern Prometheus* in 1817?

12 What was the pseudonym of author Cicily Isabel Fairfield (1892–1983)?

13 Georgette Heyer is well known for her historical romances. What other kind of books did she also write?

14 Who is the author of *The Women's Room* (1977)?

15 For which Yorkshire-based novelists of the 19th century were Sarah and Nancy Garrs nursemaids?

LITERATURE & ART ANSWERS

1 *Novelist Jane Austen*

2 *Currer Bell*

3 *Gertrude Stein and Alice B. Toklas*

4 *Full equality between women and men*

5 *Marge Piercy*

6 *CBE (Commander (of the Order) of the British Empire)*

7 Mrs Beeton's Book of Household Management

8 *Winifred Holtby's (1898–1935)*

9 The Mousetrap

10 *Christina Rossetti*

11 *A dream*

12 *Rebecca West*

13 *Crime novels*

14 *Marilyn French*

15 *The Brontë sisters*

1 To whom did British artist Elizabeth Thompson (1846–1933) give her acclaimed painting *'The Roll Call'* as a present?
2 Which other pen name did Cicily Fairfield sometimes use, early in her writing career, apart from Rebecca West?
3 What is the title of the work of art created by American Judy Chicago (with 400 co-workers) in 1974–79, which celebrates women's art and history?
4 What is the subtitle of Susan Brownmiller's book *Against Our Will*, published by Simon & Schuster (New York) in 1975?
5 Which baby was British art student Fiona Quinn commissioned to paint in 1993?
6 Which was Jane Austen's (1775–1817) first completed full-length novel?
7 For which satirical British magazine did cellist Dorothy Churchill Pratt (1905–92) write as a music and ballet critic?
8 Which College of Art in northern England did Dame Barbara Hepworth (1903–75) attend from 1920 to 1921?
9 Which branch of the UK armed forces was poet Babs Diplock a member of during the Second World War?
10 Which artistic innovation were Grete Stern and Ellen Auerbach leaders in?
11 What event does Caryl Churchill's play *Mad Forest* deal with?
12 What is the title of writer and psychoanalyst Marion Milner's autobiography (1934)?
13 Who published Carolivia Herron's book *Thereafter Johnnie* in 1992?
14 In the graveyard of which chapel in Cheshire is novelist Elizabeth Gaskell (1810–65) buried?
15 How many of Emily Dickinson's (1830–86) poems were published during her lifetime?

LITERATURE & ART ANSWERS

1 *Queen Victoria*

2 *Rachel East*

3 'The Dinner Party'

4 Men, Women and Rape

5 *The Miss Pears Baby Competition winner*

6 Pride and Prejudice

7 Punch

8 *Leeds College of Art*

9 *WAAF (Women's Army and Air Force)*

10 *Experimental photography*

11 *The Romanian Revolution*

12 A Life of One's Own

13 *Virago Press Ltd*

14 *Brook Street Chapel, Knutsford, Cheshire*

15 *Two*

1 What did feminist Mary Hays (1760–1843) publish six volumes of in 1803?
2 In the 17th century, how much did artist Mary Beale (1632–99) charge for painting a three-quarter-length portrait?
3 Under what pseudonym did Finnish poet Karin Alice Heikel (1901–44) write?
4 In the 14th century, why did the first recorded playwright, Katherine of Sutton, Abbess of Barking nunnery, rewrite the Easter dramas performed for her congregation?
5 Who was the only woman artist to have her work shown in the London surrealist exhibition of 1936?
6 What did Anna Atkins (1797–1871) use to illustrate the botanical specimens in her book *British Algae, Cyanotype Impressions*, published in 1853?
7 What is the title of the first book about her travels that Dame Freya Stark (1893–1993) had published in 1937?
8 If you were a collector and had an 18th-century Hester Bateman cream jug, what would it be made of?
9 Why were Egyptian feminist and novelist Nawal El Saadawi (b. 1930) and several other women arrested and imprisoned in 1981, on the orders of Egypt's President Sadat?
10 When the first, edited, version of Anne Frank's (1930–45) diary was published in 1947, what was it called?
11 Which English city elected novelist Sara Grand (1855–1943) as its mayor in 1927?
12 How old was American artist Georgia O'Keeffe when she died in 1986?
13 Which two Welsh sisters set up the company Grgynog Press?
14 What problems does Japanese novelist Sawako Ariyoshi (1921–84) tackle in her novel *Kokotsuno Hito* (The Twilight Years)?
15 Which British newspaper was author Angela Carter (1940–93) apprenticed to at the age of 18?

20 LITERATURE & ART

hard

1 Dictionary of Female Biography

2 £10

3 Katri Vala

4 To keep the congregation awake

5 Eileen Agar (b. 1904)

6 Photographs

7 Baghdad Sketches

8 Silver

9 For publishing Confrontation, *a feminist magazine*

10 Het Achterhuis *(later translated as* Diary of a Young Girl*)*

11 Bath

12 99

13 Margaret and Gwendoline Davies

14 The problems involved in caring for and living with a senile relative

15 Croydon Advertiser

1 Which political party did the first woman elected as a Member of Parliament (Constance Markiewicz) belong to?

2 In 1968 Mary Daly (b. 1928) was employed as a teacher in the Theology Department of a Boston (US) college run by Jesuits. What happened when her book *The Church and the Second Sex* was published?

3 Which was the first English refuge for battered women, opened in 1971?

4 Which daughter of Emmeline Pankhurst went to live in Australia?

5 What is the name of the group of missionaries founded by Mother Theresa?

6 For which constituency was Margaret Thatcher Member of Parliament?

7 Which place of pilgrimage is St Bernadette (1844–79) associated with, where she saw 18 apparitions of the Virgin Mary?

8 In which year did Queen Elizabeth II succeed to the throne?

9 Of which army did Eva Burrows become general in 1986?

10 What is special about the Reeves Hotel in West London?

11 For how many hours did French nursery teacher Laurence Dreyfus keep her class of nursery school children calm and occupied while they were held hostage in May 1993?

12 What relation were Doctor Elizabeth Garrett Anderson (1836–1917) and suffragette Millicent Garrett Fawcett (1847–1929)?

13 Of which children's charity is Princess Anne president?

14 Why did Vera Brittain (1893–1970) take time out from her studies at Somerville College, Oxford, after only one year?

15 Which writer and South African revolutionary was killed by a letter bomb in August 1982?

HERSTORY ANSWERS

1 *Sinn Fein (now the political wing of the IRA)*

2 *She was sacked*

3 *Chiswick Women's Aid*

4 *Adela Pankhurst (1885–1961)*

5 *Missionaries of Charity*

6 *Finchley*

7 *Lourdes*

8 *1952 (6th February)*

9 *The Salvation Army*

10 *It is owned by women, run by women and is for women guests only*

11 *46*

12 *Sisters*

13 *Save the Children Fund*

14 *She went to work as a voluntary nurse at home and abroad during the First World War*

15 *Ruth First*

1 In 1209, what was Agnes, referred to as 'Wife of Odo', the first woman to be accused of?

2 In which year did Barbara Castle become the UK's first female Secretary of State, as Minister of Transport?

3 Which was the first British Civil Service department to employ women, as female 'typewriters' in 1888?

4 In 1338, when her home Dunbar Castle was under siege from the army, what did Agnes Dunbar, Countess of March and Dunbar do?

5 At which High School in northeastern England was novelist E. H. Young educated?

6 Which commission was African-American Eleanor Holmes Norton (b. 1937) appointed chairperson of in 1977?

7 What was the result of the Ten Hours Act of 1847?

8 In which year did Victoria become Queen of England?

9 In the 19th century, why were women forbidden by the Bishop of London from attending Wheatstone's 'Lecture on Electricity', at Kings College?

10 Who was the United States' first self-made woman millionaire?

11 Which is the only statue of a (named) woman in Manchester city centre?

12 Which group of women were called up to join the British Armed Forces in January 1942?

13 On Wednesday, 18th March 1987, how did Reverend Sylvia Mutch make history?

14 In 1945 Barbara Castle became Member of Parliament for which constituency?

15 How did Boudicca, Queen of Iceni, die?

21 HERSTORY ANSWERS

medium

1 *Witchcraft*

2 *1965*

3 *Inland Revenue*

4 *She defended the castle, so well that the siege was abandoned*

5 *Gateshead High School*

6 *Equal Employment Opportunity Commission*

7 *The work hours of women and young persons were limited to 10 hours a day*

8 *1837*

9 *Too many women were attending the lectures*

10 *Madame C. J. Walker*

11 *The statue of Queen Victoria*

12 *All single women between the ages of 20 and 21*

13 *She became the first woman to conduct a church wedding ceremony in Britain*

14 *Blackburn*

15 *She poisoned herself*

1 Who was said to have had a lover in every town she conquered in 16th-century Africa?
2 What was the German Hanna Reitsch's job during the Second World War?
3 In the 5th century Ia, a noble-born Irishwoman, founded a religious settlement in St Ives, Cornwall. What is it said she used, instead of a boat, to cross the sea from Ireland to Cornwall?
4 What was the main difference between the first real schools for females—Queen's College and Bedford College (both in London)?
5 What UK Congress did Anna Loughlin become president of in 1943?
6 Objects made by businesswoman Louisa Courtauld (1729–1807) can be seen in London's Victoria & Albert Museum. What precious metal are they made of?
7 Which ancient language did Elizabeth Elstob (1683–1756), from Newcastle upon Tyne, become a noted scholar of?
8 While prisoners in the Maison de Correction de Fresnes, during the Second World War, why were Odette (Lise) Sansom and others taken to 84 Avenue Foch?
9 What is Áte the Greek Goddess of?
10 What qualification did aviator Amy Johnson (1903–41) graduate from the University of Sheffield with in 1925?
11 By 1926 Miss Gordon Holmes had risen to the position of Stockbroker for the UK's National Securities Corporation. What had she started her career as?
12 What is the aim of the Pepperell Unit, launched by Britain's Industrial Society in 1984 and named after businesswoman Elizabeth Pepperell (1915–69)?
13 Women in South Australia could vote from 1894. When were women in New Zealand given the vote?
14 What is the Tamil Goddess, Korrawi, Goddess of?
15 The 1888 strike by women workers at Britain's Bryant and May match company for better pay and conditions is well known. In which four other trades did women go on strike in Britain in the same year?

HERSTORY ANSWERS

1 *Amina (of Hausaland)*

2 *Test-pilot for the Luftwaffe*

3 *A leaf*

4 *Queen's was governed by men only, Bedford by women and men*

5 *The TUC (Trades Union Congress)*

6 *Silver*

7 *Anglo-Saxon*

8 *To be interrogated by the Commissars of the Gestapo*

9 *Disaster*

10 *BA in Economics, Latin and French*

11 *A typist*

12 *The improvement of women's conditions at work*

13 *1893*

14 *Battle and Victory*

15 *Mill-workers (Kilmarnock); cotton and jute workers (Dundee); cigar makers (Nottingham); and blanket weavers (Yorkshire)*

1 Where was Angie off to in September 1993?

2 For which mission was Ena Sharples caretaker?

3 Who is Tracy Barlow's mother?

4 Why did Raquel go to Croydon in September 1993?

5 Who was appointed manageress of the *Rovers Return* on 4th February 1985?

6 Where did Audrey refuse to move in 1993?

7 Who became manageress of the *'Kabin'* in 1992?

8 Who own and run the café?

9 What kind of business does Denise own and run?

10 Where does Hilda Ogden's daughter now live?

11 Which pub did Liz MacDonald become manageress of in 1993?

12 Where was Elsie Tanner heading for when she left the Street in January 1984?

13 What kind of shop does Maggie Redman own and run?

14 Who owns a budgie called Harry (originally Harriet)?

15 Which character was played by Violet Carson?

CORONATION STREET ANSWERS

1 *Mexico*

2 *Glad Tidings Mission*

3 *Deirdre Barlow*

4 *She went on a modelling course*

5 *Bet Lynch*

6 *To Lytham St Annes*

7 *Mavis Wilton*

8 *Alma Baldwin and Gail Platt*

9 *A hairdresser's*

10 *Canada*

11 The Queens

12 *Portugal*

13 *A flower shop*

14 *Mavis Wilton*

15 *Ena Sharples*

1 Why did Paula stop seeing so much of Andy McDonald?

2 What rumour did Ena Sharples start in March 1961 after she visited the Town Hall to complain about her water pressure?

3 Which comedy actress arrived in *Coronation Street* as Maureen Naylor, assistant at Bettabuys?

4 Who owned the corner shop before Florrie Lindley?

5 What was Marion Willis's CB handle?

6 What did Hilda Ogden inherit in 1983?

7 Which barmaid owned her own pub in Cheshire in real life?

8 With whom did Suzie Birchall and Gail Potter lodge when they first arrived in the Street?

9 Which member of the *Coronation Street* cast played Cleopatra in *Carry on Cleopatra*?

10 What kind of car did Annie Walker buy in 1976 after passing her driving test?

11 What relation is Bet Gilroy to 'posh' Vicky?

12 Who became Mayoress of Weatherfield in 1973?

13 Which exam did Lucille Hewitt pass in August 1961?

14 Which shop did Renée Roberts buy in 1976?

15 What did the Queen award Violet Carson (Ena Sharples) in 1965?

22 CORONATION STREET ANSWERS

1. *To concentrate on her 'A' levels*
2. *That Coronation Street was to be demolished*
3. *Sherrie Hewson*
4. *Elsie Lappin*
5. *'Stardust Lil'*
6. *A chip shop*
7. *Betty Turpin*
8. *Elsie Howard (Tanner)*
9. *Amanda Barrie (Alma Baldwin)*
10. *A Rover 2000*
11. *Step-grandmother*
12. *Annie Walker*
13. *Her 11-plus exam*
14. *The corner shop*
15. *OBE (Order of the British Empire)*

1 Who was left Number 11, Coronation Street in a will in January 1965?

2 What was Elsie Tanner charged with in November 1969 that resulted in her having to appear in court?

3 In which year did Emily Nugent pass her driving test?

4 What did Emily sell to pay the bills in July 1976?

5 Which member of *Are You Being Served?* played landlady Nellie Harvey of the Lady Victuallers?

6 Why did Ena Sharples not wear a wedding ring?

7 What did the Queen award Doris Speed (Annie Walker) in 1977?

8 What was Prunella Scales' job when she appeared in the Street as Eileen Hughes in 1961?

9 Who played the organ at Emily Nugent's first wedding in 1979?

10 At which shop did Dot Greenhalgh and Elsie Tanner work together?

11 In which year was Gail Tilsley's first child born?

12 Who worked at the Imperial Hotel until her death in 1961?

13 At which club did Rita Littlewood make her first appearance in *Coronation Street*, as a dancer?

14 Why was an eviction order served on Elsie Tanner in April 1963?

15 Who was the first *Coronation Street* character to die?

CORONATION STREET ANSWERS

1 *Ena Sharples*

2 *Shoplifting*

3 *1965*

4 *Her engagement ring*

5 *Mollie Sugden*

6 *In 1941 it got too tight so she had it cut off; she could never afford another one*

7 *MBE*

8 *Bus conductress*

9 *Ena Sharples*

10 'Miami Modes'

11 *1980*

12 *Ida Barlow*

13 The Orinoco Club

14 *She had refused to pay a rent increase*

15 *May Hardman*

1 Which ex-assistant Chief Constable wrote *No Way up the Greasy Pole*, published in May 1993?

2 After whom did author Sarah Dreher name the heroine of her crime novels, Stoner McTavish?

3 Who ran the *Whistle Stop Café* near Birmingham, Alabama?

4 What is the name of the dog private investigator V.I. Warshawski shares with her neighbour downstairs?

5 What is the title of the novel written by Toni Morrison which was awarded the Pulitzer Prize for Fiction in 1988?

6 Who are the publishers of comedian Su Pollard's favourite romantic novels?

7 What did Maria Brontë (1813–25) die of?

8 In which Jane Austen novel will you come across Mrs Cole?

9 Which writer of detective fiction wrote romantic novels under the pseudonym Mary Westmacott?

10 Who wrote a series of alphabetically-titled detective novels, starting with *A is for Alibi*?

11 In which language was the novel *Egalias døtre* (1977), written by Gerd Brantenberg and translated as *The Daughters of Egalia* in 1985, originally written?

12 In which Charlotte Brontë novel does she use her days at the Clergy Daughters' School at Cowan Bridge as the basis for her portrayal of Lowood School?

13 Who published the first British *Directory of Women Co-operatives and Other Enterprises* in 1990?

14 Which Agatha Christie novel, published in 1930, introduced Miss Marple?

15 Which British poet wrote the novel-poem *Aurora Leigh*?

LITERATURE & ART ANSWERS

1 *Alison Halford*
2 *The American feminist, Lucy B. Stone*
3 *Idgie Threadgoode and Ruth Jamison*
4 *Peppy*
5 Beloved
6 *Mills and Boon*
7 *Consumption*
8 Emma
9 *Dame Agatha Christie (1890–1976)*
10 *Sue Grafton*
11 *Norwegian*
12 Jane Eyre
13 Everywoman *magazine*
14 Murder at the Vicarage
15 *Elizabeth Barrett Browning (1806–61)*

1 For how many years did British author Charlotte M. Yonge (1823–1901) teach at Sunday school?
2 What kind of plant did British artist Marianne North (1830–90) discover on her travels in the Seychelles (1883), which was then named after her?
3 Jane Austen (1775–1817) started writing *Sense and Sensibility* after she had completed writing *Pride and Prejudice*. Which one was published first?
4 Only two of Emily Dickinson's (1830–86) poems were published while she was alive. How many poems were found after her death?
5 What does the book by Ruth First (1925–82) *117 Days* (1965) describe?
6 Which Channel Island did Jacquetta Hawkes (b. 1910) write a book about the archaeology of in 1910?
7 Whose autobiography, of her experiences during the Second World War, is entitled *Granny Was a Spy*?
8 What request, made by Emily Dickinson (1830–86) as she was dying, was ignored after her death?
9 For which British Sunday newspaper did Joyce Grenfell write radio criticisms at the beginning of her career?
10 For how much did Jane Austen (1775–1817) originally sell her novel *Northanger Abbey* to a publisher in Bath?
11 Who signed her column in the *New Yorker* 'Constant Reader'?
12 In the novel *Three Weeks*, written by Elinor Glyn (1864–1943), where did the sensual scene that caused a scandal in the US take place?
13 In 1969, which of her novels did Elizabeth Jane Howard adapt for Britain's Thames TV as a serial, produced and directed by Moira Armstrong?
14 Which British broadsheet was persuaded by Caroline Lejeune, film critic, to let her write a weekly column entitled *'The Week on the Screen'* in 1922?
15 Who wrote the novel *The Way of an Eagle*, which, when it was published in 1912, was an instant success?

LITERATURE & ART ANSWERS

1 *71*

2 *A capucin tree,* Northia seychellana

3 Sense and Sensibility *(1811)*

4 *Over 1700*

5 *Her experiences in prison, when she was held in solitary confinement for six months*

6 *Jersey*

7 *José Villiers*

8 *That all her poems, over 1700 of them, be destroyed*

9 The Observer

10 *£10*

11 *Dorothy Parker*

12 *On a tiger skin*

13 Something in Disguise

14 The Guardian

15 *Ethel M. Dell (1881–1939)*

1 What was the title of the very first Sunday newspaper in the UK, started by Mrs Johnson in 1779?

2 What was the title of British author Elizabeth Jane Howard's first published novel?

3 Under what name did Amandine-Aurore-Lucie Dupin Dudevant write her novels?

4 How is it difficult to find out anything about the early history of *The Society of Female Artists*, founded in Britain in 1857?

5 Who edited the book *Greenham Common: Women at the Wire* in 1984?

6 Which Brontë sister (author of *Agnes Grey*) did Winifred Gérin write a biography of in 1959?

7 For a time the novelist Frances Trollope lived in Cincinnati, Ohio. While there, how did she try and make a living?

8 Why did British author Eliza Carter wake up early each morning?

9 Which disease did British writer May Sinclair (1863–1946) suffer from in later life?

10 What is the title of scriptwriter and author Anita Loos' autobiography (1966)?

11 What was Dame Elisabeth Frink's last commission, which she finished just before she died in April 1993?

12 Where did American artist Sandra Fisher (b. 1947) graduate from in 1968?

13 Which three languages did 19th-century British writer Eliza Lynn Linton (1822–98) teach herself as a child?

14 Which novel by Kate Chopin, published in 1899, was made into a film called *The End of August*, released in 1981?

15 Which painting by Elizabeth Thompson (1846–1933), when shown by London's Royal Academy in 1874, needed extra police to keep back the crowds who had come to see it?

LITERATURE & ART ANSWERS

1 British Gazette and Sunday Monitor

2 The Beautiful Visit

3 *George Sand*

4 *Its archives were destroyed during the Second World War*

5 *Barbara Harford and Sarah Hopkins*

6 *Anne (*Anne Brontë: A Biography*)*

7 *As a shopkeeper*

8 *To teach herself Greek*

9 *Parkinson's Disease*

10 A Girl Like

11 *Figure of Christ for the facade of Liverpool's Anglican Cathedral*

12 *California Institute of the Arts*

13 *Hebrew, Latin and Greek*

14 The Awakening

15 'The Roll Call'

1 In the 17th century, why did Britain's Overseers of the Poor (Parish Officials) employ local wise-women instead of university-trained (male) doctors to look after the poor?

2 What dangerous chemical is used to bleach paper and sanitary products?

3 Who invented the computer term 'bug'?

4 Why did mathematician Mary Somerville (1880–72) never get to see the bust of herself placed in the Great Hall of the Royal Astronomical Society?

5 What did British entomologist Eleanor Ormerod (1828–1901) study?

6 Why did the UK's Society of Apothecaries change its rules in 1865?

7 Why are the notebooks Marie Curie used in the 19th century, during her search for radium, still kept in a strong room lined with lead?

8 Which ancient city did British archaeologist Kathleen Kenyon (1906–78) spend the years 1952 to 1958 excavating?

9 Who was the second woman, after Florence Nightingale, to be awarded Britain's Order of Merit, in 1965?

10 Which British university did Miranda Barry attend, disguised as a man called James Barry, and qualify at as a surgeon?

11 What does the acronym WISE stand for?

12 What kind of clinic did Marie Stopes open in London in 1921?

13 In a survey by UK soap manufactures, who proved to spend least time in the bathroom, women or men?

14 What do the initials IVF stand for?

15 In 19th-century fashion, what was a 'cage'?

SCIENCE ANSWERS

1 *It was cheaper*

2 *Dioxin*

3 *American computer expert Grace Hopper*

4 *Women weren't allowed in*

5 *Insects*

6 *To make sure no woman, after the success of Elizabeth Garrett (1836–1917) could again sit and pass their exams*

7 *They are radioactive*

8 *Jericho, in Jordan*

9 *Dorothy Hodgkin (b. 1910), English biochemist*

10 *Edinburgh*

11 *Women into Science and Engineering*

12 *Birth control clinic*

13 *Women*

14 *In vitro fertilization*

15 *A steel frame crinoline*

1 What were workers who died of 'radium jaw' using radioactive paint on?

2 Which famous physicist was born on 7th November 1867 in Warsaw?

3 In various studies done in the US in the 1980s, what one factor was consistently found to improve the health of single women?

4 Which subject did Catherine North, sister of Marianne North, paint?

5 In which category did British biochemist Dorothy Hodgkin (b. 1910) win a Nobel Prize in 1964?

6 Who became the first Italian woman doctor in 1896?

7 In the early 20th century, why was Margaret Sanger arrested in New York?

8 In the 1990s what is the average number of children born to each women in EC (European Community) countries?

9 When Elizabeth Garrett Anderson (1836–1917) refused to leave the first meeting she attended of the British Medical Association, what was the result?

10 In 1891 what forced Gertrude Jekyll to give up embroidery and painting and take up gardening instead?

11 What form of gruesome death was suffered by mathematician Hypatia in the 4th century?

12 What were called the 'Little Curies' and used at the battlefront during the First World War?

13 In which year did astronomer Caroline Herschel (1750–1848) observe her first comet?

14 Which modern movement for the terminally ill was started by Briton Cicely Saunders?

15 Which mother and daughter scientists received the Nobel Prize for Chemistry (the mother in 1911, the daughter in 1935)?

SCIENCE ANSWERS

1 *Luminous watches*

2 *Marie Curie (née Sklodowska)*

3 *Being in paid employment*

4 *Flowers*

5 *Chemistry*

6 *Maria Montessori*

7 *For opening a birth control clinic*

8 *1.6*

9 *A new rule was created to ensure no other woman could become a member of the BMA*

10 *Acute myopia (she could no longer see very well)*

11 *She was torn apart by a Christian mob*

12 *Mobile x-ray units*

13 *1786 (August)*

14 *The Hospice Movement*

15 *Marie Curie (1867–1934) and her daughter Irené Joliot-Curie (1897–1956)*

1 Astronomer Caroline Herschel (1750–1848) discovered more comets than any other astronomer of the time. How many did she discover between 1786 and 1797?
2 In 1824 paleontologist Mary Anning (1799–1847) discovered the fossil of a dinosaur in Lyme Regis. What kind of dinosaur?
3 How was crystallographer, physicist and chemist Kathleen Lonsdale (1903–71) able to go back to work (research into x-ray diffraction of crystals) after the birth of her children?
4 In the 1740s, how did Mrs Giles try and earn a living?
5 Whose daughter (Louise) became Chief Surgeon of London's Endell Street Military Hospital during the First World War?
6 What two factors did mental health researchers Myrna Weissman and G. Klerman find were the main causes of depression in women?
7 Of which Institute was archaeologist Jacquetta Hawkes (b. 1910) governor from 1950 to 1955?
8 In what area of biology is American Sylvia Earle Mead (b. 1935) a renowned specialist?
9 Which two women were awarded Honorary Membership of the Royal Astronomical Society in 1835?
10 Who wrote, and illustrated, the five-volume *Flowering Plants and Ferns of Great Britain*, published in 1855?
11 Which subject was Italian Maria Agnei (1718–99) professor of at Bologna University?
12 What area of research did Dr Mary Edward Chinn specialize in before her death in 1980?
13 What is the name of the former New Hospital for Women, opened in London in 1872?
14 What did Briton Eleanor Davis-Colley become the first Woman Fellow of in 1911?
15 In the 17th century, which subject did Bathsua Makin advocate should be taught to girls in school?

SCIENCE ANSWERS

1 *Eight*
2 *A plesiosaurus (marine reptile)*
3 *She was offered a grant to cover the cost of child care*
4 *By getting rid of people's unwanted hair*
5 *Dr Elizabeth Garrett Anderson's (1836–1917)*
6 *Low social status and marriage*
7 *British Film Institute*
8 *Marine biology*
9 *Caroline Herschel (astronomer) and Mary Somerville (mathematician)*
10 *Anne Pratt (1806–93)*
11 *Mathematics*
12 *Cancer research*
13 *Elizabeth Garrett Anderson Hospital*
14 *Royal College of Surgeons*
15 *Science*

1 On her marriage in 1832, what did French socialist and feminist Jeanne Deroin (1810–94) refuse to do?

2 Who was the only child of Catherine of Aragon (1485–1536) to survive?

3 In 1988, for which London Borough did Valda James become the first black woman mayor?

4 What was Elizabeth, dowager Countess of Shrewsbury (1520–1608) more generally known as?

5 Who paid Nina Masel, and other British women, to write diaries about what they observed during the Second World War?

6 Who became Prime Minister of India on 24th January 1966 – and again in January, 1980?

7 What do the letters ANCWL, of South Africa, stand for?

8 In 1993 which honour was awarded to Laurence Dreyfus, heroine of the 46-hour nursery school siege?

9 In 1987 what title was Princess Anne given?

10 In the 1990s, which partner requests 70 per cent of divorces?

11 As part of an anti-nuclear demonstration in July 1993, which British Royal palace did 15 women members of the Anti-Nuclear Testing Network climb over and wander around the grounds of?

12 Who took the throne as the first Queen of England in her own right?

13 How many arms does the Buddhist Goddess Astābhuja-Kurukulla have?

14 Who launched Vivair, an aircharter broker which achieved a turnover of £20 million in 1990 and of which Vivien Padwick is Managing Director?

15 What do the initials WEDA stand for?

25 HERSTORY ANSWERS

1 *She refused to change her name*
2 *Mary I*
3 *Islington*
4 *Bess of Hardwick*
5 *The Mass Observation Unit*
6 *Indira Gandhi (1917–84)*
7 *African National Congress Women's League*
8 *Légion d'Honneur*
9 *Princess Royal*
10 *The wife*
11 *Buckingham Palace*
12 *Mary I (Mary Tudor, 1516–58)*
13 *Eight*
14 *Vivien Padwick*
15 *Women's Enterprise Development Agency*

medium

1 What did Christian Davies do in 1692 when her husband disappeared?

2 Between the two World Wars, what did most people in Britain consider the 'natural sphere of employment' for women to be?

3 After the UK Government's *Sex Disqualifications Removal Act* of 1919 all professions except two had to admit women. Which were the two exceptions?

4 What world event was British journalist Kate Adie reporting when she was shot in the arm?

5 Women over 21 were given the vote in Britain in 1928. When was the first time they could use their vote?

6 When nurse Edith Cavell was court-martialled in 1915, approximately how many people did she admit to helping to escape German-occupied Belgium?

7 Which undercover group was Odette Sansom a member of during the Second World War?

8 Where did Cleopatra VII succeed to the throne in 51 BC?

9 In 1919, which UK children's charity was set up by Eglantyne Jebb and her sister Dorothy as an emergency relief fund?

10 Which of Queen Victoria's children was given the nickname 'die Englanderin'?

11 In which century did Lady Godiva ride naked through the streets of Coventry?

12 In 1890, in which subject did Philippa Fawcett win top place in the Cambridge University finals?

13 Who was the last person buried in Westminster Abbey, in 1906?

14 Why did Mrs Frances Bell have to give back her Victoria Cross, which had been presented to her by Queen Victoria in recognition of her extreme bravery during the Boer War (1899–1902)?

15 From which funeral firm in England's northeast did Joyce Patterson (b. 1924) retire as general manager in 1988?

HERSTORY ANSWERS

1. *She dressed up as a man, then enlisted as a foot soldier in order to go looking for him (she found him after 12 years of searching, then stayed on fighting until the end of the campaign)*
2. *Domestic service*
3. *The Church and top Civil Servants*
4. *The killings in Tiananmen Square (China)*
5. *May, 1929*
6. *200*
7. *Special Operations Executive*
8. *Alexandria*
9. *Save the Children Fund*
10. *Victoria (Empress of Germany)*
11. *11th century*
12. *Mathematics*
13. *Angela Burdett-Coutts (1814–1906)*
14. *It was discovered after it had been given to her that women were not eligible to receive this award*
15. *(British) North-Eastern Co-op Funeral Group*

1 In which year was Saint Teresa of Avila canonized?

2 A statue of the Aztec Goddess of Earth and Fire, Coatlicue, stands in Mexico City. What does her necklace consist of?

3 Which Women's Guild was founded in Britain in 1883?

4 In 1929 the Member of Parliament for Northampton became the first woman in the Cabinet. Who was she?

5 Louisa Courtauld ran a very successful business in London in the 18th century. What was it?

6 What was Odette Sansom's codename as a Special Operations Executive (British Agent) in France during the Second World War?

7 Which royal personage was mother of Margaret Douglas, Countess of Lennox (b. 1515)?

8 Who was the last woman in England to be executed for a political offence (in this case high treason, in 1685)?

9 Why did Betty Harvie Anderson retire as Deputy Speaker of the House of Commons in 1973?

10 Which Scottish school of medicine was founded by Sophia Jex-Blake in the 19th century?

11 In the 1960s, how long did it take Sheila Scott to fly the longest solo flight ever undertaken?

12 What was the newspaper of Britain's National Federation of Women Workers (NFWW) called?

13 Who were the three British Agents shot at Ravensbruck Concentration Camp on 26th January 1945?

14 When did the UK's Amalgamated Engineering Union (AEU) accept its first woman member?

15 What did Unity Valkyrie Mitford (1914–48) usually wear round her neck when she attended dances?

HERSTORY ANSWERS

1 *1622*

2 *The hands and hearts of human beings*

3 *The Co-operative Women's Guild*

4 *Margaret Bondfield*

5 *She was a silversmith*

6 *Lise*

7 *Margaret Tudor (Queen of Scotland)*

8 *Elizabeth Gaunt*

9 *To be free to oppose Scottish devolution*

10 *The Edinburgh School of Medicine for Women*

11 *33 days and three minutes*

12 The Woman Worker

13 *Violette Szabo, Lilian Rolfe and Denise Bloche*

14 *1943*

15 *Her pet grass snake, Enid*

1 Who had a number one hit in the UK with *'Don't Cry for Me, Argentina'* in December, 1976?

2 What song did Julee Cruise take into the UK top 10 in November 1990?

3 What relation are Dionne Warwick and Whitney Houston to each other?

4 Which song did Kylie Minogue take to Britain's number one in January 1990?

5 Who paired up with Elaine Paige to have a number one hit in the UK with *'I Know Him So Well'* in January 1985?

6 Who are the backing group for Martha Reeves?

7 Which song did Tina Turner take to number 3 in the UK charts in June 1984?

8 Who wrote *'Poor Man's Blues'*, recorded by Bessie Smith in 1928?

9 Which UK female vocal trio *'saw Mammy kissing Santa Claus'* in 1953?

10 What did Tammy Wynette spell out in 1975?

11 Who rapped *'Twist and Shout'* in November 1988?

12 What was the title of Marianne Faithfull's first album?

13 Which British talent-spotting show did Mary Hopkin appear on in 1968?

14 Siobhan Fahey forms half of which group?

15 What was the title of the song Sandy Shaw sang when she won the Eurovision Song Contest?

MUSIC ANSWERS

1 *Julie Covington*

2 'Falling'

3 *They are cousins*

4 'Tears on My Pillow'

5 *Barbara Dickson*

6 *The Vandellas*

7 'What's Love Got to Do with It?'

8 *Bessie Smith*

9 *The Beverley Sisters*

10 *'D.I.V.O.R.C.E'*

11 *Salt 'n' Pepa*

12 Marianne Faithfull

13 Opportunity Knocks

14 *Shakespear's Sister*

15 'Puppet on a String'

1 Who took *'Walk on By'* to number six in the UK charts for nine weeks in 1990?

2 Which record label was American soul singer Mary Wells signed to?

3 Which major department store chain did singer Betty Boo work for part-time, as a florist, when she was a teenager?

4 In 1993 which Dolly Parton song contained the lines, 'I may not be in love/But let me tell you, I'm in heat'?

5 In December 1987 where did Belinda Carlisle tell us 'heaven is'?

6 What is the title of Mary Margaret O'Hara's album, released in 1988?

7 What was the name of Judy Collins' first album?

8 Who sang about a mockingbird in 1982?

9 Who wrote the song *'Clouds'*, sung by Judy Collins?

10 What did Polly Brown 'go up in' in September 1974?

11 What kind of singer is 'Dimples D'?

12 Which song did Diana Ross take to number one in the UK in July 1971 and, as a re-mix, to number 21 in July 1990?

13 Which female vocal/instrumental group sang *'Love Is the Slug'* in November 1986?

14 What couldn't Kim Wilde say in December 1990?

15 Who were the first group to get to number one in the US twice in the 1990s?

MUSIC ANSWERS

1 *Sybil*
2 *Tamla Motown*
3 *Marks and Spencer*
4 'Romeo'
5 *A place on Earth* ('Heaven is a Place on Earth')
6 Miss America
7 A Maid of Constant Sorrow
8 *The Belle Stars*
9 *Joni Mitchell*
10 *in a puff of smoke* ('Up in a Puff of Smoke')
11 *A rapper*
12 'I'm Still Waiting'
13 *We've Got a Fuzzbox and We're Going to Use It*
14 *Goodbye* ('I Can't Say Goodbye')
15 *Wilson Phillips*

1 Which American country singer was born Virginia Hensley?

2 Who manages singer Lulu?

3 How many Marvelettes were there originally?

4 What reason did the Manchester Hallé Orchestra give for sacking all its women members in 1920?

5 When was the first phonograph record by a blues singer, *'That Thing Called Love'* by Mamie Smith, cut?

6 How many different labels issued Lucille Hegamin's hit, *'Arkansas Blues'*?

7 Which Des'ree album, released in 1992, includes her UK hit single, *'Feel So High'*?

8 Who released an album entitled *And Still I Rise* in 1992?

9 Which popular Scottish ballad was written by Baroness Caroline Nairne, born in 1766?

10 Denise La Salle released two albums on one CD in 1992. One album was called *On the Loose*; what was the other one?

11 Who released the single *'One True Woman'* in 1992?

12 Which hymn was written by Sarah Adams and set to music by her sister Eliza Flower?

13 At what number did Tori Amos' debut album, *Little Earthquakes*, enter the UK charts in 1992?

14 What is the name of the pop group from New York consisting of Stephanie, Jill, Claudine and Debby?

15 What action did Briton Ethel Smyth (1858–1944) take in order to make her parents agree to allow her go to the Leipzig Conservatory in Germany and study music?

MUSIC ANSWERS

1. *Patsy Cline*
2. *Marion Massey*
3. *Five*
4. *The orchestra wanted 'unity of style'*
5. *1920*
6. *11*
7. Mind Adventures
8. *Alison Limerick*
9. 'Charlie is My Darling'
10. Tripped by a Thing Called Love
11. *Yazz*
12. 'Nearer, My God, to Thee'
13. *15*
14. *The Aquanettes*
15. *She barricaded herself into her bedroom until they agreed to let her go*

1 Who was the author of *The Yellow Wallpaper* (1892)?

2 What does author Shelley Bovey think about being fat?

3 On whose life story is the character Julia Almond in *A Pin To See the Peepshow* (written by F. Tennyson Jesse in 1934) based?

4 Which famous novelist was Anne Thackeray's step-niece?

5 What is the title of the only book written by aviator and race-horse trainer Beryl Markham (b. 1902)?

6 What event resulted in Revlon refusing to advertise in Ms. magazine?

7 What other name does Ruth Rendell write under?

8 Who was 'the Tenant of Wildfell Hall' in the book of the same name?

9 Where is playwright Aphra Behn (1640–89) buried?

10 Which British women's art society was founded in 1855 and still exists today?

11 Who was the mother of author Mary Shelley (1797–1851)?

12 Which magazine was edited by American Amelia Bloomer?

13 What was 'the colour of hope' for Russian poet Irina Ratushinskaya?

14 Who is the author of the children's book *The Secret Garden* (1911)?

15 Whose first novel was entitled *Mary Barton: a Tale of Manchester Life*, published in 1848?

LITERATURE & ART ANSWERS

1 *Charlotte Perkins Gilman*

2 *That it's not a sin (from her book,* Being Fat Is Not a Sin, *also known under the title* The Forbidden Body*)*

3 *Murderer Edith Thompson's*

4 *Virginia Woolf (1882–1941)*

5 West With The Night *(1942)*

6 *A front cover photo showing Soviet women without make-up*

7 *Barbara Vine*

8 *Helen Huntingdon*

9 *Westminster Abbey*

10 *The Society of Women Artists*

11 *Mary Wollstonecraft (1759–97)*

12 The Lily

13 *Grey (in her book* Grey Is the Colour of Hope*)*

14 *Frances Hodgson Burnett*

15 *Mrs Gaskell (1810–65)*

1 Who sculpted the statue *'Horse and Rider'* which was commissioned by Trafalgar House and stands in Dover Street, London?

2 Who published the first *Directory of Women's Businesses in London*?

3 What kind of artist was Jamaican Edna Manley?

4 Ellen Sturgis Hooper wrote a poem about going to sleep thinking life was beauty. What did she say you found life was when you woke?

5 Which book launched Naomi Mitchison's writing career?

6 What was the title of Fanny Burney's first novel, published (anonymously) in 1778?

7 What was so important to women about London's Slade School of Fine Art when it was founded in 1871?

8 On whom is the character Helen Burns, in Charlotte Brontë's *Jane Eyre* (1847) based?

9 Which Frenchwoman did Christine de Pisan write a song in honour of in 1429?

10 In which year did Adrienne Rich win (and reject) the US National Book Award for Poetry for her book, *Diving into the Wreck*?

11 Which British newspaper was founded (in 1958) and edited by Claudia Jones (1915–64)?

12 Who took over from Wendy Henry as editor of Britain's *News of the World* in 1988?

13 Which UK publishing house was founded by Emily Faithful (1835–95)?

14 What was the title of Aphra Behn's first play (1670)?

15 During which World War was Olive Edis the only woman commissioned by officials and the press to take photographs?

1 *Dame Elisabeth Frink*

2 *Springboard*

3 *Sculptor*

4 *'Duty'*

5 The Conquered *(1923)*

6 Evelina

7 *It was co-educational*

8 *Charlotte's sister Maria Brontë (1813–25)*

9 *Joan of Arc*

10 *1974 (She later accepted it, along with Alice Walker and Audrey Rich, on behalf of all women)*

11 The West Indian Gazette

12 *Patsy Chapman*

13 *Victoria Press*

14 The Forc'd Marriage *or* The Jealous Bridegroom

15 *First World War*

1 Which British novelist, poet and fighter for the rights of a divorced woman is the book *A Scandalous Woman* (by Allen Chedzoy, published in 1992) the story of?
2 What qualification did novelist Margaret Drabble (b. 1939) leave Cambridge University with?
3 What is Rule Number 21 in John Kirkby's subjective book, *Eighty-Eight Grammatical Rules*, written in 1746?
4 Where was Aphra Behn's first play, *The Forc'd Marriage* or *The Jealous Bridegroom*, performed on 20th September 1670?
5 How long did it take novelist and journalist Antonia White (1899–1980) to write *Frost in May*?
6 Which private art exhibiting society was founded by Vanessa Bell in 1905?
7 What was Jane Austen's novel *Northanger Abbey* originally called?
8 What was the title of Mary Wollstonecraft's first published book?
9 Who said 'One can't paint New York as it is but rather as it is felt'?
10 Susanna Blamire is known for the songs she wrote in Scottish dialect. She also wrote story-poems in a different dialect – which?
11 Anne Puddicome (1836–1908) wrote under the pseudonym Allen Raine. How was the name suggested to her?
12 Gwen Rowerat was an artist and book illustrator What technique did she use to illustrate books such as *The Cambridge Book of Poetry for Children*, published in 1932?
13 What was author Agnes Strickland (1796—-1874) and her sister Elizabeth Strickland's best-known work?
14 Alison Uttley is known for her children's books, but what job did she take after leaving Manchester University in 1903?
15 What pseudonym did Olive Schreiner use when she published her book *The Story of an African Farm* in 1883?

LITERATURE & ART ANSWERS

1 *Caroline Norton (1808–77)*

2 *A double first in English*

3 *'The "male" gender is more comprehensive than the "female" '*

4 *Lincoln's Inn Fields, London*

5 *17 years*

6 *The Friday Club*

7 Susan

8 Thoughts on the Education of Daughters

9 *Georgia O'Keeffe*

10 *Cumbrian dialect*

11 *In a dream*

12 *Wood engraving*

13 Lives of the Queens of England

14 *Science teacher*

15 *Ralph Iron*

1 In 1960, why did Irish traveller Dervla Murphy deliberately wear clothes that were too big for her while walking through Bulgaria and Turkey?

2 When she was on her travels, whom did Isabella Bird (1834–1904) write to every night?

3 What did Marianne North (1830–90) paint and study on her travels?

4 Where did Margery Kempe make her first journey to, as a pilgrimage, in 1413?

5 What did Mary Kingsley (1862–1900) use as 'small change' when travelling in Africa?

6 Which country did Christian Miller cross from east to west on a folding bike (at the age of 57)?

7 In 1912, Suffragette Fanny Workman reached the summit of Karakoram. What was the message on the poster she then held up high?

8 Which Victorian traveller was grand-daughter of the Second Countess Stanhope?

9 In which year did Mary Kingsley (1862–1900) make her first trip to Africa?

10 Having completed the fourth stage of her round-the-world walk by travelling the length of Africa (in 1993), where does Fyona Campbell intend to walk next?

11 Which explorer was the first Englishwoman to enter the South Yemen alone?

12 What saved the life of Victorian explorer Mary Kingsley (1862–1900) in Africa when she fell into a pit lined with sharp upright spikes?

13 What form of transport did Bettina Selby use when travelling through India (at age 47)?

14 Off the coast of which country did Lucy Irvine live on a desert island for over a year?

15 What did Sarah Hobson disguise herself as when she travelled through Iran in 1970?

EXPLORERS & TRAVELLERS ANSWERS

1 *She was pregnant at the time*
2 *Her sister (Hennie)*
3 *Plants*
4 *Jerusalem*
5 *Fish hooks*
6 *United States*
7 *'Votes for Women'*
8 *Lady Hester Stanhope*
9 *1893*
10 *Across Europe*
11 *Dame Freya Stark (1893–1993)*
12 *The thickness of the skirt she was wearing at the time*
13 *A bicycle*
14 *Australia (on the island of Tuin)*
15 *A man*

1 Which desert was Alexine Tinné travelling across when she was killed by Tuareg horsemen?

2 What form of transport did Dervla Murphy use to travel overland to India (at the age of 30)?

3 In 1924 what did Alexandra David-Neel (1869–1968) disguise herself as in order to enter Lhasa, Tibet?

4 On what animals did Robyn Davidson travel across 1,700 miles of Australian scrubland?

5 In 1909 Canadian traveller Agnes Cameron (1863–1912) was travelling north to the Arctic when she met a grey wolf. What happened?

6 Along which river did Mary Kingsley (1862–1900) travel during her first visit to West Africa in 1893?

7 How old was Isabella Bird Bishop (1831–1904) when she set out on her last journey, to Morocco?

8 Which country did Celia Fiennes (1662–1741) travel around and write about?

9 In 1908, of which British women's league did traveller and archaelogist Gertrude Bell (1868–1926) become a founder member?

10 Where was Isabella Bird Bishop all packed and ready to go when she died in 1904?

11 Which part of the world did traveller Dame Freya Stark (1893–1993) describe in her book *The Southern Gates of Arabia* (1936)?

12 What was the name of the 53-ft yacht in which Naomi James (b. 1949) sailed around the world?

13 Where was Rosita Forbes (1893–1967) travelling to in 1920 when she disguised herself as a Bedouin to prevent herself being killed?

14 In which country did explorer Freya Stark (1893–1993) work as a nurse during the First World War?

15 In which country was Mary Kingsley working as a nurse when she died in 1900?

EXPLORERS & TRAVELLERS ANSWERS

1 *The Sahara*
2 *A bicycle*
3 *A poor beggar*
4 *Camels*
5 *The wolf turned tail and left*
6 *The Congo*
7 *70*
8 *England*
9 *The Women's Anti-Suffrage League*
10 *China*
11 *South Yemen*
12 Crusader
13 *Kufara, in the eastern Sahara*
14 *Italy*
15 *South Africa (Simon's Town, near Cape Town)*

1 In 1924 while explorer Alexandra David-Neel (1869–1968) was in Lhasa, Tibet, why was she beaten by a police officer?
2 How much did it cost Mary Kingsley (1862–1900) for her second trip to Africa?
3 How did Fanny Workman spend the winter before she set the women's altitude record of 21,000 ft by climbing Mount Gunge?
4 In which county of northeast England was traveller and archaeologist Gertrude Bell (1868–1926) born?
5 While deep in the African bush, what was Christina Dodwell so desperate for that she traded her only pair of sandals for it?
6 In 1838 Henriette D'Angeville became the second woman to climb Mont Blanc. How did she send news of her successful arrival at the summit to those down below?
7 What rare honour (for a woman!) was bestowed on Isabella Bird Bishop in 1892?
8 How did Alexandra David-Neel (1869–1968) spend the winter of 1914/15 when she was in Sikkim?
9 On her long flight through Africa in 1928, how did aviator Sophie Heath pass the time?
10 In 1808, who became the first woman to climb to the summit of Mount Blanc, Europe's highest mountain?
11 In 1873 while travelling through the Rocky Mountains, Isabella Bird Bishop (1834–1904) got lost. She found some kernels of cherry stones to eat. Where did she find them?
12 In which part of Syria did Lady Hester Stanhope (1776–1839) live after 1810?
13 How long did Evangeline French, her sister Francesca French and her friend Mildred Cable spend evangelizing in China in the 1920s and 1930s?
14 What did Christina Dodwell use to get herself and her bike across a river, swollen with melted snow and ice, when high in the Himalayas?
15 Which journey does Gertrude Bell (1868–1926) describe in her book *The Desert and the Sown* (1907)?

EXPLORERS & TRAVELLERS ANSWERS

1 *She was walking on a place reserved for the rich*

2 *£300*

3 *Travelling around India on a bicycle*

4 *County Durham*

5 *Tobacco*

6 *By carrier pigeon*

7 *She was made Fellow of the Royal Geographical Society*

8 *As a hermit in a cave*

9 *By eating chocolates and reading*

10 *Marie Paradis, of Chamonix*

11 *In the stomach of a dead bear*

12 *Djouni, on the slopes of Mount Lebanon*

13 *15 years*

14 *A small black cow*

15 *Her 1905 journey from Jerusalem through Syria to Asia Minor*

1 Whose life and bravery does the museum run by the Royal National Lifeboat Institute in Bamburgh, Northumberland, commemorate?
2 Which British Government Department was the first to employ women as clerical workers, in the mid-19th century?
3 Which Goddess is the month of June named after?
4 What did former slave Isabella Baumfree (1797–1883) change her name to when, at the age of 46, she began her own campaign to end slavery?
5 Which political office did American Congresswoman Shirley Chisholm (b. 1924) run for in 1972?
6 Which television station was foreign correspondent Kate Adie working for when she reported the 1987 American bombings of Libya?
7 How did American physicist Sally Ride (b. 1951) make history in June 1983?
8 What contest did women demonstrate against in New Jersey in 1968?
9 What is the aim of Britain's '300 Group', set up in 1980?
10 Which charity for the homeless did Member of Parliament Joan Ruddock begin work for in 1968?
11 Which member of the Royal Family celebrated her 93rd birthday on 4th August 1993?
12 At which university in northern England did Marie Stopes become the first woman lecturer?
13 Which British women's magazine was started by journalist and freelance writer Nancy Spain (1917–64) and Joan Werner Laurie?
14 Who became the first black woman Member of Parliament (1987)?
15 What career did Gertrude Jekyll (1843–1932) turn to, and become the first woman to do, when her eyesight began to fail?

HERSTORY ANSWERS

1 *Grace Darling's*
2 *The Post Office*
3 *The Roman Goddess Juno*
4 *Sojourner Truth*
5 *President of the United States*
6 *The BBC*
7 *She became the first American woman to go into space*
8 *The Miss America Pageant*
9 *To get 300 women politicians into the House of Commons*
10 *SHELTER*
11 *The Queen Mother*
12 *University of Manchester*
13 She
14 *Diane Abbott*
15 *Garden designer*

1 Women could officially work as clerks at the Post Office from 1871. When was the marriage bar introduced?
2 Which Roman Goddess was said to be the protector of married women?
3 In which occupied country was José de la Barre (now José Villiers) active in the anti-Nazi resistance during the Second World War?
4 What did Sally Ride (physicist), Rhea Seddon (physician) and Kathy Sullivan (geologist) apply for and be chosen to do in 1978?
5 Which Acts of Parliament was the 19th-century Ladies' National Association, led by Josephine Butler, founded to fight?
6 Why were Britons Lily Webb and Maud Brown on the march in 1932?
7 Who published the autobiography of British suffragette and city of Manchester magistrate Hannah Mitchell (1871–1956), *The Hard Way Up*, in 1977?
8 Which self-help group was started by Manchester teenager Niki Winnard in 1989?
9 In the 19th century, dressed as a man, Helen Bruce had a varied working career, in Newcastle, Leith and London. What were her main reasons for dressing as a man?
10 What did the British Association of Headmistresses in Endowed and Proprietary Schools, founded by Frances Mary Buss in 1874, change its name to in 1896?
11 Of which British guild was Margaret Llewelyn Davies general secretary from 1883 (the year it was founded) to 1915?
12 In 1863 a group of 91 girls were allowed to sit the Cambridge University Local Examinations. To what did the maths examiner ascribe the fact that they all failed the arithmetic part of the exam?
13 What is the name of the league of which South African Lillian Masediba was the first president?
14 In which Belgian city did First World War heroine Edith Cavell nurse?
15 How old was Isabella of Valois (1387–1410) when she was married to Richard II of England?

HERSTORY ANSWERS

1 *1875*

2 *Juno (Goddess of Marriage)*

3 *Belgium*

4 *Train as astronaut mission specialist scientists and go into space*

5 *The Contagious Diseases Acts of the 1870s*

6 *They were leaders of the women's section of the 1932 Hunger March*

7 *Virago Press Ltd*

8 *HAWC (Help Adolescents with Cancer)*

9 *Men got paid more and were not asked for references as women were, and she found men's clothes more convenient*

10 *The Association of Headmistresses*

11 *Women's Co-operative Guild*

12 *Lack of proper instruction*

13 *ANC (African National Congress) Women's League*

14 *Brussels*

15 *Eight*

1 What did Yaa Asantewa do to the British Army Officer who arrested her in 1900?

2 In the 1940s how did women in the Blackburn Labour Women's Section get a woman on the shortlist for prospective Members of Parliament?

3 Which Kingdom chose Aelfwyn as a ruler in her own right in 918?

4 As a businesswoman in 1470 Alice Chester traded with Spain and Flanders. She exported cloth; what did she import?

5 In 1627 what did the Pope give Catalina de Erauzo (1592–1650) ecclesiastical permission to do?

6 Who was imprisoned as a political prisoner in the Maison de Correction de Fresnes for a total of one year and four days in 1943?

7 What did Katherine Parr die of on 5th September 1548?

8 What part does the demon Ammit play in the Egyptian Day of Judgement?

9 What was Ananker the Greek Goddess of?

10 In 1936 there were three women in the French Government. When were women given the vote in France?

11 In what unusual place did American geologist Kathy Sullivan take a walk, in October 1984?

12 Which British society, campaigning for equal rights for women, did Eleanor Rathbone become president of in 1926?

13 Which political figure in England's northwest was a magistrate from 1926 to 1946?

14 Which British association was founded by Dora Russell (1894–1987) and Stella Browne in 1936?

15 Apart from French sailors, who else was rescued from the sea during the Battle of Trafalgar?

1 *She spat in his face*

2 *They threatened they would stop making tea for the men unless a woman was shortlisted*

3 *Mercia*

4 *Iron*

5 *Dress as a man*

6 *British Agent Odette (Lise) Sansom, working for the French Section of the War Office*

7 *Puerperal fever, brought on by childbirth*

8 *It is her responsibility to devour anyone who is judged to be a sinner*

9 *Fate, or inevitability*

10 *1944*

11 *In space outside the space shuttle Challenger*

12 *NUSEC (National Union of Societies for Equal Citizenship)*

13 *Hannah Mitchell (1871–1956)*

14 *The Abortion Law Reform Association*

15 *The wife of a French naval officer*

1 Who starred as Eliza Doolittle in the 1956–59 production of *My Fair Lady* in London's West End and on Broadway?

2 Which 1938 film won Bette Davis her second Oscar?

3 What is the name of author Sara Paretsky's Chicago detective?

4 Whose autobiography is called *Ginger*?

5 Who is the mother of Darlene and Becky?

6 In the American comedy *The Golden Girls*, what relation is Sophia to Dorothy?

7 Who was actress and singer Liza Minelli's mother?

8 Which 1991 film, starring Laura Dern, was directed by Martha Coolidge?

9 Which American list was actress/director Lee Grant's name added to, which resulted in her being labelled a Communist and unable to get a job in film-making for 12 years?

10 In which country is the 1989 film *A Dry White Season* set?

11 What have Sophie (in the Australian soap *Home and Away*) and Pheobe (in *Neighbours*) got in common?

12 For which film, directed by Sherry Lansing, did Jodie Foster win an Academy Award?

13 Which film, written by Elinor Glyn, made Clara Bow a star in 1927?

14 Who played Lucy in the American comedy series *I Love Lucy*?

15 How old was Hayley Mills when she made her first film, *Tiger Bay*?

ENTERTAINMENT ANSWERS

1 *Julie Andrews (b. 1935)*

2 Jezebel

3 *V. I. Warshawski*

4 *Ginger Rogers'*

5 *Roseanne Connor (on the TV sitcom* Roseanne*)*

6 *Sophia is Dorothy's mother*

7 *Judy Garland*

8 Rambling Rose

9 *Senator Joseph McCarthy's blacklist of suspected Communist sympathizers*

10 *South Africa*

11 *They both became pregnant while still teenagers and both their boyfriends were killed in road accidents before their baby was born*

12 The Accused

13 It

14 *Lucille Ball*

15 *12*

1 Which serial starring Helen Holmes (1892–1950), then Helen Gibson (1894–1971) became the longest-running movie serial?
2 In the 1970s, why were some of the films made by Iranian women never released?
3 Which soap did Dame Judith Anderson sign a long-term contract to appear in at the age of 86?
4 Which 1952 film starred Lauren Bacall, Marilyn Monroe and Betty Grable? D QL
5 Which American actress, born in New York City in 1924, changed her name from Betty Joan Perske?
6 What is the title of the 1918 film which portrayed the life of Helen Keller (1880–1968)?
7 Who played aviator Beryl Markham in the film *West by the Night*?
8 Which 1988 comedy film starred Katharine Hepburn as an aged novelist?
9 Which 1992 film, set in Alabama, starred Kathy Bates, Jessica Tandy, Mary-Louise Parker and Mary Stuart Masterson?
10 What did singer Sinead O'Connor give to charity in November 1992, which was worth £340,00?
11 Who directed the film *Christopher Strong*, which starred Katharine Hepburn?
12 Which TV acting role made American film director Penny Marshall famous?
13 Who is in the *Guinness Book of Records* as the first woman in history to win an Oscar, a Tony, a Grammy and two Emmys?
14 In which 1968 horror film featured Ruth Gordon (1896–1985), in a role for which she won an Oscar?
15 In 1987 why could the American Women in Radio and Television not award its annual prize to an advert that treated women positively?

1 Hazards of Helen

2 *Their production coincided with the 1977–79 uprisings*

3 Santa Barbara

4 How to Marry a Millionaire

5 *Lauren Bacall*

6 Deliverance

7 *Geena Davis*

8 Laura Lansing Slept Here

9 Fried Green Tomatoes at the Whistle Stop Café

10 *Her Los Angeles mansion*

11 *Dorothy Arzner (1900–79)*

12 *Laverne in* Laverne and Shirley

13 *Rita Moreno*

14 Rosemary's Baby

15 *They could not find an advert that qualified*

1 What was the name of the film company formed by actress Lule Warrenton (1863–1932) in 1917?

2 What is the title of the first film Ida Lupino acted in?

3 Which 1971 film was both written by and starred Elaine May?

4 What is the title of the 1990 film about the pregnancy of a teenage girl, directed by Ruby Oliver?

5 What have Peaches Jones (1952–88), Louise Johnson and Evelyn Coffee in common?

6 In which year did Jodie David start her career as a stuntwoman?

7 Which 1980 film made by Michelle Parkerson was featured in the 1981 Berlin Film Festival?

8 Which Hollywood scriptwriter wrote *Dinner at Eight* (1933)?

9 Where did producer Hannah Weinstein (1911–84), born in New York, move to in 1950?

10 What was the last film written by prolific scriptwriter Anita Loos, in 1942?

11 What did Ruth Gordon do for the first time (at the age of 87) in the film *Maxie* (1985)?

12 Lotte Reiniger (1899–1981) was commissioned to make the first full-length animated feature film, which she completed in 1926. What was it called?

13 In *Gone With the Wind*, who was Vivien Leigh's stunt double in the dramatic tumble down the stairs which resulted in the loss of the character Scarlett O'Hara's baby?

14 For which 1989 film did Geena Davis win an Oscar for best supporting actress?

15 Who starred in the 1978 film *A Question of Love*?

30 ENTERTAINMENT ANSWERS

1. *Frieder Film Corporation*
2. Her First Affair *(1932)*
3. A New Leaf
4. Love Your Mama
5. *They are all professional stuntwomen*
6. *1971*
7. But Then She's Betty Carter
8. *Frances Marion*
9. *London*
10. I Married an Angel
11. *She rode a motorcycle*
12. The Adventures of Prince Achmed
13. *Aline Goodwin*
14. The Accidental Tourist
15. *Gena Rowlands*

1 Who was the author of the *Pippi Longstocking* children's books?

2 Which original (and now sometimes controversial) British educational material is Maria Edgeworth credited with inventing?

3 Which English reformist publication was founded in 1858 by Bessie Raynor Parkes?

4 Under what name did novelist Mary Challans write?

5 Of which British women's magazine, which ceased publication in 1993, was Rosie Boycott (b. 1951) a co-founder?

6 Who is the author of *The Second Sex*, published in 1949?

7 Who wrote *Little Women*?

8 What was the sequel to *What Katy Did*, by Susan M. Coolidge?

9 Who wrote *The Bell Jar*, which was published in the year of her death (1963)?

10 Which British author wrote *The Tale of Jemima Puddleduck* in 1908?

11 Who was Jane Eyre's handmaiden at her cottage near Moreton?

12 In the original Kate Greenaway book of nursery rhymes, written in 1881, what did the girls do that made Georgie Porgie run away?

13 Who wrote *Gone with the Wind* (1936)?

14 Anita Loos' book claimed that *Gentlemen Prefer Blondes.* What kind of women do they marry, according to the title of the book she wrote in 1927?

15 Who wrote *Travels in West Africa*, published in January 1897?

LITERATURE & ART ANSWERS

1 *Astrid Lindgren*
2 *The first Reading Scheme*
3 English Woman's Journal
4 *Mary Renault (1905–83)*
5 Spare Rib
6 *Simone de Beauvoir (1908–86)*
7 *Louisa May Alcott (1832–88)*
8 What Katy Did Next
9 *Poet Sylvia Plath (1932–63)*
10 *Beatrix Potter (1866–1943)*
11 *Alice Wood*
12 *They* 'began to play'
13 *Margaret Mitchell*
14 *Brunettes (*But Gentlemen Marry Brunettes*)*
15 *Mary Kingsley (1862–1900)*

1 For which country did Dame Laura Knight (1877–1970) become a war artist in 1916?

2 What is the title of the children's book written by poet Sylvia Plath?

3 Which British artist sculpted the *Winged Figure* (1963) outside the John Lewis store in London's Oxford Street?

4 After publishing her first book (*Elizabeth and Her German Garden*, 1898) anonymously, how did Elizabeth Von Armin sign her next 20 books?

5 What kind of paintings did Annie Swynnerton (1844–1933) specialize in?

6 When not in London, in which part of coastal Yorkshire did painter Dame Ethel Walker (1861–1951) work?

7 Who wrote the children's book *Ballet Shoes* (1936)?

8 What nationality is author Margaret Atwood (b. 1939)?

9 Who modelled the death masks of many of the victims of the guillotine during the French Revolution?

10 What kind of factory did British novelist Sylvia Townsend Warner (1893–1978) work in during the First World War?

11 The first volume of which British artist's autobiography is entitled *Oil Paint and Greasepaint* (1936)?

12 Which children's writer and illustrator of children's books, resident of the Lake District, became an expert on breeding Herdwick sheep?

13 What kind of poetry is *The Forgotten Army* (1991), edited by Nora Jones and Liz Ward, an anthology of?

14 What was the title of Enid Blyton's (1897–1968) first book about the '*Famous Five*'?

15 Which romantic novelist has a place in the Guinness Book of Records as the most prolific living author?

LITERATURE & ART ANSWERS

1 *Canada*

2 The Bed Book

3 *Barbara Hepworth (1903–75)*

4 *By the author of* Elizabeth and her German Garden

5 *Watercolours*

6 *Robin Hood's Bay*

7 *Noel Streatfield (1895–1986)*

8 *Canadian*

9 *Anne Marie Tussaud (1760–1850)*

10 *A munitions factory*

11 *Dame Laura Knight (1877–1970)*

12 *Beatrix Potter (1866–1943)*

13 *First World War poetry by women*

14 Five on a Treasure Island

15 *Barbara Cartland (b. 1901)*

1 What nationality was painter Angelica Kauffmann, who, in 1768, was one of the founding members of the London-based Royal Academy of Arts?

2 Who was author of the religious poem '*Lamentation or Complaint of a Sinner*' (1547)?

3 Who sculpted the '*Single Form*' for the United Nations Building in New York, in 1964?

4 Why was British novelist Marie Corelli (1855–1924) arrested during the First World War?

5 In which African country are the novels of Bessie Head (1937–86) set?

6 Of whom did the city of San Francisco commission Harriet Hosmer to sculpt a statue, which she finished in 1894?

7 What did novelist Edith Somerville (1858–1949) become Master of?

8 Which British Institute did Brenda Colvin help found in 1929, and became president of in 1951?

9 What was the subtitle of the Charlotte Perkins Gilman book published in 1911 as *The Man-Made World*?

10 Under what pseudonym did Italian Rina Faccio (1876–1960) write her poetry and fiction?

11 What medium did 18th-century artist Anne Morritt specialize in?

12 Who wrote the poem '*The White Cliffs*' (1940), which was extremely popular and read by actress Lynne Fontanne over the radio station NBC Blue Network?

13 Which New Zealand feminist of the 19th century wrote under the pseudonym 'Femina'?

14 Which magazine did American photographer Esther Bubley work for, temporarily, before going to work for the Farm Security Administration?

15 In which Marcia Muller detective novel does Sharon McCone make her first appearance?

31 LITERATURE & ART ANSWERS

1 *Swiss*

2 *Katherine Parr (1512–48)*

3 *Barbara Hepworth*

4 *For hoarding sugar*

5 *Botswana*

6 *Queen Isabella*

7 *Foxhounds*

8 *Institute of Landscape Architects*

9 Our Androcentric Culture

10 *Sibilla Alerama*

11 *Embroidery and tapestries*

12 *Alice Duer Miller*

13 *Mary Muller (1820–1902)*

14 Vogue

15 Edwin of the Iron Shoes

1 Which American island did Australian Shelley Taylor swim around in 6 hours 29 seconds on 15th October 1985?

2 In which sport does Klondyke Kate compete?

3 Who became Britain's first World Judo Champion in 1980, in the World Championships held in New York?

4 In 1992, of which 4th division British football club was Vicky Oyston a director?

5 Why was it suggested women should not do archery in 1836?

6 Which medal did Briton Janet Salt win at the World Disabled Water Ski Championships, held in the United States in 1991?

7 What nationality was tennis champion Suzanne Lenglen?

8 What was uncomfortable and impracticable about the saddle of the Ladies Ordinary bicycle, invented in 1874?

9 In 1978, why was Theresa Bennett banned by the British Football Association from playing for the Muskham United under-12s team?

10 What was the major cause of the demise of British women's football?

11 Which is the most popular outdoor sporting activity of women?

12 In ancient Greece, which animal raised Atlanta the huntress, wrestler and runner?

13 Whom did tennis champion Suzanne Lenglen insult at Wimbledon in 1926?

14 Which Swiss mountain was Lucy Walker the first Englishwoman to climb, in 1871?

15 In 1978, which American marathon did Norwegian Grete Waitz run in a women's world record time of 2 hours 32:29.8 minutes?

SPORTS ANSWERS

1 *Manhattan*

2 *Wrestling*

3 *Jane Bridge*

4 *Blackpool*

5 *It was suggested it could result in asymmetrical physical development*

6 *Gold medal*

7 *French*

8 *It was a side-saddle*

9 *She was a girl*

10 *Women and girls were banned from playing football on Council pitches*

11 *Walking or rambling*

12 *A she-bear*

13 *Queen Mary*

14 *The Matterhorn*

15 *The New York Marathon*

1 For which Olympics did power-lifter Barbara Dalton light the opening flame?

2 In 1984 Georgina Clark became the first woman to umpire a final at Wimbledon. Which final?

3 After setting a new world record for the 400 metre hurdles at the 1993 World Athletics Championships in Stuttgart, who said 'I've rehearsed this many times'?

4 In which Swedish city were the 1993 IBM Women's Open Golf Championships held?

5 Between which two teams was the final of the 1991 Women's Rugby World Cup?

6 What was British runner Paula Dunn's paid job during the 1980s?

7 In 1822, why did the boxing match between Martha Flaharty and Peg Carey start at 5.30 in the morning?

8 When was the first National Tennis Championship for women played at Wimbledon?

9 What are the names of the three British women who have won Wimbledon since the Second World War?

10 When women were banned from speedway racing, what did champion speedway racer Fay Taylour (1908–83) race instead?

11 Why did Roberta Gibb not have a number when she ran in the Boston Marathon in 1966 and 1967?

12 What was the size of the crowd at the 1920 Boxing Day football match between St Helen's Ladies and Dick Kerr Ladies?

13 In which year was the Women's Football League set up in Britain?

14 How many times did Charlotte Dod win the Ladies' Lawn Tennis Championship at Wimbledon between 1887 and 1893?

15 Ancient Greeks shared the spoils of their successful hunts by offering sacrifices to the god Apollo and who else?

SPORTS ANSWERS

1 *The UK Summer Special Olympic Games, Sheffield 1993*

2 *Ladies' Singles*

3 *Sally Gunnell*

4 *Stockholm*

5 *England and the United States*

6 *Clerk in Manchester City Council's Housing Department*

7 *It was before the participants and spectators went to work*

8 *1884*

9 *Angela Mortimer (1961), Ann Jones (1969) and Virginia Wade (1977)*

10 *Motor cars*

11 *The marathon was thought an unsuitable race for women and they were therefore not allowed to enter; she ran unofficially*

12 *53,000 supporters*

13 *1991*

14 *Five*

15 *Artemis (the huntress)*

1 In 1913 what did world champion cyclist Hélène Dutrie become on giving up cycling?
2 Which ball game was banned by the American women's college Smith in 1878 and reinstated in 1892?
3 In which year did the Jockey Club officially allow women to become jockeys?
4 How many Grand Slam Tennis Championship titles are held by Margaret Smith?
5 Who became the unofficial British Lightweight Boxing champion in 1983?
6 Who was the first left-handed player to win the Ladies' Singles Championship at Wimbledon?
7 Which mountain did Irene Miller and Vera Komarkova reach the summit of in October 1978?
8 How did British runner Priscilla Welch reduce her weight before competing in the women's Olympic marathon in August 1984?
9 Why was Mildred 'Babe' Didrikson offered a job as a stenographer, at an inflated wage of $900 a year, in 1930?
10 In which year did the St Andrews Ladies' Golf Club come into existence?
11 How old was tennis champion Suzanne Lenglen when she got her first tennis racquet?
12 What did Dawn Fraser, Australian swimming champion of the 1960s, try and steal from the palace of Emperor Hirohito of Japan?
13 How many siblings did track and field champion athlete Wilma Rudolph have?
14 What dangerous team did Dolly Sheperd join in 1903?
15 At which races was the 'Mrs Mapp Plate' (inspired by bone-setter Sarah Mapp) run in 18th-century Britain?

SPORTS ANSWERS

1 *An aviator*

2 *Baseball*

3 *1972 (May)*

4 *66*

5 *Sue Atkins*

6 *Ann Jones (1969)*

7 *Annapurna*

8 *She took off her watch and wedding ring*

9 *In order that she could play in the company's basketball team*

10 *1867*

11 *11*

12 *The Japanese flag*

13 *21*

14 *A parachute team*

15 *Epsom Races*

1 In the spring of 1928 aviator Lady Heath flew from the Cape of South Africa – to where?
2 During 1643–44 against whom did Charlotte, Countess of Derby defend Lathom House?
3 Which former British politician is the daughter of Vera Brittain (1893–1970)?
4 Which successful British designer and businesswoman was born in 1925 and called Laura Mountney?
5 Which subject did Ellen Wilkinson (1891–1947) study at Manchester University?
6 What job did Princess Diana (Princess of Wales) have before her marriage in 1981?
7 In 1985, what reason did two thirds of women graduates with children, asked in a survey by researchers at Bristol University, give as their reason for working?
8 While Minister of Parliament for Jarrow, voted in in 1935, which march was Ellen Wilkinson (1891–1947) leader of for much of the way?
9 Who became deputy leader of Britain's Labour Party in 1993?
10 At the time (1926), what was unique about the Managing Director of the National Securities Corporation?
11 In which space shuttle did astronaut Dr Sally Ride travel and work in space (in June 1983 and October 1984)?
12 Later leader of Britain's Conservative Party, who was leader of the Opposition from 1975–79?
13 Who was appointed as the first woman assistant Chief Constable by Merseyside in 1983?
14 Who were 'the Ladies of Llangollen', whose lives in the 18th century are described in *The Ladies of Llangollen*, published in 1984?
15 Which country swore Kim Campbell in as their 19th Prime Minister on 25th June 1993?

33 HERSTORY ANSWERS

1 *England*

2 *The Roundheads*

3 *Shirley Williams*

4 *Laura Ashley (1925–85)*

5 *History*

6 *Nursery school teacher*

7 *Because they enjoyed it*

8 *Jarrow March*

9 *Margaret Beckett*

10 *She was, at the time, the only female stockbroker in England*

11 *Challenger*

12 *Margaret Thatcher (b.1925)*

13 *Alison Halford*

14 *The Honourable Sarah Ponsonby and Lady Eleanor Butler*

15 *Canada*

HERSTORY QUIZ 33

1 In 1857 there were more women than men in Britain. What did the press suggest should be done with the 'surplus' women?
2 In which century was Amina queen warrior of Nigeria?
3 How do we know about the life of 15th-century Englishwoman Margaret Paston?
4 What subterfuge did Agnodice have to adopt to practise gynaecology in Ancient Greece?
5 Who, allegedly, joined the German Secret Service in 1907 and passed on secret information for the next 10 years?
6 When Lady Godiva rode naked through the streets of Coventry only one man looked at her. What happened to him?
7 Jahan Nur (1571–1634) was the only woman ruler in India to issue coins in her own name. From which dynasty did she come?
8 Which Austrian-born queen of the 18th century is credited with saying of the French lower classes, 'Let them eat cake'?
9 Gertrud Sigurdsen (b. 1923) became a leading politician in which European country?
10 Nzinga Mbande was the Angolan leader in the 17th-century struggle against which colonial power?
11 Why was Angela Burdett made Baroness Burdett-Coutts of Highgate and Brookfield, Middlesex, in 1871?
12 For whom did Violette Szabo work during the Second World War?
13 In 1991 which British Local Authority was voted best employer for working mothers?
14 Which school was opened by Millicent, Penelope and Dorothy Lawrence at Brighton in 1855?
15 During the Second World War, a wartime Social Survey asked women, 'If you have any objection to War Work, what is it?' What were the two objections given by the majority of women?

33 HERSTORY ANSWERS

medium

1 *They should be exported to marry overseas*

2 *16th*

3 *She wrote many letters that have been preserved, and published (as* Paston Letters, *ed. N. Davis)*

4 *She dressed as a man*

5 *Mata Hari*

6 *He was struck blind*

7 *Moghuls*

8 *Marie Antoinette*

9 *Sweden*

10 *Portugal*

11 *In recognition of her benevolence to the poor and needy*

12 *The Special Operations Executive*

13 *Oxfordshire County Council*

14 *Roedean*

15 *That war work was 'too monotonous and uncongenial'*

1 What did Hanna Reitsch and Melitta Schiller of Germany do during the Second World War?
2 In 1827, aboard the naval ship *Genoa* there were nine women, wives of the Petty Officers. What did the women do during battles?
3 Which constituency in northeast England voted Margaret Bondfield in as Labour Member of Parliament in 1926?
4 When the Greek Goddess Empusa decides not to appear as a beautiful maiden, what other form does she take?
5 At her execution in May 1928, how was Xiang Jingyu (1895–1928), Chinese feminist and revolutionary, prevented from making a final speech?
6 During the Second World War what official position did Briton Mary Adams (1899–1984) hold?
7 How many times was Katherine Parr (1514–48) married?
8 In ancient Rome, which Goddess was honoured with a feast at the end of April each year?
9 To which constituency was Labour Member of Parliament Judith Hart (b. 1924, later Dame Judith Hart) elected in 1959?
10 Which airline employed Sophia Heath (1896–1936) as its first pilot?
11 On which circuit was Dame Rose Heilbron (b. 1914) presiding judge from 1979 to 1982?
12 What did Margaret Knight (1838–1914) invent and patent in 1870?
13 What 'cover story' did British Agent Giliana Balmaceda (Madam Gerson) of the Special Operations Executive use when in France collecting information in 1941?
14 In 1786 what did Mary Broad steal that resulted in her being sent to Botany Bay, Australia, for seven years?
15 In what did aviator Amy Johnson gain an honours degree at Sheffield University?

HERSTORY ANSWERS

1 *They tested fighter planes (they were experienced pilots)*

2 *They acted as nurses to the injured aboard ship*

3 *Wallsend*

4 *She takes the form of a hideous ghost that has the feet of an ass*

5 *She was gagged*

6 *Director of Home Intelligence at the Ministry of Information*

7 *Four*

8 *Flora (The Feast of Floralia), Roman Goddess of Growing Corn and Blossoming Flowers*

9 *Lanark*

10 *KLM/Royal Dutch Airline*

11 *The Northern Circuit*

12 *A machine which made square-bottomed paper bags*

13 *That she was an actress looking for work*

14 *A lady's cloak*

15 *Latin, French and Economics*

1 What do the initials k. d. in k. d. lang stand for?
2 Which song did Lena Zavaroni sing when she appeared on talent show *Opportunity Knocks* in 1973?
3 What was the title of the song Dana sang when she won the Eurovision Song Contest for Ireland in 1970?
4 Which singer's real name is Alison Clarkson?
5 What was the title of the suffragettes' unofficial theme tune, composed by Ethel Smyth (1858–1944) in 1911?
6 Which 'Holiday Camp' TV personality and star of *Hi-de-Hi* went to Britain's number two with *'Starting Together'* in February, 1986?
7 Who represented Britain in the 1970 Eurovision Song Contest with *'Knock Knock Who's There?'*?
8 Who released an album called *Arkansas Traveller* in 1992?
9 What was the title of Canadian singer k. d. lang's album released in 1992?
10 Who wrote the country and western song *'Romeo'*, sung by Dolly Parton?
11 During their 1991 tour, how did Sweet Honey and the Rock accompany their singing?
12 Which Liverpudlian singer reached the UK's number one with *'Anyone Who Had a Heart'* in 1964? Jarry
13 Which Irish singer had a UK number one with *'Nothing Compares 2 U'* in January 1990?
14 To which female vocal group did one member of Shakespear's Sister originally belong?
15 Which American singer was the 1993 film *What's Love Got to Do with It?* a biopic of?

MUSIC ANSWERS

1 *kathy dawn*
2 'Ma, He's Making Eyes at Me'
3 'All Kinds of Everything'
4 *Betty Boo*
5 'March of the Women'
6 *Su Pollard*
7 *Mary Hopkin*
8 *Michelle Shocked*
9 Ingenue
10 *Dolly Parton*
11 *With body and hand percussion instruments*
12 *Cilla Black*
13 *Sinead O'Connor*
14 *Bananarama*
15 *Tina Turner*

1 Dusty Springfield was the first woman singer to appear on *Top of the Pops*, on its very first programme. What song was she singing?

2 In which year did Kate Bush become the first woman to reach number one in the UK album charts with *Never for Ever*?

3 In 1993 who caused controversy in Nashville with her song *'Romeo'*?

4 Who was *'Rockin' Around the Christmas Tree'* in November 1962?

5 Which African-American singer became famous in 1946 with her recording of *'Move On Up a Little Higher'*?

6 When did Sonia have a UK number one hit with *'You'll Never Stop Me Loving You'*?

7 How many women make up the group Strawberry Switchblade?

8 What did Pat Suzuki 'enjoy being' in April 1960?

9 What is the name of the album by Nanci Griffith produced in 1987?

10 During which world tour was Kylie Minogue's video *Kylie Live* recorded?

11 How many 'kinds of loneliness' did singer Tanita Tikaram produce in 1992?

12 What was the title of Jerry Burns' first single, released in April 1992?

13 In which Romanian city was internationally famous concert pianist Clara Haskil (1895–1960) born?

14 Who was named Best Female Folk Singer by the *New Musical Express* in 1971?

15 On which Caribbean Island was singer Joan Armatrading born in 1950?

MUSIC ANSWERS

1 'I Only Want to be With You'

2 *1980*

3 *Dolly Parton*

4 *Brenda Lee*

5 *Mahalia Jackson*

6 *1989 (June)*

7 *Two*

8 *A girl* ('I Enjoy Being a Girl')

9 Lone Star State of Mind

10 *1991* ('Let's Get it Together')

11 *11* (Eleven Kinds of Loneliness)

12 'Burns Night'

13 *Bucharest*

14 *Isla St Clair*

15 *St Kitts*

1 Which opera by Thea Musgrave was first performed in 1974?

2 Where was Ethel Smyth's (1858–1944) composition *'Mass in D'* performed in 1891?

3 What was the name of the album released by Ranch Romance in 1991?

4 Who wrote *'A False Designe to be Cruel'* and was the first female composer to have her work published?

5 Which album by the Forester Sisters was produced in 1990 by Wendy Waldman?

6 Who composed *'The Road is Wider than Long'* (1991)?

7 Who is the mother of British composer Nicola LeFanu?

8 What is the title of Isla St Clair's first LP?

9 What instrument is played by musician Phillippa Schuyler?

10 Jane Glover, Odaline de la Martinez and Sian Edwards are all top of their profession – which is?

11 Which song did Chaka Khan take to a British number one in 1984 and number 45 in 1989?

12 As well as three top-10 hits, what else did Brenda Lee produce in 1962?

13 Which song by duo Donna Summer and Barbara Streisand was released simultaneously on two labels – in 7-inch format on Casablanca Records and 12-inch on CBS – in 1979?

14 What was the title of the single released by The Aquanettes on 15th June 1992?

15 What is the name of the first all-woman record label, set up in 1979?

1 Voice of Ariadne
2 *The Royal Albert Hall, London*
3 Blue Blazes
4 *Mary Harvey (Lady Dering, 1629–1704)*
5 Come Hold Me
6 *Lindsay Cooper*
7 *Elizabeth Maconchy*
8 Traditional Scottish Ballads
9 *Piano*
10 *Conducting*
11 'I Feel for You'
12 *A comic book about her life story*
13 'No More Tears (Enough Is Enough)'
14 'Whoa!'
15 *Stroppy Cow*

GEOGRAPHY QUIZ 35

easier

1 Naomi James (b. 1949) was the first woman to sail solo around the world in 1977. Off which Cape did her boat capsize, nearly causing Naomi to drown?

2 Of which country did Queen Victoria become Empress in 1877?

3 Which country did missionary Gladys Aylward (1903–70) become a citizen of in 1931?

4 In which country did nurse Susie Whighton and surgeon Pauline Cutting risk their lives working with Palestinian refugees in the 1980s?

5 In which British county was the Greenham Common Peace Camp?

6 Which ocean was Ann Davison the first woman to sail solo across?

7 Where were British wildlife film-makers Cindy Buxton and Annie Price filming when the Argentineans landed on the other side of the island?

8 In which city in England's northeast did Ethel Bentham practise medicine until 1909?

9 In which city in northwest England did novelist Mrs Gaskell live after her marriage?

10 Where did doctor/nurse Mary Seacole (1805–81) set up her own hospital, called The British Hotel?

11 In which country was British Agent of the Second World War Violette Szabo born?

12 What was the name of the women's peace camp outside the gates of the US Airforce Base near Newbury, England?

13 In which country did Elizabeth Blackwell (1821–1910) qualify as a doctor in 1849?

14 Whereabouts in Lincolnshire is the birthplace of Margaret Thatcher?

15 In which city can the women's college (founded in 1879) named after mathematician Mary Somerville (1780–1872) be found?

GEOGRAPHY ANSWERS

1 *Cape Horn*
2 *India*
3 *China*
4 *Lebanon*
5 *Berkshire*
6 *Atlantic*
7 *South Georgia, Falkland Islands*
8 *Newcastle upon Tyne*
9 *Manchester*
10 *Spring Hill, near Balaclava, Crimea*
11 *France*
12 *Greenham Common Peace Camp*
13 *United States*
14 *Grantham*
15 *Oxford*

1 Which American mountains did British traveller Isabella Bird (1831–1904) travel 800 miles through—alone?

2 Where was aviator Amelia Earhart flying when she disappeared in her Lockheed Electra?

3 Where did Robyn Davidson live for a year in order to learn everything she needed to know before crossing 1700 miles of Australian scrubland?

4 In which part of Russia did Kate Marsden set up a hospital for lepers in the 19th century?

5 At the age of 57, which country did Christian Miller cycle across, east to west?

6 Which village in Cheshire is Mrs Gaskell's book *Cranford* (1853) based on?

7 In which British county will you find the *'Hen House'*, a Women's Holiday and Study Centre?

8 In 1992, which European country had more female film directors than any other?

9 In which English northeastern coastal town was Dame Flora Robson born in 1902?

10 In which town in New York State was the first Women's Rights Convention held on 19–20 July 1848?

11 In the 19th century, in which town in southern England did fossil collectors Mary, Margaret and Elizabeth Philpot live?

12 In which city in northeast England was doctor and TV presenter Miriam Stoppard born in 1937?

13 In which African country was actress Diane Keen brought up?

14 In which country did Liza Goddard start her TV acting career?

15 In which northern English town did educational campaigner Emily Davies (1830–1921) spend her childhood?

GEOGRAPHY ANSWERS

1 *The Rocky Mountains*

2 *Around the world*

3 *Alice Springs (Northern Territory)*

4 *Siberia*

5 *United States*

6 *Knutsford*

7 *Lincolnshire*

8 *Germany*

9 *South Shields*

10 *Seneca Falls*

11 *Lyme Regis, Dorset*

12 *Newcastle upon Tyne*

13 *Kenya*

14 *Australia*

15 *Gateshead*

1 Which nation did Rebecca West write about in her books *Black Lamb* and *Grey Falcon*?

2 Where was Britain's first major women's conference on pornography held, on 25th November 1989?

3 After which Celtic Goddess are the two hills called Da Chich Anann (near Killarney, Munster, Ireland) named?

4 Of which Asian country was Sirimavo Bandaranaike Prime Minister?

5 In which part of Manchester was Charlotte Brontë living when she began to write *Jane Eyre*?

6 Where did the Fifth International Feminist Book Fair take place?

7 What was the birthplace of singer Patsy Cline?

8 Where was explorer Alexandra David-Neel (1869–1968) the first European woman to reach?

9 In which country did British traveller Hester Stanhope (1776–1839) make her home after she left England in 1810?

10 After which American mountaineer was the north peak of Huascaran named?

11 On which moor in the northwest of England will you find the Ellen Strange Memorial cairn?

12 From which university did British TV presenter Sue Lawley graduate?

13 In which village in northwest England can you find a plaque referring to the *Female Union Society of 1824* above the doorway of 238 Bolton Road?

14 When Peggy Braithwaite became the first woman lighthouse keeper in 1975, where was the lighthouse she was responsible for?

15 In which British city, famous for its lace-making, was artist Laura Knight (1877–1970) born?

GEOGRAPHY ANSWERS

1 *The Yugoslav nation*
2 *Nottingham Polytechnic*
3 *Ana, Goddess of Earth and Fertility*
4 *Sri Lanka*
5 *Hulme*
6 *Amsterdam, Holland*
7 *(Winchester) Virginia, USA*
8 *Lhasa, Tibet*
9 *Syria*
10 *Annie Peck (1850–1935)*
11 *Holcombe Moor*
12 *Bristol*
13 *Haslingden*
14 *Walney Island Lighthouse, Port of Lancaster*
15 *Nottingham*

1 Which British sporting body declared in October 1921 that 'the game of football [soccer] is quite unsuitable for females and ought not to be encouraged'?

2 Of which track sport are British northwesterners Paula Dunn and Di Edwards stars?

3 Anne Boleyn was passionate about which sport?

4 What stopped Suzanne Lenglen playing tennis at Wimbledon before 1919?

5 Why did Wilma Rudolph, American track and field champion, have to wear a brace on her leg as a child?

6 Who won the Ladies' Singles Championship at Wimbledon in the year of Queen Elizabeth's Silver Jubilee (1977)?

7 Which Channel was British swimmer Manda Topp the 329th person to cross?

8 What admission by Billie Jean King resulted in Avon Products dropping their sponsorship of women's tennis?

9 In 1986 who was voted runner-up as the BBC Sports Personality of the Year?

10 At Wimbledon in 1927, why did crowds boo Billie Tapscott?

11 Which royal personage officially invented racing for money in 1914?

12 Which Channel did Alison Streeter take less than 10 hours to swim in 1988?

13 Of which British Athletics Club in northwest England is runner Diane Edwards a member?

14 In which year did Chris Evert win her first Wimbledon final?

15 In which outdoor ball sport is British northwesterner Joanne Morley top woman amateur?

SPORTS ANSWERS

1 *The Football Association*

2 *Running*

3 *Archery*

4 *The First World War*

5 *She had polio*

6 *Virginia Wade*

7 *The English Channel*

8 *That she was bi-sexual*

9 *Fatima Whitbread*

10 *For not wearing stockings*

11 *Queen Anne*

12 *The Irish Channel*

13 *Sale Harriers*

14 *1974*

15 *Golf*

1 In a broadsword contest in 1887, what made Sergeant Owen Davis so angry he charged and threatened the referee?
2 In 1884 Maud Watson won the first National Tennis Championships for Women at Wimbledon. Who was her opponent?
3 On what did Frankie Nelson win the six-day race in New York in 1895?
4 In 1979, when qualified referee Belinda Petty took the British Judo Association to court for refusing to allow her to referee a men's judo international, what argument was used to say she couldn't referee the match?
5 Which two British players met in the final of the Ladies' Singles at Wimbledon in 1961?
6 When Grete Waitz ran the New York Marathon in 1978, what was her overall finishing position?
7 Which American basketball team did Lynette Woodward and Jackie White play for?
8 Which track event was Tatyana Kazankina the first woman to run in less than four minutes, in 1980?
9 Which type of horse races did the Spartan woman Cynisca win in 396 and 392 BC?
10 In 1832, what kind of exercises did Catherine Beecher suggest women who had servants–and who therefore would not get exercise through housework–should do?
11 In 19th-century Britain, why did owners of cycling tracks not allow women to race on them?
12 Which record did Amelia Earhart set in 1921 in her Kinner Canary?
13 Which mountain did Briton Rebecca Stevens reach the summit of in May 1993?
14 In which indoor sport are Lesley McIlraith (Australia) and Karen Corr (Britain) champions?
15 Which British tennis player did Billie Jean King beat at Wimbledon in 1967, only to lose to her in 1969?

SPORTS ANSWERS

1. *He had been defeated by a woman (Jaguarina)*
2. *Her older sister Lilian*
3. *A bicycle*
4. *That, as a woman, she would be too weak to be properly in control*
5. *Angela Mortimer and Christine Trueman*
6. *104th*
7. *Harlem Globetrotters*
8. *1,500 metres (in a time of 3:56.6 minutes)*
9. *Chariot races*
10. *Calisthenics*
11. *They lost their licence if they allowed women to race*
12. *Women's altitude record (14,000 ft)*
13. *Everest*
14. *Snooker*
15. *Ann Jones*

1 Which Ladies' Sport Union was inaugurated in Britain in 1893?

2 Who became the first black woman pilot in 1922?

3 Why did qualified referee Belinda Petty take the British Judo Association to court in 1979?

4 How many women played in the first Ladies' Championship at Wimbledon in 1884?

5 For which sport did tennis champion Lottie Dod win a silver medal at the 1908 Olympics?

6 Why did pugilist Lydia Harris have to leave London and move to Paris?

7 Who captained Great Britain in the first women's rugby international, in 1986, when Britain played France?

8 Which British athletics champion was voted BBC Sports Personality of the year in 1991?

9 What did Lady Sophie Heath (1896–1936) do which resulted in the end to the ban on women becoming commercial pilots?

10 How long did it take 16-year-old Tessie Reynolds to ride her bicycle from Brighton to London and back (120 miles), in 1893?

11 Sue Atkins became the British Boxing unofficial Lightweight champion in 1983. What is her day job?

12 At what time did Rebecca Stevens reach the summit of Everest on Monday 17th May 1993?

13 By how many seconds did Merlene Ottey miss winning the gold medal in the 100 metres at the World Athletics Championships at Stuttgart in 1993?

14 In 1993, which category of golf was Mrs Margaret Rodges of Danbury, Essex, champion of?

15 Who was the first British woman to win a mixed athletic race, cycling, in 1967?

1 *Ladies' Golf Union*

2 *Bessie Coleman*

3 *She had been refused permission to officiate at a men's judo international. (She won!)*

4 *13*

5 *Archery*

6 *Her punches were so powerful she seriously injured her opponent and the police were called*

7 *Carol Isherwood*

8 *Liz McColgan*

9 *She proved she could take off and land just as skilfully as any man, at any time*

10 *Eight and a half hours*

11 *Landscape gardener*

12 *7.41 BST (British Summer Time)*

13 *0.0001 seconds*

14 *Over-80s Female Golf Champion*

15 *Beryl Burton*

1 Who was the first American woman to go into space, in 1983?

2 In which year was Anne Frank's secret annexe discovered by German Security Police?

3 Which Labour Member of Parliament was Minister of State for Education and Science between 1967 and 1969?

4 When eventually captured, why were 18th-century pirates Anne Bonny and Mary Read put in prison instead of being hanged?

5 What had Miss Beale and Miss Buss in common?

6 In 1963, in what kind of spacecraft did cosmonaut Valentina Tereshkova orbit the Earth for three days?

7 What career was Dipika Chikhlia very successful at before becoming a member of the Indian Parliament?

8 What happened to non-British women married to British Citizens on 31st December 1987?

9 Which British Government froze the level of Child Benefit between April 1988 and April 1991?

10 In which month is the Feminist Book Fortnight held in Britain?

11 In 1984 *Newsweek* produced their research report on women who work. Of the women they interviewed, what did 70 per cent say they would rather have: high-pressure jobs with the possibility of advancement or low-pressure jobs with no advancement?

12 What does NAWO stand for?

13 What is the name of the Tudor ship Margaret Rule found and raised?

14 After her capture during the Second World War, why was wireless operator Noor Inayat Khan (1914–44) kept in chains?

15 Which Italian knitwear company was founded by Giuliana Benetton?

HERSTORY ANSWERS

1 *Sally Ride*

2 *1944*

3 *Shirley Williams*

4 *They claimed they were pregnant*

5 *They were both Principals of the first official Schools for Girls*

6 *A Vostok 6*

7 *Acting*

8 *They lost their automatic right to British Citizenship*

9 *The Conservative Government*

10 *June*

11 *High-pressure jobs with the possibility of advancement*

12 *National Alliance for Women's Organizations*

13 *The* Mary Rose

14 *She kept trying to escape*

15 *Benetton*

1 What were established as a result of Britain's *Maternity and Child Welfare Act* of 1918?

2 How did traveller Hester Stanhope (1776–1839) lose all her possessions in 1811?

3 On which British Island were women granted the vote in 1881?

4 Of which British lawful service was Mary Allen co-founder and head in 1915?

5 Who was the first person to have a statue erected in her honour as a First World War hero, in 1923? ✓ PA

6 Where does the phrase 'hiding behind the women's petticoats' originate?

7 Of which northern area of England was Lurminburg Queen in the 7th century?

8 What did Maria Rye (1829–1902) suggest, in *The Englishwoman's Journal*, would be a good idea for middle-class women who couldn't find work in Britain?

9 Who was born in Werowocomoco, Virginia (US) in about 1596?

10 In 1762 Hannah Baddaley tried to commit suicide by jumping off a cliff at Stoney Middleton in Derbyshire. What slowed her descent and saved her life?

11 In 1916 Constance Markiewicz was sentenced to prison for life, due to her part in the Easter Risings in Dublin. How long was she actually in prison?

12 What was the subject of Member of Parliament Nancy Astor's maiden speech in the House of Commons?

13 What life-saver, used in the trenches during the First World War, was developed by British engineer Hertha Ayrton (1854–1923)?

14 What unfortunate suggestion was made by surgeon Frances Morgan while she was working at the Elizabeth Garrett Anderson Hospital – which resulted in lost work for herself?

15 Of which British Trade Union League did Emily Dilke (1840–1904) become president in 1876?

HERSTORY ANSWERS

1 *Welfare Clinics*

2 *In a shipwreck*

3 *The Isle of Man*

4 *Women's Police Service*

5 *Edith Cavell*

6 *The request made in the 19th century, by men, that women's and children's hours of work should be reduced, so theirs would be too!*

7 *Northumbria*

8 *Emigration*

9 *Native American princess Pocahontas*

10 *Her crinoline, which opened up and acted like a parachute*

11 *One year*

12 *The perils of drink*

13 *Ayrton fans, used to get rid of poisonous gases*

14 *That a male surgeon be employed to help with the increase in patients*

15 *The Women's Freedom League*

1 Why was Catharina Regina von Greiffenberg (major woman poet of the German Baroque) exiled from Germany in the 17th century?
2 In which village in France was British Agent Odette (Lise) Sansom working as a courier when she was taken prisoner in April, 1943?
3 Which Irish Goddess, the Goddess of War, would often take the form of a crow?
4 *The Sex Discrimination Act* was passed in Britain in 1975. In which year was the *Equal Pay Act* passed, whereby women had to be paid the same rate as men for work that was broadly similar?
5 What job did Hilda Hewlett, pilot, have during the First World War?
6 In the midst of the battle of the Nile and The Glorious First of June, what were some of the women doing aboard His Majesty's warships, apart from nursing the wounded?
7 What did the Greek Goddess Daphne finally do in order to avoid the advances of Apollo?
8 How many women did Maria Rye (1829–1902) help to emigrate from Britain in 1862?
9 Who was the originator of Britain's *Workhouse Reform Act* which, in 1875, allowed women to be Poor Law Guardians?
10 Which religious group, believers in the second coming of Christ, was led by Mother Ann Lee?
11 In which British town did the Native American princess Pocahontas die in 1617?
12 In 1908 Elizabeth Garrett Anderson became the first woman Mayor in England. Of which town?
13 How old was Charlotte Hughes, from Redcar, when she died on 1st August 1992?
14 In February of which year was the First National Women's Liberation Conference held at Ruskin College, Oxford?
15 Which Order of Carmelites did Teresa of Avila (1515–1582) travel through Spain establishing in the 16th century?

37 HERSTORY ANSWERS

1 *Because of her Protestant beliefs*
2 *Annecy*
3 *Badb*
4 *1970*
5 *Instructor for fighter pilots*
6 *Giving birth*
7 *She had herself changed into a laurel tree*
8 *400*
9 *Louisa Twining*
10 *Shakers*
11 *Gravesend*
12 *Aldeburgh*
13 *115*
14 *1970*
15 *Barefoot, or Discalced, Order of Carmelites*

1 Who played Patsy in the BBC 2 comedy series *Absolutely Fabulous*, by Jennifer Saunders?

2 Which British actress was born Diana Fluck in 1931?

3 Which former star of the Channel 4 soap *Brookside* went on to star in *Goodbye Cruel World* as Barbara, sufferer from a wasting disease?

4 Of which ill-fated BBC soap of 1993 was Corrine Hollingworth producer?

5 Who energetically presents *Challenge Anneka*?

6 Which actress became Member of Parliament for Hampstead and Highgate in 1992?

7 Who was originally a television presenter on *Blue Peter*, and one of the Radio 4's *5p.m.* presenters in 1993?

8 In which square is Sharon landlady of the pub and Kath owner of the *Bistro*?

9 Who starred in the film *The Prime of Miss Jean Brodie*?

10 In which BBC TV cupboard could you find Philippa Forrester?

11 For which children's television programme was Biddy Baxter long-time producer?

12 Which BBC sitcom series stars Pauline Quirke and Linda Robson, with Lesley Joseph as their neighbour?

13 What can you listen to every weekday on Radio 4 between 10.30 and 11.30 a.m ?

14 Who played a doctor in *Tenko* and the redoubtable Diana in *Waiting for God*?

15 What does Gaby Roslin serve up every weekday morning from 7 to 9 a.m?

BRITISH ENTERTAINMENT ANSWERS

1 *Joanna Lumley*

2 *Diana Dors (1931–84)*

3 *Sue Johnston*

4 Eldorado

5 *Anneka Rice*

6 *Glenda Jackson*

7 *Valerie Singleton*

8 *Albert Square (on* Eastenders*)*

9 *Dame Maggie Smith*

10 The Broom Cupboard *(Children's BBC)*

11 Blue Peter

12 Birds of a Feather

13 Woman's Hour

14 *Stephanie Cole*

15 The Big Breakfast

1 In which 1960s TV series did Rosemary Nicols play Annabelle Hurst?

2 Who moved from advertising *Oxo* on TV to *Second Thoughts* on both radio and TV?

3 On which BBC 2 television football fanzine is Shelley Webb a presenter?

4 What did Anne Nightingale become the first woman to work as in 1970?

5 Which character in the BBC hospital series *Casualty* was played by Cathy Shipton?

6 Which series of TV detective dramas starred Helen Mirren?

7 Which new ITV series of 1993 starred Wendy Craig, Sheila Hancock, Jean Boht and Sheila Gish?

8 Which Australian TV fly-on-the-wall documentary, of 1993, starred Noeline Baker?

9 Which ITV drama series about a doctor in Colorado Springs, in the 1860s, starred Jane Seymour as the doctor?

10 Which Margaret Forster novel was made into a 1966 film starring Lynn Redgrave, with Charlotte Rampling as her flatmate Meredith?

11 Which information book is edited by Annete Kuhn and Susannah Radstone?

12 On 28th August 1992, which American medical sitcom created by Susan Harris began on Channel 4?

13 Who became the first black woman newsreader on ITV in June 1981?

14 Which Agatha Christie novel was adapted as the West End play, *The Mousetrap*?

15 Who played Diana Longden in *Screen One: Wide-Eyed and Legless*, the true and tragic story of a woman suffering from ME?

38 BRITISH ENTERTAINMENT ANSWERS

medium

1. Department S
2. *Lynda Bellingham*
3. Standing Room Only
4. *Radio 1 disc jockey*
5. *Lisa Duffin (Duffy)*
6. Prime Suspect 1, 2 and 3
7. Brighton Belles
8. Sylvania Waters
9. Dr Quinn: Medicine Woman
10. Georgy Girl
11. The Women's Companion to International Films
12. Nurses
13. *Moira Stewart*
14. Three Blind Mice
15. *Julie Walters*

BRITISH ENTERTAINMENT QUIZ

1 Which ballet dancer was born Peggy Hookham in 1919?

2 When Lynsey de Paul was paid £10,000 for telling a Sunday paper about her affair with Sean Connery, to whom did she give the money?

3 Which daily Radio 4 women's programme is presented by Jenni Murray?

4 Why did Nessa, in the BBC soap *Eldorado*, use a wheelchair?

5 Which Manchester High School did actress Beryl Reid attend?

6 In which area of British dramatic arts can Clara Webster (d. 1844) be credited as having been the first?

7 Who was voted Funniest Female on TV 1981–82 by *TV Times* readers?

8 Which Trinidadian-born actress worked in a bank before turning to acting?

9 What is the stage name of comedy duo Shelly Ambury and Helen Austin?

10 In the 1960s stage production of *The Prime of Miss Jean Brodie*, who played Jean Brodie?

11 Barbara Mandell became the first British woman newscaster on 22nd September 1955. For which commercial station did she read the news?

12 Who was the first recorded playwright?

13 Which ITV morning children's series is presented by Yvette Fielding and produced by Vanessa Hill?

14 In 1993, who was the producer of Radio 4's *Woman's Hour*?

15 In which year was the Theatre of Black Women, the first all-black-womens theatre company in Britain, founded?

1 *Margot Fonteyn*
2 *A shelter for battered women*
3 Woman's Hour
4 *She had brittle bone disease (osteoporosis)*
5 *Levenshulme High School for Girls*
6 *British ballet dancer*
7 *Dame Judi Dench*
8 *Floella Benjamin*
9 'Two Girls What Sing'
10 *Vanessa Redgrave*
11 *ITN*
12 *Katherine of Sutton (14th-century abbess)*
13 What's Up, Doc?
14 *Sally Feldman*
15 *1982*

1 Who was Agatha Christie's famous detective from St Mary Mead?

2 In what year did Mary Wollstonecraft write *The Vindication of the Rights of Women*?

3 Which US feminist magazine did Gloria Steinem found in 1973?

4 What two things did Virginia Woolf (1882–1941) believe all women should have?

5 What was the title of Carol-Anne Courtney's autobiographical book?

6 Who was the author of *Casabianca* or *The boy stood on the burning deck* (1825)?

7 Which is the only novel Emily Brontë wrote?

8 George Eliot was the pseudonym of which great British novelist?

9 Which London Art Gallery held an exhibition of Beatrix Potter's work in 1987?

10 Which 1930 book written by actress/producer/director Nell Shipman was serialized in *McCalls* magazine as *M'Sieu Sweetheart*?

11 What nationality is the heroine of Liza Cody's mysteries, Anna Lee?

12 What was the title of Charlotte Perkins Gilman's shocking book, written in 1892?

13 In what year is *Body of Glass*, by Marge Piercy, set?

14 What was the title of New Zealand novelist Janet Frame's three-volume autobiography?

15 Who wrote about the 'second' sex?

LITERATURE & ART ANSWERS

1. *Miss Marple*
2. *1792*
3. Ms.
4. *£500 a year and a room of their own*
5. Morphine and Dolly Mixture
6. *Felicia Hemans (1793–1835)*
7. Wuthering Heights
8. *Mary Ann Evans (1819–80)*
9. *The Tate Gallery*
10. Get the Woman
11. *English*
12. The Yellow Wallpaper
13. *2061*
14. Faces in the Water
15. *Simone de Beauvoir*

1 Whose first collection of poetry, published in 1966, was entitled *The Circle Games*?

2 Which unfinished novel was Jane Austen (1775–1817) writing when she died in 1817?

3 Whose life story was written by her friend Elizabeth Gaskell (1810–65) and published in 1857?

4 Who wrote *The Well of Loneliness*?

5 Which African-American writer was born Marguerite Johnson in St Louis, Missouri, in 1928?

6 Who wrote *The Tenant of Wildfell Hall*? D|L

7 Who edited *Ms Murder* and *More Ms Murder*, collections of mysteries by women about women detectives?

8 Which children's story writer was editor of Britain's *Sunny Stories for Little Folks* from 1926–52?

9 Who wrote about Lady Molly of Scotland Yard in 1910?

10 Who wrote the American *'Battle Hymn of the Republic'* in 1861?

11 Which job was British author Fanny Burney (1752–1840) given in 1786?

12 Which two Gothic novels were written by Ann Radcliffe (1764–1823)?

13 Aphra Behn and Agnes Maria Bennett wrote in different centuries. When writing proved too poorly paid to live on, how did each of these women support herself?

14 What kind of painter was Mary Beale (1632/33–99)?

15 What is the title of the first crime novel Agatha Christie wrote (in 1920)?

LITERATURE & ART ANSWERS

1 *Margaret Atwood's (b. 1939)*

2 Sanditon

3 *Charlotte Brontë's (*Life of Charlotte Brontë*)*

4 *Radclyffe Hall (1886–1943)*

5 *Maya Angelou*

6 *Anne Brontë (1820–49)*

7 *Marie Smith*

8 *Enid Blyton*

9 *Baroness Orczy (1865–1947)*

10 *Julia Ward Howe (1819–1910)*

11 *Second keeper of the robes to the Queen*

12 Mysteries of Udolpho *and* The Italian

13 *By becoming a mistress to a wealthy 'patron'*

14 *Portrait painter*

15 The Mysterious Affair at Styles

1 Why was Angela Webster expelled from the Art School in South Kensington, London?

2 What did novelist Naomi Mitchison say was 'a rather splendid thing'?

3 In 1907 what was the name of the feminist magazine founded in Japan by Kageyama Hideko?

4 On what were the panels painted by Paula Rego in her studio at London's National Gallery (while she was artist-in-residence) based?

5 Which British magazine was established by Eliza Howarth in April 1744?

6 What was British novelist Lady Morgan (Sydney Owenson) the first woman to be granted in 1837?

7 Scenes of which British mountain range won Marie Walkerhast the Druce Constable Award for British Landscape Painting in 1988?

8 At what age did Katherine Moore, author of *Summer at the Haven*, begin to write?

9 What nationality are the artists Gisele Amantea and Mina Totino?

10 Who was Julian of Norwich?

11 Why did 16th-century poet Lady Mary Wroth have to withdraw her only published novel, *The Countesse of Montgomerie's Urania* (1621), six months after its publication?

12 As Britain's first woman journalist, what was Eliza Lynn Linton's salary in 1851?

13 Who wrote *Marriage as a Trade* in 1909?

14 In which century was it first decided and then recorded by male grammarians that 'man' should come before 'woman' as in, e.g., male and female, husband and wife?

15 What was Muriel Spark's book *The Driver's Seat* (1970) about?

LITERATURE & ART ANSWERS

hard

1 *For whistling*

2 *To be a woman*

3 Women of the World

4 *The lives of female saints*

5 The Female Spectator

6 *A literary pension*

7 *The Pennines*

8 *85*

9 *Canadian*

10 *A woman of medieval times who wrote religious and spiritual works*

11 *Because of accusations of libel*

12 *20 guineas a month*

13 *Cicely Hamilton (1872–1952)*

14 *16th (1553)*

15 *A woman obsessed with death*

1 Under Britain's 19th-century *Contagious Diseases Acts*, who could the police declare were 'common prostitutes'?

2 Who made nursing a respectable job for women to do?

3 Which sex chromosome is carried by a woman's egg?

4 In 1860 the British Medical Association decided to allow only those who had studied at a British University to become registered doctors. What effect did this have on women?

5 What was introduced for school children by Member of Parliament Ellen Wilkinson and withdrawn by Member of Parliament Margaret Thatcher?

6 Who discovered, through x-rays, the essential information that DNA is a helical structure?

7 Who defined 'the problem that has no name', in 1963?

8 What was the real name of British Army doctor James Barry (1795–1865)?

9 When was American mathematician Grace Hopper, a member of the US Naval Reserves, promoted to Captain?

10 When Elizabeth Garrett Anderson (1836–1917) sat the Society of Apothecaries exams in 1865, how well did she do?

11 Who was the first woman to become a Professor at the Sorbonne and the only person to win the Nobel Prize twice?

12 In which town in northwest England was the world's first test-tube baby born in 1978?

13 Which medical body was Elizabeth Garrett Anderson (1836–1917) the only member of from 1873 to 1892?

14 What did scientist Mary Leakey (b. 1913) discover in the volcanic ash of the Olduvai Gorge, Tanzania, in 1976?

15 Whom is the computer programming language ADA named after?

1 *All women living in main ports and garrison towns*

2 *Florence Nightingale*

3 *The 'X' chromosome*

4 *It effectively stopped them from becoming doctors (as at the time British women were not allowed to study at University)*

5 *Free school milk*

6 *Rosalind Franklin*

7 *Author Betty Friedan (in her book* The Feminine Mystique*)*

8 *Miranda Barry*

9 *1973*

10 *She passed, and did better than all the men*

11 *Physicist Marie Curie (1867–1934)*

12 *Oldham, Lancashire*

13 *The British Medical Association*

14 *Human-like footprints which were 3.5 million years old*

15 *Ada, Countess of Lovelace (1815–52), in honour of her work in and understanding of early computers*

1 How did American physician and chemotherapist Dr Jane C. Wright make history in July 1967?

2 Where did paleontologist Mary Anning (1799–1847) discover a complete skeleton of the Ichthyosaurus dinosaur?

3 Which British School of Medicine did Eleanor Davis-Colley graduate from in 1907?

4 What does the term 'biophilic', coined by Mary Daly in her book *Gyn/Ecology* (1978), mean?

5 During the time of the *Contagious Diseases Acts* of 1864 to 1869, who (in addition to prostitutes) did Sir Henry Storks think should be brought under the control of the police?

6 How did so many of the women who painted watches with radioactive paint to make them luminous get 'radium jaw' and die as a result?

7 What mammals are studied at Britain's Jane Goodall Institute for Wildlife Research, Education and Conservation?

8 What did sociologist Jessie Bernard warn may be hazardous to women's health, in 1972?

9 Which society awarded astronomer Caroline Herschel (1750–1848) their Gold Medal in 1828?

10 In which gallery of London's Kew Gardens are over 800 of the botanical works by scientific illustrator Marianne North (1830–90) displayed?

11 In what area of science did Janet Taylor and Margaret Bryan publish works in 1820?

12 What were the names of physicist Marie Curie's two daughters?

13 What did the British War Office say to Dr Elsie Inglis in 1914 when, after raising the money and setting up the Scottish Field Hospital, she offered it to them, fully staffed?

14 What area of research is American Dr Jane C. Wright (b. 1919), physician and chemotherapist, an expert in?

15 Because of her research into which disease has Dr Clarice Reid (b. 1931) helped many people of African descent?

SCIENCE ANSWERS

1 *She became the first black woman to be made Dean of a medical centre in the US (at the New York Medical Centre)*

2 *Lyme Regis, Dorset*

3 *London (Royal Free Hospital) School of Medicine for Women*

4 *Life-loving*

5 *The wives of soldiers*

6 *They sucked or licked the paint brushes to get as fine a point as possible*

7 *Chimpanzees*

8 *Marriage*

9 *The Royal Astronomical Society*

10 *The North Gallery*

11 *Astronomy*

12 *Irené and Eve*

13 *'Go sit quietly at home dear Lady'*

14 *Cancer research*

15 *Sickle-cell anaemia*

1 To whom did the ancient Egyptians pray when anyone was ill?
2 What did Lady Montagu introduce into England in the 18th century?
3 What kind of space sickness is American Dr Patricia Cowings-Johnson working to prevent?
4 Mary Anning (1797–1847) discovered the fossil skeleton of a prehistoric sea creature (a plesiosaur). How much did she sell it for in 1821?
5 In which area of geology was Mary Horner (1803–73) an expert?
6 When scientist Marjory Stephenson (1885–1948) found she could not afford to study medicine, what did she do instead?
7 What reason did Lillian Murray (1871–1960), first woman member of the British Dental Association, generally give for deciding to become a dentist?
8 What was physicist Marie Curie (1867–1934) presented with during her tour of the United States in 1921?
9 What was the Tektite 2 project, which took place in 1970?
10 In which area of science was Maria Winkelmann an expert during the 18th century?
11 What was astronomer Caroline Herschel (1750–1848) awarded by the King of Prussia in 1846?
12 An invalid for many years, Anne Pratt (1806–93) wrote and illustrated a five-volume work about the flowering plants and ferns of Britain. Who collected the plants she drew and wrote about?
13 In the 18th century, which bodily stones did Joanna Stephens (d. 1774) find a remedy to dissolve?
14 Who were the first female medical graduates of London University, after women were allowed to take full degrees in 1882?
15 In which subject was Austrian scientist Lise Meitner (1878–1968) a professor at the University of Berlin in the 1920s?

SCIENCE ANSWERS

1 *Goddess Isis*

2 *Inoculation against smallpox*

3 *Zero-gravity sickness*

4 *£200*

5 *Mollusc shells*

6 *She got a job as a domestic science teacher*

7 *To annoy her headteacher Miss Buss, who thought she should become a teacher*

8 *One gram of Radium*

9 *A project in which 17 women lived underwater for two weeks in order to study fish and marine life in their natural habitat*

10 *Astronomy*

11 *The Gold Medal for Science*

12 *Her sister*

13 *Bladder stones*

14 *Mary Scharlieb and Edith Shove*

15 *Physics*

1 In which year did the first Biba boutique open in London?

2 In 19th-century Britain, which was the only profession seen as appropriate to women of 'gentle birth'?

3 In 1892, what freed Mary Kingsley to travel through Africa?

4 Which British political party had most Women Members of Parliament in 1991?

5 Who was the mother of Queen Elizabeth I?

6 On Saturday 18th July 1992 who became Deputy Leader of the Labour Party?

7 In 1926, which political party did Emmeline Pankhurst join?

8 Whose gravestone in St Margaret's Churchyard, East Wellow, Hampshire, starkly states only her date of birth (12th May 1820), date of death (13th August 1910) and her initials (FN)?

9 Who became the first woman Labour MP when she became Member of Parliament for Middlesborough in 1924?

10 Which guild, committed to peace, introduced the white poppy as a symbol of peace in 1933?

11 In 1906 Christabel Pankhurst gained a first-class degree in law from Victoria University (now Manchester University) and came top of her year. What prevented her from then practising at the bar?

12 In what kind of plane did aviator Amy Johnson fly solo to Australia?

13 In which year was the *Mary Rose*, which sank in the 16th century, raised to the surface again?

14 In the 19th century which women were given the nickname 'Lucy Stoners'?

15 Why did male workers in Britain's factories in the 19th century ask for a limit to be put on the number of hours women and children worked?

HERSTORY ANSWERS

1 *1964*

2 *Governess*

3 *The death of her parents*

4 *The Labour Party*

5 *Anne Boleyn*

6 *Margaret Beckett MP*

7 *The Conservative Party*

8 *Florence Nightingale's*

9 *Ellen Wilkinson (1891–1947)*

10 *The Women's Co-operative Guild*

11 *Her sex*

12 *A Gypsy Moth*

13 *1982*

14 ***Women who kept their maiden name on marriage***

15 ***They believed that if women's and children's hours were reduced it would result in the reduction of their own working hours***

1 After 1963 and before 1973, who were the only women allowed in the Gallery of the London Stock Exchange?

2 Which company, now called the FI Group, was set up by Stephanie (Steve) Shirley (b. 1933) in the 1960s?

3 What does the acronym C.O.Y.O.T.E., founded in San Francisco in 1973, stand for?

4 Where did Sojourner Truth make her famous 'Ain't I a woman?' speech in 1851?

5 What was the name of the first black women's suffrage organization in the US, founded by Ida Wells Barnett in Chicago in 1900?

6 Who was born Agnes Goxha Bedjanxhui in Skopje in 1910?

7 In which subject did Margaret Thatcher gain a second-class honours degree at university?

8 Why did doctor and health worker Josephine Butler (1873–1945) refuse a lectureship at New York University?

9 Whom did revue dancer Josephine Baker (1906–75) secretly work for during the First World War?

10 Why was Emma Goldman (1869–1940), American anarchist, sentenced to five years' penal servitude in 1917?

11 Which ministerial post did Labour Member of Parliament Judith Hart hold three times (1969–70, 1974–75 and 1977–79)?

12 Who was the mother of traveller Anne Blunt (1837–1917)?

13 Goddess Mari of Southern India is Goddess of both Rain and a virulent disease. Which disease?

14 In which year was Britain's *Sex Disqualification (Removal) Act* passed?

15 Which British company did Mair Barnes, as Managing Director, turn around from a £4 million deficit to a £45 million profit in two years?

41 HERSTORY ANSWERS

1 *Guides who showed visitors around*

2 *Freelance Programmers Ltd*

3 *Call Off Your Old Tired Ethics*

4 *The Second Annual Women's Rights Convention in Akron, Ohio*

5 *Alpha Suffrage Club*

6 *Mother Theresa of Calcutta*

7 *Chemistry*

8 *The university would not admit women as post-graduate students*

9 *The French Resistance*

10 *For opposing conscription during the First World War*

11 *Minister of Overseas Development*

12 *Mathematician Ada, Countess of Lovelace (1815–52)*

13 *Smallpox*

14 *1919*

15 *Woolworths*

1 Who was the first woman Member of Parliament to be elected and take up her seat, in the House of Commons, in her own right?

2 What was the title of Canada's first anti-slavery newspaper, published by Mary Ann Shadd Cary (1823–93)?

3 During the First World War, where did German poet Gertrud Kölmar (1894–1943?) work as an interpreter?

4 What animal form did the Egyptian Goddess Heket, symbol of fertility and life, take?

5 In 1929 Margaret Bondfield (1873–1953) became the first female Cabinet Minister (Labour). What post did she hold?

6 Who now owns the tenement house at 145 Buccleugh Street, Garnethill, Glasgow, which was lived in by the same woman, Agnes Toward, from 1911 to 1975?

7 In which year was Equality Now, an international human rights organization acting on the behalf of girls and women, founded?

8 What does CAP campaign against?

9 What was Violette Szabo, courier with the French Section of the SOE, doing on 10th June 1944, at Salon-la-Tour?

10 When did American aviator Harriet Quimby become the first woman to fly across the English Channel?

11 Which 8th-century Saxon Queen issued coins which carried her own portrait?

12 Why was thief Moll Cutpurse (c.1589–c.1662) arrested on Christmas Day 1611, in St Paul's Cathedral, London?

13 In India, what was freedom-fighter Rani Gaidinliu (b. 1915) leading her guerillas against?

14 Who became the first woman in the French navy to be promoted to take overall command of a naval vessel?

15 In 16th-century Nigeria, Queen Amina is reputed to have taken a lover in every city she conquered. What is she said to have done with them 'the morning after'?

HERSTORY ANSWERS

1 *Susan Lawrence (Labour Member of Parliament for East Ham, 1923)*

2 The Provincial Freeman

3 *In a prison camp (Doberitz)*

4 *A frog*

5 *Minister of Labour*

6 *The National Trust for Scotland*

7 *1992*

8 *Pornography (CAP = Campaign Against Pornography)*

9 *She was keeping an advance guard of 400 members of the Das Reich SS Panzer Division pinned down with her shooting, while her comrade Anastasie took shelter in a nearby farmyard*

10 *(April) 1912*

11 *Queen Cynethryth*

12 *For wearing men's clothes in the cathedral*

13 *British rule in India*

14 *José Lenzini*

15 *She had them beheaded*

1 Whose life story is the 1965 film *The Sound of Music*, starring Julie Andrews, based on?

2 In the film *Thelma and Louise*, who played Louise?

3 In which Australian soap did Gillian and Gayle Blakeney play twin sisters Caroline and Christina Alessi?

4 Who starred in the film *Red-Headed Woman* (1932), written by Anita Loos?

5 In which medical Australian soap, set in Coopers Crossing and shown on BBC TV, did Liz Burch play Dr Chris Randall?

6 In which movie, based on an Alice Walker novel of the same name, did Whoopie Goldberg play Celie?

7 Which female lead of *Cliffhanger* was a mainstay of Northern Exposure?

8 Who starred as Stella in the 1937 film *Stella Dallas*?

9 When directing a film, what did actress/director Ida Lupino (b. 1918) say she did to get more co-operation from the cameramen?

10 Who played the rock star Rose in the 1979 film *The Rose*?

11 In which film did Oprah Winfrey make her acting debut?

12 Which 1950s star appeared in the films *Bus Stop* and *Some Like It Hot*?

13 Which dramatic actress was born Ruth Elizabeth Davis in 1908?

14 In which 1960s comedy series did Elizabeth Montgomery twitch her nose?

15 Who sang about her home town in *Nutbush City Limits*?

ENTERTAINMENT ANSWERS

1. *Maria von Trapp's*
2. *Susan Sarandon*
3. Neighbours
4. *Jean Harlow*
5. The Flying Doctors
6. The Color Purple
7. *Janine Turner*
8. *Barbara Stanwyck*
9. *She pretended to know less than they did*
10. *Bette Midler*
11. The Color Purple
12. *Marilyn Monroe*
13. *Bette Davis*
14. Bewitched
15. *Tina Turner*

1 For which film did Katharine Hepburn (b. 1907) win her first Academy Award in 1933?

2 In the science fiction film *In the Year 2000* (1912), produced by Alice Guy Blaché (1875–1968), who ruled the world?

3 Who starred in the film *Sweet Charity*?

4 Actress Carrie Fisher is the step-daughter of Elizabeth Taylor. Who was her mother?

5 What was the stage name of Polish ballerina Marie Rambam?

6 What was the name of the show in which revue artist Josephine Baker made her New York debut in 1923?

7 Who were the two stars of the 1941 film *The Great Lie*?

8 What was the title of the final film Joan Crawford made for Warner Bros in 1952?

9 Which film festival did the town of Creteil (near Paris) host in March 1989?

10 What happened to Marilyn Monroe's part in the 1948 film *Scudda Hoo! Scudda Hay!*?

11 Which famous film star was born Lucille LeSueur in San Antonio, Texas?

12 Who always wrote either all, or the majority, of the script for any Mae West film?

13 In which 1932 film did Katharine Hepburn make her film debut?

14 Which novel by Jane Rule was adapted and became the film *Desert Hearts* (1985)?

15 Why did Sinead O'Connor donate her mansion in Los Angeles to charity in November 1992?

ENTERTAINMENT ANSWERS

1 Morning Glory
2 *Women*
3 *Shirley MacLaine*
4 *Debbie Reynolds*
5 *Marie Rambert*
6 Chocolate Dandies
7 *Mary Astor and Bette Davis*
8 This Woman Is Dangerous
9 *The Eleventh International Women's Film Festival*
10 *It was cut out*
11 *Joan Crawford*
12 *Mae West herself*
13 Bill of Divorcement
14 Desert of the Heart (1964)
15 *To help the refugees in war-torn Somalia*

1 For which two films has scriptwriter Ruth Prawer Jhabvala won Oscars?

2 For which 1975 drama did Ellen Burstyn win an Oscar?

3 Which Australian actress starred as Mrs Danvers in 1940 and had a Broadway theatre named after her in 1984?

4 In what aspect of the theatre did Harriet Anderson (b. 1932) start her acting career?

5 Which American writer toured Africa and Europe in the late 1940s as one of the cast in *Porgy and Bess*?

6 Which American film actress became the first woman director on the board of Pepsi-Cola?

7 What is the name of the production company founded by French film director Alice Guy-Blaché (1875–1968) in 1910?

8 What were the two reasons Warner Brothers gave for turning Rita Hayworth down after her screen test?

9 In what kind of factory was Marylin Monroe working at the end of the Second World War?

10 How was Lucille LeSueur's new name (Joan Crawford) chosen?

11 Anita Loos made a very successful transition from silent films to talkies. What as?

12 In Katharine Hepburn's second film, *Christopher Strong*, she played Cynthia Darrington. What was Cynthia's ambition?

13 In the 1943 film *Millions Like Us*, where did all the women portrayed work?

14 What did film director Martha Coolidge think were the most important things for a director to have?

15 In 1929, what important achievement in talking pictures was invented by director Dorothy Arzner, during the filming of *The Wild Party*?

ENTERTAINMENT ANSWERS

1. A Room with a View *and* Howards End
2. Alice Doesn't Live Here Anymore
3. *Dame Judith Anderson (b. 1898)*
4. *As a music hall dancer*
5. *Maya Angelou (b. 1928)*
6. *Joan Crawford*
7. *Solax*
8. *They said she was overweight and that her hairline was too low*
9. *An aircraft factory (testing parachutes)*
10. *Through a competition organized by MGM*
11. *A scriptwriter*
12. *To be an aviator*
13. *In an aircraft factory*
14. *'A good pair of shoes (it's murder on your feet)'*
15. *The boom microphone*

THE SUFFRAGETTES QUIZ 43

1 For which British suffragette organization was WSPU an acronym?

2 What was the motto of the WSPU?

3 Which British Government resisted giving women the vote in the early 20th century?

4 How did British suffragette Emily Wilding Davison (1872–1913) die?

5 Why did Emmeline Pankhurst stop fighting for votes for British women in 1914?

6 For which British organization is NUWSS an acronym?

7 In which year were women over 30 years old given the vote in Britain?

8 Why was Britain's *Cat and Mouse Act* introduced?

9 Which British university did Christabel Pankhurst attend?

10 What was the badge, designed by Sylvia Pankhurst (in 1909) and awarded to any member of the WSPU who had been imprisoned for the cause, called?

11 On whose tombstone are the words 'DEEDS NOT WORDS' inscribed?

12 How long were 14 suffragettes imprisoned in Holloway Gaol, London, after smashing the windows of Whitehall on 29 June 1909?

13 What is Britain's *Prisoner's Temporary Discharge for Ill-Health Act*, of 1913, more commonly called?

14 Which part of northwest England did mill-worker Annie Kenney (1879–1949) come from?

15 What was the title of the newspaper published by the NUWSS?

THE SUFFRAGETTES

1 *Women's Social and Political Union*

2 *'Deeds Not Words'*

3 *Liberal Government*

4 *She threw herself under the King's horse on Derby Day and died from the injuries she received*

5 *To put her energies into helping the war effort (First World War) instead*

6 *National Union of Women's Suffrage Societies*

7 *1918*

8 *To prevent suffragette hunger-strikers getting unconditional release from prison*

9 *Manchester University*

10 *The Holloway Brooch*

11 *Emily Wilding Davison's*

12 *One month*

13 *The Cat and Mouse Act*

14 *Oldham, Lancashire*

15 The Common Cause

1 What caused the death of Lady Constance Lytton and many other suffragettes?

2 When were women over 21 years old first given the vote in Britain?

3 In which city in northwest England was Emmeline Pankhurst (1858–1928) born?

4 On 18th November 1910 over 300 members of the WSPU marched on the House of Commons. The marchers suffered terrible violence at the hands of the police. What did this day become known as?

5 What were considered to be the Women's Social and Political Union's greatest weapons in the fight for Votes for Women?

6 Which newspaper gave members of the WSPU the nickname 'Suffragettes' in 1906?

7 In which year did Emmeline Pankhurst found the WSPU, in Manchester?

8 Who were the first two suffragettes to be imprisoned?

9 Why did Lady Constance Lytton change her name, temporarily, to Jane Wharton?

10 In which year were the first suffragettes imprisoned?

11 In 1915 what did *The Suffragette* magazine change its name to?

12 In 1911 which composer wrote the music for the song which became the official anthem of the WSPU, *'March of the Women'*?

13 Where did Adela Pankhurst (1885–1961) go to live in 1914?

14 Of which British suffragette group did Charlotte Despard (1844–1939) become president?

15 Through a window of which London Office did Victoria Lidiard throw a stone, which resulted in her being sent to prison for two months (1912)?

43 THE SUFFRAGETTES ANSWERS

1 *Ill-health brought on by hunger strikes and force-feeding*

2 *1928*

3 *Manchester*

4 *Black Friday*

5 *Publicity and advertisement*

6 *The* Daily Mail

7 *1903*

8 *Christabel Pankhurst and Annie Kenney*

9 *She wanted to prove that a suffragette with connections was treated differently to ordinary suffragettes in prison*

10 *1905*

11 Britannia

12 *Ethel Smyth (1858–1944)*

13 *Melbourne, Australia*

14 *Women's Freedom League*

15 *The War Office*

1 What was the rallying call of American Suffragette Susan B. Anthony (1820–1906)?

2 Which British Suffrage Society was formed in 1861?

3 When was the forced feeding of suffragettes on hunger strike in prison first introduced?

4 In which year was the first petition for Women's Suffrage presented in Parliament?

5 What was Adela Pankhurst's (1885–1961) career before becoming a paid organizer for the WSPU?

6 When did Edith New and Mary Leigh smash the first windows as part of the British suffragette campaign?

7 What did Mary Richardson ('Slasher Mary') do that resulted in her being sentenced to 18 months in prison, with hard labour, in March 1914?

8 Why was Scottish suffragette Flora Drummond (1869–1949) not allowed to become a postmistress?

9 In which year did Charlotte Despard (1844–1939) leave the WSPU and found the WFL (Women's Freedom League)?

10 When women won the vote, what did the NUWSS (National Union of Women's Suffrage Societies) change its name to?

11 In the *Free Thought Magazine* of September 1896, what two things did suffragette and abolitionist Elizabeth Cady Stanton (1875–1902) suggest were the 'greatest stumbling block in the way of women's emancipation'?

12 When was the Cat and Mouse Act introduced?

13 Where did the WSPU move its headquarters to in 1906?

14 Which volume of Sylvia Pankhurst's autobiography was drafted but not published?

15 What did Mrs Pethick Lawrence successfully lead a group of women to do on 21st November 1910?

THE SUFFRAGETTES ANSWERS

1 *'Failure is impossible'*

2 *The National Union of Women's Suffrage Societies*

3 *(24th) September 1909*

4 *1866*

5 *Elementary school teacher*

6 *30th June, 1908*

7 *She attacked* The Rokeby Venus *painting in the National Gallery*

8 *She was not tall enough*

9 *1907*

10 *NUSEC (National Union of Societies for Equal Citizenship)*

11 *The Bible and the Church*

12 *(25th) March 1913*

13 *London*

14 *The third volume, entitled* In The Red Twilight

15 *Break windows–in the Home Office, War Office, Board of Trade, Board of Education, National Liberal Club, Foreign Office, Somerset House, National Liberal Club, the Old Banqueting Hall, the London and South-Western Bank, the houses of Lord Haldene and Mr John Burns, and several post offices*

1 When was the first sex test used on Olympic athletes?

2 How many women were officially allowed to compete in the revival of the Olympic Games at Athens in 1896?

3 What prevented the Olympic Games of 1916 from being held?

4 Why was Germany's best high jumper, Gretel Bergmann, not allowed to take part in the 1936 (Berlin) Olympic Games?

5 In the 1972 Olympic Games, why did Olga Korbut receive a score of only 7.5 on the uneven parallel bars?

6 What medal did British athlete Sally Gunnell win for the 400 metre hurdles at the 1992 (Barcelona) Olympics?

7 In the 1984 Olympics, in which event did Britons Tina Lillat and Fatima Whitbread win silver and bronze respectively?

8 Who set a new world record on winning the 1972 pentathlon?

9 For which race were gold medals won by Lucy Morton in the 1924 Olympics and Anita Lonsbrough in the 1960 Olympics?

10 Who was the oldest woman ever to win an Olympic gold medal?

11 In which northern English county was Olympic gold medallist (1972) Bridget Parker born in 1939?

12 Which track event was won by Wyomia Tyus twice in a row, at the 1964 Olympics in Tokyo and the 1968 Olympics in Mexico City?

13 Why was there no pentathlon event for women in the Olympics after 1980?

14 Which two Olympic sports, which women can enter, have no equivalent for men?

15 In the 1908 Olympics, for which sport did Sybil Newall (1854–1929) win a gold medal for Britain, with a lead of 43 points?

THE OLYMPICS ANSWERS

1 *440 BC*
2 *None*
3 *The First World War*
4 *She was Jewish*
5 *She slipped and this cost her marks*
6 *Gold*
7 *The javelin throw*
8 *Mary Peters*
9 *200 metres breast stroke*
10 *Sybil Newall, at age 54 in the 1908 Olympics*
11 *Northumberland*
12 *100 metres*
13 *It was replaced by the heptathlon (seven events rather than five)*
14 *Synchronized Swimming and Rhythmic Gymnastics*
15 *Archery*

1 In the 1960 Olympics, how many gold medals were won by American sprinter Wilma Rudolph?
2 Which indoor women's sport was introduced in the 1912 Olympic Games in Stockholm?
3 Which town in northeast England does Olympic swimmer Samantha Foggo come from?
4 Which team event could women first compete in at the 1980 Olympics?
5 In the 1956 Olympics, who became the first Briton to win a gold medal for fencing?
6 How many women competed in the Lawn Tennis Championships in the 1908 Olympics?
7 For which equestrian event did Jane Bullen win a gold medal for Britain in the 1968 Olympics?
8 In 1922, why did women decide to hold their own Women's Olympics?
9 In the year ice skater Jeannette Altwegg (b. 1930) won a gold medal for Britain in the Oslo Olympics, what other honour was awarded to her?
10 In 1948, after Fanny Blankers-Koen had won the second of her four medals at the London Olympics, the Daily Graphic accorded her the headline, *'Fastest Woman in the World Is an Expert Cook.'* What was the sub-heading that followed this?
11 Who organized the first Women's World Games (originally called the Women's Olympics) in 1922?
12 In which year did Mary Peters win the gold for Britain in the pentathlon?
13 For which track-and-field event did Salford Harrier Dorothy Shirley win a gold medal in the 1960 (Rome) Olympics?
14 In the 1912 Olympics Jennie Fletcher won a gold medal for her part in the 4 x 100 metres relay. Which leg of the race did she swim?
15 Which race, for women, was introduced into the Olympics in 1928, won by Lina Radke of Germany, then withdrawn until it was re-introduced in 1960?

THE OLYMPICS ANSWERS

1. *Three*
2. *Swimming*
3. *Killingworth*
4. *Hockey*
5. *Gillian Sheen*
6. *Seven*
7. *The three-day event*
8. *There were no track-and-field events open to women in the male-orientated Olympic Games*
9. *OBE* (Order of the British Empire)
10. *'I shall train my two children to be athletes as well'*
11. *The Fédération Sportive Feminine Internationale (FSFI)*
12. *1972*
13. *High-jump*
14. *The second leg*
15. *The 800 metres*

1 In which year were women first allowed to enter track-and-field events in the Olympic Games?

2 In the 1976 Olympic Games, 49 medals were won by female athletes. How many of these were won by women from the Soviet Bloc?

3 What reason did Norwegian Grete Waitz give for not running faster in the 1984 Women's Olympic Marathon?

4 For which race did Briton Sandra Douglas win a bronze medal at the 1992 (Barcelona) Olympics?

5 In 1984, in which race did Carrie Steinseifer (US) and Nancy Hogshead (US) tie for gold?

6 In the 1964 Olympics Mary Rand (née Bignall) won three medals: a gold, silver and bronze. For which events?

7 In which year was a cycling event for women first included in the Olympics?

8 What was unusual about two of the competitors in the butterfly swimming event in the 1980 Games?

9 How old was gold medallist Judith Grinham when she retired from competitive swimming?

10 In 1956 Gillian Sheen became the first Briton to win a gold medal for fencing. What was her full-time job?

11 What did Hitler give Helen Stephens, American winner of the 100 metre dash, at the 1936 Olympic Games?

12 By 1908 women were allowed to enter three events in the Olympic Games: tennis, archery – and which other?

13 For which newspaper did gold medallist Anita Porter (née Lonsbrough) become swimming correspondent after retiring from swimming?

14 Charlotte Cooper became the first woman to win an Olympic medal (in 1900). For which sport?

15 When was the 5,000 metres for women introduced at the Olympics?

THE OLYMPICS ANSWERS

1 *1928*

2 *44*

3 *It was so hot she was afraid of dying*

4 *4 x 400 metre relay*

5 *100 metre freestyle swimming*

6 *Long jump (gold), pentathlon (silver) and 4 x 100 metres relay (bronze)*

7 *1984*

8 *They were twin sisters (Ann and Janet Osgerby)*

9 *20*

10 *Dental surgeon*

11 *His autograph*

12 *Figure skating*

13 *The* Telegraph

14 *Lawn tennis*

15 *1988*

1 Who was the 155th Speaker (moderator) in the House of Commons?

2 What was cosmonaut Svetlana Savitskaya the first woman to do, in 1984?

3 Who became president of the Republic of Ireland in 1990?

4 During the English Civil War the career of a soldier called Private Clarke, a woman dressed as a man, came to a sudden end. What happened to cause the end of her career?

5 Who became the first female Education Minister of Britain?

6 What became free for all women on the NHS (National Health Service) in 1974?

7 When did Judith Ward, given a life sentence for her alleged part in the bombing of the M62 motorway, eventually have her conviction quashed by a Court of Appeal?

8 Who was the eldest child (b. 1840) of Queen Victoria?

9 In which area of London did Laura Ashley open her first shop in 1967?

10 Which university has Lady Margaret Thatcher (b. 1925) been Chancellor of since 1992?

11 Where did UK Government reports in the 1830s and 1840s suggest women should work, if they had to work?

12 The founder of which company won the British Business Woman of the Year Award in 1984?

13 What article of clothing did Lady Haberton, President of the Rational Dress Society (founded in 1881) argue that all women should wear?

14 In Hebrew mythology, who was Lilith?

15 In 1869 which association in the US was founded by Elizabeth Cady Stanton (1815–1902) and Susan B. Anthony (1820–1906)?

HERSTORY ANSWERS

1 *Betty Boothroyd*

2 *Walk outside a spaceship, while in space*

3 *Mary Robinson*

4 *The birth of her child*

5 *Ellen Wilkinson (Labour)*

6 *Contraceptives*

7 *4th June 1992 (after serving 18 years)*

8 *Victoria*

9 *Kensington*

10 *University of Buckingham*

11 *At home, where they couldn't be seen*

12 *Anita Roddick (The Body Shop)*

13 *Trousers*

14 *The first woman to be created, from the dust of the earth, as Adam's equal*

15 *National Woman's Suffrage Association*

1 What was British artist Dorothy Coke's job during the Second World War?

2 Who won the Indian General Election of 1971, and was voted in as Prime Minister?

3 Which year was declared by the United Nations as International Women's Year?

4 In which British churchyard can you find the tombstone of suffragette Emily Wilding Davison?

5 To whom do the initials ES, which decorate the six towers of Hardwick Hall, Derbyshire, refer?

6 According to a survey undertaken in the 1980s of 106,000 women carried out by *Cosmopolitan*, what kind of women not only have better health but make more money and have a regular sex life?

7 Which Goddess is Ireland named after?

8 To which country did aviator Amy Johnson (1903–41) fly her first solo flight, in a Gypsy Moth, in 1930?

9 Who became the first American woman astronaut to work in space, aboard the shuttle *Challenger*, in June 1983?

10 What did Duchess Gaita of Lombardy do in 1880 when her husband went to war?

11 Which soldier was awarded Britain's Kara-George Star for active service during the First World War?

12 Surgeon Pauline Cutting went to work in a Palestinian refugee camp, Bourj al Barajneh, for three months in 1985. How long did she stay?

13 Which caravan was led by Briton Dora Russell in 1958?

14 Which non-European country gave women the vote in 1917?

15 What was the first living creature to be sent into space, on 3rd November 1957?

HERSTORY ANSWERS

1 *Official War Artist*

2 *Indira Gandhi (1917–84)*

3 *1975*

4 *Morpeth, Northumberland*

5 *Elizabeth, dowager Countess of Shrewsbury (Bess of Hardwick)*

6 *Single women*

7 *Eriu (Eire)*

8 *Australia (Port Darwin)*

9 *Sally Ride*

10 *She donned full armour and rode into war herself*

11 *Flora Sandes (1876–1956)*

12 *A year and a half*

13 *The Women's Caravan of Peace, which was protesting against the Cold War*

14 *Russia*

15 *Laika, a female black-and-white fox terrier*

1 When no seat was provided for her at a meeting with the Portuguese Governor of Launda, what did Queen Nzinga (c.1582–1663) do?
2 During the American Civil War (1861–65) for which side was Mary Elizabeth Bowser a spy?
3 In 1922 Victoria Drummond (1894–1978) went to sea with the British Merchant Navy. As what?
4 What careers did Moll Cutpurse (c. 1589–c. 1662) follow successfully before becoming a receiver of stolen goods?
5 After the death of her daughter, Josephine Butler (1828–1906) was so devastated she took to her bed. Eventually Elizabeth Garrett Anderson inspired her to get up. Before this, how many male doctors had told her she'd never be strong again?
6 What was Emily Faithful, founder of the Victoria Press, sent in 1892 as a recognition of her achievement in the interests of her sex?
7 In what gardening capacity could women find work at Hampton Court in 1516, for three pennies a day?
8 Who appointed Celia of Oxford as her personal surgeon in the 13th century?
9 In the British Census of 1931, how many women were working as shepherds?
10 What kind of agency did Annette Kerner (c. 1900–?) set up in the 1920s in Baker Street, Mayfair?
11 In honour of whom did the Spanish explorers rename Canada?
12 What was the name of the 13th-century women's movement where women lived together, outside the control of men, in self-supporting communities throughout northern Europe?
13 What was the codename of British Agent Pearl Witherington, member of the Special Operations Executive, who commanded and organized an army of 2,000 men during the Second World War?
14 What did the parents of Sophie Germain (1776–1831) do to try and stop her learning geometry?
15 Why was British WAAF Daphne Pearson awarded the George Cross in 1940?

45 HERSTORY ANSWERS

hard

1 *She sat on one of her women attendants*

2 *North/Union Army*

3 *Ship's engineer*

4 *Pickpocket, then highway robber*

5 *Nine*

6 *A signed photograph of Queen Victoria*

7 *Weeding*

8 *Queen Philippa*

9 *25*

10 *A detective agency*

11 *Califia, fictional Queen of the Amazons*

12 *Beguine*

13 *Marie*

14 *They refused to allow her heat or light in her room*

15 *For risking her own life to save the life of a pilot*

BIBLIOGRAPHY

Ally Acker, *Reel Women* (B. T. Batsford, 1991)

B. Adams and T. Tate (eds), *That Kind of Woman* (Virago, 1991)

Carol Adams and Rue Laurikietis, *The Gender Trap 3: Messages and Images* (Virago, 1980)

Maria Aitken, *A Girdle Round the Earth* (Constable, 1987)

W. Amos, *The Originals: Who's Really Who in Fiction* (Jonathan Cape, 1985)

Elizabeth Von Armin, *Elizabeth and her German Garden* (Virago, 1985)

Diane Atkinson, *The Purple White and Green: Suffragettes in London 1906–14* (Museum of London, 1992)

D. Bindman (ed.), *Encyclopedia of British Art* (Thames & Hudson, 1985)

Beverley Birch, *Marie Curie* (Living and Learning, 1989)

Isabella Bird, *A Lady's Life in the Rocky Mountains* (Folio Society, 1988)

Catriona Blake, *Charge of the Parasols* (The Women's Press, 1990)

Adrienne Blue, *Grace Under Pressure* (Sidgwick & Jackson, 1987)

– *Faster, Higher, Further: Women's Triumphs and Disasters at the Olympics* (Virago, 1988)

Karen Briggs and N. Soames, *Judo Champion* (The Crowood Press, 1988)

I. Buchanan, *British Olympians* (Guinness Publishing, 1991)

Leonie Caldecott, *Women of Our Century* (Ariel Books, 1985)

A. Calder, *The Myth of the Blitz* (Pimlico, 1992)

Whitney Chadwick, *Women, Art & Society* (Thames & Hudson, 1990)

Brenda Clarke, *Women in History: Women and Science* (Wayland, 1989)

BIBLIOGRAPHY

Carol Cosman, Joan Keefe and Kathleen Weaver (eds), *The Penguin Book of Women Poets* (Penguin, 1981)

A. Crawford, A. Hughes, T. Hayler, F. Prochaska, P. Stafford and E. Vallance, *The Europa Biographical Dictionary of British Women* (Europa Press Publications, 1983)

C. Daniel, *Derbyshire Portraits* (Dalesman Books, 1978)

G. Dangerfield, *The Strange Death of Liberal England* (Paladin, 1983)

Denise Dennis, *Black History for Beginners* (Writer and Readers, 1984)

Barbara Einhorn, *Let's Discuss: Women's Rights* (Wayland, 1988)

H. Elson and J. Brunton, *Whatever happened to?* (Proteus, 1981)

Andrea Fisher, *Let Us Now Praise Famous Women* (Pandora, 1987)

M. R. D. Foot, *SOE: The Special Operations Executive 1940–46* (BBC Books, 1985)

Janet Frame, *Faces in the Water* (The Women's Press, 1991)

Antonia Fraser (ed.), *Heroes and Heroines* (Weidenfeld & Nicolson, 1980)

Pamela Gerrish Nunn, *Victorian Women Artists* (The Women's Press, 1987)

Mary Gostelow, *Art of Embroidery* (Weidenfeld & Nicolson, 1979)

F. Graham, *Famous Northumbrian Women* (F. Graham, 1969)

T. Grimes, J. Collins and O. Baddeley, *Five Women Painters* (Lennard Publications, 1989)

D. Greenwood, *Who's Buried Where in England* (Constable, 1982)

A. Guttmann, *Women's Sports* (Columbia University Press, 1991)

Evelyn Hall-King, *Passionate Lives* (Piatkus, 1985)

P. Hanks and F. Hodges, *A Dictionary of First Names* (Oxford University Press, 1990)

Nikki Henriques, *Inspirational Women* (Grapevine, 1988)

J. Hislop and D. Swannell (eds), *The Faber Book of the Turf* (Faber & Faber, 1992)

Angela Holdsworth, *Out of the Dolls House* (BBC Books, 1988)

W. Hudson and Valerie Wilson Wesley, *Afro-Bets Book of Black Heroes from A–Z* (Just Us Books, 1988)

Ann Kramer, *Women in History: Women and Politics* (Wayland, 1988)

Nicole Lagneau (ed.), *Women History Makers: Solidarity* (Macdonald, 1987)

– *Women History Makers: Working for Equality* (Macdonald, 1987)

– *Women History Makers: A Chance to Learn* (Macdonald, 1988)

– *Women History Makers: Health and Science* (Macdonald, 1988)

– *Women History Makers: Into the Unknown* (Macdonald, 1988)

– *Women History Makers: New Ideas in Industry* (Macdonald, 1988)

Glenda Leeming, *Who's Who in Jane Austen and the Brontës* (Elmtree Books, 1974)

Jane Legget, *Local Heroines:A Local History Gazetteer to England, Scotland and Wales* (Pandora, 1988)

Dorothy M. Love (ed.), *A Salute to Historic Black Women* (Empak, 1984)

M. Lurker, *Dictionary of Gods and Goddesses, Devils and Demons* (Routledge & Kegan Paul, 1987)

BIBLIOGRAPHY

D. Lynam and Caroline Searle, *Olympic Games: Official British Guide* (BBC Books, 1992)

Diana de Marly, *A History of Occupational Clothing* (B. T. Batsford, 1986)

Jan Marsh and Pamela Gerrish Nunn, *Women Artists and the Pre-Raphaelite Movement* (Virago, 1989)

R. J. Minney, *Carve Her Name With Pride* (Chivers Press, 1983)

Miriam Moss, *Women in History: Women in Business* (Wayland, 1990)

Kate Murphy, *Firsts: British Women Achievers* (The Women's Press, 1990)

G. Nown (ed.), *Coronation Street: 25 Years* (Ward Lock, 1985)

G. Oakley, *The Devil's Music* (BBC Books, 1976)

Patricia Owen, *Women in History: Women and Work* (Wayland, 1989)

A. Palmer, *Who's Who in Modern History 1860–1980* (Weidenfeld & Nicolson, 1980)

E. Pedder (ed.), *Who's Who on Television* (ITV & Michael Joseph, 1985)

Irina Ratushinskaya, *Grey is the Colour of Hope* (Hodder & Stoughton, 1988)

J. and T. Rice, P. Gambaccini and M. Read, *The Guinness Book of British Hit Singles 4* (Guinness Superlatives Ltd, 1983)

– *The Guinness Book of British Hit Singles 8* (Guinness Publishing, 1991)

Sheila Rowbotham, *Hidden from History* (Pluto Press, 1989)

Mary Russell, *The Blessings of a Good Thick Skirt* (Collins, 1988)

P. Salveson, *The People's Monuments* (WEA, 1987)

W. Smethurst, *The Archers: The New Official Companion* (Weidenfeld & Nicolson, 1987)

Dale Spender, *Man Made Language* (Routledge & Kegan Paul, 1985)

Dale Spender and Janet Todd (eds), *Anthology of British Women Writers* (Pandora, 1990)

Anna Sproule, *Women in History: Women and the Arts* (Wayland, 1989)

L. Stanley, *A History of Golf* (Weidenfeld & Nicolson, 1991)

R. Storey (ed.), *Women at Work and in Society* (University of Warwick Library Occasional Publication No 7; University of Warwick, 1991)

Ray Strachey, *The Cause* (Virago, 1979)

Penny Summerfield, *Women Workers in the Second World War* (Routledge, 1989)

D. Sweetman, *Women Leaders in African History* (Heinemann, 1987)

J. Tickell, *Odette* (Chivers Press, 1949)

Lisa Tuttle, *Encyclopedia of Feminism* (Arrow Books, 1987)

Jennifer Uglow (ed.), *The Macmillan Dictionary of Women's Biography* (Macmillan, 2nd edition, 1989)

José Villiers, *Granny Was a Spy* (Quartet Books, 1988)

Virginia Wade, with Jean Rafferty *Ladies of the Court: A Century of Women at Wimbledon* (Pavilion, 1984)

Sophia Watson, *Winning Women* (Weidenfeld & Nicolson, 1989)

Norah Waugh, *Corsets & Crinolines* (Theatre Art Books, 1981)

Julie Wheelwright, *Amazons and Military Maids* (Pandora, 1990)

A. Susan Williams, *Women in History: Women and War* (Wayland, 1989)

Sue Wise and Liz Stanley, *Georgie Porgie: Sexual Harassment in Everyday Life* (Pandora, 1987)